A GIRL CALLED SAMSON

ALSO BY AMY HARMON

Young Adult and Paranormal Romance

Slow Dance in Purgatory
Prom Night in Purgatory

Inspirational Romance

A Different Blue
Running Barefoot
Making Faces
Infinity + One
The Law of Moses
The Song of David
The Smallest Part

Historical Fiction

From Sand and Ash
What the Wind Knows
Where the Lost Wander
The Songbook of Benny Lament
The Unknown Beloved

Romantic Fantasy

The Bird and the Sword
The Queen and the Cure
The First Girl Child
The Second Blind Son

A GIRL CALLED SAMSON

A Novel

AMY HARMON

LAKE UNION
PUBLISHING

This is a work of fiction. Names, characters, organizations, places, events, and incidents are either products of the author's imagination or are used fictitiously.

Published by Lake Union Publishing, Seattle

www.apub.com

ISBN-13: 9781542039741 (paperback)
ISBN-13: 9781542039734 (digital)

Cover design by Faceout Studio, Tim Green
Cover image: ©Joanna Czogala / ArcAngel; ©caesart / Shutterstock; ©swp23 / Shutterstock; ©alexandre zveiger / Shutterstock; ©Raland / Shutterstock; ©VRVIRUS / Shutterstock; ©Fotokvadrat / Shutterstock; ©Chvan Ilona / Shutterstock; ©getgg / Shutterstock; ©Sapan Unhale / Shutterstock; ©Tony Marturano / Shutterstock; ©Josef Hanus / Shutterstock; ©jessicahyde / Shutterstock; ©Vasya Kobelev / Shutterstock

Printed in the United States of America

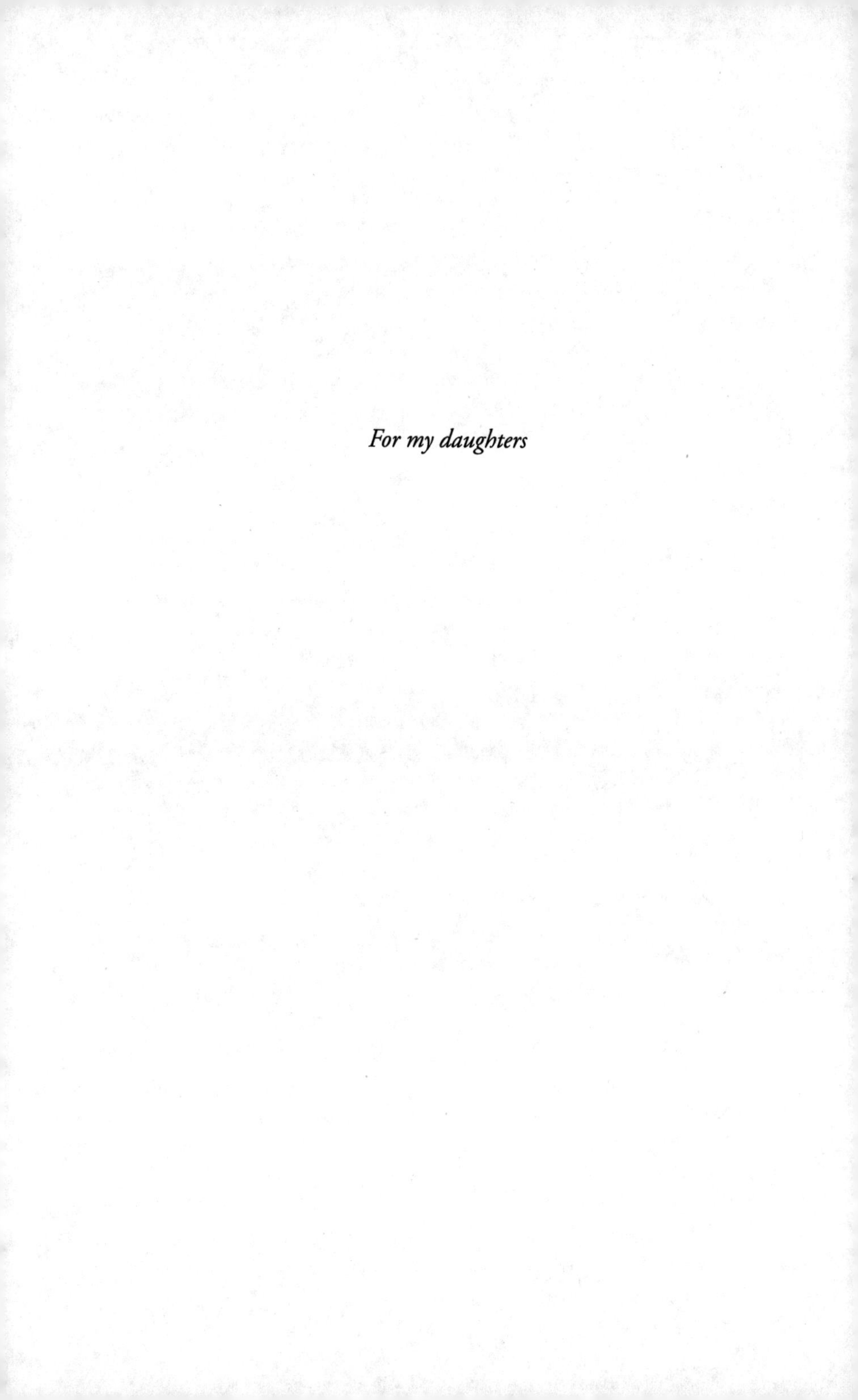

For my daughters

Strength and honor are her clothing; and she shall rejoice in time to come.

Proverbs 31:25

January 3, 1827

Dear Elizabeth,

You have not been far from my mind today. It is a new year, though I suspect it will be my last. I find myself lost in thought more than I am present, and though I've told parts of my story, I've never written it all down from beginning to end.

Many of the things I will write, you already know, but this record will be for your children. And mine. And for generations of little girls who have not even been born.

A newspaper columnist named Herman Mann—he calls himself a novelist—interviewed me at length for a book, and I had hopes that he would write my story as I conveyed it to him. But I find some things are impossible to express, especially to a stranger. The pages he has shared with me bear little resemblance to the tale I lived, and one must understand my history to understand my choices.

It is better that I write it myself, even if it shocks sensibilities.

I am accustomed to that.

The records I kept during the final years of the Revolution were scant and insufficient, but the events are burned into my memory, and I relive them in my sleep. It seems like another life, though the remnants of that life are with me still, in my flesh and in my posterity.

I thought nothing could be worse than the small, painful existence I was living. I also feared the war would end, and I would miss my only shot at deliverance. As it turned out, I saw all the bloodshed I could bear. I watched boys die and grown men weep. I saw cowardice reign and bravery falter. And I witnessed what dreams cost, up close and personal.

If I'd known, I might have avoided it all, the pain in my leg and the price of independence—my own and that of my country. But then I wouldn't have met him. And I wouldn't have come to truly know myself.

People ask me why I did it. Mr. Mann kept returning to that question, and I had no simple answer. Such a question demands the entire story. All I know is that once the desire took root in me, it grew and grew, until to deny it would have choked the hope from my breast. And hope is what keeps us alive.

Had I been pretty and small, I might have had different dreams. I've pondered on that many times. Our aspirations are so often influenced by our appearance. I wonder how mine might have changed me.

I was named after my mother, who was named after the biblical prophetess Deborah. But I didn't want to be a prophet. I wanted to be a warrior like Jael, the woman who slayed a mighty general and liberated her people from the fist of oppression. Mostly, I wanted to free myself.

At five years old, I was alone in the world. At eight, I became a servant to a widow who treated me like a dog. At ten, I was indentured to a farmer until I turned eighteen.

It is impossible to describe how it feels to have no say in one's own life, to be at the mercy of others, and to be sent away. I was only a child then, but being bound out marked me deeply and lit a rebellion in my veins I have never quelled.

Maybe that was the moment I became a soldier.

Maybe that was the day it all began.

~ 1 ~

THE COURSE OF HUMAN EVENTS

March 15, 1770

Winter had begun her retreat, but summer was still a long way off, and the horse we rode picked his way over the thawing, gouged road with a bowed head and an uneven gait. The man in front of me shielded me from the bite of early morning, but I huddled in misery behind him, ignoring the crouching countryside and the bare branches prodding the sky for signs of spring. My legs bounced against the horse's flanks, and I tucked my skirts more securely around my knees. My dress was too small, my wool stockings too large, and a patch of skin between the two was being rubbed raw. I wore every piece of clothing I owned and carried a satchel across my back that held a blanket, a hairbrush, and a Bible that had once belonged to my mother.

"Can you read, Deborah?" Reverend Sylvanus Conant asked. He tossed the question over his shoulder like crumbs for a bird. He hadn't spoken since we'd set off, and I considered not answering. On the occasions he had visited Widow Thatcher, he had been kind to me, but today I was angry with him. Today he had come to take me away. Widow Thatcher no longer needed me, and I would be moving again. I would not miss her slaps, the harsh criticisms, or the endless tasks that were never done to her satisfaction, but I had no confidence that my new situation would be any better.

This time, I would be living with a family. Not my family. My family was gone, tossed into the wind and scattered. My brothers and my sister were all in servitude somewhere to someone. Mother couldn't provide for us. She could barely provide for herself. I hadn't seen her in ages, and I would see her even less living in Middleborough.

"Yes. I can read very well," I relented. Conversation was preferable to stewing in my discontent. "My mother taught me when I was four years old."

"Is that so?" he asked. The horse that carried us whinnied in disbelief. I shifted, trying not to cling to the man, but I was not accustomed to riding thus, and the ridge of the old mare's back made an uncomfortable seat.

"My mother said reading is in my blood. She is the great-granddaughter of William Bradford. Do you know William Bradford? He was aboard the *Mayflower*. The people made him their governor." I felt the need to defend my mother if only to defend myself.

"I do indeed. It is a heritage you can be proud of."

"My father is a Samson. There was a Samson aboard the *Mayflower* too. Henry Samson. Mother said he came to the New World all alone."

"He must have been very brave."

"Yes. But my father is not brave."

Reverend Conant did not disagree, and I sank into shamed silence, embarrassed by my admission.

"Do you know your Bible?" he asked, as if offering me redemption.

"Yes. And I have memorized the catechisms."

"Oh?"

I began to prattle off the questions and answers outlined by the Assembly of Divines.

"My goodness, child!" he interrupted after several minutes of recitation. I was not finished, but I stopped. Widow Thatcher had been unimpressed by my achievement. She'd scolded me for my pride. I expected the reverend to do the same.

"That is highly commendable," he said instead. "Very impressive."

"I can keep going," I proposed, biting my lips to hide my pleasure. "I know it all."

"And can you write?" he asked.

I hesitated, slightly deflated. Reading was easier than writing, and Widow Thatcher had wanted me to read to her, sometimes for hours on end, but she hadn't been keen on me scratching away at my letters.

"I can," I said. "But not as well as I read. I need more practice."

"It is one thing to read another man's thoughts. It is another to express one's own. And paper is expensive," the reverend said.

"Yes. And I have no money." I was surprised that he'd even asked. I was a girl, after all, and a servant, but his queries made me hopeful.

"Do you think the Thomases might allow me to go to school?" I asked.

It was his turn to hesitate. "Mistress Thomas is sorely in need of help."

I sighed, unsurprised. I would not be going to school.

"But I will bring you books, if you like," he offered.

I came close to toppling from my perch behind him.

"What kind?" I blurted, though I hardly cared. The Bible, the catechisms, and a collection of maps and journals that had belonged to Reverend Thatcher were the only books Widow Thatcher had in her house. I read them all out loud to the old woman, even the journals, though they were filled with sermons and little else. The pages my mother had copied from the records of William Bradford were much more interesting, but I dearly wanted something new.

"What kind of books would you like?" the reverend asked.

"Stories. I would like stories. Adventures."

"All right. And I will bring paper and ink as well so you will have the means to practice your writing. You could compose letters."

"Who will I write to?"

He didn't respond immediately, and I feared I'd been impertinent. Widow Thatcher often accused me of such, though I'd always performed every task to exactness and only spoke when spoken to.

"I would like someone to practice with," I explained. I was hungry for a friend. I'd spent the last five years with old women who were spent and weary. "Perhaps Mistress Thomas will allow that."

"Perhaps." He said no more on the matter, and I did not allow myself to hope that he would do as he promised.

"The Thomases live about two miles from town. It's a good stretch of the legs. Nothing more. They have a farm, a pretty place. You might find it very agreeable."

I looked beyond my misery enough to take in the day around me. The mud of early spring slowed our journey, and the earth sucked at the horse's hooves, but the morning sky was turning blue, the sun had begun to warm my back, and the breeze stirred my pale hair. I'd spent too many days shut inside, hovering near Widow Thatcher so her every command could be attended to. The world beyond those stifling rooms and stagnant air had called to me, and my limbs and lungs had longed for speed and motion. If I'd thought the reverend would allow it, I would've asked to be let down so I could run alongside the horse. I loved to run. But the road was churned up from travel, and I had no confidence that my wishes would be considered, so I swallowed them.

The first time I got a glimpse of the house in the middle of forest and fields, I felt a glimmer of hope. It was well kept, and the windows made a friendly face with the front door and the little gate that separated the yard from the road. The door flew open upon our approach, and a woman, her skirts in hand, ran to greet us, a little black-haired boy on her heels. A burly man, a hat on his head and his sleeves rolled as if he'd just stepped away from his labors, called out to the reverend as we drew to a halt.

"Don't be afraid, Deborah," the reverend said gently. "You will not be mistreated here."

Boys tumbled out of the barn and came in from the fields, boys of all sizes, though most appeared older than me. Reverend Conant seemed to know all their names and greeted each one, but I didn't know which name belonged to whom. There were so many, and I had very little experience with other children, especially boys. They watched their father help me down from the mare, though it was not an inability to disembark as much as trepidation that had kept me rooted to my seat instead of sliding to the ground.

Deacon Jeremiah Thomas wore two frowns, one on his brow and one on his lips, but his wife, Susannah, a woman who barely reached his shoulder, was his opposite in every way. His soberness, I would come to find, was not cruelty. He was not jolly, but he was just, which was a far better quality in my opinion. Susannah Thomas smiled at me and grasped my hands.

"Sylvanus did not tell us you were so grown. You are so tall for ten and already a young woman."

I nodded but did not smile. I expect I looked rather fierce too, though I was simply afraid. She introduced me to her sons, oldest to youngest. Nathaniel, Jacob, and Benjamin were eighteen, seventeen, and sixteen. All three were midheight and slim with dark hair and freckled noses, which they wrinkled at me. I don't know what they were expecting, but I was clearly not it. Elijah was heavier set with lighter hair and an easier smile. He was fourteen, and thirteen-year-old Edward was his mirror image, as if Mrs. Thomas had birthed her sons in sets, whether they were born at the same time or not.

Twelve-year-old Francis and Phineas were actual twins, and the dark hair and sparer frames of their older brothers reemerged with them. I was taller than both, and the one named Phineas scowled when his mother cooed over my height. David and Daniel were twins as well, and ten like me, with curly brown mops that needed grooming. I was a sight taller than them too.

Jeremiah was the youngest, at six, and the only one who didn't seem to have a double. I was hopeful, for Mrs. Thomas's sake, that the six years after Jeremiah meant she wouldn't be having any more.

"We will try not to overwhelm you, Deborah, though we are very excited to have you here. It will be good to have another female in the house. You will help civilize my sons."

Someone snorted at that, though I could not be sure who. Mrs. Thomas turned and looped her arm through Reverend Conant's and announced that supper was ready.

"Wash and come inside, boys. Deborah, bring your things. I will show you where you'll sleep."

Mrs. Thomas turned her attention to Reverend Conant, and they walked into the house, chatting like old friends. Deacon Thomas was already leading the horse to the trough, and I hoisted my satchel, hiked my sagging stockings, and prepared to follow. The Thomas boys had fallen into quiet conference, and I froze, my back toward them, straining to hear.

"She's plain as a fence post."

"Shaped like one too."

"And her hair is the color of straw." Whoever was speaking snickered. "Maybe she could stand in the field and scare away the birds."

"Her eyes are pretty. I don't think I've ever seen eyes like hers."

"They're creepy! We'll have to set up a watch each night, to keep her from slaying us all in our beds."

I laughed at that, the bark of mirth surprising us all, and I turned to flash a wicked grin in their direction. Better they fear me than dismiss me.

"Her teeth are good," someone muttered, and I laughed again.

"She's downright peculiar," the oldest brother said, but the boy named Phineas had begun laughing too, and one by one, the others joined him.

~

I did not civilize the boys.

It might even be said that they radicalized me.

They slept in the big loft above the great room in berths built into the slope of the roof. Only David and Daniel, the youngest set of twins, slept in a regular bed, and it was hardly big enough for the two of them. They slept with their heads on opposite ends, their feet tickling each other's noses.

I was given a room of my own. It was but a closet, separated from the kitchen by a thin wall and a door, but it was big enough to hold a narrow berth, a pair of drawers, and a table a foot deep and two feet wide. And it was mine. I had my own bed, my own space. Being a female in a house full of sons had its benefits, even if one occupied the position of servant.

In the early days, the Thomas brothers kept their distance, eyeing me like I was a thief or a leper. It was Jeremiah, the littlest one, who warmed to me first. Perhaps it was that we were both loose ends, but he latched on to me quickly and made me his cohort. We were even born on the same day. I turned eleven the day he turned seven, and Jeremiah took that as a sign.

"Will you be my twin, Deborah?" Jeremiah asked, looking up at me with mournful eyes. "I have no one."

I laughed. "You have nine brothers, Jeremiah."

"But I'm the runt. I have no one who belongs to me. And you don't even have a ma or a pa or sisters and brothers."

"I do . . . somewhere."

"Well, what good is that?"

"Not much good, Jerry. Not much," I agreed, and my heart was oddly lighter for speaking the truth of it.

"So you can be my twin."

"And what do twins do?"

"A twin is the person you love most. Do you think you could love me most?"

"That will be easy."

"It will?" His toothy smile made my heart swell.

"It will."

"I love Ma an awful lot, but loving Ma is kinda like loving God. She's not really a person."

"Jeremiah!" I gasped. "She is too."

"I just mean . . . that she belongs to all of us. I want someone who just belongs to me," he repeated.

"All right. But I will try to love your brothers too, because that is what Reverend Conant says I must do."

"Even Nathaniel?" He looked doubtful. "And Phineas? He's mean. He told you no man would ever have you."

"No man will ever have me because I won't have him. And I won't need him."

"I'll have you, Deborah."

"You won't, Jeremiah. You're seven years old. And we're twins now, remember?"

"We don't look like twins . . . but that's okay, isn't it?" Jerry was small and dark, and I was tall and blonde, as different as night and day.

"Looks don't matter at all if your hearts are the same," I declared, hoping it was true.

He'd grinned at me like I'd given him the world. I suppose I had. At least the little bit of the world that was mine. I doted on him like a mother and treated him like a prince, and he got me into all manner of trouble I would not have dared get into alone. Jeremiah was the first to call me Rob—short for Deborah—and the reason I answered to it without hesitation later on.

The Thomases did not treat me poorly. I was not family, but I *was* valued. The work was never-ending with so many mouths to feed and bodies to clothe. Reverend Conant was right. I was greatly needed, and I could not be spared for school, but no matter how many chores I was given or tasks I completed, I could not shake the restlessness that consumed me. I squeezed the Thomas boys for every drop of learning they would share, often doing their chores and mine for a peek at their primers.

And Reverend Conant did not forget me.

Over the following year, he brought me several books. My favorites were a collection by Shakespeare and a four-part work called *Travels into Several Remote Nations of the World*. Reverend Conant called it *Gulliver's Travels*. I read it after supper to the brothers and was lauded as a great orator.

Reverend Conant was quite the orator himself, and I sat on the pews of the First Congregational Church with the Thomases and listened to him preach. He believed every word he said. In a way, he radicalized me too, if faith can be called radical. I've come to think it might be the most rebellious thing of all.

I don't know why Reverend Conant cared about my learning or my happiness, but he did, and it was because of him—a man who loved God and loved me, two ends of the mighty spectrum—that I began to see what a father's love looked like. To him I was simply Deborah, worthy of expectation and affection, and the things that mattered to him came to matter deeply to me.

"You must continue with your memorization. I have known no greater comfort in my life than to be able to call upon God's words when I am at a loss for my own," he would frequently say, and I memorized everything, just to show him I could. Just to hear his praise.

He also found me a tutor of sorts, an "epistolatory correspondent" in Farmington, Connecticut.

"Her name is Elizabeth. She's my sister's daughter. My niece. She is grown, a young wife and a mother, and a woman of consequence. I have asked her if she will engage in correspondence with you, to expose you to the wider world, and she has happily agreed."

"What will I say?" I cried. I thrilled and quaked at the idea. I was not yet a woman and could not imagine what interest she would have in someone like me.

"You must say whatever you wish."

"Is she . . . kind?" I did not want to exchange letters with someone who would scold me.

"Yes. Very kind. You will learn from her what I can't teach and even what Mrs. Thomas can't teach."

"Mrs. Thomas can read and write, though her writing isn't fine," I said, wanting to defend the woman who treated me so well. It was not her fault she was not a woman of "consequence."

"Yes, but you *live* with Mrs. Thomas. No need to write her letters," Reverend Conant said, always judicious. I'd never heard him mutter a bad word about anyone, especially good people, and the Thomases were good people.

"How many letters may I write?" I asked, breathless.

"You may write as often as you like, as often as you're able."

"That will be a great many. I like practicing."

His eyes crinkled, but he didn't laugh at me. "Yes. I know you do. And Elizabeth will welcome your letters."

"What should I call her? Cousin Elizabeth . . . or Mrs. Paterson . . . or maybe I can call her Lady Elizabeth?" The thought thrilled me.

"She's not a duchess, Deborah. We don't have titles in America. I'm sure Elizabeth will do."

"Why do they have titles in England?"

"Tradition. England is married to tradition and enamored with station. It is different here. A man is what he makes of himself. It is not something bestowed on him." The reverend sounded so proud.

"And women too?"

"What?"

"Is a woman what she makes of herself?"

"Yes. A woman is what she makes of herself . . . with God's direction, of course. We all need God's direction."

"But what if we don't want to go in the direction God wants for us?"

"Then I suppose we're on our own. I shouldn't like to be on my own. Not completely."

"No," I whispered, though I often felt on my own. Completely. "What about King George?" I pressed.

"What about him?"

"You said we don't have titles here. But he is still our king. Isn't he? After the massacre in Boston, some are saying he shouldn't be."

"The only king I worship is the King of Kings, Lord of Lords, the Everlasting Father, the Prince of Peace." Reverend Conant was frowning, and his jaw was tight.

I nodded seriously, but my heart was pounding too. Sylvanus Conant might be loyal, but he'd just spoken the words of a rebel.

March 27, 1771

Dear Miss Elizabeth,

My name is Deborah Samson. I'm certain you've been warned that I would be writing. I am not an accomplished writer, but I hope to be. I promise I will work very hard to make my letters interesting so you will enjoy reading them and allow me to continue.

Reverend Conant tells me you are kind and beautiful and smart. I am not beautiful, but I try to be kind, and I am very smart.

I love to read, and I love to run, though I have little time for either, as there is always work to be done. But I read the Bible every day, and I am memorizing verses from Proverbs. Do you have a favorite? I will write one that I have mastered below, just for practice.

Proverbs 28:1, "The wicked flee when no man pursues: but the righteous are bold as a lion."

I told Mistress Thomas that running is not the same thing as fleeing. I thought that was quite bold, like a lion. She did not laugh, though I saw Phineas grin. I am quite rebellious, I fear. I attend the First Congregational Church with the Thomases. Your uncle Sylvanus preaches each week, and though I am very fond of him, and he is very convincing, the hours of inactivity are torture.

Last Sunday, I lied and said I wasn't feeling well and left before the final hour. I ran straight for the woods and spent a blessed afternoon climbing the trees and swinging from the branches. I know the path that cuts behind the tree line all the way back to the Thomas farm, and I have begun to clear it of roots and stones that would trip a girl up if she were running as fast as she were able—that girl being me.

Mrs. Thomas asked me what I was doing in my free time between chores and supper. I told her I was clearing the walking path. I even quoted scripture so she was assured it was a righteous endeavor.

Proverbs 4:26 says, "Ponder the path of your feet, and let all your ways be established."

That is exactly what I have been doing. Pondering the path of my feet and establishing my ways. Mrs. Thomas seemed amiable to the activity, and even said it was a kind service to others who might use that path, but I did not tell her everything.

I call it my dashing path. I've claimed ownership of it since I've done all the work. It gives me a place to run where no one will see. I told the boys I could beat them all, maybe even Phineas, who is very fast, if I were allowed to race without my skirts hampering me. They have taken my challenge and presented me with a very worn pair of breeches that fit me quite well and a shirt to go with them. I can run so swiftly in them that I am convinced they are magic.

I hope you will not think me wicked, but if running is a sin, I will simply have to remain a sinner, as it is the only thing that quiets my mind.

Your obedient servant,
Deborah Samson
PS I will tell you all about the race,
even if I do not win.

~ 2 ~

It Becomes Necessary

Though I kept my grievances close to my heart, putting them on the page was a waste of precious paper and ink. To sharpen a quill just to sharpen the axe did nothing to lessen the sting of my circumstances. I made lists of my weaknesses instead. Not to punish myself—that was not productive either. I made an accounting so I might better myself. The Bible made mention of weak things becoming strong, and I was determined to be strong. Each day, when I was not too weary to write, I would itemize the ways I fell short and count the ways I'd succeeded, always seeking to lengthen the latter column. But there were many things I could not teach myself, and I sought instruction wherever I could find it.

"The younger boys complain mightily about their lessons," I told Reverend Conant on one of his visits. "I help them as much as I can, but I wish I had lessons of my own."

Reverend Conant always timed his visits with supper. I couldn't blame him. He didn't have a wife. He claimed he was married to the gospel, and Mrs. Thomas said he "tended to everyone in his flock," but I liked to think he kept a special eye on me. He always asked me a string of questions when he stopped in.

Deacon Thomas and his sons had come in for the midday meal, but most had eaten and scattered, uninterested in the political talk that inevitably ensued when the reverend was present. Nathaniel and Benjamin still remained, eating as though they were starving, and Jeremiah had set up his tiny soldiers in the corner of the room and was plotting an ambush.

"She helps them too much," Mrs. Thomas chided. "They take advantage of her curiosity."

Deacon Thomas slathered butter on his bread. "They want to be outside. I was the same."

"I too want to be outside," I blurted. "But I am restless, even out of doors. I find I cannot get full, no matter what I do."

"You are not getting enough to eat?" Mrs. Thomas asked, stunned. Nathaniel and Benjamin even paused in their shoveling.

"I am. Yes." My cheeks warmed with embarrassment. "Pardon me, mistress. I do not mean food. I am hungry . . . to know."

"To know what, child?" Mrs. Thomas said.

"The world, I suppose. I want to go to Boston and to New York and to Philadelphia. I want to go to Paris and London and to places that have no names . . . at least not yet. Elizabeth went to London and Paris." I bit my lip and lowered my eyes. "And I would like to know God."

I added the last bit because I felt I must. It was true . . . just not as true as the first part. Deacon Thomas was frowning at me, and Mrs. Thomas was wringing her hands.

"Continue to study Holy Writ," Reverend Conant responded. "There is no better way to know Him. It is a marvelous gift to have His words. You don't have to go anywhere. He is right there."

"But I *want* to go somewhere," I confessed.

Reverend Conant laughed, and I loved him for it.

"Proverbs nineteen says the soul that be without knowledge is not good," I argued. "It is sinful not to educate oneself." I thought my reasoning sound.

"Proverbs nineteen also says he that hasteth with his feet sinneth," Deacon Thomas quoted, his cheeks full. "I'd say you're in trouble, Deborah." His tone was mild, and his eyes did not even lift from his trencher, and for a moment all was hushed. Then laughter engulfed the entire table.

"Pa got you good, didn't he, Rob?" Nathaniel chuckled. It was all they ever called me.

"Now stop that," Mrs. Thomas reprimanded, but her lips were twitching too. "I don't know why you call Deborah *Rob*. It is not becoming at all. A woman deserves a woman's name."

"Are you a woman, Rob?" Jeremiah lifted his head from his toys, astonished, and the laughter grew.

No, I did not civilize the boys. Not at all.

"I will bring you more books. Perhaps that will help your wanderlust. And here is a letter from Elizabeth. A very long one," the reverend reassured me when Benjamin and Nat finally rose and left the table.

I snatched it up, begging to be excused, and Mrs. Thomas waved me off while reminding me that there were chores that still needed to be done and to not be long. I rushed to my little room and shut the door behind me, but I could still hear the conversation between Reverend Conant and Mr. and Mrs. Thomas.

"She is headstrong, Sylvanus," Deacon Thomas said, and I made a note to add that to my list of faults. "And proud. And she cannot always hold her tongue."

"I only hope she is a blessing to you," Reverend Conant replied.

"I cannot complain," Mrs. Thomas said. "Not at all. I don't know how I ever got by without her. She accomplishes far more—and does it well—than I do in a day. I've never seen a person more driven."

"But driven toward what?" Deacon Thomas grumbled. He watched me with trepidation when he looked at me at all, and he'd hardly said two words to me in the two years I'd lived under his roof.

He was wrong, though.

I could hold my tongue.

I held it more often than not. He would be appalled if he knew all the things I didn't say.

"She has great energy," Mrs. Thomas was saying. "She handles the spinning wheel like a master and has a gift at the loom. Nathaniel has taught her how to shoot. He says she is already a better aim than he is. In truth, there is little she can't do."

I smiled at that, despite the sting in Deacon Thomas's criticism, and turned away from my eavesdropping to the letter in my hands. Elizabeth didn't write as often as I wrote her. I'd written dozens but sent only a few, as to not abuse her kindness or trample on her goodwill, but this letter was delightfully long.

She had lovely handwriting, like geese in formation, winging across the page. I had begun trying to copy it, to train my hand to pattern hers. My writing looked like waves in a brewing storm, rough and relentless. Like me. Funny how a person's penmanship revealed so much.

April 15, 1772

Dearest Deborah,

You make me laugh, darling girl, and I read your letters with both wonder and glee. It is odd to think we are but eight years apart. In some ways, I feel ancient compared to you, though I am convinced you could instruct me in many ways. I have scoured Proverbs for something to inspire you, but found myself giggling, trying to imagine how you might apply each one.

I read your letters to my John. Even he, a man who has never done an irresponsible thing in his life, had a good laugh when you recounted the episode of the magic breeches. I would have liked to see the Thomas boys being trounced in that footrace. You've made me curious about donning a pair and finding a dashing path of my own.

I do hope someday you will experience the joy of turning a gentleman's head with more than your speed or strength. You have such a fine mind and a strong will, and your character shines through your letters. I suspect you will grow to be a woman who inspires much admiration. Do not be so quick to dismiss the blessings or power of our sex, my young friend. My grandmother told me once that men may run the world, but women rule men. Something to ponder, certainly. You must let the brothers win sometimes, just to encourage them. I find men are more apt to let us play if they believe they will triumph.

Uncle Sylvanus tells me you are the brightest girl he's ever met. He frets that you are unable to attend school but says there is little any country school could teach you. There is little I can teach you! Still, you must ask me any questions you have, and I will labor to answer them in a way that both instructs and entertains, as you have done for me.

Your constant friend,
Elizabeth

PS Proverbs 31 is my favorite, though I recognize I am at a different juncture in my life than you are. I particularly like this section:

"She opens her mouth with wisdom; and in her tongue is the law of kindness. She looks well to the ways of her household, and eats not the bread of idleness. Her children arise up, and call her blessed; her husband also, and he praises her."

I folded the letter carefully and put it in the growing stack of communications from Elizabeth. I had so few possessions, and I cherished each one. My Bible, the one my mother had given me, sat beside the pile. My mother had neatly recorded her lineage on the inside cover from the marriage of William Bradford and Alice Carpenter in 1623 to the union of Deborah Bradford and Jonathan Samson in 1751. My mother was a Deborah too.

I'd added my siblings—Robert, Ephraim, Sylvia, Dorothy—and myself in a neat line beneath my parents' names, an effort to connect us to the branch and to each other, even though we'd been snipped and scattered.

I turned to Proverbs 31 and read it through, trying to imagine myself being a woman more valuable than rubies, a woman who spoke with wisdom and clothed herself in honor and strength. I clothed myself in homespun cloth and borrowed breeches, at least when I could get away with it. The boys had never tattled on me, though Phineas had threatened to after I'd bested him in a wrestling match.

I certainly did not eat the bread of idleness. That should count for something.

I closed the Bible and took out my ledger. I added headstrong to my list of faults and stared at it before crossing it out and adding it to the other side. I wrote *Of strong mind.* That's what I was. I was of strong mind. And that was not a sin.

I left the ledger open to dry and left my room, determined to looketh well to the ways of the household, at least until I was eighteen.

~

Middleborough was a small community about thirty miles south of Boston, but the people boasted two churches: the First Congregational Church, where Reverend Conant presided, and the Third Baptist Church, which seemed to have an equal and passionate following. I once asked what the difference was, besides the minister, and Mrs. Thomas said one was true and one was not. I asked which one, and Mrs. Thomas was not amused, though I wasn't trying to be humorous.

I did like that there was a choice and no one was forced to attend either—except if one was a child or an indentured servant—though choosing not to attend one or the other seemed to make folks wary and strain relationships. Both read the Bible, both sang similar hymns, and both prayed to a similar God, according to Reverend Conant. The reverend seemed more concerned by the presence of British troops in Boston than he was by the existence of another church in Middleborough, so I didn't concern myself overmuch either, though my insatiable curiosity had me listening to debates in the public square after Sunday meetings when most of the other young people wandered away.

But the arguments about which church was true and which version of God even truer paled in comparison to the political fervor that had gripped the colonies, or at least Massachusetts. In a letter, Elizabeth claimed it was everywhere.

July 28, 1773

My dear Deborah,

Many of John's associates and our friends want no part of the rebellion brewing in Boston, but as John says, the trouble in one colony affects all colonies. A clear delineation is brewing between the wealthy and the common folk, those who don't profit from trade with Britain and who resent the taxes, regulation, and orders from on high.

John worries what the troubles will mean for our future and the future of every colony. He says oppression not resisted eventually becomes slavery, and he has begun preparations to move the family to a place called Lenox in western Massachusetts. His cousin lives there, and John wants the family away from the conflict if there is to be one, though he is likely to get pulled into the fray, wherever we go. He has wide shoulders, a level head, and a patriotic heart.

Lenox sits on the edge of the frontier, and I confess to not being enthusiastic about the move. But I suppose if John's mother and his sisters and their families come with us, I will not mind it. Of course my daughters will keep me busy.

I cannot fathom how circumstances continue to devolve. Surely, England does not want war. John says the British do not think the colonists capable of prolonged resistance or organized revolt. They are disdainful of us and call us pestilents. A certain British lord, I cannot remember his name at present, boasted that he could flatten all the rebellion in the colonies by nightfall with a single regiment and not suffer a wrinkle or a scratch.

You are so young, and I do not want to frighten you. I often forget that you are but thirteen! Your questions are those of a scholar, and I confess to not having the answers much of the time. Perhaps I will entreat John to write to you on subjects in which I am not well versed.

We must also write of simpler things, more pleasant things. There is little you or I can do about the trouble brewing, so we must not let it darken our correspondence. The doctor has just confirmed I am with child again and we want to be settled in Lenox before the baby is born. Our home is almost finished. John promises it will be grand, and I will bring culture and civilization to that place, though given the size of the town, I don't think that will be difficult.

I remain your constant friend,
Elizabeth

~

The Patersons moved to Lenox and Elizabeth gave birth to her third daughter, Ruth, named after John's favorite sister. Baby Ruth joined four-year-old Hannah and two-year-old Polly in the Paterson brood. John had four sisters, all older than he, and Elizabeth said he was destined to be surrounded by females. She still managed to write regularly, though the letters were slow, and I often wrote three to every one of hers.

I had only my own thoughts to fill the pages, but she didn't seem to mind. She indulged my analysis of Shakespeare and offered some of her own. She shared my disappointment in Othello—*he killed Desdemona!*—and enjoyed my defense of poor Shylock from *The Merchant of Venice*, though she did not share my sense of injustice in his case. I had a soft spot when it came to the outcast, even when the outcast was portrayed as the villain. I thought it most likely because I was one as well.

The following May, news of the Boston Port Bill reached American shores. Parliament had proclaimed all ports in New England closed. Nothing in and nothing out. Deacon Thomas said the British meant to kill the resistance, to force everyone out and punish the merchants for skirting their regulations.

The king revoked the Massachusetts Bay Charter, which was essentially the colony's license to operate independently from the Crown in any manner. All the governing officials in the colony were paid and appointed by the British. No trials would take place in Massachusetts, and no meeting, assembly, or speech would be allowed without permission from the Crown's governor.

They'd also demanded the people quarter the British troops in their homes, and that alarmed Mrs. Thomas most of all. She was certain a regiment would march into Middleborough any day and seize the house and farm.

The "Intolerable Acts" was what people were calling them, but such things had been happening as long as I could remember, and the people had tolerated them. I didn't know a time when people didn't complain about the Crown. No taxation without representation was something people loved to say, and the previous December, a group of rebels that called themselves the Sons of Liberty had climbed aboard three ships in Boston Harbor, ships owned by the British East India Company, and dumped all the tea into the water to protest King George's ban on tea imports from anywhere but England.

It was all very exciting.

I sent a letter to Elizabeth asking her the definition of "habeas corpus" and the dozens of other terms repeatedly used by those who considered themselves authorities on the subject. Her husband, John, replied very kindly with an answer to each of my questions. Elizabeth had mentioned that he studied the law at Yale and even taught school for a time, and I could hardly keep my eyes on the words, so greedy was I for the content. He did not converse with me like a child, but wrote in language clear and concise, as if he'd taken the time to think each point through. He was a very fine teacher, and I found my understanding much improved. I read the letter so many times, I was able to recite his explanations by heart.

In Massachusetts, the counties held congresses to consider the alarming state of public affairs and to establish their own governance, separate from the "agents of the Crown." John Paterson was elected as a delegate from Lenox, though he and Elizabeth had been residents for less than a year, but he seemed disenchanted with the assemblies.

He closed one letter with, *"Every man in attendance insists on blathering on, impressing no one but himself, and we leave these congresses with nothing of real substance. The Crown needs to see a unified force. We will save lives—mainly our own—if we can be clear in our demands and collective in our approach, but men are torn by the allegiance we all feel to Britain, and I don't think anyone believes we could defeat them in an actual war. Britain is a nation that excels in such conflicts, an empire that has dominated for centuries. It is David and Goliath, but then I remind myself who won that contest, and I am not so fearful. If God wants an independent America, He will make it so."*

It was all anyone talked about. Every conversation, every visit, every passing word was about the brewing conflict with England. Everyone had an opinion, though most repeated the same points over and over, as if they'd seen them printed in a pamphlet or heard them spoken by someone more learned than they. Even Reverend Conant preached about tyranny and liberty in his sermons, but he was careful not to call the congregation to revolution. Still, no one questioned where he stood.

"Honor thy father and thy mother, that thy days may be long upon the land," he would begin, and the congregation would sit up, knowing what was coming. "But how long will we remain children in the eyes of King George? How long will they claim that lofty position? England is not our home. It has not been for a very long time."

There *were* many folks who prattled on about loyalty to the "mother country." It always put my teeth on edge. Mother country. I hated that name, but I guessed others might have different reactions. I felt very little allegiance to my own mother and even less to the country that ran my ancestors out onto the sea because they would not conform.

Reverend Conant said we might have been the freest people in all the world, yet the colonies were viewed the way kings and nobles have always viewed the common man. Not as people, but as profit.

"It is time we put an end to the idea that people are made for their rulers," he told Deacon Thomas one evening at dinner, and we all nodded, every head bobbing like we understood the historical significance of such a statement.

"If we do not exist for the king, what do we exist for?" I asked. I was not sitting. I was serving, carving the meat from the roast that I'd turned on a spit all day. I thought I'd done a fair job of it, but the family was seated and hungry, and I was not confident my efforts would be well received. The cat swiped a piece and scampered away before I could grab it back. She ate it, licking her lips, and I shrugged, putting the platter on the table and taking a bevy of orders—a cup of milk, another bowl of butter, a knife to cut the bread.

"The governors are appointed by the Crown, and their loyalty is to the Crown, not to the people they have authority over," Deacon Thomas said, ignoring my question. "We see these things as simple rights, but the governors claim they are concessions to be revoked at whim."

"The Lords of Trade have become threatened by the liberty that fills our lungs," Reverend Conant said, and I resisted the urge to interject again. John Paterson had told me all about the Lords of Trade. They looked on the colonies as landed estates and the colonists as laborers working those estates. I imagined them in black robes and white wigs, doling out freedom or favor, collecting their gold, with no knowledge of the people whose lives they affected.

"If we do not exist for the king, what do we exist for?" I asked again. I was not ill-treated, but I was not free. And I did not know my purpose, beyond work. "If we aren't governed by King George or the Lords of Trade, who will we be governed by?"

"That is the question, isn't it, Deborah?" Reverend Conant answered, chasing his peas around his trencher. But nobody answered it.

~ 3 ~

One People

Though I was only five when he left, I had very clear memories of my father, and they weren't pleasant. I looked like him. His eyes were the same hazel and our hair the same hue as the wheat in the fields he hated. My father did not like farming, he did not like Plympton, and he did not like me or my siblings. He fretted endlessly, and my mother was always seeking to soothe him, though she had five children hanging from her skirts. I did not hang. It was crowded around her feet.

It was his departure that precipitated my being sent to live with Cousin Fuller with nothing but my name and Mother's stories to remind me who I was. Mother moved in with her sister, and the house we'd lived in before Father ran off was occupied by someone else.

Instead of a farmer, Father thought he'd try to be a sailor or a sea captain—the story often changed—or a merchant of trade. Mother told us for the longest time that he would return. Or maybe that's just what she told me, the few times I saw her. My sister Sylvia and my brothers, Robert and Ephraim, all whom were older than I, were sent away too.

Mother kept the baby. Her name was Dorothy, and Mother called her Dot. She died of croup sometime after our family ceased to be.

I don't remember Dorothy at all. She was a faceless cry, a little *dot* on the landscape of a truncated life. Perhaps Mother should have given her a different name. Every Dorothy in the family tree had a tragic end.

I never saw my siblings again, and I have no notion of what they were told, but I assume Mother drilled their identity into them like she did to me. Mother taught us our heritage.

I learned to read from William Bradford's journal and to write by copying his words into the dirt. The journal I read was not the original. His descendants had made painstaking copies so the record wouldn't be lost. The version we had was printed in my mother's handwriting, giving his sentiments an almost feminine flair, like it was Mother experiencing his trials and triumphs. His story was woven through every early memory I had of her. I think her pedigree was the only thing of which she was proud.

Like I had done with the catechisms, she recited line after line of her great-grandfather's writings and wonderings. His life filled our bedtime stories. One of the first letters I received from her after moving in with the Thomases was a desperate summation of his life, like she couldn't bear for me to forget the details. She wrote:

> *My great-grandfather, William Bradford, was born in 1590 in Yorkshire, the son of a wealthy landowner, but his life would not be that of a cherished son. His father died when he was but a babe, and he was orphaned at seven years old when his mother too passed away.*
>
> *He was curious, like you, Deborah, with a love of books and learning. He was fascinated with religion, not just God Himself, but in the rights of men to worship as they believed.*

William began to attend secret meetings with a small congregation who called themselves Separatists, but King James vowed to destroy all reform movements and imprison those guilty of religious disobedience. People were fined, jailed, and hunted, betrayed by their neighbors and shunned by their friends. William and a small group of reformers fled England for the Dutch Republic, where religious freedom was permitted.

At eighteen, he was a stranger in a strange land, with no family and few friends. He worked at the most menial of jobs and eked out the barest of existences, but he was a weaver of fine cloth—a skill that has been passed down through our family. I can weave, and you can too. His blood runs in our veins, his courage, his talent, and his curiosity too.

He could have remained in the Netherlands, but that was not to be. He was compelled to seek a different life. He helped to secure a charter and a boat called the Speedwell, but alas, it did not speed well. It was not seaworthy at all, and the Separatists and the small group of tradesmen they'd hired all boarded the remaining ship, the Mayflower, and left everything else behind.

They made it all the way across the sea, crowded and sick, with icy water streaming down on them from quaking beams and rolling waves. Great miracles were wrought on their journey, but miracles do not make life easy. Most often, miracles just make the next step possible.

It was December when they arrived, and they had no shelter but the ship. William had disembarked with a small group and gone ashore to explore the area. He was gone for many days, and when he returned, he was told his wife, Dorothy, was dead. She had been fished from the water and was laid out on the deck.

She'd drowned in the harbor. She could see land, she'd reached her destination, but she had no desire to continue. Some say it was an accident. Others say she threw herself overboard. She'd left her young son John behind in Holland with her parents and feared she would never see him again. Perhaps she thought William would not return either. I think of her sometimes when I am at my lowest. She lost hope, but we must not. God willing, we will be together again.

That is the hope that kept William striving, a better world for his children. That is what keeps me striving too. Like Isaiah says of the Lord, William Bradford was a man of sorrows and acquainted with grief. But he did not succumb to that grief, and neither will we.

Mother

It was after that letter from my mother that the dream started. Vivid dreams were not new to me. In my dreams I could fly and swim and run without touching the earth. My sleep was never filled with fear, only freedom. But in this dream, I was drowning, my skirts pulling me down to the ocean floor, my lungs screaming for breath.

I would wake up tangled in my bedclothes, sobbing for another chance, and furious with my mother. She rarely wrote more than a few lines, once or twice a year, letting me know she was well and asking after my welfare in return, but for whatever reason, she thought I needed to know about a woman who drowned in the harbor, a story that gave me nightmares ever after.

Dorothy May Bradford was not my ancestor. My mother descended from Joseph, a son of William Bradford's second marriage, and Dorothy May's blood did not run in my veins. Her tragic death was not a burden I should carry. Yet every once in a while, she came to me, and we drowned together in my sleep.

She cried for her son and begged him for forgiveness. *I'm sorry, John, forgive me, John.*

I fought to wake, but she never did, and if she ever changed her mind, it was always too late.

~

In February of 1775, Boston was controlled by the redcoats—the derogatory term for the British soldiers—but the countryside was bristling with activity. It had long been the law that every town have its own militia to protect from Indian attacks, and every boy over the age of sixteen was required to serve, to have his own gun, and to know how to shoot it. But those militias took on new life and purpose. A general agreement had been reached throughout the colonies that a local government would be established, and supplies and arms were being hoarded and military leaders were being elected.

In April, the British general Thomas Gage sent seven hundred British troops marching out of Boston toward Concord, about twenty miles northwest of the city, both to destroy the stores being held there and to arrest a handful of the Sons of Liberty holed up in nearby Lexington.

They were met with forty armed men—farmers mostly—in an open field, and a battle ensued. The redcoats routed the farmers and then proceeded to destroy the supplies, but on the way back to Boston, every Massachusetts man for miles grabbed his gun and took to the trees. They picked off the redcoats, one by one, as they marched through the countryside, making the mission a bloody one. Eighty-eight colonials died, but the British lost more than two hundred fifty soldiers.

After the events in Lexington and Concord, Nathaniel was made a lieutenant of the Middleborough Militia, and when he wasn't drilling in the village square, he was drilling his brothers in the barnyard, yelling out commands and prodding them back in line with a stick when they turned the wrong direction.

He let David, Daniel, and Jeremiah drill with them, though David and Daniel weren't yet sixteen and Jerry was only eleven years old and a little on the short side. But what Jeremiah didn't have in height or age he made up for in enthusiasm. I watched their little brigade, giggling at Jerry's serious face and Nat's furrowed brow, and joined in, matching their steps and holding my broom like a musket.

Nat turned on me, angrily. "This is serious, Rob."

I glared back at him. I knew it was, but they'd always let me join in before. It was Nathaniel himself who taught me to shoot.

"I know the drills as well as any of you do. And I can load twice as fast," I said.

"This isn't a footrace, Rob. And we won't be killing rabbits," Phineas said. "This is one thing you can't do."

"Women can't be soldiers, Deborah," Nat said, and pulled the broom from my hands like it was loaded and dangerous.

"I'm going to Boston just as soon as we get the word," Phineas said, puffing out his chest. He'd passed me up a while back and made a big deal about looking down on me from his lofty height a mere inch above me. Phineas was always in competition with me. He'd never really forgiven me for that footrace years before. He was faster now, a fact I secretly mourned, but my endurance was greater, and I never let him forget it.

"You're not going anywhere," Nathaniel said, shoving Phin's shoulder, trying to maintain order in his unruly ranks. "Someone has to help

Mother and Father. There's a farm to run, if you haven't noticed. And Deborah can't do it by herself, even though she thinks she can."

I wanted to strike Nathaniel so badly my fist curled and my mouth watered. I snatched my broom from his hands and marched toward the barn so I didn't beat him with it.

I didn't need Nat's permission. I could do the maneuvers on my own. I'd sat on a rise in town plenty and watched the men drill, performing the evolutions in my head, counting paces, and tensing my arms as my imaginary musket twirled in my head. I knew what came next and what came after that. I'd practiced each drill in the barn, calling the signals out to myself.

A man had to be five feet and five inches to serve in the militia. It was the height it took to load the long barrel of a musket. I had three inches to spare, but height was not strength. I knew that. I was strong for a woman, but I had never been blind to my own weakness. Each night, since the men had begun drilling, I pushed myself off the floor and lowered myself back down, repeating the action until I could not continue. Then I held my gun over my head, arms extended, the weakest position for me, by far. I don't know why I did it. It was a foolish enterprise and a waste of my time, but the need to prove myself and to compete was an impossible habit to break, even if I was barred from participation.

"I'll drill with you, Rob," Phineas said, coming up behind me, but he plucked my cap from my head and pulled it on his own. He looked ridiculous, the ruffle flopping against his cheeks, and I chased him around the barnyard using the broom as a sword and trying to retrieve my cap. He parried my blows with the handle of a shovel, and when he knocked my broom aside, I sprinted through the barn door, scooped up a handful of dirt and straw, and tossed it at his face as he tumbled inside behind me. He roared and caught me about my waist, his cheek pressed between my shoulder blades, and brought me down on a bed of hay. I'd used the same maneuver on him more than once. It was how Deacon Thomas caught pigs.

Phineas had gotten stronger in recent years, and I'd simply sprouted breasts and rounder hips, which hadn't helped me at all. If anything, they got in the way, and I was in a dress to boot. He rolled me over and pressed my shoulders into the ground, calling himself the victor. "You're pinned."

I wriggled and bucked, and he bore down harder, his upper body pressed to mine.

"You run like a boy. You shoot like a boy, fight like a boy, and you even look like a boy when you wear your britches. But you don't feel like a boy, Rob." I kicked and spat and swung my arms, humiliated by his words, but his eyes were frank as he pinned me with his knees and stared down into my face. I thought he would dribble spittle and exact promises, like he'd done a dozen times before, but he didn't. Or maybe he just didn't get the chance.

Phineas was suddenly knocked aside, and a red-faced Nat stood over me, his rage apparent.

"That's enough, you two," Nat thundered, though his anger was directed at me. Phineas stood, brushing at his clothes, and he was no longer smiling. Bits of hay sprouted from his hair and clothes, and he was glaring at his brother.

"Why are you so mad, Nat?" he asked, still trying to catch his breath.

"You know full well. I told you this had to end. Now get," Nat snapped. "And shut the barn door on your way out. I need to speak with Deborah."

Phineas looked at me and then back at his brother, his face growing crimson, though I wasn't sure if it was fury or embarrassment. He turned and left, his departure marked by squawking chickens trying to get out of his way. He swung the door so hard the whole structure shook.

"You need to apologize to Phineas," I said.

"Phineas needs to apologize to you," he shot back.

"Why?"

"Because a man doesn't handle a lady that way. He says he's old enough to fight. He's not even old enough to know that."

"I'm not a lady." I laughed. "I'm just . . . Rob. We've always been like this. You know that, Nat. He didn't do anything wrong. He doesn't see me that way. He never has. That's why I like him."

"Do you like him, Rob? I need you to think on that long and hard. Do you like him?"

"Of course I do. I know we fight. But that's the fun part."

He reached down and offered me a hand. I swatted it away and stood on my own, brushing at my arms and shaking my skirts. I didn't know where my cap was. Darn that Phineas.

"Phineas needs to grow up. He shouldn't be tossing you around like you're one of the brothers. You aren't. Never have been. Never will be."

His voice was so vehement that for a moment I couldn't see for the hurt that sprang to my eyes, but Nat continued, undeterred.

"You aren't ten anymore, Rob. You're a young woman. And you should act like it."

"I do!" I cried.

His brows shot up, and his mouth fell open.

"Well . . . most of the time, I do!" I insisted. "But acting like a young woman usually means not having any fun. Acting like a woman means working like a dog. It's perfectly fine that I churn the butter and milk the cows and wash the clothes. And somehow it's ladylike to scrub the floors, beat the rugs, and do all the chores. But I can't march in the yard, race up the hill, or wrestle Phin in the barn. Who decides these things, Nat?"

He shook his head. "For someone so smart, you are awfully dumb, Deborah Samson."

I gritted my teeth, and my palm itched, just like before.

"You heard what he said, didn't you?" The anger was back in his voice. "What Phineas said? That you didn't *feel* like a boy. Well, you don't. And you don't look like one either . . . because you aren't one. And don't think Phineas and all the rest of us haven't noticed. Why do you think Benjamin avoids you all of a sudden? He won't even look you in the eyes."

Benjamin *had* been acting oddly for some time. But he'd always been a little quieter, stuck right in the middle of the pack. He was the obedient one, the peacemaker, and sometimes keeping the peace in a big family meant you stayed silent. That's what Mrs. Thomas told me anyway, when I asked if something was bothering him.

"If you're not careful, Phin is going to think that wrestling means something different than it does. If that's what you want, so be it. But he's got some growing up to do. If he isn't what you want, then you'd best decide who it's going to be and make it known."

"What? Make what known?"

"You're beautiful. We all think so."

It was my turn to gape at him. "I am not," I scoffed. "And no you don't."

His nose wrinkled and his mouth twitched. He scratched at his cheek like he was trying to find the words. "Maybe not in the regular sense."

"Not in *any* sense."

"That's not true, Deborah. You're not pretty—"

"I've never tried to be," I interrupted.

"I don't say that to hurt you. I'm trying to explain."

"I'm not hurt." I would have been hurt had he lied to me and said that I was. I knew my worth was not in my looks.

"You're not pretty," he repeated. "But there's something about you. And it makes a person take note. Something in your eyes. Ma has it too, though with her it's because she knows and loves us so well. It's something different with you. It's like you're daring a man to challenge you, to tell you no, or to take you on."

"What has gotten into you, Nathaniel?" I asked, stunned. "First you're mad, and now you're going on about my looks. And why are you suddenly calling me Deborah?"

"That is your name," he ground out, angry again. Nathaniel was wiry and slim, and not much taller than me, but he'd always held himself above me. Above us all. Perhaps it was his position in the family. He was twenty-three, yet he acted as old as the deacon, though his opinions weren't always as predictable.

A shock of dark hair fell over his forehead, but he kept the back and sides shorter than the fashion, because he couldn't stand the brush of it against his neck. Mrs. Thomas or I took the shears to his hair once a month and the blade to his cheeks every morning to keep his thick, black beard at bay.

He wore his responsibility as eldest well and often spoke for his brothers; I wasn't surprised that he was speaking for them all now. I was simply stunned at the subject matter.

"I think we're all a little bit in love with you. Or maybe it's just admiration. But you could have your pick of the lot of us. David, Daniel, and Jeremiah are too young. Francis and Phineas are too, if you ask me, even though they're both older than you."

"Jacob is sweet on Margaret Huxley."

"All right. Well maybe not Jacob," he snapped. "But if you don't decide which one of us you like, and soon, it's going to cause problems between us. It already has."

"It already has?" My head was spinning. Nat had lost his mind. "But you're full grown . . . Why would you want me? I'm only fifteen."

"Ma was sixteen when she married Pa. He was my age."

"B-b-but . . . I'm b-b-bound until I'm eighteen."

"I'm not asking you to go anywhere."

"What *are* you asking me?"

He folded his arms and then unfolded them, like he wasn't certain where to put them. Then his jaw hardened and he reached for me, his hands on my shoulders, like he was about to deliver some very bad news and wanted to hold me up.

Then he kissed me. It was just a firm press of his lips on mine, though I'd had no time to purse them or prepare at all.

"Nathaniel!" I was so surprised, he could have pushed me over with the straw still stuck in my hair. "You don't even like me," I whispered.

"Yes, I do." His dark eyes flashed and he kissed me again, though his hands never left my shoulders.

His lips were dry and his cheeks were prickly, but it was not unpleasant. It was an odd sensation, his face so close to mine, feeling the tickle of his breath and seeing the spike of his lashes before I closed my eyes.

I wasn't sure I liked it. I wasn't sure I didn't. But I did not kiss him back. I didn't know how. Nathaniel may have taught me to shoot, but he gave no instruction now. He stepped back, his hands falling away, and I blinked at him in wonder.

"You can't say it never occurred to you," he said softly.

I shook my head. It had *never* occurred to me.

"I would have waited. But the world feels upside down. I'm out of time."

"But . . . you have been like brothers to me. And none of you ever let on."

"Sure we have. If you paid more attention to being what you are instead of trying to be what you aren't, you'd have set your cap on one of us a long time ago."

I didn't much care for that assessment. "You really want me to choose?"

He studied me for a moment, and his eyes dropped to my mouth, considering. I wouldn't have minded if he kissed me again, especially now that I was expecting it. It might help me decipher how I felt.

He picked a piece of straw out of my hair. “Yes. I want you to choose. I want you to choose me.”

The barn door squealed and Nat stepped back, well out of reach. There would be no more kisses and no more clarity.

“Nathaniel?” It was Mrs. Thomas, and her voice was sharp and her step quick. “Phineas says he’s leaving. Heading for Boston. He says you can’t stop him. Nobody can. What in heaven’s name happened?”

Nat sighed and I flushed, and he strode from the barn without explaining anything to his mother or me. Mrs. Thomas watched him go, but she didn’t follow him.

“War is coming,” Mrs. Thomas murmured, raising her eyes to mine.

I didn’t know what to say. I wasn’t certain whether she spoke of the country or the battle building in the house, and I was too shaken by Nathaniel’s declaration to focus on anything else.

“I have ten sons . . . and war is coming. God help us.”

“I need more time,” I said, though I was not really speaking to her at all. “I’m not ready.”

“I’m not ready either,” she said, “but no one ever asks us.”

– 4 –

Dissolve the Bands

One night, weary and rushed, I sat down to compose a letter to Elizabeth and wrote the entire thing in my journal before I realized my mistake. The journal was brand new, a present from Reverend Conant for my fifteenth birthday, and to rip the pages from the book would damage the binding. Plus, my orderly, exacting self could not abide the thought of a missing or torn page right at the beginning. So I left it, copying the words I had written onto loose paper the following day.

The letter to Elizabeth, there at the front of my journal, was an odd beginning to the book, but in many ways it captured my life and circumstances better than any essay or bit of self-reflection could, and I found the format freeing. I began with the salutation from then on, addressing Elizabeth and often copying bits of my entries into the letters I sent her, the diary becoming a more honest, unfiltered draft of what I could not say to her . . . or to anyone.

I was still careful. I was growing up in a house full of boys who were endlessly curious about what I was scribbling, and I knew better than to write anything that would devastate me were someone to read it. I resented that, but I had never been a fool. To be a fool required a level of fantasy no one had ever indulged in me. The only privacy I truly had was in the space between my ears.

But that night, even at the risk of having it discovered, I recounted the scene with Nathaniel in my journal and considered, for the first time, a future with each of the brothers, from Nathaniel down to Phineas. I felt ridiculous doing it. Nathaniel said they were all a "little in love with me," but I'd seen no evidence of that. Part of me was convinced Nat was pulling a cruel prank, though he'd never been prone to such things before.

Whatever Nathaniel had said to Phineas, it must have worked, because Phin didn't leave. At supper, with his eyes averted, he stiffly apologized to me for his "roughness," and promised it would not happen again. Benjamin, seated beside him at the table, clapped him on the shoulder, as if to comfort him. The conversation then moved to redcoats and blue skies, and if any of the boys were green with envy over Nathaniel's sudden interest, they didn't let on.

Nathaniel seated himself beside me at the table, and from the searching gazes of his brothers, I suspected he'd consulted with them. Deacon and Mrs. Thomas too. Nat had a private conference with his parents when supper was over, which I was thankfully not invited to. I did my evening chores, fled to my room, and bolted the door, needing the comfort of my letters and the clarity that came with writing my thoughts down.

I was as honest as I could be in my assessments, dissecting each brother's attributes down to the smallest thing, but when I finished, I felt no closer to a preference than I had when I started. On paper, Nathaniel made the most sense. He was the oldest. He was also handsome, hardworking, and the most ready to make a commitment. And he had kissed me.

But I wasn't sure Nathaniel and I would suit. He was always trying to make me still, and stillness wasn't in my nature. Nathaniel might make me unhappy. Even worse, I might make *him* unhappy.

Benjamin had a stillness all his own, and he didn't try to force it on me. It just moved with him, making him easy to be around. I liked that about him and wondered if I should ask him to kiss me so I could make a full comparison. That thought appealed, and I made a note to find a moment alone with him. Of course, if I made Benjamin unhappy, he would never say, and that too was unacceptable.

I could not imagine kissing Francis or Edward or Elijah. I thought that might be a crucial piece, though I could easily list their strengths and weaknesses. The thought of kissing Phineas made me laugh. We would argue about who kissed who the best and end up in some sort of match to settle it.

My laughter sounded a bit like a sob, and I shoved the list aside and began a letter to Elizabeth. I dearly needed a woman's advice, a woman other than Mrs. Thomas, who would not be able to see clearly through my dilemma. She was their mother, and Nathaniel, especially, was the apple of her eye.

Elizabeth had told me once about her courtship with John. *"I never doubted him for a moment. We were young, but he was so handsome and so confident, but without the bluster or arrogance of the other Yale boys."*

They'd married when he was twenty and she was seventeen, and for her, it had been an easy decision. It would not be an easy decision for me. I would not be seventeen for a while yet, and perhaps that was the only difference. But I didn't think so.

When a soft knock interrupted my musings, I ignored it, pretending I was asleep. I had not yet recovered from one interaction with Nathaniel and feared it was him.

"I can see the candle flickering beneath the door, Rob. I know you're awake." It was Phineas. I rose, abandoning the letter I was composing to Elizabeth, and cracked the door.

His hair was mussed and his shirt untucked, and he looked as wretched as I felt. Wordlessly, he handed me my cap. It was soiled and the ruffle was torn, and looking at it made me even more forlorn.

"I'm sorry," he said. "Can you fix it?"

"Of course."

"You can fix anything, can't you, Rob?"

I wasn't sure I could fix the new discomfort between us. It made me angry, and I blamed Nathaniel. It was yet another mark against him.

I bid Phineas a tired good night and made to shut the door, but he stopped me with a foot shoved in the opening.

"Let's run," he said in a rush. "We'll go as far as you want. I'll even let you win."

I gaped at him, though I immediately considered it. "It's dark, you'll get us both in trouble, and I don't want you to let me win, Phineas Thomas."

A ghost of a smile slid past his lips. "I know."

We studied each other for a moment, still awkward and uncertain. Then he squared his shoulders and folded his arms. "Are you going to let Nat win?" His voice had turned slightly belligerent, but that was Phineas too.

Elizabeth's counsel from long ago rose in my mind's eye. *"You must let the brothers win sometimes, just to encourage them. I find men are more apt to let us play if they believe they will triumph."*

But I didn't want to encourage Nat. I didn't want to encourage Phineas either, though I still wasn't certain that's what he wanted from me.

"I didn't even know we were racing," I answered softly.

"No . . . neither did I."

"I'd rather things stay the way they are," I begged.

He nodded slowly. "That can't happen if you let Nat win. Everything will change."

"It's not a competition, Phineas."

He smirked. "Sure it is."

I was suddenly spent. "No. It's my life. And I don't know how many prospects I have. I have to consider them all."

"Just wait, Rob. Wait. I'm not ready yet. Nat's right about that. But wait for me."

"For how long?"

"I gotta get out of here. I don't want to be a farmer. I want to see the world. Climb some mountains. Kill some redcoats." He grinned again.

"Sounds like I'll be waiting a long time." There was no sting in my words, but he wilted a little.

"I'd take you with me if I could," he muttered.

"I know you would." And what an adventure that would be.

"I'll come back for you, Rob. If you'll wait for me . . . I'll come back," he said, earnest.

His face was dear in the flickering candlelight, and I reached out and touched his cheek. It was still smooth, like my own, and such talk was as fanciful as fairies and Lilliputians. He had a life to live, and I wanted him to live it.

"Don't you worry about me, Phineas Thomas. You start running and never stop. If I were you, that's what I would do."

~

June 15, 1775

Dear Elizabeth,

It is odd to think of you in a different place. When I picture you, it is on a grand street in Farmington, writing to me from rooms that are so different from the one I occupy. But now you are in Lenox, on the edge of the frontier, and I am envious. How thrilling it would be to walk out one's door, turn west, and just keep on going. To see things no one has yet described, at least not in written words.

I don't know if I would have the courage to explore, and yet it would call to me. To be separate from all that is familiar would be terrifying and yet exhilarating. You have your children and Mr. Paterson, but I have nothing that binds me to my home, nothing but my servitude, and the time will come when that is done too. I think on that day with both eagerness and trepidation; there are many ways in which one can be bound.

Nathaniel, the oldest of the Thomas brothers, says he wants to marry me, but when I think of marriage, I see my poor mother and the heartache and vulnerability her union brought her, and I want something else. Something more. I should like to see the world and test my mettle. To go on a quest. To do something no one has done before.

I know these aren't sensible dreams, yet I still have them. As Antonio says in The Merchant of Venice, "I hold the world but as the world, a stage where every man must play a part. And mine is a sad one."

Do you think it is true, that every man must play a part? I should like a new one, if that is so. But as Mrs. Thomas said, no one ever asks us.

I remain your most humble and grateful servant,

Deborah Samson

~

My favorite time of day was dawn, and more often than not, when time and the weather allowed, I would climb up Mayflower Hill—I'd named it for my ancestors—and watch the sun come. But days started early on a farm, and I'd already gathered eggs, pulled the weeds from the garden, hung out a load of wash, and helped Mrs. Thomas put out breakfast on the table before I could even think about slipping away.

I was out of sorts, and so was she. The entire household was on tenterhooks, and she shooed me off after breakfast, telling me not to come back until supper so she could "have a moment's peace."

I'd been halfway up my hill, moving at a good clip, when I heard Jeremiah calling for me to wait for him.

"Rob! Wait for me. I'll come with you," Jerry hollered. I wanted to be alone, and Jerry liked to chatter, but I found a seat and settled in, waiting for him to catch up.

He plopped down beside me, though we still had half a hill to climb. I let him rest, suddenly in no hurry to reach my destination. I hadn't slept well. I'd dreamed of Dorothy May Bradford being pulled into the deep, her skirts wrapped around my legs, her hopelessness filling my chest.

"If this was all the world you ever got to see . . . just the view from this hill, would that be enough?" I asked Jerry.

"I suppose. It's a pretty good view."

It was. It was a spectacular view, and the pressure in my lungs eased. Perhaps it would be all right if I never saw another.

"It's beautiful. Looking at it, I can imagine what falling in love feels like." The thought made my throat ache. I didn't think I would ever feel that way about Nathaniel. I could admit that to myself now, with a little perspective.

Jeremiah scowled at me. "I don't like it when you say stuff like that. You don't sound like Rob."

"What do I sound like?"

"You sound like a girl."

"Well, I am one. And there is nothing else that makes me feel like this. Just look at it, Jerry."

"I'm lookin'."

"In some of my dreams I'm drowning," I told him. "But in some of my dreams I can fly. I rise up over the earth and look down on fields and forest, on rivers that crisscross the land and waters that slap against the shore."

"Do you have wings?"

"No. I just . . . rise up. The air doesn't whoosh around me. It doesn't take any effort at all. And I'm not afraid of falling. I see the farms and the trees and the sky. I sometimes fly all the way to Boston, following the road below me, though I'm moving much faster than a horse or even a bird. Then I see the ships in the harbor—sails of every height and size, and the air smells of brine and fish. I fly higher so I will not be seen. There is nothing to hide behind, and my skirts billow about me. I worry that someone will look up and see me floating there."

"And see straight up your skirts."

"Yes . . . and they will call me a witch and shoot me down with cannon fire. So I fly higher and faster, heading inland, though I've lost my sense of direction. I don't recognize the land or hills below me. I fly one way and then the next, trying to find my way back here, to this hill where I started from, but I can't."

"Are you scared?"

"I wake up cold and terrified every time. And yet . . . I still want to fly."

"I want to sail. Someday I'm going to go on a ship. I'll catch whales. You can come with me if you want to. You can be my cook."

"I don't want to be your cook, Jeremiah."

"Well, you can't be the captain."

I thought about that. "I could if I put my mind to it."

"The sailors would throw you overboard. Nobody likes taking orders from a girl unless she's his mother. That's why Nat gets so mad at you. You're always telling everyone what to do."

"I don't want to be in charge of anyone but myself." That's what I wanted most in the world, to be responsible for and to no one but myself. "But if you captain a ship someday, Jer, I wouldn't mind going for a sail."

A distant popping commenced, and we sat, our eyes trained toward the sound even though Boston was thirty miles away.

"Do you hear that?" I asked.

"Do I hear what?" Jerry grumbled. He didn't like climbing near as much as I did and was ready to head back down. I clutched at his arm and shushed him. The sound came again, a faint rumbling, like thunder in the sky, but the air did not smell wet and the sun blazed hot overhead.

"It's gonna rain, and we're up here," he whined again. "I'm hungry too. Let me have that apple."

I mimicked the sound, popping the air between my lips, so faint, so far away, and suddenly I knew. "It's cannon fire, Jerry. It's a cannonade!"

"It is not! You've never heard cannons, Rob."

I had begun to run, scrabbling up to the top so I could see even farther. Jerry wasn't far behind. He knew I was right. We watched as smoke rose into the June sky.

"Do you think that's coming from Boston?" he asked, awed.

"Yes. I do. It's . . . happening."

It was beginning. Not just a skirmish or a protest or throwing tea into the harbor. It wasn't pamphlets and speeches and practice drills on town greens. It wasn't even a skirmish in the woods. It was cannons. Warships. Thousands wounded. Hundreds killed.

It was war.

~

I slept in fits and starts for days afterward. One would think I'd seen the battle up close instead of from a green hill thirty miles away. The sounds of battle followed me into sleep and became mocking voices urging me to join the fight. I did not believe the dreams were from God. They were too much in my own mind and heart to give Him the blame or the glory.

But the boom and the bellow of warships and cannons had awakened something in me, and I wasn't the only one. We were all caught up in the swell. That is what it felt like—a great, sweeping wave that carried us into the sea of revolution.

Every young man felt the beckoning, I think. I felt it too. More than anything, it was a call to adventure, to heroism, and no one wanted to miss out.

They were calling it a Pyrrhic victory for the Crown, which meant the objective was reached but great losses were taken in the process. The Americans had built a redoubt and other smaller fortifications on the hills overlooking the harbor on the Charlestown side. The British had far superior numbers in addition to gunships, and their men were ordered up the hill in a full-frontal assault. It wasn't until after the third wave and many British deaths that the colonials, out of ammunition and powder, abandoned the redoubt and retreated down the other side of Breed's Hill. British losses were over a thousand men dead or wounded, including one hundred officers. Colonial forces lost less than half that number, but among the fallen was Dr. Joseph Warren, one of the famous Sons of Liberty. Overnight, his name became a rallying cry.

Nathaniel, Benjamin, and Phineas left for Boston with a local regiment of one hundred men right after the battle at Breed's Hill. Elizabeth's husband, John, was already in Boston. He'd gathered a militia from Lenox after Lexington and Concord, and arrived, ready to serve, the following day. Elizabeth wrote of his fervor, and she seemed to share it, though she was under the assumption he would return in a few days' time.

He didn't. None of the men did. John Paterson was elected captain by his regiment and then made a colonel within days of their arrival.

Nathaniel left without an answer from me. He'd been right. Time had run out, and though I knew I did not love him and would not marry him when he came home, I was grateful I had not been forced to declare myself, one way or the other.

"It is better this way. You're too young, and it wasn't fair of me to speak," he had conceded. "But I haven't changed my mind, and I can wait for you to make up yours."

"Will you write to us, Nathaniel?"

"I'm no good at that, Rob, but you must write to me." His use of my nickname made me smile. I didn't much care for *Deborah* on Nat's lips. It felt like a corset pulled too tight.

"But I'll be back before you know it," he vowed.

"I'm not coming back until every redcoat has been booted out of Boston. And maybe not even then," Phineas said, darting an apologetic look my way.

Benjamin simply gave me a smile and patted my shoulder, and the three of them left amid waves and tears.

General Washington took command of all colonial forces in July, and Jacob slipped off in August, telling Margaret, the girl he planned to marry, he would be back when the conflict was over.

Fall came, and Elizabeth reported that the men who had enlisted in haste in spring were ill-prepared for service in winter, and Mrs. Thomas and I worked feverishly to card and spin wool from the Thomases' herd and then weave two dozen blankets. I became so fast on the loom, the town commissioned me to produce the cloth for a hundred more, and I set up my operation in a room at Sproat's Tavern, accepting donations of carded wool for the soldiers. I spun and wove for long hours into the night and rode the old mare back home in the dark so I could fulfill my duties at home.

The days passed in a blur, the clap and the clack of the loom and the whir of the spinning wheel accompanied me into the winter and propelled me toward spring, waiting for news that never came.

Then, on March 17, 1776, General William Howe, commander of the British forces occupying Boston, boarded a ship and evacuated the city, ending the siege that had lasted almost a year. Washington and his army had managed, in the dead of night, with a storm rolling in, to mount cannons in Dorchester Heights, the highest point in the harbor, and train them on the British warships anchored below. It was a stunning victory, and Reverend Conant brought us word of the triumph with a bottle of wine and utter conviction that the trial would soon be over.

"They had to get the cannons onto the heights, but the ground was frozen, so digging trenches was out of the question. Old Put—that's what General Putnam's men call him—came up with a plan to build the fortifications in sections. Then they hauled the sections up the hills, quiet as church mice. They even put hay bales between the path and the harbor to keep the sound from carrying. Building parapets and hauling cannons isn't quiet. Neither are twenty-five hundred troops. Still, by 4:00 a.m., they'd done it. General Howe said the rebels had done more in one night than his whole army could have done in a month."

Deacon Thomas slapped the table in triumph, and Mrs. Thomas began to cry tears of pride and joy, but Sylvanus wasn't finished.

"The general also agreed not to burn the city if his men were able to leave unmolested." He threw up his hands, triumphant. "They're gone."

"Are they going back to England?" I asked. "Is it over?"

"Not quite. The British forces that were in Boston have taken temporary cover in Nova Scotia, but they've lost control of the ports in New England. General Washington is heading to New York. Some think the British will strike there next."

Phineas said he wasn't coming home until every redcoat had been booted from Boston, and that had just been accomplished.

But Phineas did not come home.

Nat, Benjamin, and Jacob did not come home either.

We expected them in June; they'd signed a one-year enlistment after Bunker Hill. Instead, buoyed by the end of the siege in Boston, they reenlisted, and Elijah and Edward joined them, whittling the number of brothers still at home to four. The deacon's shoulders began to droop, and Mrs. Thomas grew quiet and gray. Gone were six of their sons, seduced by a revolution that had grown significantly more trying and considerably less exciting.

I continued to labor and wait, though for what I did not know.

~ 5 ~

Of the Earth

In the early months of 1776, a pamphlet was widely distributed throughout the colonies, one I read and reread with paper and quill at the ready. Written by an anonymous author, it was titled *Common Sense*, and it called not just for redress from England but independence.

The pamphlet was too long for the papers to print, and too lengthy to nail to a tree, but Sylvanus Conant read sections aloud from the pulpit, though some hissed when he said "independence" and a few stood and left.

"Independence" was not a word that had been bandied about, and it was a step too far for many. Yet the word became a battle cry.

Not everyone agreed with the war. In truth, the yeas were but a slim majority, even in and around Middleborough, where a hundred sons from the area had marched to join George Washington in the last year and more were constantly going.

Treason became a common attack, and those who wanted to remain under England's flag had begun to call themselves loyalists, as if those who disagreed were guilty of a deeper offense, even a flaw in their characters.

"Who are they loyal to? A king and a flag? I think it a greater thing to be loyal to one's own countrymen," Deacon Thomas muttered.

I wrote to Elizabeth, full of questions and commentary, and she wrote back with her usual aplomb, promising that she would share my thoughts with John in her next letter to him and ask him for his insights.

A few months later, I received a stained and filthy letter with a *JP* in the wax seal and *Col. J Paterson, 26th Regiment* in the corner. I carefully broke it, marveling that a letter had reached me at all; we'd received nothing from the brothers. It was not more than a few paragraphs, with short, clear answers to the questions I'd asked Elizabeth, but he closed with this:

> *People must be convinced. Persuaded. The pamphlet is but a precursor, a softening of the populace toward these ideas, but it is a powerful one. The man who penned it could not have offered stronger arguments.*

The author of the pamphlet was still unknown, at least to the general public, and I had harbored secret fantasies about it being written by a woman. By someone like me. And why not? A woman could hide behind an anonymous signature as well as a man. The author intrigued me almost as much as the pamphlet itself.

But John Paterson proved right. Late that summer, the Continental Congress, in a statement written by Thomas Jefferson of Virginia, declared the united colonies "free and independent states."

I wrote to Mr. Paterson directly, saving poor Elizabeth from my idealistic ramblings.

August 14, 1776

Dear Colonel Paterson,

I have begun to record the beauty that is free—the smell of the earth, the colors of the sky at sunrise and sunset, the quiet of the morning, the chirping of the birds, the rush of falling water. So many of the most wonderful things are available to everyone, and such things bring me great comfort.

But nothing has given me more comfort or hope than the words of the declaration that has just been published. Life, liberty, and the pursuit of happiness. I have repeated these words until they run together in a new language, and every step I take rings with their rhythm. Life, liberty, and the pursuit of happiness. Never have words penetrated deeper or lifted me higher. For what good is life without liberty, and what good is liberty without pursuit?

Do you think it means all men? And women too? All mankind? Because either it is true for all, or it is true for none. A man cannot be given "certain unalienable rights" and then say they are only unalienable for some. Reverend Conant says "unalienable" means that they are not given by man but by God, by the nature of our mere existence.

It is something to ponder, indeed, and something that fills me with hope and purpose. The signers pledged their lives, their fortunes, and their sacred honor to the declaration. I have no fortune, and my life has never been mine, but I would pledge it if I could.

I remain, dear Mr. Paterson, your humble servant,

Deborah Samson

~

Francis enlisted in January of '77 after the rallying news of the battles in Trenton and Princeton. General Washington had crossed the Delaware in the dead of night, in hail and snow, on Christmas Day no less, and surprised the Hessians. A routing of Lord Cornwallis followed, and hope was restored. Francis could hold out no longer.

I went with him to the home of Reverend Calder of the Third Baptist Church, where the muster man rallied the locals, and a month later, we watched him march away. We'd all known he would go.

The day David and Daniel left, they didn't tell their mother or father; they begged me to do it for them.

"I can't," I protested, vehement. Sad. "You boys always want me to cover for you . . . to do your chores. But this is one I won't do."

"You're not going to try and stop us, are you, Rob?"

"No. I would go too. If I could, I would go too. But you have to tell them yourself. At least leave a letter."

"We don't write like you do. You tell them, and you take care of them too. You'll take care of them, won't you?" David asked. He'd always had a softer heart.

I nodded, though I could not promise. I was not a daughter, and my servitude would come to an end. I would not be bound by a contract or blood, and the need to run was growing in my belly. I wanted to go too.

~

"Soon your bond will be lifted. You will be eighteen. Do you think you might marry?" Sylvanus Conant asked me one week after meetings. He'd walked out into the sunshine to mill among his parishioners and eventually made his way to me, as he was wont to do.

"Marry? Who? They have all gone to war. And I am taller than the boys and old men who remain," I said.

"Yes. As tall as I," he marveled. "When did that happen?"

By the time I was fourteen I was almost a full foot taller than the diminutive Mrs. Thomas, who at four foot nine was shorter than the average woman, but not terribly so. I was not average at all, at least not in height, but Sylvanus Conant had shrunk as of late.

"I do not want to look down on my husband," I said.

"So find a man of stature."

"Psalms 68:6: 'God setteth the solitary in families: he bringeth out those which are bound with chains: but the rebellious dwell in dry land,'" I said. "I am solitary, indentured, and rebellious. I fear it is dry land for me."

"We should liken the scriptures unto ourselves, Deborah, but you have never been chained," Reverend Conant said, though he chuckled at my application of the text. "You are a woman of great fortune," he added.

My eyebrows surged beneath my cap, and he amended his words. "You are a woman of great *worth*, and I warrant the Thomases would be hurt if they heard you dismiss them that way."

"I warrant they would," I agreed.

His brow was furrowed and his blue eyes troubled as he continued. "You have been such a joy to me. I have no daughters of my own, but in my heart, I claimed you the first time I saw you. You looked like a foal, big-eyed and long-limbed, so eager to please, so precocious and precious. You deserved more than Mistress Thatcher, fond as I was of the old widow. You haven't missed her too much, have you, Deborah?"

"I have not missed her at all," I said frankly. Reverend Conant laughed again. He never seemed to mind the irreverence that slipped off my tongue. He'd always valued honesty more than propriety. Perhaps it was partly his fault I was the way I was.

"She was harsh, and"—he seemed to search for the right word—"jealous."

"Jealous?" I gasped.

"Widow Thatcher was old. Her life near over. You were young, with boundless energy and a mind unclouded by age and suffering."

"I suffered plenty."

He frowned at that, and the groove between his eyes deepened. He looked old, I realized suddenly, and his color was off.

"You have been happy here, though, haven't you? With the Thomases?" he asked again. "Mistress Thomas tells me there is nothing you can't do. You plant, you build, you cook, you sew. Young Jeremiah says you're a better shot than all of the brothers."

"There is much I can't do." I sighed. "But I have little control over that." I sounded bitter, which was unlike me. I did not complain. Especially not to Reverend Sylvanus Conant, who had been my true friend and advocate. "If I am skilled or at all accomplished, it is because you believed in me," I said, moderating my tone.

"You needed so little encouragement," he said.

"Yet you gave it abundantly," I answered, a lump rising in my throat. He was so dear to me.

"Put an old man's mind at ease, child," he begged. "Tell me I did not fail you."

"Never. Not even once. I would have memorized the entire Bible had you asked."

"You almost did."

"And I have a new recitation to share," I said.

"Oh yes? And what is that? The Book of Revelation or perhaps the entirety of *Hamlet*?" He was teasing me, but I had memorized the Divine Assembly for a pat on the head and a bit of praise.

"The declaration, have you read it?"

"I have."

"And what did you think of it?" I asked, impatient.

His eyes twinkled. "I haven't formed any firm opinions. Remind me what it says."

He had always been thus, encouraging my education in whatever form it took, and so full of admiration when I learned something new.

"'When in the course of human events,'" I began earnestly, and he stayed silent as I spoke the words, my voice ringing like his had from the pulpit an hour earlier.

One Sunday, Reverend Conant did not attend meetings. The congregation gathered, filing into a church that was ominously empty. After fifteen minutes of impatient waiting, Deacon Thomas was sent to check his quarters to see what delayed him. He was toppled over by his bed, still wearing his nightshirt and his cap. Deacon Thomas said it appeared as though he'd knelt to pray and his heart had failed him. The town grieved his loss, but no one more than I. I wrote to Elizabeth of his passing:

> *I have lost my truest friend and protector. I can't imagine my life without him. He was your uncle, and I should be sending my condolences to you, yet I am inconsolable myself. I know I should not complain when so many have died and while your beloved John is in harm's way, but I loved the reverend and he is gone, and I cannot grasp it. Who will listen to my recitations and marvel at my wit? Who will challenge me without censure? And how will I ever sit through another Sunday sermon?*
>
> *The Thomases have said I must continue to attend, that Sylvanus would wish me present, but*

I cannot bear it, and if the dead can see us, I would hope he can forgive me.

It was never fealty for the church that kept me going, but fealty to him. He loved God, so I do too, though I'm not certain God is in the churches. I attended the Third Baptist meetings last Sabbath, just to see if He might be there. Perhaps He peeked in through the windows, but I didn't feel Him. At least I didn't ache for my friend, so I might go again.

The Baptists are delighted to have me, as if they have won me over to their side. There are so few converts to fight over in Middleborough these days. It feels good to be wanted, though I am sure the attention will soon wane, especially when they realize I am not nearly so obedient or faithful as I now seem. My peculiarities will seep out soon enough, and they will be glad that I was never really one of them.

It makes me realize what a gift you are, dear Elizabeth. All these years you could have scolded me, shamed me, or simply chosen not to answer. Instead you have shared your life and your loves, your faith and your fortitude, and most of all your warm acceptance. Of all the gifts your uncle gave me, it has been correspondence with you that has most blessed my life. I will be forever in his debt.

I am, dear Elizabeth, with perfect regard, your most obedient and very humble servant,
Deborah Samson

Some men came home, straggling into town with their feet wrapped in rags and their clothing tattered, telling tales of terrible things. Their enlistment was up, and they'd seen enough. It was too much to ask a man with a family left destitute by his absence to continue on. But many men did.

News arrived in tatters too, bits and pieces of battles, rumors of glory and whispers of loss. And then one day a rider approached with a letter sealed with wax and addressed to Deacon and Mrs. Thomas. The rider did not smile or water his horse. He did not want to stay.

Nathaniel was dead. Killed in a battle near Brandywine Creek. A beautiful name for a terrible defeat.

A month later, the rider came again.

Elijah died in Germantown. Edward had died beside him.

The third time he came, the rider could not meet Mr. Thomas's gaze, and the deacon handed the letter to me. "Which son?" he whispered. "Which one now?"

David, who had worried over his parents, had succumbed to his inoculation of smallpox in a Philadelphia hospital. I wondered if Daniel was with him, and prayed Nathaniel, Elijah, and Edward were there to greet him in the end. Pennsylvania had claimed them all.

We'd grown accustomed to their absence, and they were absent still, but now their absence was final. We tortured ourselves with thoughts of their suffering and didn't know what to do with our own. We had no bodies to bury or cold hands to clasp. We had memories. A prickly kiss and a possibility. That was all Nathaniel had given me, and he would never be anything more. I would never have to refuse him or be tempted to accept his offer.

It would have been so easy to do. Had he come home and extended his hand, I think I would have taken it. It might not have been right, and I may not have loved him the way I suspected I was capable of loving. But I might have taken it.

One. Two. Three. Four. All in one fell swoop. We no longer believed there wouldn't be five. Or six, or all. Loss is not spread equally. I have learned that lesson well. It is a lumpy porridge and a thin gruel, and fate does not consider the suffering of a mother and say, *Perhaps I'll spare her this time.*

There were many times in our season of death when I sat upon my hill, surveyed the bit of the world I was allowed to see, and pleaded for God to rein fate in. Fate was cruel, but I did not believe God was.

But fate was not done, and God did not stop her.

~ 6 ~

The Equal Station

The day I turned eighteen, December 17, 1777, was like the day before it and the day after. I had waited for it since I'd been bound to the Thomases almost eight years prior, thinking that I would have plotted a course, a path that led to a life of my choosing, where no one could keep me and no one could control my steps. But freedom is not left or right, up or down. It exists in degrees.

A bird has more freedom than a horse. A dog has more freedom than a sheep, though it might depend on the value—or the lack of value—of the beast. A man has more freedom than a woman, but only a few men have any real freedom at all. Freedom takes health and money and even wisdom, and I had two of the three, but I had no more freedom the day I turned eighteen than I'd had before. In fact, I cried bitterly into my pillow and wished for a little more time.

"You must stay here, Deborah. You have earned a place with us for as long as you need, and I cannot bear the thought of you leaving," Mrs. Thomas said, and I gratefully accepted the reprieve.

"I have nowhere else to go," I said, and grieved anew that it was true.

Death had unmoored me. It didn't help that my birthday fell in deep December, when the days were short and dark and the spring still so far away. I'd saved enough for a spinning wheel and a loom, and spent long hours at both, but I needed the sun on my face and had no outlet for the boundless energy that bubbled and spit during the dormancy of winter. I chopped more wood than we could use and cleared the entire barnyard of snow. Jerry complained that I made him look bad, but with his brothers gone, there was more work for everyone.

I received a letter from John Paterson. It was dated six months earlier. Before Sylvanus died, before David and Daniel left. Before. Before. Before. But that it arrived on my birthday, a day I had looked forward to for so many years and now mourned, seemed providential.

He'd been made a brigadier general. His name, rank, and *Newburgh Encampment* were written above the wax seal. He had received my letter about the declaration, though that seemed a lifetime ago. I wondered how long it had bounced through the inconsistent and beleaguered post to finally catch up to him. We'd received a letter from Nat, the only letter we'd ever received, after he was already gone. My zest for the conversation, in the face of all that had been lost, had waned considerably, but as I read, my passion was restored.

Elizabeth said John had been sent to Canada with four brigades and sent back again when the campaign was abandoned. His regiment had been ravaged by disease and exposure, and the six hundred men he'd left New York with had been whittled down to half that when he rejoined General Lee just in time for Fort Washington to be taken by the British and Lee to be taken prisoner and then branded a traitor. John Paterson should have been disconsolate, but the letter held not a word of complaint.

June 23, 1777

Dear Miss Samson,

It is not for the man who has everything and wants more that we fight, but for the man who has nothing. In no place on earth can a man or woman who is born into certain circumstances ever hope to truly escape them. Our lots are cast from the moment we inhabit our mothers' wombs, from the moment we draw breath. But perhaps that can change here, in this land.

Our lives are so short. Very little of what you or I do will be felt in this generation or even in the next. Your forefathers—such a pedigree you have—set foot on this continent more than 150 years ago. We will never know what it cost them to cross a sea toward a dream, yet here we are.

What will life look like 150 years from now? I suspect our descendants will take us for granted, just like we take our ancestors for granted. No one will remember John Paterson when that time comes. Even my children's children will have no real knowledge of me or what I dreamed of, but God willing, they will reap the rewards of my efforts.

Many wonder what it is all for. I wonder what it is all for. And yet that truth, the truth of the ages, is that it is not for ourselves that we act. It is not our lives we are building, but the lives of generations that will come. America will be a beacon to the world—I believe that with all my heart—but that beacon is lit with sacrifice.

You should go to Lenox, to Paterson House. Elizabeth would welcome you. She calls you little sister. It is not Paris, but should you need a new frontier, you are welcome in our home. Two of my sisters and my mother live nearby—my beloved sister Ruth passed away last January—and it is a great comfort to me that they all have each other. As for me, I do not know when I will return. I hardly know what I have gotten myself into, and pray only for the strength to see it through.

John Paterson, Brigadier General

It was a speech so beautiful and impassioned that I wore it out with rereading and memorized whole passages, marveling endlessly that I'd even received such a communication. I suspected it was not so much a letter for me as it was a reminder to himself, as if John Paterson had needed to buoy himself up in a moment of frailty. It was his declaration to the world, and I'd simply been fortunate enough to read it.

~

All the best young men were gone, the educated and unlearned alike, and Middleborough had no one to teach the children their lessons. When I learned of the position, I volunteered, and Deacon and Mrs. Thomas vouched for my abilities.

"She knows much of the Bible by heart and reads and writes like a true scholar," Deacon Thomas attested, and I was given the position, though my compensation was limited to the generosity of the families I served.

"We will consider more pay when you have proven yourself," the local magistrate said, and I agreed, though I never saw a single shilling from him in the time I taught in the one-room schoolhouse near the Third Baptist Church.

We practiced our letters, did our figures, and made a study of the maps in our possession. It was not a Yale education, but I didn't do too badly, and I had only to level my "fearsome" gaze on the children and they did as they were instructed, for the most part.

I had inherited all Reverend Conant's books, and I was generous with them, but the children—I was glad to see almost as many girls as boys—weren't ready for Shakespeare. I told them the stories instead, reading sections and adding my own narrative.

We had arm wrestles and footraces at recess, and I did not let any of them best me. It was not dignified, but the boys were quite impressed and the little girls delighted.

I dedicated a small portion of our time each day to learning sundry things: tying knots and learning stitches and identifying the local flora and fauna. An education was about more than reading and arithmetic. It was about wonder too, and becoming able and useful people.

I told the children they need not enjoy or be good at everything, though I felt a right hypocrite, given that I had always demanded excellence from myself in all things. There were no lessons or assignments tailored to just the boys or only the girls. All my instruction was for every child, and surprisingly, there was very little resistance, even from the parents.

Perhaps they had low expectations of the female schoolteacher. Perhaps they knew it was only temporary, and when the war ended and life "returned to normal" I would be gone. But "normal" changed, and though I was the first female schoolteacher in Middleborough, I doubted I would be the last. It only took one person to climb a mountain or reach a summit before others followed and sought new heights.

To Elizabeth I wrote:

I am finally attending school, a place so long denied me, and I am ecstatic. It is only in the winter months for a few hours a day, and I am still able to do my weaving and assist the Thomases in the evenings and in the early mornings before school starts.

Jeremiah is the oldest of my students, and it is a joy to have him there, grinning at me from the back row. I don't know how long he'll attend. He is aching to join the fight, and I have no doubt that when he is of age, he will go as all the others have done, though I am praying he doesn't. I will miss him too much.

Teaching has helped to ease my restlessness and given me purpose. I am striving to be a Proverbs 31 woman, as you are, but Romans 12:2 is more to my liking: "And be not conformed to this world: but be you transformed by the renewing of your mind."

I fear I will be conformed to my very small world forever, but perhaps the boundaries are not as rigid or unforgiving as I once believed. It will not come as a surprise to you that I am enjoying pushing up against them.

I think of you every day, my friend, and pray for you, your daughters, and your beloved John. You must write and reassure me that you are well.

—Deborah

The summer of 1780 brought longer days and a journey to Plympton to see my mother for the first time in the decade since I'd left. She'd sent for me, begging me to come to her, and Deacon and Mrs. Thomas accompanied me there before continuing on to Boston to see the deacon's brother, whom they'd not seen since before the siege had gutted the town in the early days of the war.

My mother was not greatly changed, though the brown of her hair was woven with sprigs of gray and the ruts between her eyes and around her lips were more pronounced. She took my hands and peered up into my face, perhaps searching for the girl I'd been.

"You are so tall," she worried, the grooves deepening with her frown. It was not how I had imagined her greeting me after so long.

"Y-yes."

"I don't know if Mr. Crewe will approve."

"Mr. Crewe?"

"Our neighbor to the north. I have told him all about you. He is quite well off, and he's looking for a wife, Deborah."

"Is that . . . why you told me to come?" I asked.

"Yes. It is an opportunity for you. You are released from your bond, and you are twenty years old. You must marry."

She thought she was helping me. I could see it in her eyes and feel it in her eager touch. The knowledge helped me maintain my composure even as my stomach clenched with disappointment and dread.

My aunt greeted me kindly, her husband too, but they left us to visit at the small table set with a bit of butter and bread and sliced tomatoes from the garden. We ate in silence, strangers to each other, and she eventually returned to the subject of Mr. Crewe.

"You say you have told him all about me. What did you tell him?" I asked, lifting my eyes from my supper.

She hesitated, caught. How could she tell any man, any being, about me? She knew so little. We'd shared a handful of letters consisting of little more than evidence that we were still living, proof that we had not succumbed to the fate of poor Dorothy May. My mother knew nothing about me.

"I told him how able you are. I've been kept abreast of all your accomplishments. And Mrs. Thomas tells me you have not been ill, even once. Your teeth are strong and straight . . . your figure too. And you are an accomplished weaver. All the Bradfords are. I daresay there is nothing he will require in a wife that you can't provide."

"But what if he is not what I require in a husband?"

She blinked at me. "You are beyond the age where you can be too particular, Deborah. And you could do much worse. He is not much to look at, though I often think good looks are a cross. Your father was a very handsome man. We both suffered for it."

I was too distracted by her last statement to be offended by her first. "Oh? How exactly did he suffer?"

"His good looks made him believe he deserved more than life gave him. Had he been plain, he might not have been so proud."

"Had he been proud, he would not have abandoned his responsibilities," I countered.

"He was lost at sea."

"Lost at sea?" I'd never heard this part of the tale. "He did not drown at sea, Mother. He left us. Do not make excuses for him."

My honesty seemed to stun her. "He was ashamed," she murmured.

"His shame was more important to him than his family?"

"He was swindled out of his inheritance. It broke him. He tried to make a living as a farmer, but he was cut out for greater things."

"Greater things?"

"He was so handsome and so smart. So gifted. 'Twould have been a waste to not pursue more than our circumstances offered. He had to try, didn't he?"

She was lying to herself. I couldn't decide whether she'd told the story so often she believed it, or if it was simply better for her to be a widow than a woman abandoned by her husband. I suspected that was so, and it made me angry at her and angry at anyone who would condemn her, as if his failures were her fault. A widow still had her dignity. A discarded wife did not.

"He wanted to see the world," she explained. "He wanted to explore."

"And you didn't?" I asked.

She chuffed as if such things were ridiculous. "You children are all grown. All healthy. All strong. My work is done." She had not really answered the question, but she wouldn't. She had learned not to want impossible things.

I did not want to hate my mother, but I did not love her, and I could not listen to her rationalizations. She had not raised me. She had not worked for my welfare. I had done that with my own sweat and my own labor.

I rose, unable to abide her presence any longer. I was supposed to remain with her until the following day, when Deacon and Mrs. Thomas returned, but I determined in that moment that I would walk back to Middleborough if I had to. I was wearing sturdy shoes.

"Your sister, Sylvia, had another baby. She has four now," she said in a rush, seeing I was ready to flee. "She writes that all are healthy and strong."

"I am glad she is well," I whispered. I hoped she was. She lived in Pennsylvania. I hadn't seen her—or any of my siblings—since I was five years old. I could not even conjure a face.

"All of my children are well. That has been my only goal."

I wanted justice—justice for her, justice for me—but as I looked at her, mercy won. It was true. She was right. I *was* well. I was healthy and strong and grown, just as she'd said. With five young children and no way to support them, she must have feared such a day would never come.

"He came back . . . for a time, just after you went to live with the Thomases," she added. "He asked about all of you. Where you were and if you were well. I thought he would stay. But he didn't. And I haven't seen him since."

"You let him come back?" Had she welcomed him into her bed with the arms that had once held his dispersed and discarded children?

"Of course I did. It was all I ever wanted." She didn't even look up from her stitching.

"Why?" The word was almost a wail.

"Because it would have meant *you* could come back," she said quietly.

I sank back into the chair I'd vacated, shamed and heartsore. My mother had given me all that she had. And I was angry that she couldn't give more.

"Why did you teach me to read?" I asked. "I was so young, and you must have had so many other things demanding your time and attention."

"I hardly did anything at all. I was teaching the older children, and you learned so quickly."

I inhaled deeply and let it go. "Thank you."

Surprise rippled over her guarded face. She had not expected such words from me.

"William Bradford believed all men and women should be able to read the word of God for themselves," she said.

"Yes. I know. You have always been so proud of your lineage."

Her back straightened and her chin rose. "Ours is a tree of strong roots and sturdy branches, filled with freedom-loving people."

I wondered what strong roots and sturdy branches were good for if I was never given the opportunity to grow or to bloom.

"William Bradford arrived in this land more than a century ago," my mother continued, her voice still ringing with pride. "The compact those Separatists made as a people became the foundation for the war we fight now. It is God's war. His plan, and His timing. And it started with them."

I thought of my dream, the one where I flew above the earth, time spread out beneath me. Nothing before, nothing after, everything one, eternal now. I imagined it was how God observed the world, moving the pieces and painting the scenes, forward and back.

"'I hold the world but as the world, a stage where every man must play a part. And mine is a sad one,'" I quoted. How often had I pondered that line?

My mother looked up at me, her head cocked quizzically. "Every part is a sad one, Deborah. And rarely one of our choosing."

I could not argue with that.

Milford Crewe was a diminutive man who must have appeared old even when he was not. He was balding on top and attempted to make up for it by allowing his hair to grow long and brush his shoulders in graying blond curls. He swept his wide-brimmed hat from his head and gave me a little bow, one hand at his waist and one in front of him, like we were about to do the minuet. He was not much to look at, it was true, but it was his manner that most repelled me.

My mother had insisted on dressing my hair, and two long curls hung down each side of my face though the style did nothing for my strong features and my square jaw. I'd learned it looked best drawn back in a long, fat plait or coiled neatly around my head underneath my cap. Everything else made me resemble a Christmas goose with a ribbon round its neck.

Upon introduction, Milford Crewe walked around me like he was inspecting a cow, even tugging at the strings of my cap like he wished I would remove it.

"Your eyes are an odd hue, aren't they?"

I felt my lip begin to curl into a sneer, and I sucked it between my teeth. "I don't know. What color should they be, Mr. Crewe?"

"Blue or green or brown would be fine. They're all three, far as I can tell."

"Yes, well. I'm temperamental. Hard to please. I doubt I'd make a good wife."

"I don't know about that." He said it as though he was bestowing a great compliment.

"I do."

"You're tall."

"Yes. I am. And you're not."

He stuck out his jaw and wrinkled his forehead. It made him look a bit like Deacon Thomas's billy goat. I half expected him to emit an impatient bawl. What a pair we would be. A goose and a goat, honking and bleating at each other, completely unsuited and forced to share the barnyard.

He claimed he was not a loyalist, but he was not a patriot either, and to me, that was unacceptable.

"When it is all said and done, we will have nothing but blood and debt to show for our efforts. I am a pragmatic man, and this war never made any sense to me." He shrugged. "But children must learn."

Mr. Crewe stayed all afternoon, chatting with my mother and considering me. He asked me questions only to shift his gaze or become impatient when I gave him more than a simple answer, and my mother grew more and more desperate on my behalf.

He was still in attendance when the Thomases arrived, the wagon wheels signaling their welcome approach. I practically leapt for the door, but my mother stood guard, trying to forestall the inevitable.

Sadly, he asked if he could see me again, and nothing I said could dissuade him.

~

The journey back home was a painful one. We traveled the same road from Plympton to Middleborough as Reverend Conant and I had done a decade earlier, but I was not the same girl. I no longer mourned the loss of my mother or feared the people beside me, but I was gutted all the same.

"You are so quiet, Deborah."

"I do not wish to speak over the clatter," I answered.

"What did you think of Mr. Crewe? He seemed quite taken with you," Mrs. Thomas said.

"He did not." Of that I was sure. Whatever he was, he was not taken with me at all. He might think his charity would profit him, but there had been no admiration in his eyes.

"He is as good as any man," Mrs. Thomas said, her eyes surveying the countryside. I could only stare at her, dumbfounded.

"Is he really?" What a pathetic thought. He was not half the man Reverend Conant was. Or Deacon Thomas. Milford Crewe didn't have Nathaniel's confidence, Benjamin's peace, Phin's passion, or Jeremiah's sweetness. I could think of nothing about him I liked.

"I would rather lie with the pigs," I said.

Mrs. Thomas gasped and the deacon glowered at me like I had spoken in tongues. I bowed my head in remorse. I hadn't meant to sound crass. Only honest. Only vehement. I would rather parade naked through the town square than disrobe in that man's presence. I knew how children were made. I knew men liked the process and women weren't supposed to. I thought I might enjoy it, but not with Mr. Crewe. Not with him.

"But . . . will you allow him to see you again?" She looked at me oddly, and I could not fathom her thoughts.

I sighed. "I have no wish to see him again."

"He has offered to buy the fields I cannot farm and build nearby," the deacon said. "It is a good offer. You must allow him to make his case." It felt like a command, and it hung in the air, as discordant as the squeaking wheels. Again, I was struck dumb.

"I would have liked very much for you to remain in the family. But this way you will be close by. And now that Nathaniel is gone," Mrs. Thomas murmured, "you must choose anew. It is time, Deborah."

I didn't have the heart to tell her that even if Nathaniel had lived, I could not imagine being a wife. And if not to Nat, then most definitely not to Milford Crewe.

"I would have liked to remain in the family too," I said, and that much was sincere. I let the rest of my thoughts go unexpressed.

~ 7 ~

The Laws of Nature

Death has a way of stripping away our inhibitions and our excuses. I'd lost so many in such a short time, but Jeremiah did not die . . . he simply left. His height had held him back thus far—a soldier had to be five feet five inches—and Jerry was too small. But the summer before he turned seventeen and I turned twenty-one, he grew two inches, gained ten pounds, and promptly signed his name to the enlistment rolls. I begged him to stay, if not for the deacon and Mrs. Thomas, then for me.

"Please don't go, Jerry."

"You would go if you were me," he shot back. I could not deny it, and he knew it.

"If you go, I'm coming with you," I threatened.

"Oh, Rob." He laughed and shook his head. "You would make a good soldier. A good sailor too. I'm sure of it. But they won't take you."

"I swear it. If you go, I'll follow you. You heard about the woman in the Battle of Monmouth. She loaded the cannon when her husband fell ill. A cannonball went right between her knees. Blew off her petticoats, but she didn't suffer a scratch. Didn't falter either." Stories of the woman had spread, though nobody seemed to know her name. There were other tales of wives who had followed their husbands to war, and I was convinced I could do it too.

"You don't have a husband, and nobody's going to let you anywhere near a cannon, Rob. And you can't make me stay. I want to be a sailor. I may be the youngest and the smallest, but I'm big enough, and I'll always wonder if I don't go. I'll wonder, and I'll be ashamed. You don't understand, because you're a girl, and no one expects it of you."

"How are we to watch out for each other if you leave?" I argued, desperate to convince him.

"How am I to face myself if I stay?"

The year 1780 became 1781, and as soon as the snow began to thaw, Jeremiah headed to Philadelphia to join the merchant marines headquartered there, his shoulders set and his gaze sure.

The day he left home, Mrs. Thomas went to her bed and refused to rise.

"I delivered ten healthy sons," she wept. "I never had any difficulty carrying them, not even the twins. I had easy births too. So many women suffered terribly. Not I. I was built for birthing sons. You wouldn't think it because I'm small, but it came easily to me. Raising them was another matter, but I never complained, because I'd been so richly blessed. I thought myself so lucky, but I wonder now. I can't help but think it would hurt less if I'd never loved them at all."

Deacon Thomas went out among his animals, to the fields he would farm alone, and I scrubbed and spun and chopped wood and forced them both to eat, and when I could find nothing else in which to occupy my time—the school season was drawing to an end—I wrote to Elizabeth and also to John, though neither of them had responded in ages. It had been six months at least.

Two letters, one for me and one for the Thomases, arrived in early April. One was from John Paterson, and one was from Benjamin. I tucked my letter into my bodice for later and coaxed Mrs. Thomas from her room to read the one addressed to her.

She made her husband read it first, though I told her it was addressed in Ben's handwriting and surely welcome news.

The deacon read it once, silently, with shaking hands, and then he read it again, out loud, to Mrs. Thomas and me.

> *We have made it through the worst winter we have ever spent. But our enlistment is up next month, and Jacob and I are satisfied that we've done our part. The news of our brothers has brought us both low. Enough Thomas blood has been spilt.*
>
> *I don't think the war will continue too much longer, and certainly not in the northern colonies. Most of the action has moved south, though Benedict Arnold's betrayal and poor Major André's hanging had us fearing an attack here at the Point. We have spent these months holed up doing little but shivering and starving and waiting for orders. We'll be home in time for planting. Don't let Rob do it all before we get there.*

"They are coming home," Mrs. Thomas moaned. "Coming home!"

The deacon nodded, his lips quivering and his eyes bright. He shoved his hat on his head and retreated to the back pasture, needing some privacy to collect himself. Mrs. Thomas bustled about, revived, and began preparations for supper as though Jacob and Ben would be arriving any minute.

I kept the letter from John Paterson tucked inside the fichu of my dress, enjoying the anticipation of more good news, and I didn't take it out again until we'd finished our afternoon meal and sat in companionable silence about the table, Deacon Thomas reading his Bible and

Mrs. Thomas carding wool. I pulled out my letter and carefully broke the seal. Mrs. Thomas looked up in interest as I unfolded it.

"What have you there, Deborah?"

"It's from General Paterson. I haven't heard from him or Elizabeth in so long," I explained. "It arrived earlier, with the letter from Benjamin."

"So kind of them to keep up a correspondence after all these years." She said something else and I think I nodded, but I was no longer listening.

I was no longer breathing.

Ice and fire warred in my chest, and I read through the scant message three times, then read it again, looking for the lie.

I had never met Elizabeth Paterson in person, but she had been my dearest friend. In every way, she gave me solace and joy. For nigh on a decade, she had never rejected me and never failed me.

And she was gone.

I laid my head down on the letter, unable to push it away, unable to deny the words even as I sought to hide them. When I closed my eyes, I could still see them on my lids, John Paterson's slanting scrawl like a line of black ants, undeterred.

Feb'y 10, 1781

My dear Miss Samson,

I regret to inform you that Elizabeth died suddenly last September. She had not been well in some time, though she was good at hiding her ailments. Especially from me. I have been released to attend to our affairs in Lenox. I know you and Elizabeth have enjoyed a long correspondence, and I am sorry to notify you of her death in such an abrupt and unfeeling manner, but I know of no other way. I find I am spent and have little compassion to spare. She was very fond of you and had the greatest hopes for your happiness.

My deepest regard,
John Paterson

Such a short missive.

Such a massive blow.

I had no compassion either. Not for poor John Paterson, or his children, or even Elizabeth herself. In that moment, I was consumed with sorrow for myself. I had not a soul left on the earth. Not a solitary soul on whom to rely or live for. No more letters. No more hope. And *nothing* to look forward to.

"What is it, Deborah?" Mrs. Thomas asked, her voice wary.

"Elizabeth Paterson has died." My voice was dull.

She nodded, oddly, as if she'd expected it. Of course she expected it. She was all too familiar with letters filled with bad news and visitors who brought tidings of horror and tears. We had both grown accustomed to terrible things.

"Her husband . . . is he still serving under General Washington?" she asked, not lifting her eyes from the wool.

"He says . . . he says . . . he has gone home to Lenox."

"As he should. The war has gone on too long."

She said nothing more, and truly there was nothing more to say. I stood, John Paterson's letter in my hand, and I thought for a moment that I would enjoy watching it burn. I held it over the candle, the page fluttering between my fingers.

I would not receive another.

Not from Elizabeth and not from her beloved John. He would have no reason to write.

I snatched it back, the corner singed, and turned to my little room.

"I'm tired," I said, though it was not weariness coursing in my veins. "I'm going to bed."

"Good night, dear," Mrs. Thomas said softly.

"Good night," I said, though it was only four o'clock. The day was dreary and dark, but bedtime was still a while off.

There is a clarity that comes when one surveys the years gone by from a perch of experience and age. Death, disappointment, and a wealth of desperation had backed me up to the cliff's edge. I can see that now, even as I marvel that I jumped.

I pulled out the breeches and the shirt that one of the boys had discarded and none of the others had claimed. They weren't the same pair that made me fleet of foot and free as the wind. They weren't magic. I'd outgrown those. I loosened my dress and tugged it off, repeating the action with my underthings until I stood naked and shivering in the waning light peering through the tiny window.

I pulled the pins from my hair and ran my brush through it, watching myself in the small mirror that hung on my wall. My hair hung past my waist, and with it brushed to a sheen and streaming around me, I felt like a creature from the sea, not constrained by fashion or station. A siren or a Greek goddess. I thought I might be beautiful this way, though I was not soft or small.

And no one would ever know.

No one would ever see this version of Deborah. No one but my husband.

Milford Crewe wanted to be my husband. He seemed intent upon it, and I suspected the sale of the deacon's land was contingent upon my agreement.

"No!" I spat, startling myself. My hairbrush clattered to the floor.

"No," I said, but this time much more softly. "No. Not him. Not ever."

My hair was my one vanity, yet my tresses made me angry too. What good was beauty to me? I was as tall as most of the men I knew—as tall as half of the Thomas boys I'd been raised among. My mouth was wide, my jaw square, and my cheekbones sharp. The bump on my nose and the thickness of my brows made me more handsome than fine, though I wasn't certain I could claim any comeliness. Even my eyes with their many colors were more strange than lovely.

"I do not want to be a wife," I whispered. "I do not want to be a *woman*." Emotion rose and broke, and my reflection became a watery smear. "I want to be a soldier."

Did I?

I swiped at my eyes, angered by my weakness, but my heart was pounding. *I did.*

"Why should I not play the part?" I said, louder now. "When it is within my power to make it happen?"

My hair shimmered around my body, beckoning me. I wouldn't have to cut it *all* off. The men I knew wore their hair gathered at their napes in short tails. I'd trimmed the boys' hair often enough. I'd shaved their stubbly cheeks too. Shaving was not something many men attempted without a good mirror, and often not even then. It was a skill better left to a barber—or a woman—and I'd shaved every one of the Thomas men, except Jeremiah, who had no more beard than I. The thought gave me courage. There were plenty of bare-faced boys in the army. But none of them had hair to their waists.

I took a hunk of my hair in my fist, and with the sharpened edge of the same blade I'd used on the boys, sheared it off at my shoulders, long enough to tame it into an oiled queue, but short enough to draw a sharp distinction between male and female. Section by section, I repeated the action until there was far more hair at my feet than on my head.

I turned my head to the right and then to the left, enjoying the new, weightless swish against my naked shoulders. My breasts seemed bigger without my long hair obscuring them. They jutted out, rosy-tipped and large enough to fill my palms, and for a moment doubt surged. I folded my arms across my chest, searching for a solution.

My corset lay discarded on my bed, and I studied it, an idea forming.

I slid out the boning, removed the ties, and cut the corset into horizontal halves. I didn't need to be winnowed from my ribs to my hips; I needed to constrain my breasts.

With careful stitches, I hemmed the newly cut edges and restrung each section with a piece of the long tie. Now I had two cinchers, each about six inches long, one to wear, and one to spare. If it didn't work, maybe I could sew the pieces back together and reinsert the boning.

I stepped into the halved corset and wriggled it up so it circled me beneath my armpits. Then I pulled the laces good and tight, and my breasts flattened obediently against my chest. It almost felt . . . good.

What an odd feeling to be bound on top and free at my middle! I knotted the ties, tucked the ends beneath the band, and bounced on my toes, watching my reflection and marveling at the lack of movement. I raised my arms, danced a little jig, and almost laughed out loud. It felt right.

With the shirt on, it was even more impressive. The swell was not any different from that of a man with a bit of muscle on his chest. My shoulders weren't broad, but they weren't narrow either. I'd developed enough strength in my back to create a tapering from my shoulders to my ribs, and my hips were narrow in the breeches I secured around my waist.

"My bottom is a bit too round," I worried, palming my backside. I thought about cinching it too, and how I might accomplish such a thing, then dismissed the idea. Most young men had no idea what a woman's bottom looked like beneath her skirts, and they certainly had no idea how one looked in breeches. I giggled, the sound high-pitched and nervous, almost a keening, and I immediately swallowed the bubble of mirth. Laughing was out. Crying too.

I was going to see the local muster man. If I was successful, I would return before morning and finish the last two weeks of school while I awaited my reporting day—I knew by now how it was done—and no one would be the wiser.

~

I went to town without a word or a note to the Thomases. They wouldn't worry. Mrs. Thomas knew I was grieving. If she noticed me gone at all, she would think I'd taken a walk in the woods or climbed to the top of my hill, as was my habit.

I'd added Reverend Conant's vest and coat to my ensemble, along with the deacon's Sunday hat. I would buy my own when I got into town and return his to the hook by the door. My shoes were Reverend Conant's too, and they needed new buckles to cinch them up tight—I had a narrow foot—but they too would do until I got into town. A soldier needed good shoes.

I walked past the tavern and onto the green, past the First Congregational Church, strolling along with legs unhampered, arms swinging at my sides. No one stared. Wagons rolled past. I did not wave. I was a stranger, I told myself, and I did not shrink or pick up my stride.

Master Israel Wood, the muster man who had enlisted every one of the Thomas sons, looked directly into my face and saw me not at all. Did a skirt wield that much power? Or were a pair of breeches so convincing a disguise? I could not believe it. Yet no one studied me with any interest.

I signed the enlistment rolls with the name Elias Paterson, a name I'd settled on during my walk into town, and was given sixty pounds, which I didn't stop to count. Instead, I purchased a pair of shoes and a hat with a green cockade, and stared at myself in the glass. I looked like a dandy, but I didn't look like a woman.

No one even questioned me. They looked me square in the eyes and no recognition flickered. I might have laughed if I wasn't so stunned. I had not altered my face. I'd simply changed my hair and donned a hat and the clothes of a man. Yet no one saw Deborah. No one saw a woman.

I marched into Sproat's Tavern and sat myself upon a stool, not looking to the right or left. I reminded myself to lounge with my knees wide and my elbows on the bar, as though I had much on my mind and something substantial between my legs.

I'd spent months in the backroom of the tavern with my loom producing bolts of cloth for the army with donations from the townspeople. I had never sat at the bar and I had never had a drink, but if I could pass the test here, I could pass it anywhere.

"What'll you have, young man?"

Sproat didn't even turn around, and I grunted out, "Rum, please," without squeaking. I didn't think I liked rum. But I didn't know, and whether I liked it or not, I was going to down it like a man, a free man, a solitary man, and then ask for another. I drank them both, suppressing the body-length shudder that they induced, and asked for one more.

"So you're off with the others?" Sproat asked. "Maybe you'll see my son, Ebenezer. He's with the Fourth. They've made him a colonel."

"Yes, sir," I said, and belched just like Jeremiah taught me. I set my hat on the bar, growing ever more confident, and ran my hands over my tidy queue.

"You'd do well to keep your hair covered. The sun will bounce off that blond and give the redcoats a shining target. My son stands a foot taller than most of the others. It's a wonder he's still got his head." He stopped pouring and offered up a prayer right then and there.

"I'm not tempting you, Lord, nor am I crediting luck when I well know it is Providence, and I am full of gratitude. Bless all the boys from Middleborough, including this lad who's not yet a man." He opened one eye and looked at me. "And may his drink make the hair sprout upon chest and cheek, that if he dies, he dies fully grown."

"Amen!" someone said, sitting at my side with a belch and a slap to my back.

"He's going to need more than hair, Sproat!"

"Oh yeah?"

"He's as spindly as a new foal. He needs meat with his rum."

I had a fish pie and another glass. I was beginning to like the flavor. "It's what freedom tastes like," I whispered, but the men around me laughed. I guess I spoke louder than I thought.

The room had grown soft around the edges, and it pulsed with the beating of my heart. I wasn't afraid anymore, but for some reason, I began to cry. My tears kept dripping down my face and wetting the bar beneath my cheek. I would sleep here, where I was prayed for and protected by all my new friends. And tomorrow I would don my dress for a little longer, until it was time to report for duty. No one would know. I'd done it. I'd become a man.

~

"Are you sure?"

"Yes. Look at her hand. She's got a felon finger. See how red and calloused it is? It's from feeding the thread into the wheel; you've seen it done. You've seen her do it! This boy is Deborah Samson."

"There's only one way to know for sure."

Their voices were muted and dreamlike, and I was not ready to wake. I was not *able* to wake, truth be told. I didn't think my eyes would open or my limbs would move, but my pickled brain was trying desperately to rouse me.

Big hands grasped my shoulders and sat me up straight. I managed to peek out beneath my right lid, to see who was handling me. It was Sproat and his frizzy-haired woman.

They were staring at me, intent, and reality crashed around me. A flood of pure terror burned off the lethargy that had held me in thrall, but Sproat and his wife weren't done with me. Mrs. Sproat ran her palms across my chest.

"She's got 'em bound up, but they're there."

I gasped and slapped at her hands, and promptly fell from the stool I'd spent several hours so happily perched upon.

"Call the constable and the muster master. I saw her sign the rolls. She took bounty under false pretenses!" someone yelled.

"Did you spend it all, Deborah Samson?" Sproat was helping me back onto the stool. His hands didn't wander to verify his wife's claims, but he seemed convinced all the same. I was caught, and I was drunk.

I shook my head. No. I hadn't spent it all . . . not all of it . . . had I? I clutched the purse at my waist that had felt so healthy and hopeful the night before. It tinkled but it didn't clank, and I counted what remained with horror. Surely I had not spent so much. Someone must have taken it.

"She's going to be sick. Get her out of here," Mrs. Sproat wailed. "I don't want to be cleaning up after her."

"I can pay it back," I stammered, rising. I would not be sick. I would not. "I've just got to go home to get the money. I'll pay him back. Please don't tell anyone," I begged Mr. Sproat.

I staggered toward the door, but Mr. and Mrs. Sproat weren't willing to let me go so easily.

"It's too late, Deborah Samson," Mrs. Sproat crowed. "You heard 'em in there. People know. Word will travel if it hasn't already. Someone's gone for the reverend and some of the church brethren. And rightly so."

"You go get the money you took, and you give it back to Israel Wood," Mr. Sproat instructed, his tone more kindly. "Do it now, and the constable will go easy. The Baptists . . . I don't know about them. But at least you won't get tossed in the clink."

~ 8 ~

The Opinions of Mankind

I was escorted back to the Thomas farm by two elder brethren of the Baptist church, Clyde Wilkins and Ezra Henderson. Both had been particularly committed to my conversion after Reverend Conant died. I rode in the back of the cart, listening to them confer, bouncing all the way and sicker than I'd ever been in my life.

It was not yet dawn, but Master Wilkins pounded on the door until it was thrown open by a weary Deacon Thomas and a hovering Mrs. Thomas. The brethren then enumerated my sins in great specificity while I stood silent, guilty of every word, clutching my jaunty hat and swaying in my new shoes. I'd lost the deacon's hat somewhere along the way.

When they left, the deacon and Mrs. Thomas stared at me, eyes bleak and mouths tight, as if I'd brought tidings of new death. The deacon pointed toward my room, his voice weary. "Go to bed, Deborah. We will talk when you aren't addled."

I did as I was told, fighting tears of humiliation, and Mrs. Thomas hurried behind me. I refused her assistance, afraid she might take my costume, and bolted the door behind me.

When I joined them at noon, pallid and penitent, they had already discussed my fate.

I handed Deacon Thomas the bounty money that remained, combined with the money I had spent. It left a dent in my paltry savings. For years I had pocketed every penny from my wool and my vegetables, and in one night I'd squandered almost a quarter of it.

"I'll take the bounty and see that it is returned to Israel Wood. I'll talk to the church elders too. I'll tell them you lost your senses, but it won't happen again." Deacon Thomas paused and raised somber eyes to mine. "It won't happen again, will it, Deborah?"

I shook my head. No. It would not happen again. Not in Middleborough. I had been a fool.

"Why did you do it, Deborah?" Mrs. Thomas asked. "The whole town will think something is wrong with you. They won't hire you for their weaving or let you in their homes. Not if they think you're not of sound mind and you're loose with your morals."

"I drank too much. I didn't mean to. But many people do that. Some get sozzled night after night. No one thinks they are nutters. No one thinks they are loose."

"The men who get drunk are not females dressed as males. They aren't schoolteachers and itinerant weavers. They aren't *women*," the deacon said gravely.

"No. They aren't women," I agreed. And that was the heart of the matter. "I should never have gone into the tavern." *Why had I gone in the tavern?*

"Going into the tavern was the least of your sins," the deacon chided.

"You signed the muster!" Mrs. Thomas cried. "Do you really want to go to war?"

"Yes. I really want to go. I want to help end it. And why shouldn't I? I can do everything the boys can do. I'm a better shot, and I make a decent trap. I ride well. I can barber, I can cook, I can sew, I can run. I'd make a good soldier. Jerry told me." *Oh, Jerry.* I was suddenly fighting tears, but I swallowed them down, refusing to be undermined by my own emotions.

"Such skill is wasted on a woman." Deacon Thomas did not speak unkindly; it was what he believed. I supposed it was the truth. Such talents *were* wasted on me.

"You have broken the law. It is forbidden for a woman to disguise herself as a man, or a man to pretend to be a woman."

I nodded.

"You cannot teach the children any longer."

I nodded again, knowing he was right. "It was always a temporary position."

"The church elders do not want you among their members. You will be removed from the rolls. I anticipate that Mr. Crewe will withdraw his offer of marriage as well. You should have married him months ago." The deacon sighed.

"I did not seek his offer, nor would I have accepted it. And I don't care about the church. Either of them." The words welled and spilled over, and unlike my tears, I could not hold them back.

"You have lost your faith," Mrs. Thomas mourned.

"My faith is not in a church. My faith is in God. I have not lost my faith," I argued softly, shaking my head. I had not lost my faith, but I was in grave danger of losing all hope.

I spent the Sabbath alone in my room, reading from my Bible and writing a useless letter to Elizabeth, growing more and more distraught as the evening deepened. Never had I felt so alone, both in my convictions and my circumstance, but it was my disappointment that was the hardest to bear. I had attempted escape, and I had failed. Miserably.

> *Oh, Elizabeth. I've been an utter fool, and I can't help but think that the line between courage and madness is a thin one. I have told myself what I did was wrong, but deep down I don't believe it. I don't believe it, and my regret is not that I acted but that I didn't succeed.*

I set my journal aside and turned back to scripture, looking for inspiration, for something to ease my disconsolation. It was in Proverbs, the thirteenth chapter, twelfth verse, where I found an answer.

"Hope deferred makes the heart sick: but when the desire comes, it is a tree of life," I read.

Then I read the verse again, slowly, as a sudden, irrevocable knowledge reverberated in my breast like the tolling of bells.

"If I don't do this, I cannot continue on," I said to the silent walls. "I would rather die."

I was not given to histrionics or overexaggerations, but in the very depth of my being, I knew it was true. I had lost my hope, and if I did not pursue it, I would be finished.

I closed my Bible and arose. I removed my frock and my petticoats and took down my hair, just as I'd done before, but it was not despondency or grief that informed my actions now. It was the tree of life, extending its branches toward me, beckoning me forward. I dressed in my male attire and gathered my things, moving quickly and silently, clarity settling on my shoulders like angel wings. I had not thought things through the first time, and I had acted desperately, rashly. I would not make the same mistakes again.

My most prized possessions—the letters from Elizabeth and John, the writings of William Bradford, the Bible with my family tree—were left behind. I even left my own journals, though I hated the thought of someone's eyes perusing the pages. Better here than where I was going. I would record my experiences on fresh pages, and I determined to buy a small book and a traveling quill and ink set when I reached my destination.

Two pairs of stockings, the extra binding for my breasts, and a small blanket tied to the bottom of my satchel were packed first. I added a loaf of bread, three apples, and a pound of dried mutton to my bag and draped my musket, a canteen, and my cartridge box over my shoulders like I'd seen the soldiers do. I had the rest of the money I'd saved and the conviction I'd come to, and I left the house without allowing myself a look back.

I did not take the mare but set out on foot. I had ridden her so often that should someone see me, they would identify the pair of us, and though the deacon had given it to me for my use, it was not mine, and I would not be able to bring her back. The Thomases had gone to bed, and the night was deep. I knew they would worry when they rose to find me gone, but I saw no way around it. I'd left them a simple goodbye and thanked them for their kindness, but I did not tell them where I was going, nor did I promise to return.

I had to enlist somewhere else, someplace where the ranks wouldn't be filled with Middleborough men, including the Thomas boys. North was Boston, east was Plympton, and west was Taunton, a community which bled into Middleborough. None were nearly far enough away for my peace of mind or my anonymity. I would have to go south until I found a village far afield and in need of recruits to fill their quota.

I also needed a new name. Something dull and typical, yet not so bland as to be suspect. A name that would provide cover by itself, and something different from the one I'd already, disastrously, used.

I played with derivations of Deborah, mixing the letters and saying it backward. Harobed? That wasn't a name. Obed? Horace? Robert? I liked Robert the best. It was the proper name for Rob, and I already answered to that. Obed and Horace were a little too distinct.

Now for a surname. I could not use Samson or Thomas or Bradford. I considered Conant, as a nod to my dear friend, and abandoned it immediately. All who knew me knew of that connection. Elizabeth's maiden name was Lee, but that was too ordinary and too simple. Johnson, James, Jones . . . too common all.

My oldest brother was named Robert Shurtliff, in honor of an obscure relative I knew nothing about. The name Shurtliff, spelled a variety of ways in Massachusetts, was just unusual enough to be realistic. I couldn't fathom anyone choosing it of their own accord, which made it ideal.

Robert Shurtliff.

It settled around me softly, and I nodded at the moonlight.

"I am Robert Shurtliff," I murmured. "I am twenty-one years old." I shook my head, rejecting that. I could pass as a boy, not a man. I would tell them I was sixteen. "I am smart. I am swift. I am able in all things. I am from . . ." I stewed over that. Where was I from? I couldn't say Middleborough or Plympton. I'd been born in Plymouth County, so that was what I'd say. I tried again, repeating my story. "I am Robert Shurtliff. Sixteen years old. From a village in Plymouth. No family to speak of."

They would think me a beardless orphan running off to join the army the first chance I got, like so many others. But that was fine. That was good. If they thought I was lying about my age, perhaps it wouldn't even occur to them that I was lying about my sex. I would tell the truth where I could, in order to make it easier on myself.

I repeated my story all night long, matching it to the rhythm of my feet upon the road, and made a pact with myself that I wouldn't cry, I wouldn't complain, and I wouldn't quit. Those things wouldn't make me a man—I knew plenty of women with such qualities—but I figured by holding my tongue and my tears, I wouldn't draw excess attention to myself.

I also wouldn't drink. I'd learned that lesson.

Then I vowed to continue what I'd done my whole life: endure and excel. That was my only plan.

~

My fear and sanity returned at dawn after walking for hours in a state of calm conviction. I'd cut through Taunton in the dark and was west of the village when a rider approached from the opposite direction, moving at a trot. I considered running into the tree line but abandoned the plan immediately. Acting suspicious would only arouse suspicion. I kept walking, my pace brisk, my shoulders back.

I braced myself and nodded politely as he passed, realizing in the final moments that I recognized him. He was a post rider. He'd been the messenger who'd visited the farm multiple times with letters from the front. His satchel was full and his destination was clear: Taunton and Middleborough.

He didn't give me a second glance, and I didn't allow myself to watch where he went, but the incident left me weak-kneed and shaking, and I found a thicket of trees about ten rods from the road where I could close my eyes and rest for a bit. I ate an apple, drank some water, and fell into a sleep so deep, an army of grim riders could not have awakened me.

It took me three days of walking, winding my way through villages and skirting farms, until I went as far south as I could go, and reached the coastal town of New Bedford. I'd been moving in a bit of a trance, intoxicated by the freedom I had never enjoyed and almost giddy in my male attire. It was a wonder to me that every woman hadn't simply donned breeches and left home to wander the world.

I walked the wharves, basking in the sunshine that reflected off the water and the breeze that snapped the sails of the vessels anchored in the harbor. New Bedford and nearby Fairhaven had been raided by the British in '78, homes, shops, and ships set afire, and the damage was still evident. It was a pretty town, even wounded and scarred. Stone and grass and gulls paid homage to the river and the ocean beyond.

I watched some fishermen come in, their nets full and their faces red with wind and exertion, and thought of sweet Jeremiah, and his dreams of sailing the seas. My own aspirations and my hunger roused me, prodding me along, and I found my way to a thatch-roofed tavern overlooking the docks with a buzzard painted on the door, his wings tucked and his eyes mean. Sailors and soldiers moved in and out, and no one spared me a glance. I bit back my grin and offered up a prayer of thanks and a proverb of my own. "Thou hast made me tall and plain, and I will never e'er complain."

Business was brisk and the dining room teemed with people, the stench of sweat and stew making my eyes water and my stomach groan. I approached the bar to order biscuits and stew, my eyes down, clutching my satchel and mentally counting my coin.

A pair of women whose breasts rose plump above their deeply squared necklines sidled up to me, one on each side, and I kept my eyes stubbornly averted. It had been a woman in Middleborough who had exposed me the first time. Women were wise to other women, and they did not so easily underestimate each other. But if I was to be among men, men who assumed because of my height, my flattened chest, and my lean hips that I couldn't possibly be female, then I might be safe. There would be no women to sniff me out. But I was not safe yet.

"Buy us a drink, handsome lad, and we'll keep you company," one said. They were plump and powdered, and both looked as though they'd kept many fellows company. I gaped down at them and then looked around, unsure of whether they were talking to me. I pulled my elbows into my sides, crossing my arms over my chest, just to be safe.

"No drink for me," I said. "Just stew, if you please."

One woman scoffed and the other sighed. "He thinks we're serving up the stew, Dolly."

"I have nothing you w-want," I stammered, and they both snickered.

"Too good for us, eh?" the younger one said.

"No, madam. Not too good. Just famished."

"Let him alone, Lydia. He's just a boy, albeit a pretty one." The one named Dolly patted my cheek. I was rigid with fear, certain that any moment they were going to pounce the way Mrs. Sproat had done, outing me to the crowded tavern, but they just laughed again and turned their attention to the sailors bellying up to the bar beside me.

"Do you want a room, boy?" the innkeeper asked.

I shook my head. "Just a bite to eat. Then I'll be on my way."

He set a bowl of fishy soup and two biscuits in front of me, and I ate it all so fast, I hardly tasted it. I drew a few coins from my pocket, and the man gave me another heaping scoop and a bit more bread. He plunked a tankard down and made to fill it, but I shook my head and slapped my hand over the rim. "No thank you, sir. Just water, please."

He shrugged and acquiesced, but he took in my satchel and the musket slung across my back. "You looking for work, lad?" he asked.

"I'm looking to join the army," I answered. "Is there a muster underway?"

"They will'na take you," he growled. "Yer barely weaned, and the war is all but over. But the captain there, in the corner, he's looking for a cabin boy."

I turned to survey the room, trying to see to which man he referred, though I had no interest in the job. The man in the corner had his head bowed over his drink, his forearms on the table, but there was something familiar about the line of his cheek and the set of his brow. He looked up, as if he heard himself mentioned, and I turned back to the bar, avoiding his searching gaze, and finished my meal.

"You'd best be moving on, boy." The woman named Dolly was back, wedged in beside me, but facing the bar as though she waited to speak to the barkeep.

"You don't want a drink or a poke. That's good," she murmured, and once again I wasn't sure if she was talking to me. "You're too young for women or for soldiering. But you don't want any part of that either." She cocked her head toward the corner of the room. "Samson's a mean one."

"Samson?" I gasped.

She kept her eyes forward, and I couldn't tell whether she was lying or if she was simply afraid.

"He doesn't know whose side he's on. Nobody can trust him. Plus, when you get out on the open sea, there's nowhere to run, and no one will notice if you don't come back to port."

"His name is Samson?" I pressed, disbelieving, but she ignored that, speaking quickly.

"Go to Bellingham. The bounty is fair and recruits harder to come by. They'll take you. I know the muster man; he's a good sort. Tell him Dolly sent you."

I took another coin from my pocket. I really couldn't spare one, but I did anyway, sliding it across the bar to the woman. She tucked it between her breasts and moved away without a backward glance, and I did as I was advised.

But I could not leave without knowing.

The day was warm and my belly full, and I found a patch of grass where I could shrug off my pack and rest myself, watching the door of the Buzzard Inn and waiting for the man named Samson to appear.

I didn't have to wait long. He strode out, his gait almost rolling, like he'd not adjusted to the land beneath his feet, or maybe he'd just had a drink too many.

I called out to him. "Jonathan Samson, is that you?"

He turned sharply, almost spinning around, and when he saw me and realized it was I who had spoken, he raised his hand to shield his eyes.

Had I not recognized myself in his face, I might not have believed it was him. My memories were faint and fraught with unhappiness. But he was the same tall, long-boned, fair-haired, hazel-eyed man, though his skin was weathered and his back slightly bent.

I stood up, needing my own height to steady me. I'd been warned away from him, but I was calm. Eerily so, the blood barely moving in my veins. I was not at all concerned that he would know me. He never had. He never would.

He looked at me with eyes like mine, eyes that didn't know which color to be.

"Who are you? Are you Ephraim?" he asked. "You're not Robert. Robert looked like a Bradford, not a Samson."

I wore my musket across my back, and it wasn't loaded, but he'd noted its presence. I'd said my piece and seen all I needed to see. I picked up my satchel and began walking in the opposite direction.

"Who are you, whelp?" he insisted again, angry, but he made no move to follow me.

"I am more a man than you'll ever be," I said, tossing the words over my shoulder. "I'll tell Mother I saw you. She told us you were lost at sea."

It was foolish of me. I was taunting him and endangering myself. I should have never engaged with him at all. I well knew the proverb about perverse tongues falling into mischief. I had proven it true time and again, and that day on the docks in New Bedford would come back to bite me.

~

I bought a journal and a traveler's ink and quill set, just as I'd said I would, but I didn't dare write as Deborah, in case it fell into the wrong hands, and I was careful to say nothing revelatory. Still, I addressed the entry the way I'd done for years, needing the comfort of my friend, even if she couldn't answer me.

Dear Elizabeth,

I saw my father in New Bedford. I was warned away from him, though I had no intention of boarding his ship. I want to be a soldier, not a sailor. It seems he's become a captain after all, but a woman in the tavern told me he's "a bad one."

She also told me to go north, to a place called Bellingham, though it's fifty miles away. She said they were mustering troops and the bounty was good. I caught a ride for most of the first day and ate my fill of turnips, though I've never liked them much. The farmer was kind and his wife took one look at me and burst into tears. They lost their son in Germantown too.

I have so much to tell you, though I wonder if you already know. I like to think you are following along, an angel on my shoulder. I am alone, but I'm not lonesome. My heart is too full of hope for sadness. It's like nothing I've felt before, and as Solomon says, my desire is a tree of life. I've nothing to do but walk, and my mind is strangely quiet, my restlessness appeased. People have been kind. They think me too young, but no one has stopped me, and I am seized by continual wonder in this new adventure. —RS

I did not speak of my identity or the specifics of my struggle. I did not write of my menses or the contraption I'd fashioned to bind my breasts. I wanted to. I wanted to document it all, but I dared not do it, and left my entries vague. It comforted me all the same, and when I signed *RS* at the bottom of each page, it did not feel like a lie.

The innkeeper's warning, "They will'na take you," haunted me all the way, but when I reached Bellingham, I was sent on to Uxbridge, where the numbers were low and recruits needed. The man behind the table did not challenge me in any way. He made me stand up to the measuring post and asked if I wanted to be a soldier. I said I did, most fervently so, and I was gratified that it was the truth.

"What's your business?" he asked.

"I was a weaver . . . and I taught school." Weaving was not simply a woman's profession. The Bradfords came from a long line of weavers. William Bradford brought a loom on the *Mayflower*.

The speculator made a note on the rolls, indicating I could read and write. Then he directed me to sign on the line, and in a moment of panic, I misspelled Shurtliff. It hardly mattered, as he didn't know the difference, but I may as well have written Shirtless, as naked as I felt. He handed me my bounty and moved on to the man behind me. I told Elizabeth of my triumph in an entry dated April 20, 1781.

I am a private in the Fourth Massachusetts Regiment. Not only did they take me, they have assigned me to a company of light infantrymen under Captain George Webb. The light infantry are those able to advance quickly, and I wish I could tell the brothers that this proves, once and for all, that I am truly one of the swiftest.

Three years or the end of the war. That is what I agreed to. My hand shook a bit when I signed the roll, but it was not fear that made me tremble. I am not the smallest soldier, nor the tallest, but my stride is just as long and my heart just as willing. I was told to report to Worcester in three days—yet another fifteen-mile walk—where I'll be mustered in.

Proverbs 13:19 says that desire accomplished is sweet to the soul.

I've never experienced anything sweeter. —RS

~ 9 ~

Declare the Causes

Every soldier was issued a uniform to immediately change into and a haversack filled with a week's worth of rations—salted pork and hard biscuits—to carry on our backs. We were told we would forage along the way as well, and I would soon learn that there was never enough food.

The men around me began to shuck off their outer layers, the soiled and mostly tattered piles rising up around their feet. I did the same, gritting my teeth and moving quickly. I could not run off behind a tree or erect a partition every time I was faced with such a situation. I had on drawers that looked no different from those of every man around me, and the half corset that kept me bound was laced tight beneath my shirt. No one was looking at me. No one had the slightest inkling that I had something to hide. Best that I not act as if I did.

The fit of the breeches gave every man the look of a plucked chicken, skinny legs and indeterminate sex, the folds and the extra fabric designed for movement obscuring what was between their legs.

That was good, but I felt scandalous, my hips and my thighs clearly defined by the fit.

"I can do this. I have done this. It is done," I chanted silently, my hands shaking. I had been wearing breeches for two weeks; I would not despair now. I slipped my arms into the white waistcoat, which was essentially a fitted vest, and immediately felt more secure. I wound the neckcloth round my neck and that too reassured me. My neck was long and slim, with no bulging Adam's apple. Better to hide it altogether.

The uniform fit me well enough. The blue coat was a little broad in the shoulders and the breeches a bit tight in all the wrong places, though I could grab a handful at the seat.

"Ya got worms, lad?" a whiskered man jeered at my actions. "Yer arse itchin'?"

I ignored him and knotted the strings at the top of the breeches to keep them from slipping down, determined to alter them when I had the chance. I didn't need to be worrying about them endlessly. Even without a corset winnowing my waist, I wasn't as straight in the middle as the men.

I yanked the stockings to my knees and secured them with the ties to keep them in place, then pulled the gaiters over them. The day was warm and the layers unwelcome, but the gaiters would protect our legs and preserve our stockings.

When I put the tricorn hat on my head, I had to bite back my grin as the green plume caressed my cheek. I'd never worn anything so jaunty or fine. In the earlier days of the war, the rebels had had no uniform. I suppose that was an advantage to arriving late to the conflict; I adored it.

I rolled the clothes I'd removed into my blanket and secured it on both ends with rope, making a little sling with which to carry it beneath my knapsack. I set about putting the rest of the gear in order—cartridge box, powder horn, canteen, musket, hatchet, knife—everything strung across my chest with yet another strap or hanging round my waist.

They'd issued me a bayonet as well, along with a sheath to store it when it wasn't attached to the end of my musket. Of all the accoutrements of war, I was least comfortable with the bayonet. If I ever had to use it, I doubted I would come out the victor.

I had my cup, bowl, and knife in my knapsack, along with a kit for sewing. My journal, my traveling inkstand, and my flint and tinderbox too. A comb, a candle, a slab of soap wrapped in oiled leather, and rags that could be used when I began to bleed, which would be a few weeks yet, thank Providence. I'd dealt with the flow on my journey from Middleborough. I'd managed well enough, but I'd been alone. It would be harder going forward.

A few hard biscuits and a small sack of dried peas would give me something to nibble on if my hunger got too great. I had an extra shirt, two pairs of stockings, and the other modified corset, just in case the one I now wore was damaged or wet and I needed to change. Anything more and I would have had too much gear.

"The less you take, the less you'll have to carry," Captain Webb shouted, echoing my thoughts, and we were hustled out into the bright midday, tugging at our uniforms and righting ourselves as we were taken through our drills.

I excelled at the drills. I'd made sure I would. A few times Captain Webb shouted out, "That's it, lad! Eyes on the boy there, men. That's the way it's done." I couldn't control the heat in my cheeks, but my back was ramrod straight and my eyes didn't slide or scurry. I just kept at it and prayed that the captain would not see fit to call attention to me again. The men liked to tease.

"Where did you learn to dance like that, Private?" Captain Webb asked me, slapping my back. I flinched but didn't shy away.

"I used to watch the men drill on the green . . . when I was young. I practiced with my . . . brothers. I like drills. They help me relax." I'd only hesitated over the bits I didn't want to explain. The Thomas boys weren't my brothers, but they might as well have been.

"And your name?"

"Robert Shurtliff, sir."

He nodded. "Can you shoot as well as you drill?"

"Yes, sir."

"Well, that's good then. Wait until the redcoats are marching across the field of battle," he muttered. "All those drills will go straight out of your head. Good thing too. A drill never killed anyone. You ever kill anyone?"

"No, sir."

"You will."

I did not fear death, oddly enough. I almost expected it. But I did not want to kill. And for the first time, it occurred to me that killing was what I'd signed up to do.

Very little is how we imagine it will be, but I'm certain that nothing, not all the running and jumping and hiding and sneaking I'd done in my twenty-one years, could have prepared me for the grueling march that followed. Each day I made it through something so unpleasant that I began to store up a well of miseries. I would tell myself, "This isn't so bad as that, and you didn't quit yesterday." One day it was the mire, the next day the flies. An unseasonable heat or an unrelenting downpour.

Sometimes the voice in my head would insist that no one knew me. I could leave and become Deborah Samson again, and Robert Shurtliff would simply cease to be. That voice was a liar, and I called it such. Robert Shurtliff could cease to be, yes, but the world of Deborah Samson was no longer available to me. She had no home, no clothes, no possessions. She had no family to welcome her or gainful employment to keep her fed. Anything would be better than this, the voice insisted, but I learned to turn my thoughts to silence, or if not silence, to fill the space with proverbs and psalms. Sylvanus was right. When my own words failed me, the things I had memorized kept defeat and despair at bay.

"What are you muttering about?" a man named John Beebe asked me several days in. He was a talker, acquiring the nickname Buzzy Beebe the first day out. He kept up a steady stream of dialogue with anyone who would listen, and he'd made his rounds as the miles stretched on, seemingly unaffected by anything but boredom.

I shook my head. "Nothing."

"Your lips are always moving, but you don't ever say anything," he argued. "You don't talk to any of us and you keep to yourself. You're mad as a hatter or you're just unfriendly. Which is it?"

"Both."

He hooted, and then he repeated what I'd said to the two fellows behind us. Jimmy Battles and Noble Sperin were their names, and I liked them. Jimmy reminded me of Jeremiah and Noble reminded me of Nat, the two bookends of the Thomas boys. Both grunted at Beebe, neither of them interested in the conversation. Or perhaps it took too much stamina to engage.

"I think you're entertaining yourself," Beebe contended. "That's just mean not to share. I'm bored. If you've got a story or a song, you should tell me."

"It's just scripture."

"Scripture?" he crowed, and turned to Noble and Jimmy again. "Did you hear that? Shurtliff would rather quote scripture than talk to me."

"He's bashful. Leave him alone," Noble insisted.

Beebe threw his heavy arm over my shoulder. "Come on, now. Share the good word with me. I'm in need of salvation."

I shrugged him off with a shudder and a hard push, and he staggered into the man on his left, sending a rippled stagger down the line.

"Bonny Robbie doesn't like to be touched," he said, laughing.

"So don't touch him," Noble interjected again. "And for hell's sake, hold your blathering tongue."

Beebe grumbled, "Seems awful unfriendly to me."

I had drawn negative attention only a few days in. My weariness became worry as the men around me dropped into exhausted silence, and Beebe fell back and found someone more amenable to conversation.

He was not a bad sort. None of them were. No one seemed mean just for the sake of meanness, and none seemed too soft or especially scared. That was good. I was scared enough for all of us, but I changed my strategy after that, making myself useful instead of holding myself apart. I couldn't roughhouse, but I could serve, and I looked for ways to ingratiate myself on my own terms. Physical distance was necessary, but comradeship was too.

I made it known that I was a decent barber—only fools used a razor on their own face without a mirror—and spent one evening shaving the whole company and greasing their hair back into tight tails. I also offered to write letters for those who lacked the skill, and even Beebe had me draft a message home. His incessant chatter didn't translate to the written word. He could read a little, though, and saw me writing to Elizabeth, who he assumed was my sweetheart. It wasn't a bad thing for my company to believe, and I let him rib me without ever setting him straight. His nickname for me stuck, unfortunately, and Bonny Robbie or Bonny Rob was what most of the men called me.

I didn't take part in the competitions, the wrestling and the races, though Jimmy challenged me and I would have liked to see how I stacked up. It was not unlike living in the Thomas house, though I heard and witnessed things that scorched my ears and my eyes. I had no idea men were so obsessed with women or with their own anatomy; the brothers had spared me that.

We traveled the entire length of Connecticut, including New Britain, and I reported to Elizabeth that it looked as I imagined it would, though like Massachusetts, there were very few places that had not been battered by the war. We moved through villages and slept where we were welcome and even where we weren't. I was so fatigued one night, I did not make it inside the house in which I was quartered. I awoke in the grass, shivering in the light drizzle, my messmates having abandoned me for a roof over their heads. Had the mistress of the house not come outside to gather eggs and taken pity on me—"Come inside, boy, with the others"—I would have thought I'd been left behind.

I became adept at sleeping on demand. I had always slept on my side, curling around myself, hands clasped between my breasts. I no longer had any sort of ritual or preferred position. I slept with my musket in my arms half the time, staring up at the sky because sleeping flat on my back on the ground was easier than any other position.

One night, I slept in a furrow of a freshly plowed field. There, in the soft dirt, the sides cradling me like a mother's arms, I enjoyed the best sleep I'd ever had. But that was not the normal way of things. I stopped keeping track of the food in my belly and the hours of rest I didn't get. My menses came halfway through the march, but the flow was so light I hardly noticed it. Either I was becoming a man in truth or I'd become too lean or depleted to bleed. I thanked God for that mercy in my prayers.

Every man had to skulk off to do his business alone sometimes. It didn't seem enough to arouse suspicions that I did so more often than the others, but I held my water until I was full to bursting. The one time another soldier caught a glimpse of my flank, squatting deep, he turned on his heel, assuming he'd caught me at something else, for which every person must sit.

No one bathed or changed their clothing to sleep. The clothes we wore when we left Worcester were the clothes we all still had on when we arrived at West Point two weeks later.

The British controlled New York City, and we did not go near it, cutting through the territory considered neutral. The miles were populated with farms and settlements that gave way to thick forests as we neared the area known as the highlands.

In every direction, an endless expanse of green hills bowed beneath a blue sky, hugging the curves of the winding river, and I could not imagine a more beautiful spot. My awe returned, my wonder and hope too, and my well of miseries dried up in the face of my new horizons.

"This is why I'm here," I whispered. "This is what I wanted."

We crossed the glassy Hudson, often simply called the North River, at King's Ferry, a landing on the east side of the river bustling with all manner of vessels and troops, and debarked on the west side of the river at Fort Clinton, a rocky edifice that overlooked the water. Having never been posted anywhere, I had nothing with which to compare the stronghold, which was actually one of several forts making up the encampment known as West Point. Constitution Island jutted out into the river directly across from it, another fort and two redoubts visible behind the batteries there as well.

Where the river curved back on itself, a massive chain was stretched across from the Point to the island to prevent British ships from passing through, though Captain Webb claimed they'd never even tried. But that was not the only marvel.

On the other side of the garrison walls and behind Fort Clinton stretched a flat, grassy plateau at least a half a mile wide with an impressive artillery park on the south end and a sprawling encampment at the rear, completely invisible from the water.

We were given a hasty tour of the layout—quartermaster, bakehouse, prison, officers' huts, headquarters, forge, commissary, hospital, stores, and rows of long wooden barracks, where we were instructed to choose a berth and drop our sacks.

A wide parade ground was centered in the encampment, and we were herded onto it and told to stand at attention as we awaited further instruction. I was not the only wide-eyed soldier, my gaze endlessly skipping over the sprawling encampment, the rugged landscape, and the silvery ribbon of water that curled through it.

It was not until a pair of drummers at the edge of the green took up a cadence, signaling the arrival of a mounted officer, that I managed to pry my attention from my surroundings. He approached from the direction of a big red house barely visible through the trees. Captain Webb indicated it had been there before the base was established.

"General Washington used it as his permanent headquarters for a time, and he still stays there when he comes to the Point," he had added.

My awe swelled again. *I might see General Washington.*

The horse the officer rode was white with a charcoal mane and tail, and though it pranced like a princess, it was built like a gunship, all muscle and mass. Beebe whistled his appreciation as the rider dismounted and handed the reins to a sentry who stood at attention nearby. Colonel Jackson, Captain Webb, and several other officers from the other regiments stepped forward to greet him.

"General Washington gave him that horse. Some say it was a bribe to return to service, though General Paterson would cut out yer tongue if he heard you say it."

"General Paterson?" I gasped, a trifle too loud. The men around me snorted at my outburst, but I was too stunned to care. "That's General Paterson?" I hissed.

"That he is," Beebe said. "He's the commander of the whole Point. We're in his brigade."

I knew John Paterson was a man of intelligence and kindness. He'd responded to the letters of an indentured girl, after all, and fielded my questions seriously, with no condescension or disdain. That was something indeed, and in my mind he had taken on the features and form of Sylvanus Conant, kindly and gray, a wise elf with a slight stoop and a soft belly.

This John Paterson was none of those things.

He was brawny and tall with a thick mane of auburn hair pulled back into a tail at his nape. He was not old—not at all—and he did not resemble the good reverend in the least.

"That's not the general," I said. "Surely that isn't him."

"It most definitely is, bonny boy," Beebe asserted. "But don't let his common-man appearance fool ya."

"C-common man?" I stammered. He looked like no man I had ever seen.

"He has no patience for sloth or sloppiness. He likes drills and rules and order and has no qualms about throwing out the rabble if rabble is what you prove to be," another man interjected.

"Robbie isn't rabble." Jimmy Battles, who stood beside me, jumped to my defense, reminding me again of Jeremiah, but I was still too caught up in my disbelief to thank him.

This was not Elizabeth's John, was it? But how many General Patersons could there be? I thought he'd gone home to Lenox, yet here he was, inspecting the newly arrived troops, pausing to exchange a word here and there, his stride long and his hands clasped behind his back.

I must have moaned out loud.

"Ya all right, Robbie?" Jimmy asked.

I was not. Not at all. "I thought he resigned."

"He did," Beebe answered. "His wife died. He went home to see to his affairs. General Washington asked him to return."

"How do you know so much about Paterson, Beebe?" Jimmy asked.

"You think soldiers don't gossip? The ranks are worse than ladies in a drawing room. They're worse than a church picnic. Poor Paterson's been in this fight so long, it's a wonder they haven't named a fort after him."

"That's not his way," an older man named Peter Knowles, a reenlistment, chimed in. "He's never cared much about the glory. That's why the men like him, and General Washington trusts him. No fancy ego on that one. Not like Arnold or some of the rest."

"Isn't he a bit young?" I asked, still unable to believe this was my John Paterson.

"Look who's talkin'," Beebe snorted.

"He's the youngest brigadier general in the whole army," Knowles answered. "Exceptin' Lafayette, but we won't count him, bein' he's French."

As the general neared, all conversation ceased. Every spine straightened and every gaze swung.

He would not recognize me. We'd never met. He'd never seen me, nor I him. But I *knew* him. And he knew me, as well as anyone on earth knew me, and I was suddenly so afraid I could barely stand.

Emotion grew in my throat and pulsed behind my eyes. I blinked furiously, outraged by my sudden loss of composure. I had prepared myself for a possible sighting of one of the Thomas boys, though none of their companies were stationed at the Point, but I'd been blindsided by Elizabeth's John. That he would be here had never even occurred to me, and I was filthy, I reeked, and I was so tired I couldn't trust myself to speak. I began to pray, frantically, silently.

In you, O Lord, I have taken refuge; let me never be put to shame; deliver me in your righteousness. Turn your ear to me, come quickly to my rescue; be my rock of refuge, a strong fortress to save me.

The general walked past me, uniform pristine, boots shining, close enough that I could have clapped my hand on his epaulet, which was level with my eyes. He stood half a head taller than most of the men. He reached the end of our company, chatting with Captain Webb and Colonel Jackson, before he turned and walked back again, his eyes sweeping over the ranks. His gaze caught on my face and held, and a frown lowered his brows. He was only ten feet away, but he closed the distance until he stood directly in front of me.

"How old are you, soldier?" he asked, voice gentle.

I cleared my throat, met his pale blue eyes, and told the lie that was more believable than the truth. "Sixteen, sir."

He grunted, signaling his displeasure with my answer. "And you, Private?" he asked Jimmy.

"I'm sixteen too, General, sir."

"What's your name?"

"Jimmy Battles."

"Hmm. Any connection to the Battles of Connecticut?"

"I don't know, sir. I don't know my father's family."

He was looking at me again. "And you . . . What's your name?"

"Robert Shurtliff," I answered, no hesitation.

"Robbie's one of our best, General," Captain Webb said, and the moisture threatened to rise again. Kindness was my undoing. "He's always willing and always able."

"Robbie?" the general repeated, as if baffled by the nickname. "Jimmy? Where are all the men, Webb? Each new round of recruits looks younger than the last."

"They're young, but they're eager, and I've been pleased with them, sir. It's not the best company I've had, but it definitely isn't the worst."

John Paterson shook his head, obviously not reassured. "God willing, this war will end before it makes them men . . . or we dig their graves," he muttered, and proceeded down the line.

May 3, 1781

Dear Elizabeth,

John is here. I did not expect him. I confess to being more shaken by his appearance than I have been by anything else thus far. They say General Washington would not accept his resignation. He seems highly esteemed and respected, and he greeted many of the new soldiers personally.

He is a very striking figure, though he was not impressed by me; my looks do not inspire confidence. Still, I was overcome by the meeting and wanted so much to extend my condolences. It seemed a great dishonesty not to greet him as a friend, though of course decorum and my circumstances dictated otherwise.

Captain Webb commended me in his presence, which touched me greatly. Webb is a good officer, as is Colonel Jackson, though I've heard tales of many who aren't. Too many think too much of their own comfort and not enough of the men in their charge, though that does not appear to be the case here at West Point. Perhaps it is the example of the general, who seems to demand much of everyone, including himself. His parting words on the parade ground were these: "There are no exceptions to the rules. You will follow them. Your officers will follow them. I will follow them. That is how we safeguard our position, how we defend each other, and how I protect you."

He is not at all what I expected, Elizabeth. He is young, but old. Gracious, but grim. Straight and tall, but weary too, though my impressions may be colored by my compassion. I pray I will not let him down or let myself down. Even if I cannot follow his every rule. —RS

~ 10 ~

The Separation

General Paterson lived in Moore House, named for the farmer who built it before the army determined his land was the perfect place for a stronghold on the Hudson and commandeered it from him. It was an enormous red-planked home with three gables, a massive stone chimney, and several stories, and it was completely at odds with the rest of the timber structures on the Point.

Everyone called it the Red House, as if it needed the distinction from the other dwellings in the garrison, and it was set apart by a smaller parade ground and a short lane north of the new barracks. My company was quartered in these, which greatly pleased my messmates. Rumors of the rats in the old barracks were the stuff of nightmares.

We were not far from the pond where we could swim, bathe, and wash our clothes if we didn't want to use one of the bathing barrels lined up in a long row near the latrines. Neither the wash barrels nor the latrines afforded any privacy at all. Two built-in benches with holes cut in the top ran the length of the latrine on each side. Twenty men could sit and empty their bowels at the same time, all while enjoying face-to-face conversation. There were two such latrines on either end of the encampment, and the officers' homes and the Red House had their own toilets, though the rank and file were prohibited from using them.

I went to bed last and rose first, using the latrine only twice a day, picking my way to the long structure in the dark, following my nose and leading with my toes, inching along so I wouldn't tumble into a hole filled with waste. I had no choice in the matter. I couldn't very well sit side by side with another man with my breeches down.

After that first night, I counted my steps and always used the same bench and hole, simply because familiarity was its own kind of sight. I tried to go after everyone else was asleep, but my exhaustion made it hard to wait, and a few men took notice when it became a ritual.

"Robbie's got a baby face and a baby bladder," Beebe said about two weeks in. I said nothing in response, as was my way, but nothing scared me more than discovery. Not pain. Not death. Not torture or starvation. I wanted nothing more than to continue on, and that meant blending in.

My messmates liked to pull pranks, even Noble and Jimmy. They said it was all in good fun, and it might have been, but a known routine invited many opportunities for sabotage, and just as I'd done on the march, I adjusted my strategy.

The next evening, I marched into the latrine right behind Beebe and found an empty spot directly across from him so my presence wouldn't be missed. I loosened my ties, dropped my breeches, and sank onto the hole in one smooth motion, my shirttails providing cover, my eyes on the floor.

I stayed long enough for Beebe to leave and a few more men to straggle in. I even managed to urinate and ease the constant ache I'd suffered since enlisting. It was the most horrific thing I'd ever done, and my neck broke out in welts of mortification afterward, but at least a dozen men had seen me, and that was my goal. I couldn't imagine making it a regular occurrence—that was tempting fate—but I'd done it.

Bathing was a different matter. I washed in the pond a full two hours before the horns of reveille woke the camp, when it was so dark I couldn't even see myself. I submerged myself in my clothes and washed them while I wore them. I became adept at shimmying off my dripping drawers and untying my altered corset beneath my shirt to avoid ever being completely naked. But I worried how I would manage when winter came.

I kept myself as neat and tidy as possible, brushing my coat, shining my boots, and maintaining my equipment, if only to avoid extra attention and inspections, which happened to some of the more slovenly soldiers.

I don't doubt many of the men noticed my beardless face and my clear complexion. My skin had always been my finest feature. I'm sure there were those who registered the unmanly shape of my hips and the comparatively narrow breadth of my shoulders. Perhaps they even laughed a little at the unfortunate "bonny boy" in their ranks who spoke softly when he spoke at all. I kept my voice pitched as deeply as I was able—it had always been husky—but it was not low enough; it wasn't even as low as Jimmy's. I imagined my company talking among themselves. *Robbie looks a little feminine. Not his fault. None of us can do much about the way we look.*

But then I kept up during the march, led them in drills, and handled my weapon with as much speed and accuracy as anyone else in my company, and they stopped seeing the parts of me that might have made them wonder before.

I was accepted as a man because for me to be a woman was unfathomable.

~

A partial solution to my problem came with picket duty. Captain Webb's company was assigned to water guard—which was exactly what it sounded like—from the Red House to the great chain. We stood sentry along the perimeter, overlooking the water, a man posted about every ten rods. Considering no vessels passed beyond the barrier, the section of river we were assigned to watch was quiet duty. The war continued mostly in the south, and for the moment, there was nothing else for the new recruits at West Point to do but watch and drill, and we were given no orders beyond that.

I volunteered for the night shift from ten until two at the northernmost end, the watch no one else wanted, though a handful of others drew the short straw and manned the positions closer to the chain.

It allowed me an excuse to sleep when the hut was relatively empty and leave the barracks when most of the men were just settling down to bed. And my latrine and bathing habits went unnoticed. The stench of soldiers in close quarters as the temperatures rose into June, as well as their tendency toward evening misadventures was not something I missed, and it was on such a night when General Paterson approached my post, surprising the line with an inspection.

I called out as I'd been instructed to do—"Who comes there?"—and he bade me to be at my ease. I had not seen him since our arrival, except from a distance, and was struck once more by his size.

He was tall, a good deal taller than me, and broad of shoulder. He didn't wear a hat or his uniform, and in the moonlight he was colorless, his pale shirt and tan breeches giving him the look of a man who couldn't sleep instead of an officer performing an examination. The planes of his face were shadowed and his expression obscured. I was comforted that mine would be as well.

"You've been on water guard every night, soldier. Surely there is someone else who can take a shift?"

I was surprised that he knew, though my post was nearest to the Red House where he resided. "I volunteered for this watch, sir," I said, keeping my voice soft and low. "I like the quiet."

"I do too," he said. I thought he would move on, but he hesitated. "Remind me of your name?"

"I am Robert Shurtliff, General." My stomach twisted as it always did when I lied outright. "Captain Webb's company."

"Ahh. That's right. Robbie. Robbie and Jimmy."

He stopped beside me, his eyes on the river, and said nothing more for several long minutes. His melancholy was palpable, and my own throat began to throb, the need to acknowledge his loss almost unbearable. I searched for something to say—anything—to distract us both.

"Have you read *Gulliver's Travels*, General?" I blurted.

He jerked and looked down at me, as if he'd forgotten I was there. "I have," he answered, almost surprised.

"Which is your favorite?"

He was silent for a moment, as if mulling that over. "I don't know. I never understood why Gulliver kept casting off. Home is the only place I long to be."

I could not relate. Home was, in some ways, as mythical a place as Gulliver's Lilliput or the land of the horses. I had never truly had one of my own.

"Where is home?" I asked, though I knew.

"Home is in Lenox, though I've hardly been there enough in the last six years for it to feel at all familiar. I was born and raised in Connecticut."

I wanted to keep him talking. I don't know why. It was certainly not my way. With every word, I endangered myself.

"And before that?" I asked. "Where are your people from?"

He studied me. I could feel his eyes on my smooth cheeks, and I kept my gaze averted, looking out over the slope of ground that led to the water, a diligent watchman on duty.

"My great-grandfather fled Scotland, a place called Dumfriesshire, during the reign of King James the Second. I have exchanged one set of highlands for another."

I knew to what he referred. They called the area around the Point the "highlands of the Hudson"—the hated highlands, to be exact.

"I should like to see Scotland," I said.

"So would I." There was a bit of irony in the general's voice, and again I seized on the chance to converse.

"It's odd, isn't it? That one's history could be all wrapped up in a place. That one's ancestors could toil in the land and walk the hills for thousands of years, and yet it be as foreign to us as the Pyramids of Egypt or the streets of Paris. Have you ever been to Paris?"

"I have never been to Paris. No."

"I should like to go there too." I made myself stop talking, and he did not pick the subject up again. I had not lifted his spirits or distracted him from his sorrow, I could see.

"You shouldn't be here," he said softly, suddenly, and it was my turn to start in surprise.

"Sir?"

"You shouldn't be here," he repeated. "You are just a boy." I knew what he saw. A tall, beardless lad with a voice that hadn't deepened into manhood and shoulders that hadn't widened with years.

"No, sir. I'm old enough. And I know why I'm here." To tell the truth felt sweet, and my words rang with the conviction of testimony. If I knew nothing else, I knew that.

"Why? Why are you here?" It seemed an existential question, and hardly one particular to me. It was as though he asked so that he would better understand himself, and the anguish I sensed underscored his words.

"'We hold these truths to be self-evident, that all men are created equal, that they are endowed by their Creator with certain unalienable rights, that among these are life, liberty, and the pursuit of happiness,'" I began.

He huffed under his breath, like I'd surprised him again, and I paused in my recitation.

"You've memorized it?" he asked.

"Yes, sir."

"Why?"

"Because I believe in it."

He grunted, considering that. "Do you know it all?"

"I haven't memorized all the injuries and usurpations, word for word. The list is long."

"Yes. It is." He laughed, though it was hardly more than a chuckle. I considered it a victory.

He sighed, and we stood in silence once more. "Will you recite what you can remember?" he asked. "I need to be reminded."

"Of course," I said, though I was rusty and afraid. I reminded myself again that the general would not—could not—find me familiar. He knew nothing of my face or form, or even my fondness for recitation. But I finished with feeling, and he pressed my shoulder in thanks, a heavy hand that rested only a moment.

I balked, afraid of detection, afraid that my very bones would give me away. The other fellows slung their arms around each other's shoulders and slept in piles half the time. Not me. I allowed them—and myself—no familiarity.

"Well done, young man. Well done. You have the gift of oration."

It was as though Reverend Conant had come to visit, and I was drenched in sudden longing for my old friend.

"Thank you, General."

He turned back toward the Red House and bid me good night.

"Good night, sir."

"Let someone else take a turn tomorrow," he instructed as he walked away.

"Yes, sir," I said. But I had no intention of obeying him.

"You're still here, Shurtliff," he said the following night, the only answer to my mandated, "Who comes there?" though I could well see it was him.

"Forgive me, sir. I prefer it. It is too warm to sleep."

"That it is. And it will only get warmer. The bugs are thick."

"They haven't bothered me."

"No?"

"I am not sweet enough," I answered frankly. It was what the Thomas brothers always said.

I did not intend it to be humorous, but the general laughed, and I exhaled, glad to see him in better spirits.

"You do have a rather piercing gaze, Private. It belies your age and your smock-face."

"My students said it was fearsome."

"Students?" Again the surprise.

"Yes, sir. I was a schoolteacher before I came here."

His gaze narrowed. Again, he didn't believe me.

"There was no one else to do it. All the men—the more educated men—were gone." That much was the truth, but I inwardly flinched, seeing as it matched what he might know about Deborah.

He cocked his head at me and lifted one brow, as though he were puzzling it all out before he committed to speak.

"I taught school once too, after my father died and before I married. It seems like a lifetime ago," he said, and his sadness returned like a shroud.

"I am so sorry about your wife, General Paterson," I blurted.

He froze.

"I mean . . . Mrs. Paterson. Forgive me. I am sorry, sir. Very sorry for you and your children. Your loss is felt . . . by many . . . of your men. They are aware of your sacrifice . . . to be here."

I had made an utter mess of it.

I mentally lashed myself, cursing my babbling tongue and my pounding heart. He had mentioned his marriage, and I had pounced on the opening. I shouldn't have said anything. I should have written a letter instead, a letter from Deborah Samson, and poured out my heart and my affection for lovely Elizabeth as well as my sorrow for him, a man I was deeply fond of and one I greatly admired.

This man was not the friend of our long correspondence. This man was not my dear Mr. Paterson. This man was a brigadier general, a man in command of me and every other man at West Point, and a man I wouldn't have dared speak to at all had I not *known* him.

He did not respond to my sloppy condolences. He simply stood, hands clasped behind his back, staring out at the water. The night was so clear and still that the stars reflected on the surface, creating an illusion of standing above them, of looking down from a godlike perch. It reminded me of my dreams.

"It is like flying," I remarked, unable to bear his painful silence any longer. I didn't care whether he thought me a fool. Perhaps it was better if he did. "It makes me hopeful."

He said nothing.

"What gives you hope, sir?" I pressed softly.

He exhaled. "The thought that it will end," he said, voice heavy.

I considered his words only long enough to reject them.

"No," I said, and my vehemence surprised us both.

"No?"

"No, sir." I swallowed. "If it was only an ending you wish for, you would not be here. None of us would."

He shook his head. "You are bold, Shurtliff. I'll warrant you that."

"Hope requires boldness, sir."

He grunted, and I warmed to my subject. "In Proverbs it says, 'Hope deferred makes the heart sick: but when the desire comes, it is a tree of life.' That is why I am here."

I had shared so many things in my life with Elizabeth, and I knew she'd shared many of my letters with John. He knew Deborah Samson—my history and my heritage—so I could hardly relay the same stories. I was at a loss, stripped of the things of which I was proud. William Bradford was a hero of sorts, and I wanted to claim him. But he was Deborah's, and I was Robert now. I trod carefully.

"My mother once told me the story of a woman who sailed to this country . . . long ago. She'd left her child behind in hopes he could join them when they settled. Her husband had gone to find shelter on land, and she waited in the boat. He was gone too long, and she feared him dead. She was cold and exhausted, and she did not want to continue on without him. She drowned herself."

His breath hissed, his shoulders sagged, and his chin dropped to his chest. I had said the wrong thing. Again. The despondency and death of a wife left too long hit close to home.

"It was an ending that she sought," I said, trying to salvage my story. "Not hope. But it is hope that will give you the desire to continue. You must resist it, that hopelessness. When God takes you, let Him take you. When He plucks you from this earthly coil, then you may rejoice. But as long as you draw breath, as long as your heart beats and the sun rises, you must stay in the fight."

Every word I uttered was heartfelt, but when Paterson raised his head, his demeanor had not changed.

"You are just a boy," he whispered. "You have no idea what you're talking about and no idea what you've gotten yourself into."

I bit my lip and swore I would hold my tongue if it killed me.

"But you have a way with words," he conceded, "and lately I cannot abide my own company."

I swallowed an apology and shifted my musket to my other shoulder. I would not argue or defend myself either. If he wanted company, I would give him that. But I would be quiet.

"Will you recite it again, Shurtliff?" he asked, and my vow of silence was instantly dashed on the rocks of my desire to please him.

"The declaration, sir?"

"The declaration."

"From the beginning?"

"From the beginning."

~

The next night was much the same. The general stopped, exchanged a few pleasantries, and asked if I would recite the declaration. Sometimes he would stop me after the preamble, sometimes he would add his voice to certain words, as if they troubled him. Or strengthened him. I did not ask.

"Would you like to hear something else, sir?" I said after the fifth straight night of the same recitation. "A sonnet or scene or a bit of the Book of Revelation?"

"Good God, no. Do you want me to throw myself over this ledge?"

I gaped, not certain whether he jested. "You do not like sonnets, General?"

"I do not like the Book of Revelation."

"I love it," I breathed. "'And no man in heaven, nor in earth, neither under the earth, was able to open the book, neither to look thereon.'" That was my favorite part. "It is wonderful. The beasts with wings, the four horsemen, and the heavens being rolled back like a scroll. What a story!"

"The earthquakes, the lamentations, the sun turning to ash, the moon turning to blood?"

"Yes!"

"You are a very odd fellow, Shurtliff."

"Yes, sir. I know." He had no idea how odd I truly was.

He began to laugh, a slow rumble that grew into a lusty, head-thrown-back howl.

"Sir?"

He covered his face with his palms, still chortling.

I didn't know whether to laugh with him or put a palm to his forehead to check for fever.

He patted my shoulder and straightened my hat, still laughing, and something shifted in my chest.

The moon bathed his face and mirth lit his eyes. I could almost see their color—a pale, wintry blue—and when he laughed, his teeth were white and strong behind well-formed lips. I immediately averted my gaze.

"There is also a rainbow throne," I mumbled. "And harps and golden vials of incense, which are the prayers of the saints."

"Yes. And a bottomless pit and locusts as big as horses with the hair of women and the teeth of lions."

"I should like to see all of those things," I confessed, sneaking a peek at his smiling face.

"And what of famine, pestilence, and death?"

"But all of those things arrive on great warhorses," I cried. "It is frightening . . . and . . . fantastic."

He shook his head and bid me good night, and his laughter echoed through the trees as he returned to the Red House.

I spent the remainder of my watch puzzling over the strange new emotions in my breast.

"It is the way he looks," I whispered. "It is only admiration for the way he looks."

The peculiar feeling bubbled again, and I tamped it down with ruthless denial.

I did not like men. Not that way. I had never found them intriguing and had never entertained the girlish fantasy of falling in love. The fact that I had noticed the shape of the general's lips was disconcerting.

"He is not at all what you expected," I told myself. His height and form would be notable to anyone. He was at least six feet two, and he was lean in the way everyone was lean—strain, toil, and war took the fat off men—but it only made his musculature more pronounced. He didn't wear a wig, and his hair was a ruddy brown that looked as though it might have been red in his youth.

He was lovely to behold.

I frowned. This realization did not reassure me. I had not had a similar reaction to anyone before. I had never dwelt on a man's looks. Not the men in Middleborough, not the Thomas brothers, and not the men in my company. My heart had never quickened or my stomach trembled when they were near.

"It is because he has startled you," I said. "You thought you knew John Paterson, and you didn't. It is only surprise that has made your insides quake. That is all."

It was as good an explanation as any, and I accepted it stubbornly. "That is all it is," I insisted to the river below. But it troubled me all the same.

~ 11 ~

We Hold These Truths

General Paterson did not come the next night or the next, and my company was given a new assignment away from West Point. The last time I saw him before we left, he was inspecting the garrison with Colonel Kosciuszko, a Polish military engineer who had drawn up the design and continued to oversee the building of fortifications in the highlands.

I watched them ride away, the colonel gesturing this way and that, pointing out new redoubts and batteries, Paterson nodding his head. They were of a similar age, and both had reddish tails beneath their hats, but that is where their similarities ended. The general was big where the colonel was small, the general was quiet and self-contained where the colonel was animated and verbose.

Colonel Kosciuszko resided at the Red House as well, along with his aide, a young African man in his midtwenties named Agrippa Hull, who accompanied the two officers on a horse of his own. Hull had a flashing smile, a direct gaze, and a set to his shoulders that bespoke self-assurance, like he knew he belonged—or perhaps didn't care to.

Everyone called him Grippy, but I thought him too impressive for the nickname and determined to call him Mr. Hull if ever I had the chance to address him.

He was a favorite at the Point, though I had not yet made his acquaintance. I wanted to. Elizabeth had mentioned him once in a letter. He'd been born a freeman in Stockbridge, near Lenox, and had helped John Paterson raise a local militia in 1775. He'd been appointed aide-de-camp to Colonel Kosciuszko at the colonel's request, but it was the general he was committed to, and the two men had stayed together for much of the war. I was almost as intrigued by him as I was with the general, and I wrote a long letter to Elizabeth in my journal, describing him in great detail and formulating questions I might ask him if given the chance.

Rumor was that the construction of a great hall would soon be underway. Colonel Kosciuszko had already drawn up the plans. It would give the soldiers stationed in the quiet highlands something to do now that the fighting was almost completely in the south.

But I was not to be spared, nor were the men in my company.

Between the highlands and New York City, which the British held, was a thirty-mile stretch of farmland referred to as no-man's-land. The territory, centered around Westchester, was considered a neutral zone, but those living there had been continually caught between the opposing armies, their property taken or burned, their cattle stolen, their crops commandeered. Most of the people had fled.

On our march to the Point, we'd cut through the area to reach the Hudson. Little remained of what once had been a vast and thriving community. Fertile countryside, rich and grassy, lay dormant. Homes were burned out and abandoned, fences listed, fruit rotted on the trees, and scavengers roamed the countryside.

The Westchester Militia, made up of men from the area, were charged with protection of the zone by General Washington. He'd assigned light infantry units to assist the militia and challenge all British troops that encroached past their lines, but six years as a battlefield had reduced the area to little more than fallow fields and hunting grounds.

Those who couldn't leave were preyed upon by a brigade of loyalists and British deserters led by a man by the name of James DeLancey, a colonist and once the sheriff of Westchester.

DeLancey and his scavengers and profiteers wore red coats and considered themselves British soldiers, but they were more akin to the Hessians—soldiers for hire—than the British regulars, though DeLancey held the rank of colonel. Entire communities had declared their loyalty to the Crown in hopes that their property—and their lives—would be spared by DeLancey's Brigade.

The acquisition and movement of supplies had become the real battle of the highlands, but it was the events at Pines Bridge, not long after my arrival at the Point, that had been the final straw. DeLancey and his men had attacked a defensive position held by the Rhode Island Regiment on the north bank of the Croton River near Yorktown in Westchester. The Rhode Island Regiment was partially made up of African soldiers, and Colonel Christopher Greene, their white commander and a cousin of General Nathanael Greene, had been dragged from his tent, mutilated, and killed. His body was found a mile from the skirmish, the excessive violence wrought upon him thought to be retribution for enlisting African Americans and encouraging them to rebel against the Crown.

In late June, a corps of light infantrymen, of which I was part, were dispatched to scout enemy positions and troop activities, including those of DeLancey's men. A shipment of goods was expected on the Connecticut coast, and my unit would be patrolling the entire area for as long as necessary in hopes of securing the much-awaited supplies. It would be the first chance at engagement for many of us, and the men around me vibrated with an enthusiasm I could not capture. Even Jimmy was flushed with excitement, and Beebe could not contain himself.

"I'm going to get me a redcoat," Beebe crowed, "if it's the last thing I do."

"Pack light—we'll be moving fast and frequently—and pack well. We may not be back until the summer's over," Captain Webb told us.

I did not talk to the general before I left and felt a fool for wishing I could say goodbye. In a moment of weakness, I penned a short letter from Deborah Samson, dated it April 1, and included it in the stack of correspondence I'd helped my bunkmates draft to their own loved ones. I delivered it to the post rider myself, certain it would eventually find its way onto the general's desk with no one being the wiser. If for some reason I did not return, which part of me expected, I wanted him to know what Elizabeth—and he—had meant to me. I was careful and brief, but felt better for having done it.

Instead of heading toward Westchester, a detachment of about fifty of us were held back as Colonel Jackson's regiment prepared to go south. We watched as they left in waves, expecting to bring up the rear, though as light infantry, we should have been at the front. We waited all day, ready to depart, only to spend another night in the barracks. None of us knew where we were going, and Captain Webb was tight-lipped about the delay. We were told, last minute, to put our blue coats in our packs, and issued hunting shirts of various browns and greens to wear instead. The plumes from our tricorns were all removed, and some men were issued wide-brimmed hats of felt or straw.

Whatever our mission, it was clear that we were to blend in, and that the fewer people who knew the plan, the better. That included us. Troop movements were tradable intelligence, and nobody was to be trusted, even the troops themselves.

We covered ten miles a day, moving steadily north, the river on our right, until on the evening of the fifth day, we arrived on the outskirts of Kingston, a settlement fifty miles above the Point, and waited for nightfall before entering the town. After dark we were herded into an empty warehouse near the wharf and directed to wait. The only one who seemed to know what was going on was Captain Webb, and he wasn't talking.

Kingston had been burned to the ground by the British in '77 to destroy the army's wheat stores kept in the town. The granaries had been rebuilt, but the residents who had returned were wary of our presence, though the American control of the North River all the way to Albany gave them far more protection than the communities in the lower river valley enjoyed.

We holed up for two days, waiting for reasons that weren't explained to us, but the rest was needed and the outhouse, complete with a latching door, a relief. My toenails had turned black from the march from Worcester and some had begun to fall off. I was sure the march back to the Point would finish the job.

But we didn't return the way we'd come. We didn't march at all.

On our second night in Kingston, we bagged and loaded two barges with grain from a nearby silo, moving silently up and down the loading dock, taking turns on armed watch until the hulls were filled and our backs breaking. We were then ferried to the other side of the river to a slaughter yard where we found barrels of salt beef in such quantities to prompt the acquisition of a fourth barge to handle all of them.

Then our detachment was divided between the vessels, a dozen men or so on each deck, where we waited for the tide to shift, nerves taut, our muskets loaded and drawn. The Hudson flowed both ways, six hours to the north followed by six hours to the south, a massive inhale, exhale that moved freight up and down her banks.

Whatever Captain Webb was afraid of, the operation went off without a hitch, and we set off down the river toward West Point at dawn, catching the change in the current and moving swiftly along. I'd never been aboard a boat of any kind, and the experience thrilled me. I stood at the rail, marveling at the scenery and the speed of travel. What had taken us days on foot was accomplished in hours, and we docked at midday below Fort Clinton, our mission accomplished. Captain Webb was jubilant with relief, as if we'd pulled off something big.

"He did it" was all he said. "Paterson did it again."

We didn't remain at the garrison but split into two smaller groups and spent the next ten days slowly moving south to scout the British line.

I couldn't wash, but no one did. The smell of the detachment would warn the redcoats of our approach when we were still miles off, though I doubt they smelled much better. As we'd done on our first march, we slept in our clothes and washed the bits—our arms and necks and faces—that could be got without stripping down or getting our clothes wet. Wet clothes weren't pleasant to march in, and no one took the time for leisurely swims in no-man's-land.

I had no appetite. The heat and the strain of my circumstances filled my belly instead. I wanted only water, and often gave my daily ration of rum to one of my messmates. I forced myself to eat to keep my strength up, but had to choke it down. The ration of bread and meat, which we sometimes drew and sometimes didn't, depending on our position between encampments, was sufficient for my needs, but the men around me suffered constant hunger.

We watched the British pickets for several days to find a weak place in the line and then moved around them, going as far as Harlem, only eight miles from the city center. We made our observations without incident—if thirst, fatigue, and three days of lying in the bushes and another three moving without sleep could be considered unworthy of commentary—and retreated back to White Plains about a month after we'd left the Point, reporting on what we'd seen.

It wasn't a whole lot.

The bulk of the British forces were still in the south fighting other campaigns, and the movements of those that remained behind the lines in New York were slow and sloppy, with no obvious designs for doing anything beyond surviving yet another summer.

Captain Webb said, "They're as desperate for supplies as we are, and it's going to get a whole lot worse come winter. The whole colony—the whole country—has been stripped bare."

"There's not enough farmin' being done. Only fightin'," Noble said, his tone bleak. He didn't say it, not with the captain nearby, but Noble regretted his enlistment. He had a wife and two young children at home. He didn't talk about them much. He shared almost as little as I did, but he'd asked me to write a letter for him, a letter to "my dear wife, Sarah," where he'd mentioned his two sons, Jesse and Paul, and expressed his love for them:

> *I shouldn't have come. I should have stayed with you and contributed another way. But pride and shame are powerful tools, so here I am, away from you and our sons, away from the land that needs my attention. I only pray that I can soon return, my duty done, my conscience clear.*

It was a funny thing, pride. It made some men leave and some men stay. My father's pride had made him selfish. Noble's pride had done the opposite. Like so many others, he'd been driven by the need to do his part.

I wasn't sure where I fit on that scale. Maybe somewhere in the middle. I wanted to do my part, to play a *new* part, but the need to prove myself, to conquer each task, to overcome every obstacle and to win . . . those things fueled me more than anything else.

Had it been a competition of sheer strength, I would have lost. Had we been engaged in hand-to-hand combat, day in and day out, running for our lives or taking lives, I would have fallen. But as is the case with so much in life, the tasks my detachment was charged with were more contests of endurance and determination than physical prowess. And in both, I refused to be bested.

We rejoined the other half of our company in White Plains and proceeded toward the Hudson, in the area of the Tappan Bay, not far from Tarrytown, where we made camp and awaited further instructions. To our surprise, General Paterson and Colonel Jackson were already there, tents pitched, awaiting us.

General Paterson told us that we would remain another day at the Tarrytown encampment before heading east toward the Connecticut border, along with Colonel Ebenezer Sproat, who was camped half a mile below us with detachments from the Massachusetts Second, Nat's old regiment. I didn't know which company Phineas was in. He'd been assigned elsewhere—the other boys too, though regiments had been reorganized and rearranged throughout the war. I hadn't seen any of the brothers, thank Providence, but I'd seen Colonel Sproat.

The old tavernkeeper's son from Middleborough was tall as a tree, and he stood out from the rest. He'd made a name for himself, and Captain Webb had sung his praises, but I was wary. I didn't want to travel with his company. He'd known me—though from a distance—for too many years, and I feared he might have heard tales from home and would recognize me.

My company was grateful for the rest, but I spent the hours of my picket duty with my stomach in knots, unimpressed by the slivered moon, the soft air, and the croaking frogs. When Beebe relieved me early, stepping out from the trees, I spun, hands on my weapon, a startled cry in my throat. The guard was thin now that we were back behind our own lines, but a man was still stationed on every side.

"Don't shoot, Robbie. It's just me."

"You're early."

"I was awake. Thought I might as well take watch if I wasn't going to sleep."

"It's quiet," I said. "Only the bullfrogs are awake."

"You callin' me a toad?" he quipped, rubbing at his bristly cheeks. The whole company—except for me and Jimmy—needed a shave. Captain Webb had been sheepish about our bedraggled appearance when we'd arrived in camp, but General Paterson had waved off his apologies, though his eyes had lingered on my face for a moment.

I just shook my head and let Beebe grumble. He loaded his musket, tearing the cartridge open with his teeth and priming the flash pan before closing the frizzen and pouring the rest of the powder into the barrel. He added the ball and paper and rammed it into the breech.

"You don't look so young and bonny anymore either," he muttered. "Your skin's leathered, and the sun has bleached your hair. If I'm a toad, you're a lizard."

I scrubbed at my face, not understanding. I'd washed all the parts that weren't covered.

"Got a mean look to you now, though your eyes gleam all the more. You'd best close 'em or the moths will circle your head." He was jesting, but he didn't laugh at me or himself like he was inclined to do.

The thought that my looks might have changed cheered me. Perhaps General Paterson had only been noting the difference.

"Go on, Robbie. Get some sleep," Beebe demanded, but I hesitated. His gloom was pronounced.

"My watch doesn't end for a bit," I offered. "I'll stay if you don't mind."

He shrugged, shifting his musket and peering up at the moon.

"You got a girl somewhere, Rob?" he asked suddenly.

"No."

He snorted. "I didn't think so."

I knew better than to let Beebe bother me, and I ignored his scoffing.

"Talking to you about this is like talking to my sister."

I didn't like that assessment at all, and immediately set about disabusing him of the notion. "What exactly are we talking about, Beebe?" I said. "Do you need advice?"

He jeered again. "From you, lad? I doubt it."

"You might be surprised."

"Have you ever even touched a girl?" he needled, and Deborah Samson, in all her contrarian wickedness, decided to goad him right back.

"Of course," I said, honesty ringing from my words.

"Liar," he snapped.

"It's the truth," I said, but shrugged, letting it go. He fidgeted and fretted and finally broke the silence.

"I'm not talking about her arm, Shurtliff. Or her hand."

"I didn't think you were." The devil on my shoulder howled with laughter and the angel felt totally justified.

"You've touched a breast?"

I ground my teeth together to keep from smiling. "Yes. Many times."

He jerked. "Many?"

"Yes. Many. More times than I could count."

"You're just a . . . a smock-faced boy."

I shrugged.

"Have you seen everything? Every part? Without clothing?"

"Yes."

"A real live woman? Full grown? Not a child running about?"

"A real live woman."

He gaped at me like I'd just sprouted a crown. "Have you slept beside one?"

"I have."

"Have you put your knob in one?" His voice was so quiet I wasn't certain I'd heard right, and it took me a minute to process what he meant.

"No." I certainly could not claim that, and I was amazed once more at the limitless names men had for their parts. I had learned a dozen of them, at least.

"Why not?" He narrowed his eyes.

"Eh . . ."

"'Tweren't offered?"

"Something like that," I said, and the grin I'd been holding back split my cheeks. I had not had this much fun since I'd beat Phineas in that footrace.

Beebe's shoulders fell and his chin hit his chest.

"Nor have I. But I dream of it. I heard it's like a bit of heaven," he said, wistful.

I grunted, my need to laugh warring with my sincere sympathy. He seemed so sad.

"That's what scares me," he added.

I stiffened, certain he was going to confess something about coupling I didn't want to hear. I suppose I deserved that.

"I'm afraid I'll die without ever finding out," he mourned. "I've had a funny feeling all day."

My mirth fled, and the demon on my shoulder vanished. I looked up at the sky and searched the woods around us, trying to summon words that might comfort him. It was odd. Terror informed my every action, but it was not the same dread felt by those around me. Oh, I shared my comrades fears as well—cowardice, death, suffering—but I was more afraid of discovery than of anything else, and it served as a huge distraction from all the other horrors. In fact, I suppose it made me bolder than I might have otherwise been.

"If you die . . . you won't just experience a little bit of heaven. It'll be heaven itself. Maybe you won't need a taste because everything will be so good."

"Do you believe that?" He seemed doubtful . . . and hopeful too.

"I'm not sure what I believe. But whoever made this world understands beauty and love. All you have to do is look around to feel it. And I don't think that ever ends. 'Whatever God does, it is forever,'" I quoted. "I imagine death is like moving into a new season."

"That's in Ecclesiastes, right?" he asked.

I nodded. "'To every thing there is a season, and a time to every purpose under heaven.'"

"Yeah. I guess that might be true. You gonna be a reverend when this is over? You could be with all the Bible quotin' you do."

I considered that, picturing myself standing at the lectern in Reverend Conant's church. Somehow I thought it might be harder to be a man of God than a man of war, and in a few years, I wouldn't be able to pass for a beardless boy. But to be a reverend appealed to me.

"I would like that," I confessed.

"Then you better stop your whorish ways," he whispered, grinning. "No more sampling from the apple dumplin' shop."

I blinked, not sure I understood, and then I remembered what I'd told him.

He sighed, but his rancor was gone. "Thanks for the talk, Robbie. Don't let the fish take your wanker while you wash. We caught a few this afternoon. They were bitin'."

I choked, and he chuckled, his humor restored. I suppose I had one advantage: I had no fear of losing my wanker.

"See that Noble and Jimmy are awake. They've got the next shift," Beebe added. "I'm watch captain until we're back at the Point."

Dawn was coming, and I wouldn't have long before the encampment was stirring, though the plan to sit tight for another day would delay their rise. Many of us had slept no more than winks and nods in several days. The morning would be slow. Still, I didn't want an audience, and sitting by the fire to dry my clothes would be a whole lot more pleasant if the sun wasn't yet up.

I shook Jimmy awake and then picked my way through the sleeping men until I found Noble. He was already up, pulling on his boots, and I watched him pick up his musket, snap his bayonet into place, and trudge to his picket point on the riverside. Jimmy was slower to follow, but once he had exited the encampment, I retrieved my pack and my blanket—it needed washing too—and headed toward the creek. I needed sleep, but I couldn't go another day without a bath.

The creek was only chest high at its deepest point and maybe ten feet wide. It emptied into the Hudson about twenty rods to the west, if that, but it made for a nice bathing spot not far from camp. I shucked off my boots, found my soap, and waded a few feet in before sinking to my knees, submerging myself to my neck. I began wringing and washing, slipping my hand beneath my billowing shirt and my loosened breeches to scour my underarms and my nether regions before attacking my clothes. The band around my breasts remained tight and tied; the proximity of my company and the dwindling time forced me to wash it while I wore it, running the soap over the outside, as I'd done a dozen times before. If I was able, I would exchange it for the dry one in my pack. If I wasn't, I would manage.

I'd been at it for mere minutes, frenzied as always, scanning the darkness for signs of unwanted company while keeping an eye on Jimmy, who sat watch farther up the creek. He'd never once even looked my way, though I'd made certain there was nothing for him to see. He was seated with his back to me, and from the way he was slumped, I doubted he was seeing anything but the backs of his eyelids.

I'd just finished rinsing the soap from my hair when a shifting and reshaping of the darkness, a ways beyond Jimmy's picket point, caught my eye. As I watched, riders began to converge, moving along the opposite side of the creek. The trees cast long shadows that gave them cover, but there were many of them, their pistols were drawn, and they were not Continentals. I tucked my lips over a shriek and inched back until my shoulders touched the bank, tying my strings beneath the water, terrified that any movement would draw their eyes toward me and equally terrified that I'd lose my breeches when I stood. Jimmy's head stayed bowed and his back remained bent.

I wriggled up the bank behind the small outcropping of rocks I'd chosen specifically to give me some privacy, though I'd never envisioned needing cover like this. I put the straps of my powder horn and my cartridge box over my head, notched my belt, and aimed my musket at the rider in the center. Discharging my weapon would be the fastest way to alert my detachment, but I wasn't going to waste a bullet, and it might make them scatter, knowing they'd lost the element of surprise. I had doubts about my actions for half a second and then discarded them. Their coats were red, their movements stealthy, and their intentions clear. Images of Colonel Greene being dragged from his tent and slaughtered cemented my resolve. These were the tactics of DeLancey's Brigade, and they weren't behind our lines to negotiate a treaty.

I pulled the trigger and I think a man fell, though I didn't stop to make sure, surging up from the bank and racing toward the encampment, separated from the marauders by trees and sheer terror. Bullets began to whiz and crack above my head, and I didn't stop to pull on my boots or shrug into my coat. My wet clothes clung and my hair stuck to my cheeks and dripped down my back, but not one of the Thomas brothers could have outrun me in that moment.

~ 12 ~

Self-Evident

As I broke through the trees into the encampment, men were coming to their feet, weapons in hand, in various states of dress, their confusion evident.

"DeLancey's coming," I shouted, though I wasn't certain who led the assault. "We're under attack."

Captain Webb was out of his tent, and Noble was running toward me from his picket on the Hudson side of our encampment. I caught a glimpse of General Paterson, gun in hand, his shirt hanging loose about his breeches, no boots, no stockings. He was shouting out orders, urging the men to move north to the tree line, and then his voice and his figure were swallowed up by the cavalry that descended upon us.

The flames of small campfires illuminated the hooves of flying horses and the legs of panicked men, but the crescent moon did nothing to alleviate the chaos or light the way to safety. I needed to reload. That was the only thought in my head, and I went through the motions, intent on my task.

"Shurtliff!" Noble yelled. "Get down. Get down!"

He was beside me, thrusting his bayonet left and right, trying to skewer a rider and keep them from hewing us down, and then his head snapped back and his arms flew wide, the back of his right hand catching me across my cheek and nose and laying me flat. I scrambled up immediately, my ears ringing and my now-loaded musket still clutched in my hands. The back of Noble's head was a puddle of blood.

"Noble?" I shouted, rolling him over. His face was gone.

"Shurtliff!" Someone was screaming my name, and another wave of riders broke through the trees. Too close to aim, too close to run. I simply thrust upward with all my might, and felt the jarring thunk and sickening slide of resistance as my bayonet met flesh. The action tore my musket from my arms and snapped the clasp that kept the bayonet secured. The rider fell back, end over end, and landed at my feet, his face planted in the earth, his buttocks in the air like he'd stopped to pray but died instead.

Someone swung at me, a broadsword that whistled and hissed through the air and sliced my sleeve from shoulder to cuff. Again, I didn't think. I didn't scream or even look to see who sought to kill me. My musket was gone, my bayonet too, so I reached for the hatchet on my belt. With both hands I sent it flying, end over end, toward the wielder of the sword. I didn't think at all, I just heaved and watched it strike.

It was an old game we had played, the Thomas brothers and I. We had a target on the barn wall and rings to tally our points, and we'd hurled the axe a thousand times. I'd excelled at the game. I excelled at every game. But this was different.

The man's eyes widened and his lips pursed, like he said "woman," though I couldn't be sure.

His eyes were bulging and his leather helmet hung from the strap beneath his chin. Curls clung to his forehead and his nape. He tried to lift his sword, but his arms did not cooperate. His horse stopped obligingly, its head tossing, feet stomping, and I reached up for the handle of my hatchet.

Then sound and scent—oh dear God, the scent—returned and General Paterson was running toward me, his mouth moving and his shirttails flapping, but I couldn't hear, and I needed my hatchet.

It came free like the man was simply a stump, a stump with crimson sap. The clutch felt exactly the same, but the sound was a squelch and a squish, and suddenly I could hear again. I could hear and smell and see and feel, but none of it was real. *It's a game. It's just like a game.*

Jeremiah had played with little toy soldiers made with lead or wood and carefully covered in paint. He'd knocked them down with clods of earth or a swath of his hands, like God on high. The second man I killed slid boneless to the ground, just like the first, and I put my hatchet back on my belt, as unfeeling as a child at play.

"Shurtliff!" General Paterson was blood-spattered, and he had a musket in each hand. He tossed the one in his right like he expected me to catch it. Somehow I did, though my palms were slick with gore.

"Get on that horse, and go for Colonel Sproat. Tell him we're pinned in here, and they're mowing us down."

I nodded, swinging up onto the dead man's horse. The saddle was warm where he'd been and soaked in his blood. I almost slid right off the other side. Captain Webb was running for a line of trees to the north. Those who could followed at his heels, those who could not were left behind. The riders had come from the east, the Hudson was west, and Colonel Sproat was south, over the creek. If the band had raided him first, there would be no one to summon or warn, but we'd have heard it and been warned ourselves.

"Go, Shurtliff!" General Paterson roared, and I dug my bare toes into the horse's sides.

DeLancey's men made a devastating pass through the camp and wheeled around and came back again, firing on the fleeing soldiers who were barely awake, only partially dressed, and shooting over their shoulders as they ran. Bullets whizzed by my head, and they were more likely than not from my compatriots. The horse beneath me shot forward, as eager as I to escape the melee.

I didn't feel the ride, nor could I remember it when it was all over. It was like sleep without dreaming, time without meaning, and none of it was real.

I had a jolt of awareness when I saw the campfires and heard the cries. Dawn was breaking, and Sproat's encampment was stirring. I almost expected to be fired upon, racing full out with no blue to identify me, no company beside me, and riding the enemy's horse.

A warning shot went up, and I knew I'd been seen. I didn't slow, but I started shouting, making my identity known.

"I'm Private Shurtliff, Fourth Massachusetts Regiment, Captain Webb's company. We've been hit by DeLancey and are pinned down half a mile north."

They had heard the gunfire and were already assembled, Colonel Sproat standing tall among them. I reined the horse in and repeated myself, panting between words.

"How many?" Colonel Sproat asked me, his hand on my reins.

"Our detachment is maybe fifty men. Half of the company moved out last night. General Paterson is camped with us. He sent me. It was dark, and they surprised us, but I'd say the attacking party was at least a hundred men, all on horseback."

I was interrupted by a sentinel, running up from the river toward his comrades.

"Colonel Sproat, British reinforcements in boats have been spotted on the Hudson, headed north," he yelled. "At least a full company. Maybe more."

"I have to go back," I shouted. "They'll be slaughtered."

"We need more men," Sproat said, shaking his head and keeping his hand on my reins. "Keep going south for four miles," he told me.

"There are always a few detachments at Dobbs Ferry and a French field hospital too. Tell them to hurry."

I nodded and spurred the horse forward, afraid it was already too late. I heard Sproat rallying his men behind me.

"Let's go!" he roared, and a cry went up, triumphant and eager, and when I looked back, they had begun to run.

~

I reached Dobbs Ferry at full light, and men were marching toward Tarrytown within fifteen minutes of my arrival, a wagon with a French surgeon named Lepien and his staff bouncing along behind them.

By the time I got back, the battle was over. Sproat and his men had turned the tide, and DeLancey's riders had fled, though DeLancey himself was not among the dead or dying. No one pursued them; no one could. We were not cavalry. The nut-brown horse with the three white stockings that had taken me on my predawn ride was picketed with the general's gray. He belonged to the Continentals now, and General Paterson said he too would be taken to the Point. There wasn't enough forage for cattle or cavalry on the hills around the garrison, and most of the livestock was kept at Peekskill, but I made sure he was watered and his gore-soaked saddle removed before I left him.

I did not look through the saddlebags. I didn't want to know anything about the man who'd ridden him into camp, the man with startled eyes and curling hair whose life I'd taken.

I knew Noble was dead, and I avoided the spot where he had fallen. But I was the one who found Jimmy. I went looking for him, knowing where he'd last been, and almost certain of what I would find. He'd not even moved from the spot by the creek. A hole gaped at the base of his throat, and his musket was still strapped to his chest. His eyes were closed like he'd walked to his picket, propped himself against a tree, and fallen back to sleep. Blood soaked his shirt and made a pool in his lap.

I couldn't carry his body back to camp by myself and went in search of help. That's when I found Beebe, who must have come from his position at the northeast corner and run right into the end of a bayonet. If he'd gotten to kill a redcoat before he died, as he'd sworn to do, I didn't know, but his premonition had proven true. He'd died without ever knowing what heaven felt like.

Death had taken his smirk and his scowl. He was gray-faced and gutted, and I crouched beside him for a moment, unable to comprehend the reality of it all. The birds warbled above me and the sky was blue. That death could exist on a beautiful day was inconceivable to me.

General Paterson had seen it all before. I could tell by the quiet in his face and the set of his shoulders. His tent was commandeered by Lepien and his staff. By the end of the day, two men had survived amputation and another two hadn't. The rest of the injured were prepared to be taken to the field hospital near Dobbs Ferry. It was closer than the Point.

Captain Webb's company had lost twelve men. Fifteen more were injured, five grievously. Our orders to head east to escort supplies were rescinded. Colonel Sproat would take another detachment and go on without us. A few of his men had been injured, but none of them lost, and they returned to their encampment to ready themselves to move the next morning.

Our dead were wrapped in their blankets and piled in the back of a wagon. They were to be taken to the Point and buried there in the graveyard overlooking the water. DeLancey's dead were buried where they'd fallen, their shoes and gear given to the men most in need. Captain Webb said no one would be back to collect the bodies. Not under the circumstances.

I took a shirt from Jimmy's sack and felt a fissure opening in my chest. I'd been moving in a state of nothingness since dawn. No pain. No anger. No horror. No shame. But when I took Jimmy's shirt, knowing he had no use for it and mine was in tatters, the nothingness became something unbearable, and I left Noble's haversack to others, Beebe's too, and wrapped myself in work until night fell and the camp grew quiet. The watch had doubled, but I was not among those assigned to duty. General Paterson had intervened when I volunteered.

"Not tonight, Shurtliff. Your nose is swollen and your eyes are turning black," he said, frowning. "You've done enough."

I touched my face, surprised, and Noble's blood-soaked visage rose in my mind. He'd struck me when he saved my life.

"You're also covered in blood," my captain informed. "Go wash and get some rest."

I looked down at my shirt, the right sleeve hanging in ribbons, but it was the sight of my long, thin feet that threatened my composure. They were splattered with the blood of men I knew and men I didn't. I couldn't decide which was worse, to be marked by those you'd killed or those you'd cared about.

My pack still sat beside the river, my boots too, and for a moment I envied what they had not seen, what they'd avoided, waiting for me to put them on again. I walked into the creek like I'd done the night before and began to wash, my sorrow billowing like the blood in the water. It was only then, when the water freed my sleeve from my skin that I realized my right arm bore a long, deep slash just below my shoulder to the middle of my arm. It was deep enough that it lay wide open, but not deep enough to expose the bone. It gaped like a toothless grin, and I moaned in protest, tears streaming down my cheeks, though it was more dread than pain, more worry than woe. It would have to be closed, and I would have to do it myself.

I dared not ask for help. What if I was asked to remove my shirt or my chest was inadvertently brushed? I tore my sleeve free and wrung it out. It would serve as a bandage when it was dry.

I waited until I was alone by the fire and the rest of the men had retired for the night. I should have waited a little longer, but I was shaking with fatigue, and I needed the light. My arm throbbed, my soul ached, and my nerves were strung tight. I wanted to be done with it.

I threaded my needle, knotted the end, and then soaked my string in my rum, hoping it would provide some protection against the wound turning bad. It was my right arm, which would make it harder, but I could stitch with my left hand.

"It is naught but pain," I whispered, but I was shaking. I threaded the needle through my flesh, making a single, wobbly stitch, and had to stop to breathe and quiet my stomach.

When I looked up, General Paterson was standing there, watching. My arm was exposed to his view. I could hardly hide it now.

"Shurtliff," he greeted.

"General."

He'd just returned from washing at the creek. His sleeves were rolled, his hair wet, and his clothes fresh. He walked to the hospital tent but returned immediately, a bottle of brandy and a bandage swinging from one hand. He turned a log onto its side and sat upon it, facing me.

"Why didn't you let Lepien attend you?" he asked. "Or Dr. Thatcher?"

Dr. James Thatcher was stationed at the Point and attached to Colonel Jackson's regiment, of which I was now part. But I'd known him before. He was from Plymouth County. I'd been in his home and brought him tea when he attended old Widow Thatcher, who happened to be his aunt. I hadn't seen him since I was ten years old, but he'd lowered his eyebrows at me once in passing, like he thought he should know me, and the look had left me paralyzed for days. I didn't want him anywhere near me.

"There were others who needed attention," I said. "And I knew I could handle my own stitches."

"I am handy with a needle," he said. "I'll help you."

"As am I," I answered, but I was trembling, and it had not gone unnoticed.

"Put your hand on my shoulder," he demanded. "I will do it."

"I can do it myself, sir."

"Quiet," he said, firm. "Now drink this." He handed me the bottle of brandy. It was half-full.

I obeyed, slugging down a few swallows, but I refused when he tried to make me drink more. I was more afraid of a loosened tongue than the pain of stitches.

"It does not agree with me," I protested. "I will be sick."

"It will hurt more without it."

"Yes, sir. I suspect it will."

He poured what was left in the bottle down my arm, and I barely flinched though it stung like holy fire.

"A tough one, aren't you, Shurtliff?"

I set my hand on his shoulder, lifting it to his view, and surrendered the needle I'd threaded. He pinched the sides of the gash together with his right hand and began sewing with his left. He didn't hesitate; he didn't even warn me. He just went to work, drawing the needle and thread through my flesh, steady and sure.

The push and pull of the needle through my skin was the worst part, but I closed my eyes and let myself rest in the pain and pleasure of reprieve. I had only to endure, not execute, and my relief was even greater than my agony. I bore the ache of his ministrations without complaint.

"Jimmy was killed," I whispered.

"Yes. I know."

"He was only sixteen."

"Too young. Just like you."

I bit back my denial. Jimmy was not like me, but it didn't matter. I looked down at the general's hands, at the row of Xs marching down my arm.

"You were right, sir."

He was almost done, and I was impressed by his handiwork. I could not have done better, and in all likelihood, I would have done considerably worse. If the wound didn't fester, it would be better in no time.

"About what?" he answered.

"You are handy with a needle."

He grunted.

"And you were right about me."

He did not raise his gaze from my arm, but he was listening.

"I had no idea what I was talking about. No idea what I signed up for."

"None of us do," he said gently. "But you did very well today."

"Jimmy Battles and Noble Sperin were my friends. John Beebe too, though he drove me crazy and liked to tease. They were my bunkmates, the men I knew best. And they're all gone. All three of them died today."

"Yes."

He didn't speak of all the others lost—I had no doubt he'd witnessed many over the years—or seek to fill the silence, and I strove for the same stoicism.

"What will happen next?" I asked, gritting my teeth to keep my lips from trembling. I wanted to know how I would endure the horrors to come, but he misunderstood.

"We will take them to the Point. They will be buried there." He knotted the thread beneath the last stitch and used his knife to cut it close to my skin.

"Do you have to write to their families?"

"Yes. Those in my brigade. Hand me that bandage." I did so, and he wound it around my arm and tied the ends securely.

"But . . . what if you didn't know them?"

"I ask their comrades. Their captain. Their colonel. I get to know them. Then I write letters that no one ever wants to receive."

None of the Thomas boys had been attached to General Paterson's brigade. The letters we'd received had been from General Howe.

"I will assist you," I said. "I helped many of them write letters home."

"Thank you, Shurtliff," he said. "I would appreciate that. Now go get some rest, Private." He rose and patted the top of my head with his big hand, like I was a child or a faithful dog.

"You must have laughed at my pretty words and inspirational ideas. I am a fool," I blurted, moisture stinging my nose. He hesitated and sat back down.

"No. Not foolish. Not at all. What was it you said? That hope is something we have to keep burning?" He studied me. "I've never heard truer words in my life."

"I killed two men. Maybe more."

"I have killed many."

"I am not sorry."

He sighed heavily. "Yes, you are."

"They were trying to kill me. They killed my friends."

"Yes. But you are still sorry. It is a terrible burden to end a life."

"Why did they attack?"

"We are at war."

I shook my head. "No. That is not why. They wanted something."

He did not answer.

"We don't have the supplies. Captain Webb said they want our supplies, but we didn't have the supplies today," I protested.

"They weren't here for the supplies. They were most likely here for me."

I gasped, and he flinched.

"You?"

He rose again, and I followed, clutching my arm to my chest.

He shook his head like he regretted speaking. "I am weary. So are you. Go to bed, Shurtliff. We have survived this day. I have no doubt we will survive tomorrow as well."

I watched him retreat to a small tent someone had erected in the trees. No one guarded his door or stood watch nearby, and I was suddenly afraid for him. The moans of the wounded and the absence of the dead tainted the night, and I doubted I would be able to sleep at all. I retrieved my blanket and made my bed beside his tent. If DeLancey came back for the general, I would be waiting.

~

August 31, 1781

Dear Elizabeth,

We returned to the Point only to leave again for Kingston two days later. General Paterson had arranged for another shipment of supplies which, given the attacks by Colonel DeLancey and his brigade, was fortunate. The supplies from Connecticut never arrived and a detachment assigned to escort the wagons has disappeared. Some think the soldiers deserted or were bribed—or threatened—to abandon the stores, but the men are gone and so are the goods.

Our second trip to Kingston did not go as smoothly as our previous assignment, and we left with half as much after twice as much trouble. Winter is coming, and the war continues, though I'm not sure anyone knows why.

My arm has healed quickly, thanks to the general, but my heart is changed yet again. I miss my mates. I was well acquainted with loss, but not with death, and the two are not the same. I told the general that I was not sorry for the men I killed, but he knew better. Sorrow has arrived, and I am permanently altered.

Noble Sperin was dutiful and brave. It occurred to me that he was much like Nathaniel, and my mourning for both has become all the more intense. What a terrible waste of good men! In the time I've been a soldier, that is the lesson that has most surprised me.

John Beebe was a lovable nuisance, but in many ways, his challenges made me better, his criticism too. And like Phineas, he made me laugh. It is not something I've done much of in my life. I have always been too intense. To laugh and play took time from the things that drove me, but Beebe brought out the rascal in me, and I am better for it.

Jimmy Battles and I were often lumped together because of our "age," and we became a bit of a pair, much like Jeremiah and I once were. I told the general that Jimmy didn't complain, he always encouraged, and he was never afraid, not even at the end. It will be a blessing to his mother to know that he died quietly and quickly, with very little suffering. It is a comfort to me as well.

Since Tarrytown, I have dreamed about Jeremiah almost every night, and I fear something has happened to him too, and he has come to tell me goodbye. Or perhaps I simply can't separate the Thomas boys from my downed comrades, and in sleep they are one and the same. They all feel like brothers to me.

We have no new recruits. No one has taken the berths of the fallen, and since they were my bunkmates, I have considerably more room, but it is not welcome space.

Autumn is here. Like a pinprick, a drop of bloodred appeared on the hillside, and then another, and another, followed by a bit of gold and a sprinkling of orange. Now the entire valley is aflame. I thought the Point glorious in spring, but the fall is beyond description. I suspect even winter will take my breath away with its beauty, but I can hardly sleep for the fear in my chest. So many things will be more difficult when the cold hits. —RS

~ 13 ~

All Men

I saw men die at Tarrytown. I watched them fall around me, and the blood and waste was beyond description, yet somehow my mind still attempted to quantify the horror, if only to consider what I might still endure.

General orders were issued for the army to prepare for movement at a moment's notice, and many of us thought an attack on New York was imminent. The capture of New York, occupied by the best troops in the British arsenal and fortified by both land and water, would be a fatal, war-ending blow to England, and the discussion in the huts abounded as to when and how it would be accomplished.

In mid-September, General Paterson's entire brigade was sent marching toward New York. We crossed the Hudson at King's Bridge, and proceeded down the river, marching to the drum and fife, making a show of our numbers and our strength, and met up with a division of French in full regalia, their uniforms white and trimmed in green.

We proceeded all the way to the enemy's post at Morrisania without challenge, but it appeared to be abandoned.

"They have retreated to New York in preparation for our attack," Captain Webb told us, and when the morning came, we were on the move again, breaking away from the bulk of the army on a foraging expedition and camping in woods near the enemy's lines, hoping to draw them out, but all was quiet. The next day we were moving again, passing through points hitherto held by the British, unimpeded.

We marched through Princeton, moving past the huge stone edifice that had once been filled with students, not soldiers. The many windows watched our progress with weary disinterest, and the weather vane atop the cupola was perfectly still. The grounds were littered with the detritus of battle, and the buildings were blackened, marked by the years of occupation by both armies. I counted the windows and longed to explore, even as we moved past and continued on to Trenton.

By the time we reached Philadelphia, it was apparent we'd been part of a grand scheme. We moved through the streets at the front of a two-mile-long parade of liveried officers, marching soldiers, mounted guns, ammunition carriages, and wagons piled with tents and provisions. The procession kicked up a cloud of dust so great I couldn't see the crowds that came to cheer us on, but I could hear them, and the French flags draped from the highest windows and waving along the route told the story.

Thirty-six French vessels had arrived in Chesapeake Bay. Count de Grasse, the French admiral, had blockaded Yorktown, which was occupied by the British. In anticipation of his arrival, Washington had been slowly moving his armies southward while engaging in tactics of deception designed to make the British believe New York was the true target.

The deception had proved successful.

Emboldened by de Grasse's fleet and seizing the opportunity to surround the enemy, General Washington ordered a rapid march of all his forces to Virginia.

We crossed rivers—sometimes aboard boats and sometimes on bridges—and saw flourishing villages and shuttered towns. We gave one such place a wide berth after hearing that disease had ravaged the population.

None of us fell ill from smallpox, but many of us became sick aboard the boat that carried us down the Elk River, so great was the tossing and lurching of the vessel loaded down with soldiers.

I had always enjoyed a hearty constitution; Phineas claimed it was my temper.

"No ailment would dare," he said. But though I'd never suffered from sickness of any sort, I succumbed to the tossing of the boat, as did most of my comrades.

We were caught in a gale that pushed us forward and didn't relent until we reached the harbor near Jamestown, Virginia, where we disembarked and camped. We had traveled over four hundred miles, most of it on foot at a punishing speed, but I would have rather marched it all again than be tossed about in that vessel. I could not stand without the world tipping and my legs trembling, and nothing remained in my stomach for a full day. But the worst was yet to come.

Lines were drawn, impassioned speeches given by every officer to his men, and we pushed forward about two miles outside Yorktown where we were joined by the three thousand French ground troops delivered by de Grasse. The digging of trenches and forming of batteries commenced, all while under an unrelenting British barrage.

My well of miseries continued to accumulate, my list of horrors, my assortment of unimaginables, but I am convinced, after living through them all, that hell could not be worse than weeks under constant cannonade.

It was not a skirmish or a glancing attack by a handful of dragoons. It was not even like the terrible night in Tarrytown. It was the culmination of six years of war.

That such horror can be beautiful is hard to imagine, but it was. Light and sound collided against the firmament like shooting stars and swooping dragons with flaming breath and fiery tails. Perhaps it was the quaking of both earth and sky and the contrast of being more alive and nearer to death than I had ever been. I was living the Book of Revelation, and I could not avert my eyes.

Great sheets of screaming fire rained down and boiled up in columns of smoke and dust coating the air and fraying our nerves until I grew numb and deaf to the boom and crackle and worked in a mindless stupor. We slept with fascines and entrenching tools in our hands and muskets strapped to our backs, catching naps propped against our earthen walls. Food—often no more than biscuits and dried salt pork—was delivered twice a day along with handcarts laden with water jugs to refill our canteens.

I used the temporary latrines maybe once a day, and always in the darkest hours of the night, but nobody bathed and nobody slept and nobody paid me any mind, except the general, who rode back and forth on the line, encouraging the men. I'd seen him from afar, riding his horse, which I had learned was called Lenox, and conferring with Kosciuszko, who was supervising the batteries being built. It was not until the early hours of October 10, when we had completed our first parallel and began a cannonade of our own, that he approached and called my name. We were all indistinguishable from each other, our faces and regimentals coated in the paste of sweat and soil, and I didn't know how he recognized me.

I tried to salute, but was unable to uncurl my fingers from the shovel. A rush of blood and water pooled in my palm as I managed to pry the handle free. General Paterson climbed from his horse and crouched by the entrenchment, beckoning me forward.

"You have been here every day since we arrived. I assume your arm is healed."

"Yes, sir. Long healed. Thanks to you. And I prefer to stay busy, General, sir."

"Show me your hands, lad."

"I am fine, sir."

He frowned at me, and I frowned back, but I did not show him my hands. It would mean a trip to the hospital tent, and if I stopped working, I didn't trust that I would be able to start again. Action was my only antidote to fear.

"You do have a fearsome gaze, Shurtliff."

I grinned at that. He remembered.

He studied me for a moment, as though there was more he wanted to say. "Godspeed, Private."

"Godspeed, General."

He rose, climbed back on his horse, and continued on, and I stopped for a moment to watch him go. I did not see him again until I was called up for a different kind of duty.

It was determined that a pair of enemy redoubts about three hundred yards in front of the main works would have to be taken in order for our artillery to move within range. Two advance columns of light infantry, French on the right, Americans on the left, were assigned to storm the defenses. My unit was among them.

My hands were so blistered I could not straighten my fingers or make a fist, and I cut a strip off the bottom of my shirt, wrapped my hands, and spent the hours leading up to the advance making peace with my maker, convinced that I could not possibly survive such a mission. I'd been lucky once. I did not expect to be so fortunate again.

General Paterson addressed the men along with General Lafayette, who had been tasked with planning the strike.

"I have no talent for pretty words," Paterson said, though I would disagree. "But we stand on the precipice of a glorious ending. Let's finish it. And let's go home."

The men around me shook their muskets and raised their voices, bellowing for themselves and for each other, and I wondered how many times General Paterson had been in such a position, how many times he'd marshaled his troops and looked into the eyes of boys who would not live to see another day . . . or even another hour. And I wondered how many of the men around me had regularly cheated death and come back again, knowing full well that it kept score. And as at Tarrytown, I was greatly humbled.

The night was so dark we walked with our hands to the shoulder of the man in front of us for almost a mile, creeping to the appointed spot where we worked in silence, doing our best to tunnel the earth without a sound.

We retreated before daylight and heard the moment the British saw our progress as a constant firing commenced, but we were well away. Shells from the opposing lines crossed each other in the sky, falling and winnowing out the earth. What damage they did in the town, I did not know, but I'd seen a horse be blown in half, his head and tail rising into the sky before his blood sprayed the trenches for fifty feet in all directions, peppering the ground like a sudden hail. A captain from the Seventh Massachusetts Regiment was tossed into the air as well, mercifully dead before he came back down.

At dark, our columns were formed. A colonel named Alexander Hamilton led the charge, and we attacked in waves, told to use only our bayonets to avoid making a sound. I could no more fight in my condition than fly, and I simply ran forward when instructed, expecting to be hewn down with every step.

Instead, the British fell back after the second wave, abandoning their positions and fleeing under the assault. Our lines closed, connecting the redoubts, and our cannons and mortars launched attack. I had sustained a hole through my hat, and the lapel of my coat hung by a thread, caught by the tip of a random bayonet, but I was still standing, my bayonet unbloodied, and the redoubt had been captured with very little loss of life.

My ears rang for days afterward and my stomach rejected its contents from my extreme fatigue, but somehow I'd survived again.

October 19, 1781

Dear Elizabeth,

I have seen two armies made up of thousands of men clash on the field of battle. We use the words "glorious" to describe victory and "terrible" to describe defeat, but such words are wholly insufficient to capture what I witnessed. The world shook, tossed about in a relentless squall, and I have still not gotten my sea legs. I saw it all, heard it all, and felt it all, yet I lack the skill to fully relay the experience.

After the capture of the two redoubts and two days of devastating bombardment, Lord Cornwallis sent out a flag and requested a cessation of hostilities. Hours later he surrendered, though he sent his surrogate, General O'Hara, to the ceremony in his stead, pleading illness. I thought that cowardly. Seven thousand British soldiers, as ragged as we, marched out to the cadence of drums and ceded their weapons, piling them high with lowered heads, before they were ushered away in slow and solemn step. They did not get to send someone in their place. Nor did the men from either side who fell on the battlefield.

General Washington was straight and fine on his pale horse, but it was General Benjamin Lincoln, second-in-command, who rode forward and accepted the articles of capitulation. The French officers stood to one side, the Americans to the other. General Paterson was among them, dashing in his gold epaulets and sash, and you would have been proud.

Many in my company wept as we watched the procession, but I could find no strength for tears. I am too spent and too dazed, caught in a dream state from which I haven't yet awakened. War is terrible, and if I survive to the end, I will bear witness to the sheer, incomprehensible waste of it all. But it is not the horror that has stricken me. It is awe that I am still here.

Virginians, both bond and free, came by the wagonload to see the departure of the British Army from Yorktown. Virginia's population consists of five hundred thousand African slaves, three times the number of whites in the colony. It does not escape me that we fight for our own emancipation while such a condition exists. It did not escape many. Colonel Kosciuszko, when we were gathered in prayer before we stormed the redoubts, said to the reverend offering the invocation:

"Here we are, contending for the rights of men with our lives while not addressing the contradiction in our own practices. It weakens our cause and our case."

The poor reverend was so distracted by the denunciation, he stood a little too close to the line and his hat was blown off by a stray shot.

"Consider that a warning, Reverend Evans," Colonel Kosciuszko said, laughing. "A warning to you

of the sin of slavery and our need to address it as soon as this war is won. Add that to your prayers so the softening can begin."

The softening has begun. My own heart is much affected, and Proverbs 18:16 keeps playing in my mind.

"A man's gift makes room for him, and brings him before great men."

I do not know what the future holds or where I will find the stamina to continue. But if we have won the war, as some believe, I will call myself blessed for the gifts—gifts Deacon Thomas thought wasted on a woman—that have brought me before great men. —RS

∾

The sticky heat that sat on our shoulders and weighed down the march from Philadelphia had retreated before us, and the exodus from Yorktown was accompanied by a full-throated fall in temperatures, heralding winter. Instead of heat and damp, we endured cold and wet, and the hot rush to battle in September became a dreary, forty-five-day slog back to the highlands.

I could not tally the miles I had marched, but my shoes, new when I enlisted, looked a hundred years old, and I felt no younger. When we stopped at night, I studied the miserable men beside me, half-dressed, half-starved, feet bleeding from walking without proper shoes or any shoes at all. They turned their bodies in front of paltry fires like rabbits on a spit, trying to warm themselves, and my awe increased.

I had never considered it a privilege to be a woman. Not even once. I had struggled at the bit of my sex, at the reins of society, at the saddle of tradition. It had not occurred to me that men had their own burdens, that they were bridled too. It was not women who died on the battlefield.

I had been denied and barred entry to a world I wanted to experience, but had I been barred because I was disdained or because I was valued? I suspected it was both. Even so, I was less inclined to complain about my lot.

We'd been promised that we would winter at the Point, rest and warmth dangled in front of us as we traversed the miles. But movement was my friend—it had always been my friend—and the dread of months spent in the barracks settled upon me.

The war was not over.

If negotiations for a treaty had begun, Congress wasn't forthcoming, and no one was being discharged. It would be spring, many said. Or maybe the fall. Surely the British knew the war was lost. Surely it couldn't go on much longer. But General Washington retreated to New Windsor, we arrived back in the highlands in mid-November, and I began to beseech God for another blessing. I had come too far to be defeated by winter quarters.

~ 14 ~

Certain Unalienable Rights

It was cold and the hunger and deprivation relentless. I was darning stockings and repairing coats far more often than I was shooting at regulars. We weren't getting the supplies General Paterson continually petitioned Congress for, so we raided instead. Every mission was sanctioned and approved, but it felt more like stealing than anything.

The scouting parties were not made up of men of the highest character, nor were they probably the worst of the lot. They were men—and I include myself in that group—that had never been given anything, so taking wasn't all that hard. Our only virtue was that we tried to take from those who had plenty, and we sought to be stealthy enough that no one would have to lose their lives over grain and whiskey and eggs. I volunteered for the scouting expeditions simply because it got me out of camp.

On our second expedition, a raid on a farmhouse that belonged to a loyalist, we came up with nothing but a few rotten bushels of fruit, a bag of cornmeal, and a cook kettle too heavy to carry back. The property had been stripped or abandoned long before we got there. We made a small fire, and I dug through the sodden fruit, cut off the salvageable bits, and put it in the stewpot with some water and my rum ration. I boiled it until it became a sticky sweet soup and then added the cornmeal, forming a yellow batter. The finished cake wasn't too bad, but it was hardly worth the effort we'd expended to conduct the raid.

Some of the men in the scouting party decided they would just keep on going. A man named Davis Dornan was the most vocal, and after a few hours spent around the fire eating my johnnycake and complaining about the conditions, he and three of the other men from our party of eight were bent on desertion.

"I'm going home," Dornan said. "I'm not going to sit up in that garrison all winter. None of us have seen a dollar since we enlisted. I heard they were promising new recruits land."

That news swayed a few more, and the grousing became louder.

"What do you think, Shurtliff? You coming with us?" Dornan asked. "You aren't a bad man to have around. You always surprise me." He picked a crumb from the cook kettle and licked his fingers.

"No." I shook my head. "I'm staying at the Point. I don't have a home to go back to."

"You can come with me, Robbie. My ma would take ya," a soldier named Oliver Johnson offered. He was amiable enough and sometimes saved me a spot in the mess line. I thought it was probably because I gave him what I didn't eat, but I appreciated kindness however it came.

"Thank you. But no. I signed up for the duration."

Davis Dornan didn't like that. He'd signed up for the duration too, I was quite certain.

"They don't honor their commitments, so how can they expect us to honor ours?" he asked, eyes shrewd. I couldn't argue with that, but I wasn't going to desert, and I just shook my head when they continued to wheedle.

"It's too damn cold to desert. I think I'm with Shurtliff. It's one hundred and fifty miles back to Uxbridge," a man named Laurence Barton concluded, and a few of the others grumbled in agreement, tipping the balance against the idea. By morning, the dangerous conversation seemed to be forgotten, and the whole scouting party made our way back to Nelson's Point across from Fort Clinton.

"You gonna tell Webb?" Dornan asked me, as we were ferried across the river to West Point landing.

"There's nothing to tell," I said quietly. "Nothing happened."

"That's right. Nothing happened," he agreed, but my desperation had risen dramatically. He was suspicious of me, and I was leery of him. I wouldn't be volunteering for another scouting mission with him or any of the others. Desertion was a crime. Plotting desertion was too.

Occasionally British and Hessian deserters would arrive at the Point, promising fealty and pleading to be taken in, but they never were. Spies abounded, and General Paterson turned them away, often assigning a detachment to escort them all the way back to the British lines to be turned over for treason. It discouraged desertions, and the word quickly spread that quarter would not be given and defectors need not apply.

Desertion and low reenlistments had been a problem from the beginning, but it was only getting worse. The Continental currency continued to plummet, and no amount of coaxing or talk of the glorious cause—as worthy as it was—could convince many to stay once their time was up. Some argued they'd never agreed to their enlistment terms, others simply felt entitled to violate them. I'd heard rumblings, especially after Yorktown, when instead of the war ending, we'd settled in for a long winter. But they'd only been rumblings. This had come dangerously close to more.

When Captain Webb pulled me aside a day later, I thought maybe someone else had talked, and I was in trouble.

"You never want to lead a team, Shurtliff, and you've turned down every opportunity to be point," he began, studying me intently. "I'd think you lacked courage, but that's clearly not it. You volunteer for the worst jobs, you perform them well, and you don't complain. I think the only thing I've ever heard you say is *yessir*."

I waited, hardly breathing.

"You don't have anything to say?" he prodded.

"No, sir." I shook my head, and he laughed.

"So I was surprised when General Paterson says he's spoken to you at length—several times—and found you to be conversant and competent in many things. He said you even taught school."

I wasn't sure if I was being commended or scolded, and I waited again, expectant.

"Lieutenant Cole, his aide-de-camp, is unwell. He's had a wasting cough for some time and another winter in the highlands would have done him in. He has been in Philadelphia since before Yorktown, and the general has been doing without. But he needs a new man, and he has asked to speak to you."

"A new man?"

"Another aide, Shurtliff. A glorified servant. You'll serve his guests, deliver messages, and whatever else he requires. But it's a promotion, one I didn't know if you'd be interested in, seeing as you haven't accepted advancement elsewhere."

"Will I still sleep in the barracks?"

"No. You'll stay in the Red House. You'll be at the general's beck and call, and you'll go where he goes. I hate to lose you, but you'll eat better, you'll sleep better, and I reckon you'll do me proud."

"I thought an aide was ch-chosen from among the officers," I stammered, hardly able to believe my good fortune.

"Usually they are. I'm not saying you've got the position. I'm just saying he wants to talk to you. You've impressed him. Consider it an interview."

"Now?" I squeaked, and Captain Webb winced.

"Lord, you are young," he grumbled. "Yes. Now, Shurtliff."

"Do I look respectable, Captain?" I asked, running my hands over my regimentals.

"You look as worn and weary as the rest of us, but nothing to be done about that now. Wash your face and hands, and clean the mud from your boots. The general seems to know what he's getting, so don't worry too much about that."

I made myself as presentable as I could in three minutes and ran all the way to the Red House, afraid that if I delayed, I would miss my opportunity.

Agrippa Hull answered the door and took a pointed gander at my feet to check for mud before scanning me from head to toe and back again, a doubtful expression on his face.

"General Paterson asked to see me," I insisted.

"For what?" he said, folding his arms over his pristine white waistcoat. I wasn't certain how he kept so clean, but he lived in the house and clearly considered himself a gatekeeper of sorts.

"My captain told me he is seeking an aide," I said, trying to hold his gaze, but I could see beyond the wide foyer to the broad staircase and the gleaming floors. It was another world—another universe—from the rest of the garrison, and my legs trembled with intimidation. The finest building I'd ever set foot in was Reverend Conant's church, and it was a simple structure with wooden pews, white walls, and a bit of colored glass.

A dining room lay to the left, a sitting room to the right, and both were furnished with heavy carpets and drapes, paneled blue walls and shelves that held more books than I could read in two decades if I dedicated myself fully to the task. Heavy gold candelabras and sconces lined the walls and adorned the tables. An enormous chandelier hung above the stairs, and a smaller version was centered over the long dining table.

"What's your name?" Hull asked.

For a moment I was so flustered by the grandeur, I could not remember. "Um . . . the general summoned me."

"Yeah. So you said. What's your name, Private?" His prompting of "private" jostled my muddled brain, and I met his lively, dark gaze and managed to respond.

"Robert Shurtliff, sir. Captain Webb's company, Fourth Regiment."

"Bonny Robbie," he said, recognition dawning. "I've heard of you."

I blanched. "You have?"

"I have. There isn't much around here I don't know." He cocked his head, considering me. I didn't squirm or lower my gaze, but my heart was pounding.

"You aren't much to look at." He sounded surprised.

"No, sir."

He grinned. "So why do they call you Bonny?"

"I suspect it's mockery, sir."

He grinned again. "All right, then. Follow me, boy. But not too close. I don't want you walkin' on my heels. I just shined my shoes. If the general is busy, you'll have to come back."

"If the general is busy, I can wait," I said firmly. I wasn't leaving without the position.

"You ever served a formal gathering?" he asked, testing me. "Because that'll be part of the job. General Washington could drop in at any time. I don't want you dumping gravy in his lap."

I had served a table full of Thomases and wrangled a room full of children countless times. Serving dignitaries could not be more difficult than that, but I didn't lie to him. Lying would come back to bite me if I needed instructions. Which I would.

"I've cooked for many and served many, but not in a formal setting. But I learn quickly. You'll only have to show me once."

"Hmm. Don't know about that." He turned left into a long hallway that was obscured by the stairs. Pictures of cherubic faces and bewigged heads watched our progress from the walls, and I wondered if the Moore family had expected to return at some point. They were a homely lot, but I didn't care for portraiture much. Everyone looked the same—plump and weak-chinned with tiny heart-shaped mouths and watery eyes.

Agrippa Hull rapped on the double doors at the end of the corridor, and General Paterson called out, bidding him enter.

"I've got a Private Bonny here, General. He says you summoned him for the aide position. He's a little too young and skinny for the job, if you ask me." He was goading me, but there was a twinkle in his eye. "But maybe that's good. He won't eat much or take up too much space."

I lifted my chin and squared my shoulders, trying to make myself look a little more formidable.

"Send him in, Agrippa," the general urged, but he sounded preoccupied.

Agrippa Hull stepped aside and pushed the door open to let me pass. When I did, he pulled the door closed behind me.

General Paterson sat at a desk, his head bowed over something that seemed to trouble him. His brow was furrowed and his hands clenched, a quill curling up from his left fist. The general was left-handed. I had noted this when he stitched my arm. That might explain the aggressive lean in the formation of his letters.

"Sir?"

He raised his head, dejection stamped across his features. He had not shaved yet, and his beard was more red than gold in the morning light streaming through the windows to his left.

"Come in, Shurtliff. And don't mind Grippy."

I took a few steps forward, my hands at my sides. I did not stand with my hands clasped behind my back unless in formation. I thought it better not to emphasize the thrust of my chest, regardless of my flattened bosom.

"Captain Webb told you the reason you are here?"

"Yes, sir. I am honored."

He grunted, his eyes falling back to the correspondence in front of him. Then he stood, shoving his chair back.

"You can read and write." It was a statement not a question, but I nodded.

"I can, General. And very well." I did not want to boast, but I could not find it in me to deny myself the truth I had worked so hard for.

"Sit here. I will dictate a letter, you will write, and I will see if your skills are sufficient."

"They are, sir."

His brows rose, but he pointed at his chair.

I settled myself in his spot, apprehension bubbling up in my chest. Would he recognize my handwriting?

He'd already begun the letter, but he moved that out of the way and provided me with a clean sheet. I dipped the quill and looked up at him expectantly. He turned away, pacing, and began stating his thoughts in broken sentences.

> *Dear Sirs,*
>
> *I esteem it my duty to inform you of the disagreeable and distressing condition of the brigade under my command. Should the enemy discover our vulnerabilities, it would take little to exploit them.*
>
> *We have no more than six days of meat provisions in the garrison. Last August we went the entire month without, our soldiers reduced to rations of flour and what little we could purchase or forage from local farms, which, considering the worthless paper we have to trade, is not much. Every department is at a stand for want of cash. Our stores are exhausted, the army unpaid and disheartened.*
>
> *Should this continue, I am fearful of the consequences. Many officers, fretted by the treatment and*

the repeated failures of Congress to honor their promises, are committed to quit the service at the close of this campaign, and I fear the soldiery will follow their example. Most are in great distress and depend solely on the rations, both in food and clothing, that they have not received.

My wish is only to see the army well supplied; resignations, mutiny, and marauding would in great degree be prevented. I am ashamed to be continually filling your ears with complaints; the crisis is difficult and dangerous, and should we survive the present, we are at constant threat of a relapse.

I will continue to do all in my power to secure supplies, though some of these means put our bravest men at much risk. The local renegades have become increasingly more violent toward our soldiers and the citizenry. Perhaps they see their own end or believe they can hasten ours, but the situation is dire.

I look forward to your response and direction.

General Paterson returned to my side and waited for me to complete the final line.

"You have a fine hand," he said.

"Thank you, sir." I hardly dared breathe as he examined my work, but he simply leaned down, took the quill, and affixed his signature on the bottom, a signature I knew well. Then he straightened once more.

"This is how I spend my time." He tossed a hand toward the letter. "Warning and worrying and writing letters that are rarely heeded." He shook his head and ran his palms over his whiskery cheeks.

"I need a shave."

"I can do that, sir." I vacated his seat. "Where is your kit?"

"I can do it myself, Shurtliff."

"Yessir, I'm sure you can. But it is an aide's job, is it not?"

"I suppose it is, yes."

"This is an evaluation of my abilities, isn't it, sir?"

He shrugged, brought me his kit and a drape to cover his clothes, and sat in his chair once more. I splashed a little water in the shallow basin nearby and brought it to his desk, but not before carefully moving the letter I'd just been dictated.

I wrapped the drape around him, created a lather on his brush, and proceeded to remove the two-day growth on his chin and cheeks.

"It might only be temporary, and I will have to talk to Colonel Jackson. He might not want to lose a good man from his ranks," he murmured as I worked.

"I would very much like the position, sir. It is a better use of my talents."

He pursed his lips, and I fought to keep my gaze steady, though my cheeks grew hot again. I'd shaved dozens of faces, but I was stricken with a sudden, painful awareness of myself and of him. I had not had a proper bath in ages, and my menses had begun that morning. The bleeding wasn't heavy, and I'd folded a rag and fashioned a sling to keep it in place beneath my breeches, but I could feel the wet and smell the distinct musk of my body, and feared he would too. I did my utmost to keep myself tidy and clean, but it was nigh on impossible.

The general, on the other hand, smelled of linseed oil and honeyed tea, and his waistcoat rivaled Agrippa Hull's. I hoped the lather beneath his nose would mask my scent, and I willed myself to be calm. It was a miracle that such an opportunity had arisen. I would not plead or press for the appointment, but I would not let my fear of his proximity make me shy from it either.

To be the general's aide would mean a bed of my own and a privacy that I had not enjoyed since my enlistment began. I would be able to wash and relieve myself without plotting and planning. I could sleep without being surrounded by men on every side.

I needed the position.

"You're quite good at that, Shurtliff," the general said after I'd cleared the stubble from one half of his face.

"Yessir. I know," I said quietly. I wasn't concentrating on my words but on the lather on the line of his left cheekbone and the scrape of the blade in my hand.

He jerked, laughing, and I gasped, my eyes flaring to his in alarm.

"Don't move, sir!"

"Sorry," he grunted. "Such confidence surprises me. Especially in one so young."

I ground my teeth and willed the embarrassment in my chest to subside as I considered my words. I hadn't meant to brag. I was distracted and had simply stated the truth.

"I am only accomplished because I try very hard at everything I do. Not because I am especially gifted."

"Hmm."

"Tuck your lip, please, sir," I asked, intent upon my task. He obeyed, and I pressed my thumb to the point of his chin to hold him steady. He did not speak again until I was finished. His eyes remained closed, his lashes thick against his cheeks, and his breath was even. His stillness made me more nervous than his speech, the necessary familiarity of the act creating an intimacy I should not feel.

I stepped back when I made my last swath and breathed in deeply, composing myself as he blinked his eyes open. He looked as though I'd come close to putting him to sleep. The man was weary, and my heart twisted in a compassion almost as great as my hope. I would be an excellent aide-de-camp, and I would take very good care of him if given the chance.

"Finished?" he asked.

"Yes, sir. The men in my company will attest to my skill."

He ran his hands across his face and rose to look at himself in the small oval mirror mounted on his office wall.

"Not bad. You have a fine hand and also a steady hand."

"Thank you, sir."

He studied himself in the mirror as if he pondered his decision. Then he squared his shoulders and drew the drape from his neck, tossing it toward me.

"Come then, Shurtliff."

I caught the drape, shook it out, and folded it neatly. "Where are we going, sir?"

He strode from the room, and I followed him obediently. The door opposite his office was identical to every other door lining the hallway, but he opened it and motioned me inside.

The room looked much like the drawing room in color and shape, though a big bed with carved posts and a deep red coverlet dominated the chamber. Two oversized leather chairs bracketed a stone fireplace, and a chest of drawers, a writing desk, and a table that held a basin and a pitcher for washing completed the furnishings. The only item of a personal nature was a painting of a dark-haired woman that hung above the bed.

"These are my quarters," the general said. "When General Washington is here, they are his quarters. You and I will move up the stairs to the servants' wing when he's at the Point."

"You and I, sir?"

"If you want the position, Shurtliff. There is a valet's closet through that door." He moved toward a section of paneling that was slightly ajar. A discreet knob was hidden in the raised whorls and vines of the woodwork.

"My last aide slept here. The room has been aired and the bedding stripped. There's a small window, a basin, and shelves and hooks, of course. It will be sufficient, I trust."

He opened the panel, and I peeked around him, almost unable to believe my good fortune. The valet's closet was bigger than the room I'd occupied at the Thomases'. An upholstered window seat in velvet blue stretched below a tall window, and a narrow berth was built into the wall below the shelves, a small table too, and judging from the cupboards from floor to ceiling, taking care of Master Moore's wardrobe had been a full-time endeavor. General Paterson's blue dress coat, two waistcoats, three shirts, and an extra pair of breeches looked very meager indeed.

"You can read and write and recite the declaration. You can barber. You can ride—"

"I do most things very well," I interrupted. "And what I don't know I will learn. Immediately."

His brows rose and his mouth twitched. I didn't blink. I wanted the job, and I knew I would not get such an opportunity again.

"Yes. As you've demonstrated." He cleared his throat. "Mr. Allen, the staff officer, will answer any questions you have about the house. He's ill-humored, but efficient. I will inform Captain Webb that you will be relieved from his ranks until further notice."

"You will?" I breathed.

"Yes. I will. I don't think I demand much . . . but the less I have to think about small matters, the better. My uniforms. My boots. The order in my quarters and the running of errands. The tasks vary and will probably feel endless . . . and thankless."

"I know what an aide does, sir. And I am honored to do it."

"Good," he clipped. "Mostly, I will need to be able to trust you. No gloating. No gossiping. No repeating what you see here or while you are at my side. Can I trust you, Shurtliff?"

My heart quaked and my belly flipped, but I nodded firmly, as curt as he. "Yes, sir, you can." And he *could*. No one worked harder or kept a secret better than I. Being a woman would not prevent me from doing any of the things he required.

"Then gather your things from the barracks, and I will tell Mr. Allen that you are now on staff. He'll be waiting for you to return."

"Thank you, General." My voice was steady, my gaze level, and he nodded once, dismissing me.

"Report back when you are settled," he said.

He followed me from his quarters and returned to his office, and I walked down the hall, through the expansive foyer, and out of the Red House with calm and measured steps, though I felt like skipping. Racing. Sprinting through the woods, leaping shrubs, and dodging the trees like I'd done when I was small.

I made it halfway down the lane before I gave in and let myself fly, joyful, strong, and imbued with new hope.

~ 15 ~

The Pursuit of Happiness

I didn't allow myself to dwell on my deception or succumb to guilt over my improved circumstances. The staff sergeant, Mr. Allen, supplied me with a new uniform, warning me that soldiers in the house could not smell like soldiers in the barracks. He issued me a nightshirt as well with instructions that I not "sleep in my filth." The nightshirt was too large, and I felt like a child when I donned it, but it did keep my berth clean and my uniform unrumpled.

Agrippa, who gave me permission to call him Grippy instead of sir, occupied a room on the second floor alongside Colonel Kosciuszko, as well as several other officers with regiments quartered in the garrison. The third floor housed Mr. and Mrs. Allen, their oldest daughter, Sophronia, and her husband, Joe, who all seemed to have come with the property. Mr. Allen took care of the house and the staff, though Agrippa told me to run everything by him. Joe took care of the animals and the stables, and Mrs. Allen and Sophronia were in charge of the cooking and general cleaning. I avoided them as much as I could, fearing they would see right through me.

On my second day, Agrippa made himself my personal instructor and escorted me through the house and around the immediate grounds, giving me a staggering verbal list of orders and instructions, which I carried out to exactness. I'm certain he had a good laugh at my expense when I pressed the general's undergarments, sat on the floor beside his bed while he slept, and tested his food for poison before presenting it to him. The general informed me kindly that such things were not necessary, warning me that Grippy had an affinity for mischief.

This penchant was on full display days later when General Paterson and Colonel Kosciuszko left the garrison for a meeting at Newburgh encampment with a small contingent that didn't include me or Agrippa Hull. They were only to be gone one night, but Grippy arranged a surprise costume party in one of the barracks—I was not invited—and attended the big event as Colonel Kosciuszko himself, wearing the colonel's dress uniform, complete with ornamental sword, banner, and beribboned hat. The only thing missing from the costume were the colonel's tall black boots, as Kosciuszko was wearing them.

Agrippa swore me to secrecy and promised me that "once I'd proved myself" I could tag along. He called it a soiree and even made a song about it, singing it softly as he stole out of the house and into the early winter darkness that descended on the Point before five and left the evenings dreary and long. I didn't mind them at all, living in the Red House with a library at my disposal.

I'd only enjoyed one chapter from a book on Revelation when the general and Colonel Kosciuszko suddenly returned, their plans scuttled by a lame horse. Still too far from Newburgh, they'd decided to return to the Point and set out again in the morning with a new mount for the colonel.

When Kosciuszko asked the whereabouts of his aide, I played dumb but volunteered to find him posthaste. I ran through the trees to the barracks, not certain where Grippy had gone, but following the sounds of laughter until I located, without much difficulty, the secret soiree. A soldier was posted at the door, but I had only to mention Colonel Kosciuszko's name with all the urgency I was feeling to be allowed inside.

Agrippa stood atop a stripped-down bunk that was being used as a stage and was entertaining the crowd with a very convincing, if theatrically embellished, impersonation of his fiery Polish employer. I pushed my way through the throng and grabbed his leg as he pranced past. It was covered from knee to toe with thick black paint to create the look of a black boot, and my hand left a streak across his shin.

"The colonel is back," I shouted up at him.

He frowned down at me and folded his arms over his chest. "I'm performing, Mr. Shurtliff," he said, still in character.

"Yes . . . I know. But the colonel is back, and he's asking for you."

He blanched, but didn't immediately jump down. The crowd begged him for a little more, and he was loath to disappoint his fans. His painted legs and feet gave the costume a comical twist, and his face was shining with laughter and sweat. He doffed his tricorn and made a sweeping bow, and I turned to go.

I'd relayed the message, done my duty, and was eager to retreat. Such gatherings were not safe for me, though I had arguably the best costume of all. I pushed out of the barracks and stooped to wash my paint-covered fingers in the snow only to realize Grippy was right behind me. He hadn't even stopped for his shoes.

He was studying my uniform, and I knew what he was thinking before the words left his mouth. I took several steps back, shaking the wet from my hands.

"No," I said.

"Give me your coat, Bonny."

"No!" I repeated, adamant. "You will not draw me into your mess, Mr. Hull. I have helped you. Do not repay me this way." I began trotting back in the direction of the Red House, putting immediate distance between us.

"Wait!" He started running too, but I bolted, using all my considerable speed to fly back the way I'd come, Grippy on my heels. We raced for a hundred yards before Grippy swore and begged me to stop. I simply sped up.

"Damnation, Bonny. You're fast," he panted, but I sensed it was more surprise than exertion that had him gasping. The snow-covered ground beneath his bare feet could not have helped either, but he was fast too.

"Give me your coat. Just your coat," he demanded again, and lunged for my arm. I heard something rip.

"I'll bring you your clothes," I yelped, skidding to a stop but warning him back, palms out. "Stay here. I'll be back. I promise. I'll bring them back."

He halted too and looked at the lights glimmering from the rear of the Red House and back at me. The night was white with moonlight, and I had no trouble seeing his indecision. He was in a predicament.

"My uniform won't fit you," I argued. "You outweigh me by two stone, if not more. And even if it did, I can't very well traipse back into the house without it," I coaxed.

"I don't know if I trust you, Bonny boy."

He had every reason to doubt me, considering the pranks he'd pulled on me, one after the other, all week, but I was not interested in vengeance nearly as much as preservation.

"I will be back," I promised. "I give you my word. Give me the colonel's uniform—"

"And wait in my drawers? It's freezing out here!"

"It will give me a reason to be in his quarters. If the colonel stops me, I will tell him you asked me to press it while I was pressing the general's."

Agrippa grumbled, but he began shucking off Kosciuszko's uniform, hopping from one bare foot to the other. "I'm going to catch my death."

"I'll hurry," I vowed, relieved that he was cooperating.

He grumbled again. "Don't make me come after you, boy. Life here can be easy or it can be hard. You leave me out here, I will make it difficult."

"Yessir." I didn't remind him he'd already made it considerably harder on me than it should have been.

He stood in nothing but a pair of woolen drawers, his painted legs offering no protection from the icy temperatures, and handed me the colonel's uniform, his teeth already chattering.

I ran with the clothing clutched to my chest, slipped into the kitchen entrance, ducked past Mrs. Allen, and scurried up the stairs, not pausing to think or even plan, my ears peeled for the colonel. *Ah, there.* He was in the drawing room with a few voices I could not distinguish.

The clothing Grippy had discarded in his zeal for his costume was in the colonel's wardrobe, awaiting his return, and I hung the dress uniform back where it belonged. The sleeve had a bit of black paint on the cuff, and the waistcoat bore a few flecks as well. Agrippa would have to address those issues when he wasn't standing half-naked in the frozen woods.

I had barreled back through the kitchen, looking neither right nor left, and was almost in the clear, when General Paterson walked out of the stable, directly in my path.

He reached out to brace me, but my arms were filled, my momentum great, and I collided with his broad chest. I bounced back instantly and managed to keep hold of the clothes, but I was caught.

"What is the meaning of this, Shurtliff?" the general asked, more surprised than indignant.

"Grippy's had a bit of a . . . mishap . . . and I'm bringing him his clothes," I said, convinced the truth would serve everyone best, especially with the colonel's uniform safely back where it belonged.

"Is this the same Agrippa Hull who sends you on a wild goose chase at least once daily?"

"Yessir. The same. But at present he is in sore need of his clothes, so I am choosing to forgive."

He chuckled, the puff of his breath in the growing darkness reminding me not to tarry, even if the general chose to follow, which he did.

I stepped around him and hurried through the trees, the general close behind, and when Agrippa stepped out, shamefaced in front of us, I simply handed him his clothing without comment.

"Do you care to explain yourself, Agrippa?" the general asked, more laughter than censure in his tone.

"Never you mind, sir. Never you mind," he said, hopping from one frozen foot to the other as he donned his breeches and stepped into his shoes, leaving off the stockings I'd included in the pile. No sense smearing them in paint too.

"And are those yours?" The general pointed at the black tracks in the snow leading off into the trees.

"Yessir," Grippy confessed.

"It was harmless fun, sir," I interjected. "Nothing more."

"Hmm," the general grunted. "Agrippa?"

"Yessir?"

"You owe the lad."

"Yessir."

"No more ridiculous lessons or instructions. No more poison testing."

"No, sir."

"Now if you will excuse me, I have other business to attend to. Alone. I trust you will both return to your duties."

"Yessir," I said, turning back to the house.

"Good night, General," Grippy said, teeth still clacking, ignoring me altogether.

~

The general demanded the full story from me when he returned.

I acquiesced, but only after obtaining a promise that he wouldn't punish Agrippa or indicate in any way that I'd divulged the details. John Paterson laughed until tears streamed from his eyes when I described Agrippa's resourceful black boots and his jaunty impersonation of the Polish engineer. His mirth only grew when I detailed our chase through the forest and recalled Agrippa wearing nothing but his drawers and his paint, awaiting my return with his clothes.

"You should not have fetched his uniform. You'd already saved him. It would have served him right to endure a shaming." The general chortled. "Someday I will have to tell Kosciuszko. No one enjoys a good story better than he."

Surprisingly, Grippy did not bring up the episode again, and he seemed to hold no animosity toward me for involving the general, but after that, I made certain to take anything he said with the proper skepticism, suspecting a prank at every turn.

~

In the months of my enlistment, I had grown accustomed to men in all states of dress, but if General Paterson were to ever discover my secret, I suspected it would be the familiarities that would make him feel the most betrayed. Thus I strove in every way to serve him, and serve him well, while keeping a respectful distance.

I had not lived in the world of ladies' maids and valets, but thankfully, General Paterson did not protest my absence while he dressed or demand that I wash his back, as Agrippa had first insisted I must do.

Every morning I shaved his face and took care of his clothes and his quarters, but he was clearly accustomed to taking care of his person, and I was more an errand boy and a clerk than I was a manservant.

Twice a week, I filled buckets of water and brought them to the kitchen, where they were heated on the great stone hearth. Then I carried them down the hall into the general's quarters and into the bathing chamber through another small door adjoining his room. The tub took an hour to fill, but when the general was finished, I was able to use the water as well, bolting the door and scrubbing myself thoroughly—unclothed—without fear of being seen.

In the barracks, I had kept myself as neat as I was able, but my clothes were stained and my skin and hair were never truly clean. The scents of crowded bodies, woodsmoke, and wet had been ever present. To be clean, naked, and alone was paradise.

Within weeks of moving into the Red House, I knew the general's schedule, his moods, his preferences, and his troubles. I anticipated his every need and ran to fulfill his every command. I also learned the portrait above his bed was Elizabeth. I'd guessed as much. Her painted gaze served as a constant reminder of my secret, and I committed myself all the more, but such dedication was not a hardship.

The winter would have been unbearable in the barracks, the close quarters, the frozen pond, the long months of cold with very little to do. Instead, I had access to an outhouse where I could bar the door, a biweekly bath, a bed of my own, and the general to look after.

I loved working in the Red House, and I adored John Paterson.

He was the finest man, in every way, that I had ever known. I feared my devotion would become obvious to him and to everyone else, and did my best to keep my eyes averted, my mouth closed, and my attention sharply attuned. But I adored him.

When he ran out of things for me to do or dismissed me, I busied myself with chores or errands for Mr. Allen and, whenever possible, browsed in the library among the books. To have access to such bounty was more than I could resist, even if it cost me sleep, and most nights I read until I couldn't keep my eyes open.

The general slept even less than I did. He took late walks, and I tried to stay awake until he returned in case he required assistance. The first time I heard him leave, I'd tried to follow him like a faithful guard dog, and he firmly sent me back home.

"You are tireless. And I am grateful. Even Agrippa has praised you, and he is not easily impressed. But after supper, your time is your own. If I need you, I know where to find you."

That night, I was still awake when the general came in. He washed and rustled about. I heard him remove his boots—I knew better than to run out to assist him—and, a few minutes later, blow out his light. He was earlier than usual, and I returned to my reading, not ready to close the book or crawl into bed.

"Shurtliff?"

"Yes, sir?"

"That candle needs to last you all week," he grumbled.

"Yes, sir."

He sighed. "It is fine, Shurtliff. I'm just in a foul temper. Are you reading?"

"Yes, sir."

"Which book?"

"I am reading a commentary on the Book of Revelation, sir."

He groaned, and I snickered softly.

"That sounds dreadful. But I will tell Mr. Allen to allot you another candle if you read loud enough for me to hear."

"You will not have nightmares, General?"

"Are you being cheeky, Shurtliff?"

"Yes, sir."

He laughed. "Just read. Start wherever you want. I don't care. I just can't abide my own thoughts anymore this night."

I rose from my chair, pulled the extra blanket from my bed to wrap around my voluminous nightshirt—breeches in bed made for dirty sheets—and opened the door between our rooms so I wouldn't have to talk through it.

He was in his large bed, and the room was dark, but I held the candle up, just a bit, so I might see his face. His arms were folded beneath his head, and the fire I'd started in his grate was now just a handful of coals. He hadn't added a log to keep the room comfortable through the night. He was frugal, and every bit of fuel, every candle, every drop of food was stretched in an attempt to make it last. It was his constant concern that the men under his command would be without.

"Are you cold?" he asked me, inclining his chin at the blanket around my shoulders and the stockings on my feet.

"No, sir," I lied. "I'm quite comfortable with the extra blanket. And I will read until you tell me to stop . . . or until the candle goes out."

"Very well."

I padded back to my chair, tucked my feet beneath me to keep them from freezing, and began where I'd left off. I found the commentary fascinating and read for at least half an hour without ceasing.

My candle flickered, spent, and the chapter ended. I set the book aside, marking my place with a wild turkey feather I'd picked up that morning when I'd hung out the wash.

The general's breathing was steady and deep, and I eased the door between us closed and crawled into my berth, filled with more peace than I'd ever known.

~

General Paterson requisitioned the chestnut horse from the Tarrytown skirmish for my use. It was kept with Lenox and the other officers' horses in the garrison stables, and I rode him all over the Point and on various errands with and on behalf of the general. The horse had a marvelous, unflappable disposition, and I called him Common Sense, which suited him perfectly and made the general smile.

In early March, we experienced a week of unseasonal warmth that thawed the ice in the Hudson and melted the snow, and the general made plans, along with Colonel Kosciuszko, to check the fortifications along the river while the weather was fair. Grippy and I packed the saddlebags and readied the horses for a few days' travel, and the four of us, along with a small mounted detachment who were returning to Verplanck's Point, set out to make inspections.

Even the horses were eager to be off, and the weather held, making the travel to Stony Point exceedingly pleasant. Agrippa and I fell into conversation, following behind the general and the colonel as they spoke of buttressing this and building that and what would happen to West Point when the war ended.

"Kosciuszko wants me to go to Poland with him when he goes back," Agrippa said abruptly, as if the matter had been weighing on him. "There's not much left for him to do here, and he's got trouble in his own country."

I gaped, thrilled for him. "Poland? He wants you to go to Poland? How wonderful. I am desperate to see the world."

Grippy screwed up his lips and furrowed his brow, like he didn't think it was wonderful at all.

"You don't want to see the world?" I asked. "To explore?"

"I want to explore *my* world. America. That's what this war is all about, isn't it? This land right here." He pointed his finger at the ground we traversed. "I don't want to go to Poland. I want to go home. Me and General Paterson both. He's a barrister, you know. He's been teaching me. Even gave me some of his books from Yale. I can read. Maybe I'll become a barrister too. So I know my rights. So I know the laws."

I wondered if the general would teach me too or if Grippy would let me see his books. He continued.

"The British put the word out to all the African folk. They said if you fight with us, we give you your freedom when the war is over. But they're promising things they won't, or can't, deliver on. What if they don't win? Then what? You fight against your neighbors? Maybe kill some of 'em? I'm not going to England or Poland when this is over. I'm staying right here. Here is better than anything they can promise. They can't give me what God already bestowed."

"Certain unalienable rights," I interjected, nodding.

"That's right. I am a free man. I was born free in Massachusetts. Going to die free in Massachusetts. When this is all over, I'm going back to Stockbridge."

"That is near Lenox, isn't it? Where the general is from?"

"That's right. I have an acre of land. I'm going to get more too. Build a house. Find a woman I like looking at, one who likes looking at me. Have some children."

"Me too," I said, not thinking. I was still stuck on the part about being born free and dying free, but Grippy laughed, a great rolling sound that shook his chest and his shoulders.

"You hear that, General? Bonny wants a woman and babies." Grippy always called me Bonny.

General Paterson and Colonel Kosciuszko had stopped talking and were looking back at us. I hunched my shoulders and bowed my head, willing Grippy to hush.

"So do you have a girl back home in . . . where did you say you were from?" Grippy asked, still grinning.

I ignored half of his question. "No, I don't have a girl. No girl."

"I think you're lying to me, Bonny. Your cheeks are all pink, and you're blinking like you've got someone in mind."

"Being free and dying free. Like you said. That's what I want. That's why I'm here."

"Huh. Okay. Well . . . white boy like you . . . shouldn't be a problem if you don't starve to death or die of sheer boredom. Most of the fightin's over, I think."

"I wasn't born free."

He frowned. "No?"

"No."

"What's that mean?"

I couldn't tell him I was born a girl. I gave him another truth instead. "I was bound out when I was a child," I said. Colonel Kosciuszko was pointing out something on the redoubt and General Paterson was nodding his head.

"You are *still* a child," Grippy said. "Are you still bound out?"

I shook my head, but he wasn't convinced.

"You a runaway?"

That's exactly what I was, though not the way he meant.

"We're all running away from something, aren't we?" I said. "But no . . . I don't belong to anyone. I don't owe anyone anything. And no one's looking for me." The last part might not be true, but I hoped it was.

Near the end of the day, as we were nearing the post at Peekskill Hollow, a man on horseback rode out to meet us, and even twenty rods out, I identified Colonel Sproat. He greeted the general with a crisp salute and acknowledged Colonel Kosciuszko. His eyes lingered on me for a moment, and I held my breath, but he simply greeted me by name and praised me for my swift action and my level head in Tarrytown.

"Private Shurtliff is my new aide-de-camp, Colonel Sproat," Paterson said.

"You are familiar to me, Shurtliff. There are Shurtliffs in Taunton. Perhaps I know your family?"

"I don't know, sir. Even I do not know my family. But I am not from Taunton." It was the truth for the most part, and it rolled from my tongue.

He nodded easily, and I was forgotten. He rode alongside the general and, in muted tones, shared some information that straightened the general's back and sharpened his gaze.

"We received some information about a trove of supplies near Eastchester in some sort of underground cavern. The man who reported it claims the supplies that never made it last August are there."

"An underground cavern? It sounds like a trick."

Colonel Sproat shrugged. "I thought the same thing. But I trust the source. He said not many know it's there, and it's not well guarded."

"He claims he's been inside?"

"Yes, sir. A couple brothers, just youngsters, were keeping an eye on the entrance. They didn't realize he wasn't part of the same gang that hired them. He told them to take him inside, and they did."

"Who's paying them?"

"Don't know. But nobody on our side. I'm guessing the detachment that went missing was bribed to desert or they're dead. I think dead. DeLancey doesn't pay when he can just take."

"No, he doesn't."

"He said it's chock-full. Wine. Hams hanging from an overhead beam. Barrels of flour. Beans. Rice. Potatoes. Molasses. Lard. Jars of fruit."

"How many wagonloads?"

Sproat blew out a breath and shook his head. "He seems to think the barrels alone would fill a barge."

"What do you propose we do?"

"We take it, sir."

"Any troop movement or wagons toward Eastchester, and they'll know. There are no secrets in the neutral zone."

"True enough. But if we send a brigade, there won't be much they can do to stop us."

"Unless they get word and move it before we get there."

Sproat scratched his head. "We need those supplies, General. Nobody knows that better than you. My men have been on half rations all winter. We've been holed up. Not scouting. Not marching, not fighting. So we don't need as much, but that can't continue."

"I know."

"DeLancey hasn't answered for the attack in Tarrytown. I would very much like to empty those stores."

"There and back, how far?" General Paterson asked.

"Thirty miles. Maybe a little less. Ten or so from White Plains."

"We'll leave at daybreak tomorrow. I will go with you."

"You, General?" Sproat sounded stunned.

"I can't devise a plan for seizing the provisions if I don't know the particulars. I need to see where they are kept, how many men and wagons we will need to move them, and if it's worth the risk to the men who might find themselves in the middle of a gunfight if my plan isn't a good one."

Sproat nodded slowly, a grin splitting his homely cheeks. "I'll be ready."

~ 16 ~

To Secure These Rights

We were already riding toward White Plains when the sky stretched and turned back her dark coverlet. Sproat had chosen a handful of trusted men, including the scout who had brought him the information. I recognized a few of them from Tarrytown but knew none of their names. Kosciuszko had remained at Peekskill, but Grippy had come along, lured by the talk of caverns and treasure, but by early afternoon, he was looking at the hovering clouds. The temperature had dropped again, and our spring thaw seemed to have changed her mind.

"You think it could snow?" Agrippa worried. "I hate being cold, I hate being cold on horseback even worse, and I hate riding said horse in the cold when I'm heading into enemy territory."

"If it's what we've been told, you'll be heading back to the Point with your own ham," General Paterson promised. "Mrs. Allen can prepare it for you, and you can eat every single bite all by yourself."

"I'm going to hold you to that."

"I'm a man of my word," the general said.

Grippy nodded and grinned. "That you are, so there better be ham. One for Bonny too. We need to fatten him up."

Our ride was uneventful, and we moved quickly under the roiling clouds, constantly on the lookout and skirting picket points and known hotbeds. The scout, a man named Williby, seemed to know where he was going, and when he suggested we stop and let him and Sproat go ahead to ascertain whether the depot was being watched or guarded, we agreed and dismounted at a creek that cut through the trees, letting our horses rest and drink while we waited. Sproat and Williby were not gone long, and Sproat was excited.

"I don't know if it's the storm coming in, but there's nobody watching it. The opening's not much more than a depression in a rocky rise, and it's easy to miss. But it's just like he said. I only had a quick look, but the barrels have the Continental mark. There's at least a hundred barrels of beans and salted meat, flour and lard, butter, molasses, all of it."

Sproat ordered five men to remain with the horses and another five to watch the door, and the rest of us went inside. Williby was waiting for us, a lantern lit, his rucksack already bulging. Sproat said nothing, and I assumed the man had been promised his own ham . . . or whatever he wanted.

The cave looked small from the outside, the opening barely tall enough for me to enter upright and only as wide as my outstretched arms. General Paterson and Colonel Sproat had to stoop, but within ten feet, the cavern opened up into much more, and just as promised, the bounty was significant.

"How did they get all this in here without anyone knowing?" Grippy marveled. "And how are we going to get it out?"

"They created a diversion," Paterson said. "That's what the strike in Tarrytown was all about. While some attacked, the rest were busy hijacking the supply line when it passed through. They just unloaded the barrels—"

"And burned the wagons," Williby finished. "There's a gulch just over the rise. The whole thing was lit up last summer. I found the hubs and the hitches. But that's all. They torched 'em good."

"How far are we from the river?" the general asked.

"Four miles, at the most," Williby answered.

"How's the terrain?"

"Easy. A man could walk it in an hour if he's moving fast."

"What are you thinking, General?" Sproat interjected. "Those barrels are too heavy to carry."

"We'll come down the North River with handcarts. On barges."

"Thirty men could empty this in less than an hour," Sproat said. "An hour here. An hour to load it all up, maybe two hours getting back to the river with the heavy carts. That leaves plenty of time to load the barges once we're there."

The general nodded. "We'll get here in the middle of the night, load up and get out, and time the return to the shift in the tide."

"Just like we do in Kingston," I said.

"Just like we do in Kingston," the general agreed.

"It could work," Sproat said, and Grippy was beaming.

"Can I have my ham now?" he asked.

~

We didn't want to sleep near the depot, but the wind howled and the night was cold. Williby led us about a mile north to the barn of a "friendly," and we hunkered down inside and ate a feast of pickled eggs and bottled peaches from the cavern. Sproat passed around a bottle of pilfered wine, but I barely wetted my lips before handing it to the general. I desperately needed to empty my bladder and would have to wait until everyone was asleep. The men had only to step outside. I would have to go a little farther.

The space was huge, and we brought the horses inside as well, sheltering them from the weather and hiding them from anyone who might pass by. I lay back against my saddle and took out my book and quill, not eager to write, but needing an excuse to sit up when the others were bedding down. Grippy and the general spread themselves out and pulled their hats over their eyes like the others, and I scratched away by the light of Williby's lantern, writing a letter to Elizabeth that was more a list of the goods we'd seen in the cavern than anything else.

I didn't want the general to see me step outside. He would be the only one who cared and would mark my absence and my return. Sproat had assigned a man to watch, but everyone seemed mellowed by the wine and unconcerned about our safety.

"I know the farmer who owns this barn. He's a patriot. We'll be fine here," Williby had reassured us.

"No book tonight, Shurtliff?" the general asked, his voice heavy.

"Perhaps. I'm not really that tired."

He grunted and lifted his hat from his eyes so he could look at me. "Liar. You're nodding off just sitting there."

I put my journal back in my saddlebag, stretched out like the others, and closed my eyes, convinced my discomfort would prevent me from sleeping.

It didn't.

I awoke hours later, the men around me already stirring, morning light seeping in through the cracks in the barn walls.

I scrambled up, stunned that I'd slept so deeply, and almost wet myself, so desperate was my need.

The general and the others were saddling their horses, talking quietly, and I hurried past them and out the door, rushing for the trees. Someone chuckled, and Grippy called after me.

"I need a moment. My bowels are feeling a little loose. Too much fruit," I babbled.

The chuckling multiplied, but no one followed.

I walked, teeth clenched, until I was certain no one could see me and no one had decided to come after me. I crouched behind a bush, my back against a tree, and wriggled my breeches down while contorting to keep the stream of urine from hitting my shoes or wetting my clothes. I'd gotten spoiled the last months at the Red House with a private perch and a locking door, and I had grown soft. I stayed crouched much longer than I usually dared, making sure I was emptied before I patted myself dry with the square of cloth I kept in my pocket in case my menses started, and secured my clothes.

The storm had passed and the air was fresh and cold. In the growing light, without the gale to distract me, the surroundings were familiar. The cherry orchard my detachment had been chased from wasn't far, and a large estate owned by a man named Jeroen Van Tassel was nearby. Captain Webb had hurried us through the area, claiming it was full of Dutch loyalists. I had no reason to doubt him, especially considering the secret depot and the gulch with the burned-out wagons.

I pulled the tie from my hair, smoothed it with my fingers, and refastened my queue. I'd left my hat in the barn and my canteen near my saddle. There was nothing more I could do to tidy myself, but I was stalling, dreading an embarrassing return after my mad dash into the trees. I had not been a good aide-de-camp that morning.

They were waiting for me, everyone mounted, when I stepped out from the shelter of the trees west of the barnyard. Grippy held my horse's reins—he too had been saddled—and my hat had been tossed over the pommel. Embarrassment flooded my chest, and I paused for courage. But none of them were looking at me. Their attention was riveted on a small rise just east of the wide, empty field. Woods crowded the cleared plot on every side, and a cabin was just visible through the trees.

The horses shimmied, suddenly nervous, and lightning rumbled and cracked. A gnat whined past my ear and then another. I slapped at it, even as I rejected the notion. It was March, not July, and the storm had passed. The swarm was not bugs but bullets.

The cluster of waiting men scattered, flowering outward across the field, and I cried out, not wanting to be left behind.

"Shurtliff," the general shouted. "Run, boy!"

But I was frozen in place, watching the drama unfold. Grippy's horse was running full out for the trees to the north, and Common Sense followed right behind him. Sproat was trying to marshal his men, but they too were barreling for the trees, some of them shooting, most of them simply running for cover. Sproat gave up and spurred his mount forward, firing at the unknown assailants as he bowed low over his horse's neck. One horse was hit, and his rider tumbled from the saddle. Williby was downed before reaching the trees. The general, still holding Lenox back, fired off a round with his musket and pulled the pistol from his hip and fired again.

A shot rang out and knocked his hat from his head, and I screamed, coming out of my stupor. He slumped, still clinging to his weapon, and Lenox bolted forward, feeling the slack in the reins. Halfway across the field, the general slid limply from his back.

I began to run toward him, my arms and legs pumping, but I didn't make it very far. Two sharp cracks split the air like a whip being drawn in quick succession across my calf and then my thigh. I staggered, fell, and stayed down, my cheek pressed to the earth.

It didn't hurt. A weird pressure reverberated in my groin, and I needed to empty my bladder again. But that was fear, not pain.

"Nothing is broken," I comforted myself. I was fairly certain that was true. I began to crawl toward General Paterson, expecting another bullet to whistle past my head or sink into my flesh, but none did.

He was not moving, but his breath continued, and his heart was steady beneath my palm. I felt around his skull, moving my fingers through his hair. Blood obscured his face, and coated the front of his uniform, but the furrow through his hair and a goose egg–shaped lump at the back of his head were his only obvious injuries. His limbs were straight and sound, but he lay like a dead man, still clutching his pistol, and I could not move him, even had I not had a bullet—maybe two—in my left leg. It was still numb, but my boot squelched with blood when I wiggled my toes. I rose to my hands and knees and surveyed the rise where the gunfire had come from. I couldn't go that way.

My horse was gone. The general's horse too, and I studied the woods around me, trying to formulate a plan. I didn't know if the attackers would return, if Sproat and the others *could* return, and I had nothing but what was on my person to aid me.

If I was right, Van Tassel's estate should be just around the bend. I would go that way. It was no more than half a mile, at the most.

It might as well have been a thousand. Walking ten feet would be a challenge.

"Elizabeth," I said. "Elizabeth, help me." I don't know what I expected, but I had no one else to beseech. I searched the woods again and begged the general to wake, feeling again for his breath and the beat of his heart. Hoofbeats and a mournful whinny sounded to my left, and I reloaded the general's empty pistol and prepared for the worst. A moment later, Lenox meandered toward me, his head low and his steps sheepish.

"Oh, thank you," I breathed, and rose, refusing to consider that my leg would not hold me. Lenox shuffled near and nuzzled at the general in apology. I took his reins, entreated him to hold steady, and raised my good foot into the stirrup, swinging myself up and onto his back in one desperate motion.

"I'll be back," I promised the general, and spurred the horse forward into a run, clinging to his back and my feeble plan.

It was as I thought, though each minute felt like an eternity. The large white structure among the trees, outbuildings and fields extending behind it, was just as I remembered. My regiment had paused for water and rest at a wide stream that fed into the river a mile north on our first march to the Point.

A young woman, her dress bright against the dull sky, sat atop a spotted pony as if she'd just set out for a ride. When she saw me, she spurred her mount back toward the house, shrieking with news of my approach. A feather danced against her pale cheek and dark ringlets bounced down her back as she called, "Papa!"

That too was a godsend. If I were to dismount, I doubted I could pull myself up again.

A man in a crimson coat and buff-colored breeches strode from the house, his large belly bouncing with every anxious step. The young woman who'd heralded my arrival dismounted and hovered at his side, smiling at me as though it was all a great adventure. He demanded she return to the house, but she ignored him. I drew up and did my utmost to steel my spine and project my voice.

"I am a soldier in the Continental army, sir. My commanding officer has been wounded and is lying in the field nearby. We were shot at and our party scattered. I cannot lift him on my own, and I require assistance and accommodations until he is fit to travel."

I didn't know whether to reveal Paterson's name or rank. A general was a valuable prisoner. In 1776, General Lee had been surrounded by a British regiment at an inn in the New Jersey countryside, much to the delight and celebration of the loyalists. The Americans had been demoralized. But this was neutral territory, and civilians were required in these parts to honor the rules of engagement, regardless of their politics.

"I require assistance," I repeated. "A cart and a horse and a man to aid me in getting the wounded officer into it."

"I have nothing more to give," the man said, lifting his chin and folding his arms over his big belly. "I have been aiding the army for seven long years. I have done enough."

I leveled the general's pistol at his face. I was not afraid of him. I was afraid General Paterson would be dead before I got back. "What is your name, sir?"

"You will leave here at once," he demanded, his face growing as florid as his coat. "I will not be bullied by every scoundrel that passes through."

"Your name is Van Tassel. Is that correct?"

The man frowned, the sides of his mouth poking at his heavy jowls.

"This is neutral territory. You cannot refuse aid to an officer. If you do not do so willingly, I will confiscate your property."

"All by yourself?" he sneered.

"It will take but one bullet to make you more agreeable. And if that officer dies, you will have an army on your doorstep. I swear it."

He stared at me a moment longer, testing my resolve. My injury was evident, I was desperate, and he knew it. But desperation makes people dangerous.

"Morris," he bellowed toward the African servant who'd emerged from around the side of the house when the daughter had started squawking. The man's clothes were worn and his face was shining with perspiration, as if I'd interrupted his work.

Van Tassel pointed at me. "Morris, assist this man. Use the barn. And do it quickly. I'm expecting guests."

The man nodded once and disappeared back in the direction he'd come, and Van Tassel pushed his daughter back toward the house and slammed the door behind them, making his displeasure and his reservations clear.

I collapsed onto the horse's neck, shaking so violently I was unable to reholster the pistol in the saddle. I gathered myself for a moment, breathing through my teeth and ignoring the blood that had turned the left leg of my breeches black and oozed from the hole in my boot. I would deal with it when I was able.

Morris reemerged around the side of the house minutes later with a horse and cart. A boy of maybe nine or ten was perched on the horse's back, a felt hat on his head and rags wrapped around his feet to protect them from the cold. His garb wasn't so different from half of the soldiers at the Point.

"Amos can ride your horse when we get your man," Morris said, indicating the boy. "The cart can hold two, and you look ready to fall out of that saddle."

I ignored that, and Morris swung up behind Amos, letting me lead the way.

The general lay where I'd left him, his eyes closed and his limbs flung wide. I slid from Lenox, gritting my teeth, and crawled to his side. He was breathing and his heart was steady, but he was no more responsive.

"Is that General Washington?" Amos squeaked.

"No. But he is a general," Morris muttered, eyeing the uniform. He looked at me, gaze frank. "You sure you want to stay with Van Tassel, soldier? He's not a friend."

"I have no choice. Help me get him into the cart. Please."

I tried to assist, but Morris swatted me away, squatting beside the general. He sat him up and then hoisted him over his back like a sack of grain. The general was a big man, but Morris was even bigger.

I scrambled into the cart, and Morris unfolded the general into my arms, easing his battered head against my chest. The general's legs were too long for the cart, and Morris draped them over the side so they wouldn't drag. I wrapped one hand around Paterson's belt and one around his chest to keep him from bouncing right back out again, and Morris helped Amos onto Lenox.

The half mile back to Van Tassel's barn was the longest and most painful I have ever spent. I was fading, my battle fever leaching into a cold sweat. Morris proceeded slowly, carefully, and I tried to muster what was left of my strength for what came next.

Morris hoisted the general across his back when we arrived, and I staggered behind him, focused on simply staying upright.

"It's not warm, but it's dry," Morris said, easing the general down into the straw. "I'll bring you water and bandages and some of Maggie's ointment for your wounds."

I didn't know who Maggie was, but I nodded, grateful.

"I'll look after the horse, and I'll ask the miss to bring you what I can't. She has a softer heart than her father."

He removed Lenox's saddle and the packs on his flanks and left me to dig through the general's things in search of something to aid us. I located his mess kit, a small bottle of brandy, and some communications that I returned to the leather pouch where I found them.

Morris brought water, rags torn to strips, and a tin of salve that smelled of butternut bark and something I couldn't distinguish. Van Tassel's daughter trailed after him, bearing two blankets and a curious expression.

"It'll keep the rot from your wounds and even numb the pain some," Morris said of the salve.

"He's dead," the girl said, prodding the general's boot with her foot. "Look at him."

I did, and he wasn't, though her words sent ice shooting through my veins.

"He's just hit his head," I said. "He'll wake and we'll leave."

She shrugged and dropped the blankets beside him.

"I will try to bring some food later. Father's having a party. I may not be able to slip away." The girl was pretty, maybe seventeen, and she'd probably seen plenty, growing up in the middle of a battleground, but if her heart was soft, I saw no sign of it. She left the barn with bouncing curls and swishing skirts.

"You'd best stay out of sight," Morris warned, as if he thought I might brandish my pistol and enter the house. "I'll keep an eye out and make sure nobody wanders in here, but if the general doesn't wake, you should go, and go as soon as you're able. These folks are not friendly to the regimentals."

"Thank you, Morris."

He nodded and left me with a lantern, closing the door and latching it behind him.

I cleaned the general's wound, layered it with salve, and covered him with a blanket, helpless to do more. Then I took the knife from his mess kit and doused it with brandy, the way I'd seen others do. It was flat with a pointed end, good for scooping and stabbing both. It was the only utensil a soldier carried.

I dumped the blood from my boot and peeled off my sock, dreading what I would find when I removed my breeches. They were stuck to my skin, and my fear was even worse than the pain.

My vision narrowed and my stomach revolted, but I peeled back the cloth and stared down at the oozing black hole in the meat of my left thigh. It didn't look too terrible, though I knew the bullet was still lodged in there somewhere.

One thing at a time. The wound that had filled my boot with blood was a different bullet altogether. It had clipped the flesh of my calf, creating a furrow not unlike the one on the general's head. It was ugly and jagged, but not deep. I gulped back the brandy, wiped a bit of ointment on the gash, and wrapped a length of bandage around it, certain a doctor could not have done any more for it than that.

I felt around the hole in my thigh with terrified fingers, hoping to find the bullet right beneath the surface and coax it out without having to dig for it. Digging might present a problem.

The breath hissed through my teeth, and the moan I denied myself burned in my chest. I sloshed a bit of brandy into the hole and almost lost my grip on the here and now.

I could not faint when I wasn't wearing any bottoms. I folded my belt and put it between my teeth, something to bite down upon when

I wanted to shriek. If a man could hold back his cries, I could hold back mine.

It took me several attempts. The small, spoon-shaped tool became slick in my hand, and sweat stung my eyes. I threw up once and had to pause, but on the fifth try, tears of agony streaming down my cheeks, I spit the belt from my mouth and freed the lead intruder from my thigh.

"Oh, thank you. Thank you, Lord. Thank you," I whispered. Blood bubbled from the hole, but my relief was so great I almost laughed. I doused it in brandy again, drained the rest of the bottle to ease the pain, and slathered the wound with Maggie's salve. I bandaged it with shaking hands before inching my caked breeches back up my legs and over my hips, securing them around my waist before I fell into an exhausted stupor, huddled at my general's side.

~ 17 ~

Just Powers

I awoke much later to the sound of voices on the other side of the barn wall. Night had fallen, and icy moonlight streamed through a high opening above our heads.

The pain in my leg reminded me immediately where I was and the danger I was in, along with the man beside me.

The voices receded—likely Morris and his boy—and I bolted upright, terrified that the general had left me while I slept. His skin was warm, but not overly so, and his lips were parted. The barn was cold enough that his breath was visible, and I took comfort in that sign of life though his continued stillness terrified me.

I willed myself to take stock of our circumstances, though I wanted only to sleep. I lit the lantern, drank some water, relieved my bladder into the dirt, and rubbed a bit more salve on my wounds. They looked terrible and felt even worse, but I wasn't bleeding or burning up with fever, and I righted my breeches and returned to the general.

He appeared to be sleeping, his big body stretched out in the straw, but he was completely unresponsive. I had slept curled beside him, sharing the warmth of my body and borrowing from the warmth of his, but I pushed aside the blanket I'd spread over him and proceeded to check his limbs and torso with more care than I'd been able to do initially. Surely I'd missed something. Something terrible.

The wound on his head was swollen and ugly, but it was the injuries I couldn't see that froze my blood. I ran my hands over his shoulders and down his long arms. His fingers did not curl or flex when I touched his palms. I unbuttoned his waistcoat and lifted his shirt, searching his skin for something I might have missed. He was warm and a tad too lean—we were all too lean—which somehow made him seem even longer, even larger, and tears rose to my eyes and tickled my nose as I ran my hands over his body, whispering my apologies as I perused. I didn't find so much as a bruise for all my boldness. His wounded head was the culprit, and I could do nothing for him.

"Wake up, John Paterson," I begged, righting his clothes and choking back my tears. "We have to get out of here."

I rolled him to his side to release the pressure on the large bump on the back of his head and dragged his saddlebag over to use as a pillow. I lay back down beside him, spent by the exertion, and pulled the blanket back over us, curling into him and resting my cheek beside his on the saddlebag. Our faces were mere inches apart, his breath even, mine harsh, but I did not close my eyes. I didn't dare. I was wracked by fear and guilt and pain, and I began to pray, demanding God's attention.

Mrs. Thomas must have prayed the same way for her ten sons.

That thought did not comfort me.

Death had come time and again to the Thomas family in spite of the desperate pleadings of righteous parents.

I was not righteous, but I was tenacious. I was like Jacob from the Old Testament. Jacob who became Israel. Jacob the usurper. The supplanter. Jacob who wrestled with God and refused to yield until he had His blessing, a blessing he did not deserve. Jacob who stole his brother's birthright.

It was not my brother's birthright that I'd taken, but his name.

"Take me, God. Take me instead," I pleaded. Perhaps God would take the general and me both. The wounds in my leg might fester. It was more likely than not, but I had never intended to survive.

I could do nothing more for John Paterson. I couldn't fight. Couldn't run. I could hardly walk. Jacob who became Israel pushed his way into my thoughts again. When God was finished with him, he'd been almost lame.

I prayed until my words slurred and my mind blanked. Before I drifted off, I entreated God once more, offering myself in John Paterson's place, a terrible deal, I knew, but a heartfelt one. And then I begged Elizabeth to send him back if he tried to join her.

"We need him, Elizabeth. I know he would rather stay with you. But send him back if you see him. Please, Elizabeth."

~

It was the rasp of his voice, barely above a rumble, that woke me again, hours later, and I jerked up, looking down into his face. Morning had broken, and I had no sense of the time that had passed. My bladder was full, my leg throbbed, but John Paterson was awake.

He'd rolled to his back at some point, and he blinked up at me slowly, as though his lids were heavy, but his blue gaze focused on my face.

"General Paterson? Can you talk to me, sir?"

"Is there a reason you're holding my hand, soldier?" he whispered, strain making the words crack.

I was too overjoyed to be embarrassed. "Yes, sir. I was afraid you would die while I slept. And I couldn't stay awake anymore. So I held your hand to keep you here."

"It seems to have worked." His hand flexed around mine, and I found myself clinging to it all the harder.

"I did not think you would ever wake." My voice broke, and I cleared my throat, trying to find control.

"Where are we?" he rasped.

"We're in a barn. It belongs to a loyalist toad named Jeroen Van Tassel. He has a home with at least a dozen rooms and, judging from his color and his girth, plenty of wine and food in his stores. I ask permission to accompany a raid on his property when we return to the Point."

"Permission granted." He blinked again, that slow, agonized lifting of his lids, and winced. "And why . . . are we in his barn?"

"What do you remember, sir?"

"The supplies. The cavern."

"We were attacked on our return. I don't know why. And I don't know who. It was chaos. Men and horses scattered. Colonel Sproat and Agrippa were still alive when I saw them last, both still on their horses. But I don't know about the others."

"DeLancey's men?"

"I don't know. Probably. But we surprised them . . . and they surprised us. I do not think it was a planned attack."

He grunted and raised his left hand to his head, feeling around the bandages. "My head feels like it's nailed to the floor."

"You took a musket ball through your hat. It parted your hair and made a furrow, but it didn't lodge. It knocked you from your horse, though. Your brow is swollen, and you have a great lump on the back of your head as well, so I tried to turn your face to the side."

"Front and back? How did I manage that?"

"I'm not sure, sir. Talent, I suppose."

"Don't make me laugh, Shurtliff," he huffed, and his mouth twitched. My tears began falling in earnest.

"You remember me then?" I choked.

His lids closed and didn't open.

"General?" He didn't answer, and I thought he'd been pulled under again. "General?" I patted his cheek, panicked.

"General!"

His eyes opened again, and his gaze was clearer.

"You were praying. Out loud. You said her name."

"Who?"

"My wife. You asked Elizabeth to send me back." His hand flexed around mine, and I realized I was still clutching his right hand in my left. I didn't dare let go.

I nodded, not trusting my emotions enough to answer. Much of my agonized beseeching had been done in silence, but someone had been listening.

"It's freezing in here," he said. "Your hand is too warm."

"I'm fine, sir."

"You aren't. You are covered in blood, you're crying, and your skin is hot."

I made myself unclench my fingers and release him.

"Most of the blood is yours, sir," I lied. "And my tears were for you too."

"You weren't injured?"

"I was. My left leg was hit, but I will heal. No permanent damage done." I hoped. "My horse ran off."

"And mine?"

"Your horse is in Van Tassel's stable."

He sighed heavily, gratefully, and we were silent again.

"How long have we been here?" he asked.

"I'm not certain. A full day . . . maybe a little longer. But we need to go. I was warned that Van Tassel is not a friend, though I didn't need the warning. The only concern shown has been by a servant named Morris and the daughter, though I think it is more curiosity than care in her case. I asked for water and blankets. She brought them, but little else."

"How do you know he's a loyalist?"

"He's fatter. Richer. More comfortable. He doesn't have the look of the harried and the careworn."

"Ahh."

"I could go alone, sir, now that you are awake. Now that I know you aren't going to die on me. And I can bring back help."

He rolled to his side and pushed himself up, assessing his head. I scrambled to assist, sitting up as well.

He swayed but caught himself immediately. "My head is pounding, but the rest of me is fine. I need a drink . . . and to take a piss."

I handed him the canteen, and he drank deeply, handing it back empty.

"Can you manage the other on your own, General?" I asked, preparing myself for the worst.

"If I can't, I sure as hell won't be able to sit on a horse."

"I don't know if you can ride yet, sir."

"You can help me stay in the saddle."

Alarm skittered down my back. *You don't feel like a boy, Rob.*

I would not be able to walk back to West Point. I knew this. I was in no condition. I didn't think my wounds had turned, but they had not even begun to heal. I would just have to hang on to him with my arms and pray my chest at his back didn't betray me.

I nodded and stood, testing my leg. It was no better and no worse than it'd been before. But now the general was watching me.

"Your breeches are blood-soaked. Where were you shot?" he asked.

I peeled my stocking down, revealing the bandage on my calf, and quickly pulled it back up. My legs, even bandaged and blood-spattered, were decidedly feminine. My hair was too fine and light, my calves too narrow.

"That doesn't account for the blood above it."

"Your head was in my lap when we brought you here."

He was silent, considering that, and I thought he might lie back down.

"I owe you my life, Shurtliff. Don't I?"

"Yes, sir. You do. So I will thank you not to lose it any time soon."

He snorted and rose gingerly, using the wall to steady himself. He closed his eyes like the barn was spinning.

"I will go get the horse, sir."

"I'm not going to ask how."

"I'll handle it."

"I trust you will."

I left him, still wobbly but standing, his hand wrapped around the nearby post. I heard him retch behind me and throw up the water he'd just guzzled. "Damnation," he moaned, but I left him to sort himself out, grateful that his misery would distract him from mine.

Morris was approaching, a bucket in one hand and a loaf of bread in the other, as I hobbled from the barn.

"We're leaving. I need the general's horse."

He stopped, the water sloshing over the edge, and then he handed both to me.

"Van Tassel won't like you taking that horse. He thinks it's his now. He's already got a buyer."

"Then I've saved him from an enormous mistake."

"I'll bring it and help you saddle him. But you'd best get gone. He left not an hour ago, but he wasn't going far."

"Just as soon as you bring the horse," I agreed, and turned back.

General Paterson was waiting for me. His color was an alarming gray, but his eyes were clear and his gaze steady. He took a hunk of the bread I offered and watched as I refilled the canteen and gathered the few things I'd removed from the packs.

"You can barely walk," he said.

"My calf is sore." I said nothing about my thigh.

Morris returned, leading Lenox, and put the saddle on his back and tied down the packs without a word. I almost moaned in relief. I didn't have the strength to pick it up off the ground. Morris held the reins as Paterson swung up into the saddle and gripped the back of his coat when he teetered. For a moment I thought the general would fall off the other side, but he held on.

"Get on, Shurtliff," Paterson clipped.

Morris stepped up, ready to assist me too, and I let him, settling on the horse's rump and leaving the saddle to the general. The horse shifted and I slipped, unable to clamp my thighs to keep my seat.

"Hold on to him, boy," Morris warned, and I did as instructed, wrapping my arms around the general's waist. He was rigid and breathing like he was about to be sick again.

"You know where you're going?" Morris asked me, his eyes on the general's ashen face.

"We're about four miles east of the river," I answered. "Peekskill is north."

Morris jerked his head in the affirmative. "Don't follow the road. Not yet. Van Tassel will be coming home that way. And who knows who'll be with him. Follow the stream until you reach the fork. Then find the road. It cuts through just east of there." He pointed into the woods, and the general thanked him.

"Should you need . . . anything . . . you come to me," the general insisted. "We welcome good men. All good men."

"I've got a woman and the boy," Morris said. "We're lucky to be together. Van Tassel could sell us off, any time he wants. I can't be a soldier."

"Tell Van Tassel the truth. We took the horse," I reminded Morris, suddenly worried about him. "He doesn't need to know you helped us. Tell him I threatened to shoot you, just like I did him."

"You should go. Now."

"Thank you, Morris," I said.

"Don't thank me. Just go," he said, urgent. "And go slow or you'll never make it." He wrapped the reins around the saddle horn and set the general's hands atop them. Then he gave Lenox a nudge.

I didn't look back, but I felt his gaze as we disappeared into the trees.

Our combined misery was palpable, and for the first mile or so, the general clung to the pommel and I clung to him, my arms quaking and my legs screaming with the effort to keep us both upright. The space I'd thought I could maintain was nonexistent.

"Our Father which art in heaven," I whispered.

"Are you still praying, Shurtliff?" The general's voice was pained.

"Yes, sir," I said. "You are heavy. And I am . . . weak."

"We will go slow, just like the man said. And we will both hold on and trust the horse."

"Yes, sir." Lenox chuffed and the clouds shifted, and I prayed silently.

"You threatened Van Tassel with a pistol?" the general asked suddenly.

"He refused to help me."

He grunted, and I wasn't sure if it was laughter or pain. "Talk to me," he demanded.

"Sir? If I am talking, I can't listen." I expected company around every bend, and we had miles to go before we reached friendly territory.

"The horse is listening." His voice was strained and his grip on the pommel had become desperate. I tightened my arms. I doubted, in his current state, that he would notice anything at all. "My head is swimming. I cannot tell the ground from the sky," he confessed.

"Close your eyes," I directed. "If the horse can listen, he can also see."

"Talk to me," he insisted again.

"Um. Do you like Shakespeare, sir?"

He grunted. It sounded like an assent.

"*King Lear*, *Much Ado about Nothing*, *Romeo and Juliet*?"

"I never cared for the latter."

"No. Neither do I. I have never been able to understand the appeal."

"Not a romantic, Shurtliff?"

"No, sir. I prefer *Hamlet. The Merchant of Venice. Othello*."

"Why?" He was doing his damnedest to hold up his end of the conversation.

"I understand the Moor. His need to prove himself. I didn't much care for the way he treated the woman in his life, but that too was understandable."

"It is the curse of manhood."

"What is, sir?"

"The need to prove oneself."

I grunted but did not disagree. I considered it a trait shared by the sexes, but thought better of arguing that point.

"I always knew what my father wanted," the general continued. "I knew exactly what was expected of me. Virtue. Strength. Integrity. The things he wanted for me became things I wanted for myself.

"He wanted me to go to school. He wanted me to study the law. To care for my mother and sisters and to have a family of my own. God, family, country. That was his motto, though country did not mean to him . . . what it means to me. I often wonder what he would think of our cause."

"He was a military man?" I knew that he was.

"Yes. His service took him away. Just like mine has done."

"Away where, sir?"

"He died in Cuba of yellow fever when I was eighteen."

"I'm sorry, sir."

"He was a good man. At least . . . I think he was. I hope he was."

"What is a good man?" I asked, trying to keep him talking.

"My father told me once that valiance is the defining quality of true greatness. Not talent. Not power. Valiance. That has been my goal. Some days, my only goal. I fear my lack of personal ambition was a great disappointment to Elizabeth."

He was almost muttering, but the conversation had taken a surprising turn. I desperately wanted him to continue.

"I will not be the kind of man history remembers. At this juncture . . . my own children will not remember me."

"The war has been hardest on the women," I said. "History won't remember them at all."

"Such an odd fellow you are, Shurtliff." He sighed. "A wise old soul in a boy's body."

My laugh was almost a sob. "I was born old, sir."

"Yes. I think you were. Tell me about your father."

"I did not know my father."

"And your mother?"

"She sent me to live with family after my father was gone." I chose my words carefully. "I have not seen her more than a handful of times since I was five years old."

"When this is over, I'll go home to Lenox, Massachusetts. Where will you go?"

"I'm not sure. I don't think that far ahead," I said. I did not *let* myself think that far ahead.

"No. I don't believe that. You are always thinking."

"Yes, sir. But not about the future. I find the present taxing enough."

I ground my forehead into his back, trying to prop him up without toppling him over. I could feel the moments he teetered on the edge of consciousness. Maybe it was exhaustion, but he swayed in intervals, and that we had managed to stay in the saddle for the last hour was nothing short of a miracle.

"Sir, if we are set upon, we are done for," I panted.

"Keep talking, Shurtliff. If you don't, then I am done for."

"I do not know what to say, sir."

"Tell me about yourself."

"I have not allowed myself to want anything too much."

He swayed, and I shook him, afraid.

"I'm here, boy. I'm here. Keep going. You don't want anything too much . . ."

"I would like to have a family one day," I said. I almost laughed at myself. I had no desire for a husband. Just children.

"Do you have a girl in mind?" he asked, slightly slurring his words.

"I do not want a wife."

"No? Children might be a difficulty then." Humor, even amid the struggle. I liked that, and I laughed.

"I want to be loved madly or not at all. I can't imagine finding anyone who would love me madly." I was babbling, but I doubted he would remember it.

"Why not?"

"Because no one ever has."

"You are young yet," he rumbled, and his chin drooped farther into his chest.

"Tell me about your children, sir," I prodded.

"I have daughters. Little daughters. Princesses, all. Like their mother. Hannah and Polly and Ruth."

I knew all about Hannah and Polly and Ruth, but I urged him on.

"Hannah and Polly are dark, like Elizabeth. Ruth looks like me, down to the divot in her chin and the furrow of her brow. Poor mite."

"Tell me about Mrs. Paterson. Did she look like the painting in your quarters?"

"She was small and . . . round, she would say, though she knew she was round in the way most women want to be round. Fair skin, dark hair, big . . . brown eyes. The painting is a fair likeness."

Small and round. Like Mrs. Thomas. Somehow, it was exactly how I had pictured her. It was only John Paterson who did not match the image I had created for him. He continued on, as if acknowledging she was worthy of a eulogy, even in his diminished state.

"Elizabeth was . . . easy . . . to love. She was intelligent . . . and good . . . and beautiful. She was the kind of woman that gets . . . snatched up quickly, and I did not hesitate. The moment she was of age, I went to her father and made my case. I never doubted it was the right decision. She gave me three children, she gave me peace of mind, she gave me friendship and support. She gave and gave . . . and now she's gone. And I am here, still fighting in this endless war, wondering what it's all for."

"I'm so sorry, General."

"So am I," he muttered.

"Hold on, sir. Not much farther now. Not much farther," I lied. We had miles to go.

"Just keep talking, Rob. Just keep talking."

He'd called me Rob, and it gave me courage, as if the Thomas brothers rallied around me, daring me on.

I began reciting everything I had ever learned, pulling the words out of the recesses of my mind, proverbs and catechisms and entire scenes from *The Merchant of Venice* to keep us both upright. The general mumbled and swayed, but he stayed in the saddle, and so did I.

We arrived at Peekskill Hollow sometime before dawn and were greeted by a guard who recognized the general's horse before he realized it was us. A bugle sounded, feet pounded, and twenty men came at a run, Grippy at the front.

"Oh, thank God," the general groaned. "Is that you, Agrippa?"

"It's me, sir. It's me. Praise the Lord."

"I thought I might not see you again, my friend." The general was swaying but smiling, and tears had begun to track down my cheeks. I too had feared the worst, and to see Agrippa Hull alive and well shattered the last bit of my control.

"General Paterson needs assistance," I called, seeking to wipe my face against his bowed back. "He's hurt."

Arms reached up to pull us down, but I was the one who found myself unable to let go, so cramped were my arms.

"Let go, Bonny," Grippy urged, but I could only shake my head helplessly.

"I can't."

The general reached down and unraveled my arms, and I slid from the saddle, trying to catch all my weight on my good leg. I landed in a heap instead.

"Get Doc Thatcher," Grippy shouted.

"No. I'm fine," I insisted, allowing Grippy to help me rise. "See to the general. I am only weary."

"You did good, Bonny. You did good," Grippy murmured, holding me upright.

Paterson managed to keep his feet as he was assisted from the saddle, and I slung my arm around his waist on one side, Grippy on his other, and we staggered to the hospital as Grippy filled us in on everything we'd missed.

~ 18 ~

The Consent of the Governed

Dr. Thatcher looked at the general's pupils and cleaned the wound that split his hair, then pronounced him in need of a tonic for his thundering head and someone to wake him every hour. "You've got some swelling, General. No doubt. But beyond a headache and an interesting scar, you should heal just fine."

I hovered by the door, wanting to assist and desperate to be alone. Grippy had gone to find us some supper and see to the general's horse, who was the real hero of the hour. Grippy was too astute, and he'd taken immediate note of my condition. I needed to get cleaned up before he returned.

"Private Shurtliff needs attention," the general said, pointing toward me.

To protest would be more conspicuous than quiet submission, and when the doctor motioned me forward, I sat where I was directed and pushed down my stocking, just as I'd done before.

Dr. Thatcher cleaned it, declared me lucky, and applied another layer of thick ointment to the furrow the bullet had created in my calf.

"There's a hole the size of a musket ball in your breeches, and you're bloodstained from hip to toe." He was peering at my thigh.

"It is the general's blood, sir, and the hole is nothing more than a tear I picked up along the way."

He harrumphed and finished bandaging my leg. "A general's aide should be neat in appearance. You should see to that immediately."

General Paterson snorted. "Go easy, Thatcher. The boy's had a bit more to worry about than a snag in his uniform."

"You can't give these men an inch, Paterson. You know that better than anyone."

"I have clothes in my saddlebags. Grippy will retrieve them, and he'll find something for Shurtliff," the general said. "My aide deserves a commendation, not a scolding."

My horse was lost, my saddle too, along with everything in the bags, and I could do nothing about it now. I had other things to worry about.

"Might I have another bandage, Dr. Thatcher?" I asked.

"What for?" he asked, frowning. He looked a great deal like his aunt when he looked at me that way.

"I would like to wash, sir, and the bandage might get wet."

"Supplies are precious, Private."

"For God's sake, Thatcher," the general snapped.

"I'll be back to check on you in a while, Paterson. You can both sleep here in the hospital." He pointed to a pair of empty cots against the wall and looked at me. "Don't forget to wake him on the hour."

I limped to an empty room, hauling a bucket of water with me, and bolted the door behind me. Then I stripped down, washed as thoroughly as I could, smeared some more of Maggie's ointment on the ugly hole in my thigh, and wrapped it tightly, praying God would mend me and heal the general too. Then I used the bucket as a chamber pot, tossed the contents out the window, and braced myself for come what may.

The general was asleep, but Agrippa had returned with fresh clothing for both of us. I panicked for a moment, knowing that to retreat to change would be odd—men did not demand privacy for such things—but Agrippa left again almost immediately, giving me a moment to whip off my soiled shirt and wiggle into the ill-fitting breeches. I drew the strings tight and dragged the remaining cot close enough to the general that I could reach out and touch him through the night.

"Don't worry, soldier. I'll watch over him. You rest," Grippy said as he came through the door, dangling a bottle of rum from one hand while dragging a rocking chair from places unknown with the other.

"Dr. Thatcher says I must wake him every hour," I insisted.

"I know. But you're hurting more than you're letting on, so you're gonna rest, and I'm gonna sit right here."

I took a long pull from the bottle of spirits he offered, hoping for a respite from the pain, and handed it back, easing myself down with a barely suppressed groan.

"Don't let him sleep too long, Grippy," I implored. "I was so afraid he would never wake again."

"I'll look after him. You hush now," Grippy said, setting the bottle on the floor. He spread a blanket over the general and pulled another over me. "You took good care of the general, Bonny, and I won't forget that. I look after my own. You don't have to be afraid anymore."

He began to rock back and forth, his presence and the slow, heavy creak of the chair soothing me far more than the rum. His kindness made my throat ache and my heart tremble, but I kept my voice steady and my eyes dry.

"Thank you, Grippy. But I'm not afraid." Not in the way he believed. Not in the way the other men were.

"No?" he murmured. "I think you are. That's why you try so hard. I've never seen anyone try so damn hard in my whole life. And I'm not the only one who's noticed. Your reputation preceded you, Bonny, even before you showed up at the Red House. There's a whole lot more to you than meets the eye."

"I'm not afraid," I insisted again, fading fast. I was too tired to be afraid. "But I look after my own too. I just don't . . . I just don't have many folks left. Almost everyone I care about is . . . here."

"That's why you're afraid. I get it. You're afraid of losin' the rest." He made a sound like he had me all figured out.

"But you're one of us now," he continued, leaning forward to pat my arm. I tried not to jerk at the contact, an involuntary reaction, but he tsked like he understood that too. "Me and the general will take care of you."

I suppose he did have me figured out, in a way. I was more afraid of losing my place than I was of losing my life. But with Grippy sitting by, I wasn't afraid of losing either, and I closed my eyes and surrendered my vigil, letting him hold it for a while.

~

Agrippa and Colonel Ebenezer Sproat had both made it back before we did. They and the others had run down the men who shot at us and killed two of them and took the rest prisoner. The shooters claimed they thought we were loyalists, but Sproat was not convinced and made them walk at the end of his gun all the way to Peekskill Hollow, where they were currently imprisoned. When they'd circled back after the firefight to find me and the general, we were gone, and they had no idea if we were dead or alive, captured or hiding.

Colonel Sproat was almost as relieved to see us as Agrippa had been, and he whistled long and low when he heard our story.

"Jeroen Van Tassel has been a thorn in our side from the beginning. You're lucky to have made it out of there. He would have turned you over to DeLancey without hesitation if he'd had the chance, although he'd have got his money's worth. I wouldn't be surprised if he helped arrange the hit on the supply train. That depot is on his land. If we're going to get those provisions, we better do it soon."

We didn't return immediately to the Point. Instead, General Paterson arranged for two schooners to take a dozen handcarts and fifty men downriver, throw anchor at Eastchester, and empty the depot that had almost gotten us killed. Colonel Sproat picked the men and led the mission. It went without a hitch, and three days later, the supplies were being unloaded at the Point.

Common Sense had not been recovered, and I was given a horse so old and swaybacked, the ride back to the Point was a long one, but neither the general nor I was in any condition for haste. Dr. Thatcher wanted to cut a small hole in his skull to make sure he didn't have a brain bleed, but General Paterson declined the offer. He insisted the doctor have another look at my calf, and Thatcher poked at it and declared it fine, but said he could bleed me if I thought it would ease the bad humors in my wound.

"Do the leeches help infection?" I asked. I was worried about the wound in my thigh. It didn't look infected, but it ached deep, like a bad tooth.

"Yes. But I don't think your calf is infected. It's ugly, and the scar will be as thick as the one on the general's head. But both wounds are healing very quickly."

I wondered if it was Maggie's salve, and kept applying it to the general's head and my leg until the little pot was completely gone. Even still, General Paterson recovered much faster than I did, though I made a valiant attempt to pretend differently. By some miracle, my leg did not fester, but I lamented that I might not ever run again without pain.

"Your limping is worse this morning," the general said when I came to shave his face, nearly a month after our narrow escape.

"It is just stiff. The more I move, the better it will feel."

He didn't argue, but his brow was furrowed as I worked. I pressed my thumb into the indentation and rubbed it. "You are scowling, sir. Is your head troubling you?"

"No," he said, but he leaned into the pressure of my fingers and closed his eyes, and a flood of affection welled in my chest. I tipped his chin up and finished my task. It was my favorite part of the day.

"There you are. All done, General. Very handsome," I said, brisk, like I was his mother and not a besotted servant.

"I have been scalped by a bullet," he said, as if that made any difference.

I touched the thick puckered line that shot back from the left side of his brow and disappeared at his crown. The fall of his hair covered it almost completely, but when it was drawn back into a queue, the scar was quite impressive.

"It gives you character, sir."

"Don't kiss my arse, Shurtliff. It makes me like you less."

"All right, General. You are hideous. Make certain you wear your hat."

He chuckled, and the air whooshed between his very fine lips. "I am going down to the stockyard today. I'll cross at Stony Point. Grippy will ride with me. You will stay. Rest your leg. I need to see how many head we have, and I will see about getting another horse for you to ride. One that doesn't have a back like a sloop."

"I should go with you, sir."

"Stay. Get off your feet. Read your commentary on Revelation."

"I have finished it, sir."

"There is a whole shelf of such commentaries. The Book of Judges is horrific. That one should appeal to you."

~

The general was right. The commentary on Judges was fascinating, and I read all day, tucked away in my quarters, and fell asleep early, lulled by my inactivity. I awoke much later, dragged from slumber by a presence in my room and a candle flickering from my small table.

General Paterson sat in my chair, his hands clasped between his knees. His hair was loose about his shoulders, his sleeves rolled, and his waistcoat unbuttoned like he'd begun to ready himself for bed and grown impatient.

"General? Do you need me, sir?" I wasn't frightened. He'd never given me reason to be. But I was unsettled by the surprise visit. I hadn't heard him return and had not expected him back until tomorrow.

He picked up the candle and held it toward my face, casting light this way and that as though he needed to reassure himself that it was me.

My eyes had not yet adjusted, and I winced and turned away.

"General?" I pressed again. "What time is it? Is there something wrong?"

"I noticed the first time we spoke that you already seemed to know me. And . . . I felt as if I knew you too, though I was quite certain we had never met. You have a very distinct look."

He sounded so pained, and ice began to form in my limbs.

"I thought it simply the rapport that happens among like-minded people. You were easy to converse with, interesting. Wise even. And so damned brave. For a boy of sixteen, that impressed me."

He paused, and in the dancing light his face was hard and hollowed out.

"But you aren't a boy of sixteen, are you, Shurtliff? You must be at least twenty-two . . . or twenty-three. And you're not a *boy* at all." He said "boy" with a note of incredulity.

I was silent, not willing to admit to anything until I knew how much trouble I was truly in.

"When you drafted that first letter for me, the day you became my aide, I was again struck with a sense of familiarity but thought nothing of it. Nothing at all. I was reminded of Elizabeth, but many things make me think of her."

"What has happened?" I whispered.

"There is a sea captain from New Bedford. He runs troops. Guns. Whatever he can get his hands on. I don't trust him. He works both sides, but I've bought supplies from him a few times. He was at King's Ferry today with his ship when Grippy and I crossed. I bought some barrels of wine from him. He had an interesting story to tell. About his daughter who wanted to be a soldier. He thought maybe, as commandant at the Point, I might have heard of her. Seen her."

"His daughter?" I asked, numb.

"His name is Samson. He has an arresting gaze. It reminded me of yours."

"Sir?"

"The chestnut horse you call Common Sense was recovered and returned to the stockyard. I have brought him back here for you. The saddle too. Your book was still in the bags."

He set my diary on the small desk beside the candle, and for a moment, I thought I might be able to wiggle free from his snare. I had been so careful in my entries. Even if he'd read them all—oh dear God—I had never once written of my identity or my deepest fear.

"Grippy opened it, just to make certain it was yours. But when he looked through it, he thought maybe the book was mine, as the entries were all letters to . . . Elizabeth."

I swallowed. "I have a dear friend named Elizabeth."

"Yes. I know," he said softly.

I was so afraid, but he didn't stop.

"I keep all my letters. It has helped me in matters of war and business more than I can say. I never destroy a letter. Those letters can save lives. I have all the letters you wrote me. Even the one you sent not long ago. The handwriting is the same." He paused and raised his eyes to mine. I could not look away. "Are you a spy, Deborah Samson?"

"Please. Please, General. I didn't . . . I don't . . ." I didn't have the words I needed. *Why didn't I have the words? Why hadn't I made a plan?*

"Why are you here? Why have you done this?" he asked, suddenly angry. "I want to hear it all. Every step, every breath, every lie you had to tell to get this far. And then I'll decide what to do with you. God knows you can't keep this up."

I slid from my bed, groping for my breeches. When I'd retired, my nightshirt had still been damp from the wash, and I'd worn my extra shirt instead. The tails hung almost to my knees, but the general cursed as if I wore nothing at all.

"What has happened to your leg?" He grabbed at the cloth and pulled it away from my thigh, and I yelped, trying to step away. I almost fell, but his fist in my shirt kept me upright.

"It's an old wound." I jerked the cloth from his hand.

"It is not," he ground out. "You are lying!"

I needed my clothes. I had to cover myself, and I turned back toward my bed, frantic. The altered corset I used to bind my breasts was folded beneath my pillow. When I'd slept among the other men, I'd learned to never take it off. But I'd grown careless in my own space, and to sleep without it pinching and pressing had been too much to resist.

There was nothing I could do about that now.

I reached for my breeches, but he grasped my arm and turned me around. "Why are you here?"

I shrugged away again, desperate to hide. To run. To wake up from this nightmare. I gathered my hair, trying to corral it into a tail, to pull myself together, but I had nothing to tie it with. I was unbound and unbuttoned. Undone. And he knew *everything*.

"I cannot believe this. I cannot believe this." He rubbed at his face like he thought himself dreaming too. "You have to go. Immediately. Tonight. Dear God, I'm beginning to think I have no instinct for character at all."

I sank to my knees, the reality of my situation too heavy to shoulder. "Please, General. Please. Don't send me away."

I had no pride, no thought in my head but survival, and I bowed before him, desperate.

"Cover yourself, Miss Samson!"

My shirt, the ties loose and my position lowered, created a gaping display of the bosom I had managed to hide from him and from everyone else. I gasped and clutched at my breasts, but it was too late.

Our combined horror pulsed in the air, and for a moment, neither of us spoke or moved. I stayed on my knees, arms folded over my chest, and he remained pressed against the door that connected our chambers.

"Please get up," he begged.

I rose, my legs shaking so badly I thought I might crumple again.

"Send me back to the ranks with my regiment," I pleaded. "I'll go now. I'll leave immediately."

"I can't. I can't do that."

"Why? I am a good soldier. I have never complained or failed to do my duty."

"You are a woman!" he shouted.

I flew at him and pressed my hands over his mouth, horrified, trying to quiet him. Someone would hear. Someone would hear, and it would truly be over.

He grabbed my wrists, betrayal in every line of his face.

"It is not for the man who has everything and wants more that we fight, but for the man who has nothing," I cried, quoting him with all the fervor in my heart. It was like begging for my life.

"What?"

"In no place on earth can a man or woman who is born into certain circumstances ever hope to truly escape them. Our lots are cast from the moment we inhabit our mothers' wombs, from the moment we draw breath. But perhaps that can change here, in this land."

He shook his head, not comprehending, but wonder had begun to replace his rage.

"Those are your words, General Paterson. Did you not mean them?" I challenged.

"My words?"

"Yes. Your words. You wrote them in a letter that I received on my eighteenth birthday. I thought they were a sign from God."

"You memorized them?"

"Yes. I did. I wore out your letter reading them. They inspired me. Were they just words?"

He shook his head again, baffled. "I wrote them a lifetime ago. It's been years. I hardly remember now."

I repeated the lines, enunciating every syllable.

"Miss Samson . . ."

"I did not want my lot. So I enlisted," I said, interrupting him. I could not bear to be Miss Samson again. Not here. I'd worked too hard and borne too much.

He searched my eyes, and when I bowed my head to collect myself, he barked out, "Look at me!"

My hair was loose about my face, and he released my wrists and brushed it back with rough palms, tipping my chin up so he could study me. He stared down at me like he was truly seeing me for the first time.

"God help me. What a bloody fool. What a bloody little fool," he breathed. "Deborah Samson. Dear God."

And then he did the most unexpected thing of all.

He drew me to his chest and embraced me.

I gasped and my knees buckled, but he held me up.

I had never been embraced. Not once in my memory had I been cradled in another's arms, but John Paterson clutched me to his heart like the prodigal son come home.

I did not return his embrace. I couldn't. My arms were folded over my bosom, keeping my heart in my chest, protecting the secret he already knew.

"Please don't send me away," I choked. "I will go back to the ranks. I'll play the fife or beat the drum. But don't make me go."

"Can you play the fife, Miss Samson?" he asked, and his voice shook, the same as mine.

"No. But give me a day or two to learn, sir. I'm certain I can master it."

I was sincere, desperately so, but his chest rumbled beneath my cheek. I'd made him laugh with my bravado.

But I could not laugh. I could not even breathe.

"I have been shot at," I hissed. "I have been wounded, and I have killed. But I have served valiantly—is not valiance the most important trait of all?—and I have served well. I have earned my right to be here. Please don't deny me that. Please don't take that away from me. When this war is over, God willing I survive, then I will have to find my place in the world. But right now, my place is here. At your side. Grippy said I was one of you now. Please let me finish what I have begun. Please let me see it through."

My throat ached with the need to weep, but I stood within the circle of his arms and awaited his verdict. He held me a moment longer, his embrace tight and his cheek resting against my hair. Then he set me away from him and left the room, pulling the door closed behind him.

I bound my breasts, dressed, and made my bed. Then I sat in my chair, too afraid to venture out and too confused about what had just occurred to form a plan. John Paterson had not insisted I go. He had not said I could stay. I could no more interpret his embrace than I could his abrupt exit.

He had left my diary sitting beside the candle that still burned. The flame was wobbling and weary, the wick a long, charred line.

I opened my book and saw my words through a new lens, reading each entry as John Paterson must have read them. It was not what I said that condemned me, though I'd foolishly mentioned Nat and Phin and Jeremiah in one entry. It was the greeting to Elizabeth in Deborah Samson's hand that must have jarred him awake. Once he'd made the connection, every careful word would have reinforced the realization.

"Oh, Elizabeth," I whispered, trying not to weep. "What should I do?"

I should gather my things and go. But . . . I was enlisted. I couldn't simply leave. If I did, I would be considered a deserter. I had not been discharged. General Paterson would have to do that, and no doubt when the morning came, he would present me with my papers and send me away. I didn't believe he would tell anyone or seek to press charges. He would just release me, and I would go. And I would never see him again.

That was the worst part of all.

Worse than private shame, worse than public censure, worse than having no future and no home. To never see John Paterson again would be unbearable.

I turned to a clean page, prepared my quill, and began writing, holding nothing back, not even to myself.

April 2, 1782

Dear Elizabeth,

You must forgive me. I did not mean to love him. Not this way. I admired him—I've admired him for so long—and was so fond of him. But this is not fondness or admiration. This is agony in my chest and fire in my belly. You are his wife. His beloved and my beloved. And my feelings shame and alarm me. But I cannot deny them.

The ache in my heart is the same as it was the day I learned that you were gone. The disbelief, the betrayal, the loss of my hope, and most of all, the gaping emptiness of a world without you in it. But now it is magnified by the guilt that I have betrayed you and John both, not just with my actions, but with my feelings.

I wish you could give me a bit of advice like you used to do. Remind me of the power and blessings of our sex—weren't those the words you used? I must return to womanhood, and I am not ready. It is not that being a man is a marvelous thing. The truth is, I am not one and never will be, nor do I even want to be one. It was never about changing myself. It has always been about freeing myself. Now here I am, bound, heart and soul, to a man who does not love me, who cannot love me—how could he?—and one I will likely never see again when I leave here.

I have looked with derision on girls who wanted only to marry, who mooned about men as if they held the power to give them the world instead of simply control their world. And now I am one of them. Now I want only to continue at his side. To care for him, to love him. And I am mortified by it. I wish you were here, and yet I am glad you are not. What a terrible thing to write. What a terrible thing to feel.

I did not sign my name or my initials at the close of the entry. I was not ready to be Deborah again, and Robert Shurtliff had been stripped away. Grippy said I was one of them, but I wasn't. I never had been.

The diary no longer mattered. I would be leaving, and nothing I said on the page would change that now. I left the book open and let the ink dry, staring down at each hideous word. Contemplating the mess I'd made.

Writing to Elizabeth, the way I'd always done, had seemed perfectly benign. If any of my bunkmates had read my words, nothing I'd said would have condemned me.

But I had not planned on John Paterson.

I should have tossed the book into the fire the day I'd moved into the Red House, but I did not think. And now all was lost.

~ 19 ~

To Alter or Abolish

The general had not slept in his bed. After our confrontation, I'd heard him leave his quarters, and he had not come back. I set out his shaving kit and tidied his room. I didn't know if he'd donned fresh clothes, so I laid them out as well and stoked the fire in the grate. March had begun with sunshine and warmth and ended with two feet of fresh snow. Traveling would be unpleasant and difficult. Especially alone.

Perhaps the general would let me stay until I'd made other arrangements. I could write to my mother, but I was sure she'd been informed of my first attempt to enlist. She'd had more public humiliation than any woman should have to endure, and all at the hands of others. I could not go to her. I *would* not.

I had an aunt and uncle in Stoughton who might let me live with them. They had a farm, and their children were grown.

I could go back to the Thomases, to Middleborough, to the church elders and beg for them to let me return. Perhaps the community would forgive me if I groveled enough.

I shook my head, scattering the thoughts that didn't serve me. The general would decide, and I would honor his wishes.

After cowering in my quarters almost an hour after reveille, I gathered my courage and walked to the kitchen to inquire whether the general had already eaten or whether I could bring him a tray.

Agrippa was alone at the kitchen table, eating his breakfast with obvious enjoyment. He looked up as I entered and answered my query as to the general's whereabouts as if nothing at all was amiss.

"He said we were to let you rest. He left with Colonel Jackson and said he was meeting Colonel Sproat at Peekskill."

"Why?" It was all I could do to keep my voice steady.

"Van Tassel—the loyalist who let you sleep in his barn—turned up dead. General got word of it, and he was gone within the hour. I would have gone, but Colonel Kosciuszko wants me here." He kept eating his breakfast, seemingly unperturbed by the general's sudden departure and the fact that I'd been left behind.

I collapsed into a chair, calling on all the fortitude I had left not to break down. I had no sympathy for Van Tassel—good riddance—but it was a mission I should have been on.

"General Paterson did not say . . . anything about . . . my position?" My heart was thundering, and I pressed my hands to my chest, bidding it slow.

"Like what?"

"My leg has been slow to heal. I fear the general needs a new aide."

"You'd best let him decide that."

"When is he expected to return?"

Agrippa shrugged. "He was worried about a slave named Morris. He'll be back when he's made arrangements. I suspect a few days is all."

"Morris," I breathed, ashamed of myself. What would become of Morris, his boy, and the woman named Maggie? I doubted I would ever know.

"I cannot just sit here. I'll go mad," I whispered. And I would. Better that I know my fate immediately than have it drawn out until the general returned. Maybe he expected me to quietly go while he was away. That thought brought a rush of new anguish, and I propped my head in my hands, jostling the breakfast Mrs. Allen placed before me.

"Are you unwell, Bonny?" she asked, laying her hand against my brow. Grippy's nickname had become common among the entire house staff.

"No, ma'am," I muttered, and she tsked, shrugging.

"The general said you were, and that I should go easy on you whilst he's away. But if you are feeling better, I can certainly keep you busy."

Grippy kept shoveling his breakfast into his mouth, not even looking up from his trencher. Unlike me, he looked as though he'd had a fine night's sleep; his clothes were pristine, and his closely cropped hair accentuated his handsome head.

"We found your horse. And did the general give you your book?" Grippy asked suddenly, as though he'd just remembered the outing of the day before.

I pulled my breakfast toward me but didn't eat. I didn't want to lie, I couldn't confess all, and I sat, staring at the healthy portion of potatoes and sausage, evidence of the haul we'd recovered from the raid on the depot.

"And who's Elizabeth? You said you didn't have a girl back home. Your book is filled with letters to Elizabeth," Grippy said. "I think it upset Paterson, seeing her name . . . Probably brought his own Elizabeth to mind. What are the odds of that?"

"My Elizabeth is his Elizabeth," I said softly, revealing yet another truth to Agrippa Hull. It probably wouldn't matter. I would soon be gone.

Grippy ceased his shoveling and raised his eyes slowly to mine.

"Elizabeth's uncle was a reverend in the town where I was raised. He looked after me," I explained. "Elizabeth looked after me too, in her way."

"So you knew General Paterson . . . before the war?"

"Yes. I knew *of* him."

"And he knew of you?"

"I had never met him." That wasn't exactly what he'd asked, and Grippy recognized the evasion.

"The general doesn't like secrets, Bonny."

I nodded inanely.

"Have you been keeping secrets from the general, boy?"

"No. No, sir." Not anymore. The general knew everything.

"Benedict Arnold was his friend. I warned him the man was no good. Too fancy. Too obsessed with his own face and form. Spendin' money and livin' like a king while everyone around him went without. The general said he wasn't always that way. He defended him . . . and then Arnold sold him and everyone else out. Paterson went home to bury his wife, and Arnold saw his chance to surrender West Point to the British. You know the rest."

I nodded. "Arnold got away, but his plan was exposed."

"And General Paterson had to come back here to clean up the mess, even though none of it was his fault. He blames himself for not seeing it. No one else does, but the general thinks he let everyone down."

Dear God, I'm beginning to think I have no instinct for character at all.

The general's words from the night before took on new meaning, and the chasm in my chest widened.

"John Paterson is always cleaning up everyone's messes." Agrippa sighed. "And he never, ever asks a thing in return."

The general did not come back to the Point the next day or the next, and I did not leave. I couldn't. I had no formal discharge and no place to go. But most of all, I could not bear to retreat or concede, though I presumed it was what the general expected.

I worked myself into a stupor each day, collapsed into my bed each night, and rose to do it all again, much to the delight of Mrs. Allen and the rest of the staff in the Red House. I tried to make a plan but mentally recoiled at the very thought of leaving, and suspended any introspection or decision until General Paterson returned and made it official.

On the sixth day of his absence, I worked all day in the commissary, and upon my return saw Joe brushing Lenox down outside the stable and Mrs. Allen fixing the general his supper.

"The general was asking for you, but the poor dear must be starving," she said.

John Paterson's beauty and appeal had not escaped Mrs. Allen. She doted on him as much as I did, and she dished up a heaping trencher of potatoes and ham. She marched down the hall, wanting to be the one to feed him. I followed at her heels, carrying a tray with coffee and tea, numb with apprehension.

"General Paterson," Mrs. Allen crooned, tapping on the door. "I've got your supper, sir."

"Where is Shurtliff?" he barked, and Mrs. Allen frowned. He was rarely short with her. He wasn't often short with anyone.

"He is here as well, General. He's got your coffee."

"Come in then."

He kept his back to us as we hurried forward and placed his supper beside the pile of correspondence he'd been working on. He wore the same shirtsleeves and waistcoat he'd been wearing the last time I'd seen him, and his jaw sported several days' growth.

I didn't dare set the steaming pot or the little tray where it could be jostled and spilled on important papers, and I stood by, waiting for his instructions.

"You can go, Mrs. Allen. Thank you. But don't feed me like this. I get the same rations as the men. It is only fair. There is enough here for two men, at least."

"Well, maybe Bonny can eat with you. He's not had his supper yet either."

His chin shot up and he glared at the woman. "What did you call Private Shurtliff?"

"Why . . . Bonny. It's what Agrippa calls him. It's actually what everyone calls him. He's a pretty boy, he is."

"You may go, Mrs. Allen. And I would prefer we call my aide-de-camp by his proper name. Please tell the staff if I hear him referred to in such a familiar manner again, I will dock a day's rations."

The woman left, her fondness for General Paterson noticeably dampened. He did not look at me, but hope quickened my heart. Why should he care what others called me if he was going to send me away?

"I don't mind the silly name. They mean no harm."

"Yes . . . well, most women like to be told they're pretty," he shot back.

The tray in my shaking hands began to clatter, and coffee sloshed over the edge, scalding my thumb where I clutched the tray. I set it down on his desk with a crash, tears pricking my eyes, though from pain or humiliation I wasn't certain, and brought my sore thumb to my mouth.

The general moved quickly, pulling me to the pitcher of cold water and the washbasin kept on the sideboard. He held my thumb beneath the stream of water and then pressed my hand into the basin, keeping it submerged. A raised red welt was already visible. I withdrew my hand and stepped back.

"It is fine, sir."

"It is most definitely not fine, Miss Samson."

"Please do not call me that."

"It is who you are!" He shook his head, dumbfounded, and ground his palms into his eyes. "And I have spent these last days trying to come to terms with it."

"Yes. It is who I am." *Oh, to admit it out loud!* "And I am . . . dreadfully sorry that I have put you in this situation. I will make arrangements to go. If only you could see that I am discharged—honorably—so that I am not considered a deserter, I would be grateful."

He raised his clear blue eyes and regarded me then.

"Is that what you want?"

I shook my head. "No, sir. I want to stay. I want to be your aide. I want to see this through until the end. Just as you do."

He said nothing but continued to study me, and encouraged, I persisted in pressing my point.

"We never have to talk of it again, sir. I have been a soldier for almost a year. There is no reason I can't continue. No one ever has to know."

"But I know," he said. "And it is against the rules."

"Yes. You know," I admitted softly. "But have I not . . . have I not performed every duty, completed every task, and been a good soldier, regardless of that fact?"

"You have. And I am indebted to you."

"You owe me nothing."

"That is not true. And we both know it. But that is not why I will allow you to stay."

"You will allow me to stay?" My heart leapt and my breath caught.

He shut his eyes as if he needed to gather strength. "Yes."

"Am I to go back to the ranks?"

"No. You will remain my aide." He was so stiff and so prickly. I wanted the old general to return, the man who trusted me and tested me, who spoke to me without carefully choosing his words and guarding his every action. His hands were even clasped behind him like he'd yanked them back from a flame.

"You must allow me to do everything you expected of me before," I insisted.

"That is out of the question," he replied, terse.

"Then I will go back to the barracks."

He gaped at me, his face flushing. "I am the commandant, and you are on very thin ice, Private."

"I do not wish to be coddled or protected. That is not why I am here," I shot back, infuriated. I could not help it. The strain of the last week had left me without reserves, and beneath my gratitude was anger that he had made me suffer so long, not knowing my fate.

"You are not in any position to make demands," he ground out.

"I am not making demands, General. I am seeking to do my job!"

We strode in opposite directions, needing space from one another, but we met back where we'd started, no calmer for the circling.

"You are exactly the same," he hissed, wagging a finger in my face. "I do not know how I missed it for so long."

"I *am* exactly the same," I cried. "Exactly the same as I was last week and the week before. When I was allowed to carry out my duties. Nothing has changed."

"That is not what I meant. You are exactly the same as in your letters. So confident and persistent and . . . and annoying!" He fisted his hands. "But I am not amused anymore."

The idea that I had annoyed him was like a slap to my face, and my cheeks grew hot in affront. "I *annoyed* you?"

He expelled a great gust of air. "You did not. Not then. But I am greatly annoyed now, and you will tread lightly and . . . and keep your distance until this thing is done."

"Keep my distance?" I asked, baffled. "How am I to do that if I am your aide?" We were mere feet apart even now.

He ran both hands through his unkempt hair and collapsed into his desk chair. His meal sat untouched, and he was visibly distraught.

I left the room and returned with his shaving kit. He still sat, dejected, his long legs stretched out in front of him. Without asking his permission, I put a cloth around his shoulders, prepared a lather, and gently spread it over his cheeks.

"This whole situation is indecent," he whispered.

"How so, sir? You have treated me with impeccable decency."

"I have treated you with incredible familiarity."

"Familiarity is not indecency."

"And you are being purposefully obtuse."

I was, and I allowed silence to settle around us as I scraped the bristles from one half of his face and then the other. I was almost finished, and his eyes were closed when I spoke again.

"Can you not . . . simply put it out of your mind?" I asked. "I expect no special treatment. I never have."

"But you deserve it," he answered, weary. "It is your right."

"My right?" I scoffed, and he opened his tired eyes. "I have so few rights, sir, but being handled like a woman, in these circumstances, is not one that I want. So if it is my right, I renounce it, and ask that you let me do the job I was selected to do."

"You renounce it?" His mouth twitched.

"I renounce it."

I finished shaving his face, blotted his cheeks, and pulled the drape free. When I attempted to dress his hair, he waved me off and tied it back himself. I poured him some coffee, and he split his supper in half, dividing it on the trencher.

"Eat, Samson," he said softly, and I sat down in the chair on the other side of his desk.

"Did you enlist to find me?" he asked.

"No. In your last letter, when you told me Elizabeth was gone, you said you'd returned home. I did not expect for you to be here. It was quite a shock. But you had never seen me, I had never seen you. There was nothing about my appearance that you would recognize."

"I can see why you used Robert, but why not Samson?"

"I didn't want anyone to think of Deborah Samson at all or be reminded of her in any way."

He nodded slowly. Deliberately. "We will not speak of this again," he said.

"Very well, sir."

"If it is discovered, I will deny any knowledge of it. You will face whatever consequences follow—"

"Of course. As I have always done," I interrupted.

"I will not be able to protect you. You must understand this."

"No one has ever protected me, General. I have only ever had myself."

He winced, and his shoulders drooped slightly. "That is a tragedy, Miss Samson."

"Please call me Rob. That is what the brothers called me. And no. It is not a tragedy. It is a victory. One I am proud of."

He was quiet then, and we ate in companionable silence.

"What has happened to Morris?" I asked softly.

"He is here."

My heart leapt. "And Maggie and Amos?"

"You know their names?"

"Yessir. Maggie made the salve that healed your wound and kept my leg from festering."

"Hmm. Well then it is good that she will be at the hospital at Robinson's house. The boy too. Morris has experience in the forge and will work there. They have not been separated. As I told him, we have much need of good men. All good men. And good . . . women."

I almost wept then, overcome by the general's goodness and God's mercy, but I tucked into my meal instead, swallowing my emotion with bits of ham and potato and gulping back my gratitude with coffee I didn't taste.

"What was it you said, 'It is not for the man who has everything and wants more that we fight,'" the general prompted.

"'But the man who has nothing,'" I finished, battling a new swell. "And it was you who said it. I only reminded you of your words."

He sighed heavily, but finished his meal without saying more.

"I will remain as your aide and nothing will change?" I clarified, after I'd cleared my entire plate and caged every wayward emotion.

He seemed to resolve something within himself and nodded once, eyes sober. "Nothing will change."

~

He said nothing would change, but it did. The easy comfort we'd enjoyed with each other was bruised. The conversation was stilted, and the general seemed to struggle with my name. He called me "private" more than anything else, and "Shurtliff" when he absolutely had to, but mostly he avoided addressing—or looking—at me at all. And one day he slipped and called me Samson again. Not Deborah, thankfully, but Samson. Agrippa overheard it and pounced.

"Samson, huh? Where did that come from?" he crowed. "I need to hear this story."

The general stiffened, and I froze.

"Shurtliff kept me in the saddle for six hours." He shrugged. "He's stronger than he looks. A veritable Samson in disguise. It is naught but a nickname."

"Ah. The mighty Samson," Grippy said, grinning. He looked at me, considering. "I like it."

I flexed my arms like the pugilists who fought in the barracks for coin and the soldiers' entertainment, and Grippy laughed, but the general dismissed us both without cracking a smile.

He was also reluctant to give me all the duties I'd had before. In the first few months as his aide, I'd delivered messages on horseback to Newburgh and Stony Point. I'd crossed King's Bridge and brought communications to officers stretched across the highlands all by myself, but that ceased the moment he discovered my identity.

"It isn't safe," he said, curt, when I questioned him on it.

"But . . . sir. The other aides are starting to notice. And complain. You've sent Grippy to King's Ferry thrice with communications. Instead of me."

"You are still recovering. You are still limping. And who is complaining? You run circles around everyone else. You shaved every face in the house, shined every boot, and did all the wash for every officer and aide in this residence just this morning. Who is complaining?" he insisted again, indignant.

I bit my lip, suddenly so disconsolate tears pricked my eyes. I was bleeding again. My flow had been minimal, a spotting that required little attention or worry since the month after I enlisted. I'd taken it as mercy from a loving God, but knew it was likely more a result of the physical taxation of being a soldier. Now, after a few months as the general's aide, with a warm bed and a full belly at least once a day, my menses had returned with regularity, putting me in my place.

"Last time Agrippa was sent in your stead, you chopped enough wood to stock the ovens and the fireplace in every room while still serving me, three high-ranking officers, and a visiting general at a formal dinner, by yourself," the general added.

"I had only to look presentable, place food on the table, and stand by, sir. The Allens did all the preparation and the cleanup."

"My point is, Samson, you do far more than your share. I don't think Agrippa or Colonel Kosciuszko mind at all."

"I mind, General."

His head snapped up, and his eyes narrowed. "*You mind?*" he asked, his voice radiating pique.

"Yes, sir." My heart was pounding. I didn't like the confrontation, but I liked the wall between us even less.

"Shut the door, Samson," he ordered.

I turned on my heel, shut the door, and returned to his desk. He watched me, grim.

"Sit."

I sat in the chair across from his desk, my back straight, my hands in my lap.

"I said we would not speak of this again," he began, but I interrupted him.

"You also said nothing would change."

"Well, pardon me, madam, if I am struggling to keep your identities straight. Pardon me for doing my damnedest to handle an impossible situation."

"You can't even look at me. You hardly speak to me. And it is not impossible!"

"I don't talk to you or about you because I am afraid I will slip and refer to you as her or she. And I cannot, for the life of me, refer to you as Robert or Robbie or Shurtliff or bloody . . . Bonny"—he spat the name—"like everyone else does. I don't know how I didn't see it from the start. You're taller than most women. You're long and lean, and you're wearing a uniform. But that's as far as it goes. You don't look like a man. Not to me. Not anymore."

"You cannot call me Samson."

"Grippy accepted my explanation," he shot back, defensive.

"Everyone who hears will think you are mocking me. They'll think it's in jest . . . like calling a fat man Slim or a big man Tiny."

He shook his head. "That's just it. It is perfectly apt. Your strength is astounding."

The compliment stunned me, and for a moment I simply stared at him. He stared back.

"You are angry . . . and cold," I said quietly. "And I miss you."

He released his breath with an audible gust. "I miss the lad I thought you were, and I have no idea what to do with the woman you are."

"I am still Shurtliff."

"No, you are Deborah Samson, and I have to be careful around her."

"Her?" I gasped. "You are talking about me, General. You have to be careful around me? Do you not trust me?"

"It is not about trust." He had dropped the volume of his voice so it rumbled between us, the sound of distant guns and approaching trouble. "It is like the scales have fallen from my eyes. I no longer see a soldier boy. I only see you," he accused, throwing up his hands.

I glared at him, but I had no response. I was a woman, after all.

He shook his head. "Except when you look at me like that. Then I remember Shurtliff's fearsome gaze."

"It was never *his* fearsome gaze. It is mine."

"Now you are doing it too, separating the woman from the boy. It is not so easy to keep them straight."

"I have served with all my heart. And I will continue to do so if you will allow it."

"I am sure that is true." His voice had changed yet again. From a blast to a rumble to a white flag of surrender. I held my breath. I didn't know yet what he was surrendering to.

"I have not known a moment's peace since I realized you are not Robert Shurtliff," he confessed.

"But I am," I pleaded.

"Deborah," he warned, and the sound of my name on his lips shocked me again.

"Please don't take him away from me. Please let me be Shurtliff until the war is over."

"What if you die here? You could have easily died at Tarrytown. Or Yorktown. Or in Eastchester, goddammit. What if you die as a soldier, as Robert Shurtliff? What then? Deborah Samson deserves more."

"But don't you see? This *is* more."

He didn't understand, and he stared at me, perplexed.

"I'm doing it for her. For me." I thumped my chest. "And if I die"—I shrugged—"then I will die a soldier, which is something Deborah Samson wasn't allowed to be."

He raised his brows, stunned. "We don't keep women out of war because they are less than."

"No?" I scoffed.

"No," the general shot back. "Men don't bring their treasure onto the battlefield. They protect it." He enunciated each word.

"I am not treasured. So I do not need protecting." We'd been over this ground before.

"But you are. Elizabeth treasured you. I treasure you."

I bowed my head, humbled by his earnest admission. For a moment, we did not speak.

"There are so few things any of us ever get to see," I entreated him. "Not just women. I know that. I am not such a fool to think men are not bound in different ways. I enlisted because I dared not board a ship. I joined because I could not go west alone. I had no means to cross the sea or set out into the world. Breeches and bound breasts aren't sufficient. A person needs money too. The war was at my doorstep, and it was the only escape available to me."

His sigh was heavy and his shoulders drooped.

"Are you going to tell?" I asked.

"Who? Who would I tell? I am the commandant for the time being. I could go to New Windsor to see General Washington and tell him my aide-de-camp is a master of disguise. After the debacle with Benedict Arnold here at the Point, right under my nose, he might start to think I'm the traitor. And he'll think you're a spy."

"You know that I am not."

"I know nothing of the sort," he grumbled.

"Truly? You don't mean that, do you, General?"

"You have no idea of the depravity and ruthlessness of men. Especially the men who profit from war."

"I swear to you on my life and my sacred honor that I am not a spy," I said, using the language of the declaration on purpose. "I am a patriot, through and through, and I will fight at your side and at your direction until this war is over. You will never have cause to mistrust me or question my loyalty. I swear on my fondness and friendship for Elizabeth."

"I do not want you to pledge me your life or fight at my side," he ground out. "I want you to stay alive. I want you to do as I say so that I am not constantly worried about your well-being. And if that means sending Agrippa to King's Ferry or wherever else I see fit, instead of you"—he pointed a finger at my face—"you will not *mind.*" He sat back in his chair and closed his ledger with a shove. His jaw was tight and his eyes were hot, and I bowed my head, contrite.

"All right, General."

"You will do as I say?"

"Yes, sir."

"And you will not question or interfere with my orders?"

"I will not question or interfere with your orders," I promised.

He exhaled with a gust. "God help us both."

I had every intention of keeping my word, but some promises are impossible to keep.

~ 20 ~

Light and Transient Causes

The month I arrived at West Point after my enlistment, sixteen soldiers charged with desertion and crimes against the local citizenry were brought out onto the open field where gallows and whipping posts were erected not far from the garrison jail.

One by one, twelve of the men were stripped to their waists, tied to a post, and, with drums playing, subjected to their punishment. Most bore it well, hardly flinching as the whip opened bloody stripes on their naked backs, their mates cheering them on.

Two men, convicted of plotting a mutiny, were marched up on the gallows to be hung, but at the last moment, Agrippa Hull had stepped forward and presented a pardon from General Paterson. The onlookers cheered, and the two men were brought back down, hardly able to stand, tears streaming down their cheeks at the mercy they'd been granted.

Two more men took their place, ropes hung around their necks, their sins read for all to hear. One man had killed a local farmer with a pitchfork, raped his wife, and set his house on fire. The other man had stood by while he did, eating the farmer's food and walking away in the farmer's boots. They were not pardoned. The thump of the platform being dropped beneath their feet brought a gasp of delight and a moan of thrilled terror from the onlookers. To remain safe and alive while others died was its own, albeit brief, transcendence.

I had watched it all in horror, not because I thought it unjust—I had no reason to believe the men were not guilty as charged—but because it had happened at all. Because such things were even necessary. My eyes were opened, yet again, to my own vulnerabilities. To be lashed would result in the discovery of my sex. But that was only a small part of my awakening. I had been steeped in revolution, indoctrinated with the language of liberty, and baptized in clear purpose. I knew, down to the soles of my feet and the depth of my spirit, that the fight was just and the cause was great. I was not without my own motivations, my own personal reasons, for engaging in the conflict, but I was a believer.

Not all the soldiers were.

Some of them were animals.

Maybe war made them that way, but I suspected that war just revealed their hooves and snouts.

A barely contained chaos bubbled beneath the order of the garrison. The barracks and the officer class housed all types, though some were better at masking it than others. Murderers, thieves, liars, and cheats were mixed in with the brave, the upright, the faithful and true. All had been tossed into the boiling pot that made up the Continental army, and the result was a simmering, seething stew.

At Yorktown, I'd watched British soldiers surrender and be led into prison ships, and I had resolved then that I would take my own life before I was taken by the enemy. Better for me to die than be captured.

The crimes of DeLancey's Brigade had only reinforced my conviction. But the British and DeLancey were one thing. To fear your fellow soldiers, the men with whom you served, was another. The experience with the talk of desertion in my scouting party had shaken me for several reasons. First, I had no wish to leave. Second, I had no desire to create conflict among my mates, and third, and most importantly, any punishment would likely result in my exposure, and I would rather die.

General Paterson had avoided a mutiny on the Point with a heavy hand but a merciful heart. His efforts to provide and advocate for the troops had not gone unnoticed, but the successful uprisings were still cited by the discontented.

In the winter of '80–81, some of the troops had marched out of their camps in an orderly and organized fashion and descended on Philadelphia with a clear list of terms. They were not spies or turncoats, and they did not consider themselves deserters. They simply wanted to be heard. Most of them were enlistees who signed up after the Battle of Saratoga, and they had committed to "three years or the war," but the war seemed no closer to an end, and they wanted to be released, stating three years was more than enough. Their terms were quietly met and most of the men were discharged and dispersed. It was only after the negotiations that the enlistment rolls were checked and the vast majority of the men granted release had not even served their three years.

Suddenly, mutinies were happening everywhere, but with more disastrous consequences. The same spirit that encouraged heroism and emboldened the men could make a mob when allowed to ferment. An officer, trying to subdue his men, was killed by a soldier who had been pardoned for leading a similar uprising only months before.

That mutiny was not treated the same way as the first. The mutineers were surrounded and disarmed, and the ringleaders shot. After that, the rebellions slowed.

But there were always murmurings. Word had spread up and down the highlands that new recruits had been promised land and bounties double those that previous enlistees had received, and discontent among the men was high.

Perhaps it was spring fever, perhaps it was the sense that it would all shortly come to an end anyway, but General Paterson was convinced the announcement of a grand celebration on the Point, in honor of the birth of the dauphin of France, would not help.

We had spent the previous day at Robinson's house, on the east side of the river about two miles south of the Point, where General Robert Howe had his headquarters. Dr. Thatcher and several other medical officers had established a hospital in the opposite wing, and the estate was a frequent meeting place to plot larger-scale military operations.

The house was formerly owned by a wealthy loyalist named Beverley Robinson who became a colonel in the British Army. When he'd fled to New York in '77 after refusing to swear fealty to the colonial cause, his home and lands were confiscated by the Americans. The rumor was he and Washington had once been friends and both were deeply hurt by the schism created by their opposing loyalties. Each thought the other terribly misguided.

Robinson's house was a sprawling home in a clearing at the base of Sugarloaf Hill. Despite being surrounded by craggy rises and inhospitable terrain, an orchard had thrived, and the estate was a village unto itself with several outbuildings that included a blacksmith and a summer kitchen and acres of land for hunting and farming set back from the rocky bluff.

I had twice accompanied General Paterson to meetings at Robinson's house, but never in such illustrious company. Forty officers, including General Washington and the Prussian Baron von Steuben, Washington's chief of staff, who had ridden the fifteen miles from New Windsor that morning, had convened in the huge central dining area that made up the entrance to the home.

Washington and Paterson were both tall and rangy, with wide shoulders, long limbs, and unyielding military posture. They also had the same comportment and presence, though my general—I caught myself—though Paterson was younger and more handsome. General

Washington always wore a powdered wig. I asked Agrippa if he had any hair beneath—Grippy always seemed to know such things—and he said he had long white hair that his valet brushed and braided every day, but it was thinning on top and the wig helped cover that fact. Bewigged or not, he was resplendent in his gold-and-blue uniform. I did my utmost not to gape or giggle like the woman I was, and was gratified to simply stand against the wall and observe, along with the other aides, as the meeting commenced.

"We owe the French military everything," General Washington said, each word deliberate and firm. Grippy also claimed that Washington's teeth bothered him, and he spoke thus to keep the false ones in place. Bad teeth might also explain why he was reluctant to grin, but I thought it more likely gravitas than vanity.

"We were not able to properly thank or honor them after Yorktown," he continued, "but without them, we would not be here."

No one could argue with that, and every head nodded with a chorus of ayes.

"This army needs to be honored as well. The anniversary of our Declaration of Independence is fast approaching, and for the first time since we embarked on this effort, I have no doubt that this new nation will survive and, indeed, thrive. That is worth celebrating. This is our opportunity to honor our friends and commemorate new life. Our country's and that of the French monarch."

General Paterson had looked aghast and immediately voiced his reservations—namely the state of food stores and the unpaid troops—but Washington was not swayed nor were his spirits dampened. "I am putting you in command, Paterson, for exactly the reasons you cite. You are in charge, and we will all support you. But we will have this celebration, and it will be in two weeks' time."

"A party?" General Paterson had murmured as I'd shaved his face the morning after. "The men have not been paid, the stores are dangerously low—morale is even lower—and I am to throw a party for King Louis's infant son?"

It was so unlike the general to complain—especially about the commander in chief—that I simply listened, sympathetic, as I scraped away at his beard.

"Kosciuszko has been plotting an open pavilion on the plain for a while. Major Villefranche, the French engineer, will be arriving sometime tomorrow morning to assist. I hope they don't kill each other. They must finish it in ten days. We are taking all the timber and boughs from the surrounding area, which will cut down on costs, but it will take a thousand men working nonstop to accomplish it." He sighed wearily. "But at least the men will be occupied. They are less likely to revolt if they are busy."

"I will help you," I reassured him.

He smirked at that. "I know you will. You are my secret weapon. Who better than a woman who has worn a disguise for more than a year to turn a garrison into a great hall?"

Spring had flowered the highlands and chased off the gray of a dreary winter, but the garrison had never hosted such a party, and the work to get everything ready would be enormous. We made lists and divvied up assignments among the regiments, and the general and I, often just the two of us because no one else could be spared, traveled up and down the highlands, from New Windsor to Peekskill Hollow, trading, twisting arms, and gathering resources.

The feast would be limited to the officers, both French and American, and their wives, but that didn't mean the support staff wouldn't need to eat. Casks of wine and rum that we'd recovered from our raid on the depot had already been depleted, and food fit for a banquet was nigh on impossible to acquire, but the general set about making it happen.

Long tables were constructed, lanterns strung, and crates of French and American flags acquired from a sailmaker in Philadelphia. He'd begun producing the tricolor banners in great quantities after the dazzling French parade down their streets before Yorktown, and was glad to sell them in bulk.

A popular portrait artist who had painted likenesses of everyone from Washington to Thomas Paine had added Lafayette and Admiral de Grasse to his collection as well. He'd agreed to set up an exhibit near the pavilion, provided the weather held, in exchange for future commissions. A military band was scrabbled together from the officers and the ranks, and daily practices began, with surprising results.

Preparations continued from sunup to sundown, the erection of the pavilion progressing at full speed. The entire thing was being constructed of timber from the wooded hills and vales surrounding the Point. The walls on the longer sides were formed up with tree trunks spaced like columns with the shorter sides left open. The ceiling was made entirely of boughs, woven together in a tight canopy. When it was completed, it would be six hundred feet long and thirty feet wide, and Major Villefranche and Colonel Kosciuszko had not yet resorted to blows, which boded well for the completion of the project.

It was only a few days before the day of the celebration when Captain Webb appeared at the Red House, asking for an audience with the general, saying it could not wait.

Mr. Allen ushered him into the general's office, and when I rose to leave the two of them alone, as was customary any time the general conferred with his officers, Captain Webb asked that I remain.

"This concerns you as well, Private Shurtliff. I had hoped to speak with you both."

Captain Webb was troubled and uncomfortable, and the general waved me back into my seat, though his eyes caught mine for an alarmed instant before he asked, "What is it, Webb?"

"One of the men in my company, a Private Laurence Barton, has come to me about talk of an uprising among some of the men in the Massachusetts line as well as the Connecticut line, in the Nelson's Point encampment. He seems to believe there might be as many as two hundred men who will participate."

"Do you know Private Barton?" the general asked me. His relief that the issue was not related to my disguise was evident, but my stomach was in knots.

"Yes, sir. We shared the same company, the same barracks, and he was in two of the scouting parties I volunteered for."

"Private Barton claims that on one of those occasions, the men in the party talked seriously of desertion. He said you refused to participate and convinced the others to go back to the garrison."

"As I recall, Private Barton was also not in favor of desertion. He was not vocal, but when asked, it was his disinterest that swung the balance."

"What were the names of the other men in the party?" General Paterson asked, his face grim.

"I only knew Oliver Johnson, Laurence Barton, and Davis Dornan. The others in the party were from another company. I believe one's name was Jones. Another was Sharpe, and there was a man they called Chuck, but the raid was unsuccessful, I kept to myself as I tend to do, and I have not been on a raid since."

"Tell us what happened, word for word, as well as you can remember it," the general insisted.

"You should have come to me, Shurtliff," Captain Webb said, when I finished my account. "Right after that happened. You should have told me."

"I should have, sir." I didn't offer an excuse. Fear of retaliation wasn't a good reason not to do the right thing. But complaints were not insubordination. Every man, even General Paterson, had his low moments.

"If Shurtliff had come to you, what would you have done?" the general asked Captain Webb.

"I would have had them all lashed."

"And Shurtliff?"

Captain Webb frowned.

"Would you have had Shurtliff lashed?" the general pressed.

"No, sir."

"Then every man in the company would have known it was Shurtliff who reported them."

"That is true, sir," Captain Webb conceded. "But now we have a much bigger problem on our hands."

"Davis Dornan was the instigator that night?" General Paterson asked, turning to me.

"Yes, sir. He started the talk and kept feeding it. He was also the one most worried about me reporting it."

"That's what Barton said," Captain Webb said, nodding. "And he says Dornan is one of the ringleaders in this new action. He thinks they will use the celebration as a distraction or a diversion. When everyone disperses the day after, they plan to leave too."

"How do you think we should handle it, Webb?" the general asked. He was upset, though I couldn't determine whether it was disappointment in me or frustration that another crisis had been placed on his shoulders.

"I think you should pull him in, General. Tell him you know what is being planned. See if he will give us the names of the others, and throw him and any others in lockup until after this whole soiree is over. Then he can be given a hearing, and sentenced accordingly."

"Do the men in your company know that Shurtliff is now my aide-de-camp?"

"Yessir. I assume they do. There aren't any secrets in the barracks."

The general's mouth actually twitched though his eyes were a flat, unhappy blue. "Have you gone to Colonel Jackson with this?"

"Yes, sir. He told me to come to you, as other regiments will need to be informed."

The general stood up abruptly and slapped his hat on his head. "Come with me, Captain."

When I made to follow as well, he shot me a warning look. "Stay here, Shurtliff."

~

When he returned hours later, he was surly and saddle sore, his uniform sweat stained and his answers clipped and short. I hauled water in for his bath and left him to it, setting his dinner on the side table in his quarters and retiring to my room until he decided whether he wanted to scold me or tell me what had occurred.

"The water's yours, Samson," he called. "Next time, you might want to use it first."

I thanked him and barricaded myself in the space, too anxious over the day's events to enjoy the soak. I washed quickly from my head to my toes and donned my clothes again, though my wet hair dripped down my collar and made me long for a nightshirt and oblivion.

The general was already in his bed, and a single candle flickered on his bedside table. His hands were crossed behind his head, his eyes on the exposed beams above him, and his lower lip tucked between his teeth. I recognized the look. He was pensive and worried, and he was waiting for me.

"We informed every colonel and every captain here and across the way, at Nelson's Point, of the possible uprising. Every company will be assembled, every man questioned."

"And Dornan?"

"He's gone."

My heart jumped to my throat. "What?"

"He must have suspected he'd been outed. He was not at his post, and he was not in the barracks. Two dozen men spent an hour combing the garrison for him instead of working on the pavilion." He sighed.

"But he's gone. Deserted. Every regiment has been made aware of his status as well."

"I became your aide only two days after that scouting expedition. It was an answer to prayer, in so many ways. Should I have told Captain Webb?"

He sat up in his bed, his gaze earnest. "No. But you should have told me."

I sighed, releasing the breath I'd been holding all day. "Sometimes it is so hard to know what the right thing is."

"I know. And a man—or woman—who can keep a confidence and hold his tongue is always to be commended. But do not hold your tongue with me."

I cocked my head. "Are you certain you want that, General?"

He quirked his brows, rueful, but the matter was done.

"What did you do this afternoon?" he inquired. "Or dare I ask?"

"I went over the menu for the banquet with Mrs. Allen and the staff in the mess hall. Everything needed for the feast is ordered and accounted for—even the geese and the chickens and the poor hogs, who are so fat they can hardly move. The butcher has been given instructions as well. I scrubbed the floor in the dining hall and dusted the chandeliers. Agrippa held the ladder. Did you know he's afraid of heights?"

"Yes. I did." He'd begun to smile.

"I decided to wash the entrance windows as well. And dust the highest shelves in the library."

"I noticed they've begun hanging the flags on the garrison wall."

"Yes . . . I thought . . . as long as I had the ladder out," I began. "Agrippa and I started at the north end—"

"Good God, Samson," he chortled, covering his face and falling back against the pillows once more. "Go to bed, woman."

I retreated to my room with a small smile on my lips, but a moment later, my nightshirt donned and my hair tucked up, I called out to him.

"Would you like me to read to you for a while?" I asked. "I need to quiet my mind."

He sighed, but the sound was one of release and even contentment. "Yes. I would like that very much."

~

French and American flags whipped in the breeze and regiments from every brigade in the Continental army lined the hills on both sides of the river, creating the illusion of a sea of blue wildflowers amid the green. The artillery had been brought out to the edge of the plain that overlooked the water, and the pavilion was complete. General Paterson had conveyed my suggestion to Colonel Kosciuszko that old and broken armaments from the armory—there were thousands of them—be used as decoration and bound to the pillars with twine. Instead of attempting to make the garrison what it was not—namely, an elegant hall—we had emphasized what it was. A fortress, a conquest, a rugged achievement carved out of nothing. And the result was magnificent.

All was in order. All that could be done had been done, and on the morning of May 31, dignitaries began to arrive.

The Red House was bursting at the seams; generals and their wives and aides and servants filled every room. Robinson's house was the same, as was every structure in between. Large white tents were erected to accommodate the overflow, but most would only remain the one night.

"Your aide cuts a fine figure, Paterson. So slim and straight. Elegant. The whole garrison is in fine form," General Henry Knox said, clapping John on the shoulders. They were the same height, but Knox was much heavier set, though his portrait in our exhibit made him look a dumpling instead of an ox, which was far more apt. He was young, probably near the same age as General Paterson, and he was one of my heroes. His father, a shipmaster, had died, leaving his wife and ten children without support, and Henry dropped out of school to provide for his family. He clerked at a bookstore in Boston and eventually opened one himself, despite being a self-educated man. Elizabeth had told me his story in one of her letters.

Contrary to his size and his peasant's face, Henry Knox had an agile mind and unflagging spirit, and in the opening days of the war, he had managed to move fifty cannons on sleds from Fort Ticonderoga to Boston, just in time for the battle of Dorchester Heights, which ended the siege and saved the day.

His wife, Lucy, was every bit the character Henry was. She'd been disowned by her wealthy loyalist family when she married Henry—they'd met at his bookstore—and had remained by his side throughout the war, moving from camp to camp. I might have been more in awe of her than I was of even Henry.

She wore a powder-blue dress, and her hair was a mass of curls above a plump cupid's face, but Lucy Knox was more intimidating than she looked. The moment she trained her eyes on me, I thought I might be done for.

"What was your name, young man?" Mrs. Knox asked, her gaze sharp.

"Robert Shurtliff, madam." I bowed politely. "Aide-de-camp to General Paterson."

"I have heard there is an exhibit with a painting of my husband on display. I should like to see it. Will you accompany me?"

The general met my fleeting, terrified glance with a lift of one brow, but I offered the woman my arm. Henry and General Paterson trailed behind us, already in deep conversation about the artillery arranged on the plain.

"Tell me about yourself, Mr. Shurtliff," the woman insisted, and it was not a casual question or polite inquiry. I resolved to tell her only truths.

"I was in the light infantry, Colonel Jackson's regiment, and stepped up as General Paterson's aide when Lieutenant Cole fell ill."

"You are not an officer?"

"No, madam."

"Samson is the best aide I've ever had. Smart, incredibly capable, and often underestimated," General Paterson interjected, saving me.

"Samson?" Henry Knox asked, and I fought the urge to loosen my neckcloth.

"I thought your name was Shurtliff," Mrs. Knox said, tipping her head quizzically.

"It is a nickname, madam. The general says I am . . . mightier than I look."

"Ahh. I do like that." Lucy Knox smiled. "I have often been underestimated myself."

"Here we are," Henry Knox boomed, stopping in front of the portrait that bore his corpulent likeness. He turned his head this way and that and even looked down at his waistcoat-covered abdomen before moving on to the others, General Paterson at his side. They praised some of them, commenting on their own knowledge of the subject in each painting. A soldier assigned to the kitchen staff circled with a tray and glasses of wine. Henry Knox helped himself and offered one to his wife, who took the glass while still holding firmly to my arm. I had begun to perspire, so great was my need to bolt.

"Do you like the portraits, Shurtliff?" Henry Knox asked kindly. I could not imagine why he would want my opinion, but he, General Paterson, and Mrs. Knox all looked at me for a response.

"No, sir." It was not a diplomatic answer, but honest speech made me feel less like an impostor.

General Knox must not have expected my candor, for he choked on his wine and set it down on a passing tray.

"Why not?" he gasped.

"I do not understand the artist's desire to add softness where there is none," I explained.

General Paterson was listening with an indecipherable expression.

"Please do go on," Mrs. Knox said.

"An itinerate artist came to our town before the war and set up his canvases on the green for people to see. I did not care for his portraits either. Not because he wasn't skilled. He was." I paused, warming to the subject.

"All the portraits had a certain style, and every subject looked the same: big, expressive eyes, pallid skin, small lips, rounded cheeks, and soft chins. It seems to be the fashion to make every man and woman look like cherubs, but I would rather immortalize people as they are and not as fashion dictates. The faces I knew—the faces I know—are gaunt and sharp, the features varied, and the skin weathered. I find that much more appealing."

"But that is not desirable," Mrs. Knox said, though her eyes twinkled merrily.

"No?" I queried.

"No. To be plump suggests wealth and status."

"Yes. I know. But we are Americans. I would rather the artist emphasize strength and character."

She grinned, and General Knox nodded. "Well said, boy."

The general simply tipped his glass.

I bowed once, attempting to make an exit while I was well regarded.

"You must save me a dance, Mr. Shurtliff. I insist. I should like to hear more of your opinions," Lucy Knox said, releasing my arm at long last.

I bowed again, promising nothing, and excused myself, leaving the exhibit with a measured stride and a racing heart. I would make certain I did not cross paths with Mrs. Knox again.

~ 21 ~

Disposed to Suffer

Dinner was served to the regimented officers and their ladies, casks were opened, wine flowed, music played, and the world was transformed. Thirteen toasts each punctuated by the firing of thirteen cannons were followed by a military presentation from both sides of the river; the sheer number of men in uniform and formation stirred the soul.

When the ball began, General Washington escorted Mrs. Knox to the pavilion and with twenty other couples, including his wife and Henry Knox, led several dances, changing partners for each one. I lurked on the far side of the pavilion throughout the evening. General Paterson did not need or want me dogging his steps, and I was intent on avoiding Mrs. Knox, though the general was not.

He danced with a dozen ladies, some of whom I could name, others I could not. I had never been to a ball, though I knew the steps for most of the dances. I'd been the only partner for ten Thomas sons and had even taught my students a few of the reels as a recess diversion, though in that instance, I'd always taken the part of the gentleman. I was convinced I could even keep up with Mrs. Knox if I was cornered but had no desire to call attention to myself.

The general did not seem to enjoy dancing as much as the commander in chief, but he performed the steps well, and I enjoyed watching him. I took a certain pride in his appearance, though I shouldn't have. I was only his aide. But his uniform was stiff and bright, his boots gleamed, and his unpowdered hair was expertly swept back from his handsome brow.

Had I not been tracking Mrs. Knox and congratulating myself on how fine the general looked and how well the event had unfolded, I would have been more aware of the people around me. When someone said my name, I turned, distracted, and came face-to-face with a piece of my past.

"Rob?" the soldier said again, his eyes wide and his voice hushed. Not Shurtliff, not Bonny, not Robbie, but Rob.

I stared, caught and cornered, not certain who I gazed upon. I did not know this man.

"Rob. Is that you?" he pressed. I began to shake my head and back away even as my heart recognized who he was.

He was no taller and no broader, but his face was etched with hollows, and his hair had thinned. A thick scar puckered his left cheek, and he'd lost some teeth, but the grin that curled his lips was the same.

"Phineas?" I said. I could not have denied him in that moment had a pistol been pressed to my brow. It would have taken acting skills I did not possess. I was too glad to see him.

He moved to embrace me, but I brought my hand to his chest, warning him back. He placed his hand over mine instead, squeezing it with quick, bruising intensity before he let me go.

"Ma wrote me and said you'd gone. No one knows where you are. But they suspected something like this after you tried the first time. Your mother showed up, asking questions about you. Said your father saw you in New Bedford, though at the time he wasn't certain it was you."

I winced. I'd been such a fool that day. "It's been over a year. I've been a soldier for over a year."

He shook his head, amazement lighting his much-changed face.

"I've been looking for you. If I hadn't, I would have looked right past you. You make a handsome lad."

"You've been looking for me?" I didn't like the sound of that. My heart had not stopped racing and my throat constricted beneath my neckcloth.

He shrugged. "I just wondered if you'd actually gone and done it. A part of me knew you had. Knew you could. So I've been looking."

"You won't tell?" I said, sounding like I was ten years old again, caught in my magic breeches. I was aware of the people around us, the movement, the eyes, and the ears. I knew better than to act as though I had something to hide, but my fear must have been evident. He stepped back, drawing me farther into the shadows.

"I won't tell, Rob," he said gently. "I've never told on you before." He smirked, giving me another glimpse of the boy who'd always made me push myself a little harder, who saw me as a worthy adversary.

"No," I murmured. "You never did."

For a moment we simply gazed at one another, old memories colliding with a new, impossible reality. It was dizzying, and we both looked away, reorienting ourselves.

"Where have you been, Phin?"

"Here. There. Everywhere. Rhode Island lately. I'm in Colonel Putnam's regiment. We're at Nelson's Point, across the river. Had to be here for the big show. My company performed a demonstration on the field. My comrades are somewhere getting drunk, but I thought I'd have a look around."

"I'm so glad you did," I whispered.

He shifted, squared his shoulders, and shifted again, as if he didn't know what to say or how to act. It had been too long, and we were both too changed.

"They throw a party for the goddamn dauphin of France when men haven't been paid all year. What are we celebrating?" he hissed under his breath.

I wasn't certain what I should say or if he was even expecting an answer, but the general and I had worked too hard on the event for me not to feel at least a little defensive.

"Life? Friendship?" I suggested softly.

He laughed mirthlessly. "Well, that's something, I guess."

"We owe a great deal to France," I parroted.

"They owe a great deal to the men who look like me." He pointed at his scarred face. "And even the ones who look like you." He sighed and turned away.

"The general expressed the same concern for the men," I conceded, "but Washington thought it would be good for morale."

"The general?" Phin asked, frowning.

I hesitated, not certain what I should divulge. "General Paterson. I'm his . . . aide-de-camp."

The old Phin would have whooped and clapped me on the back or sulked and said he could do better. This Phineas did neither, though the hint of a smirk reappeared. "Does he know?"

"No. Of course not," I lied. If I went down, I would not take John Paterson with me.

"Aide-de-camp in a year. No rank. How did you manage that?"

"Pure dumb luck. And hard work too, I suppose."

He nodded his head slowly, like he could picture it. "You haven't stopped running. You just keep on running until you win, don't you, Deborah Samson?"

My name was just a murmur on his lips, but I flinched, afraid that someone would hear. "Yes. That is what I do. That is what we both do, Phineas Thomas."

"Not me. I'm done running," he said. "I'm tired."

My heart twisted at his sad admission. "You have served so long."

"I'm a lieutenant with the Fifth."

"A lieutenant! Well done, Lieutenant Thomas."

"It just means everyone else has quit . . . or died. So many of my brothers are gone, and all were better men than me. The best men don't make it as long, though I don't know if, at this point, I can be counted among the living."

I didn't know how to respond to that and searched for something to say, something hopeful. Something good.

"Benjamin and Jacob . . . they made it home, didn't they?" I prompted.

"They did." He nodded. "Jake married Margaret."

"And Jeremiah? What do you know of him?"

He stiffened and searched my eyes. Then he shrugged and looked away. "Last I heard, he was a sailor. Just like he wanted."

"Oh, Jerry," I murmured. "I have missed him so much."

Phin's voice was pained when he spoke again. "When I left home, Jeremiah was a little boy. I can't even picture his face."

"He still looks like Jerry. You would recognize him. You recognized me."

He nodded, and his rheumy eyes refocused on my face. "But I was looking for you."

He was so different, and his gloom made the hair rise on my neck. I didn't understand this Phin. This Phin was a worn soldier with frayed edges and missing teeth, and I didn't know what to say or do to reconnect with my old friend. Maybe we just needed more time or more privacy, but we weren't going to get it.

His discomfort was as obvious as my own, and he had begun to fidget, his eyes scanning the grounds and the soldiers of every rank enjoying the fireworks that had begun over the water. He flinched and ducked at a particularly loud clap and crackle.

I touched his arm in farewell, giving him my silent permission to slip away. After Yorktown, I wasn't fond of the sounds of cannonade myself.

"It was wonderful to see you," I said. "I hope we can talk again. I haven't been able to write to your parents . . . to anyone at all . . . and I would like to write to you."

"You always had a way with words. But don't do anything that might get you caught. I'm not worth the trouble, and you've got a good thing going, seems like."

"You've always been worth the trouble, Phineas Thomas."

He grinned, giving me a glimpse of the boy I'd known, and saluted me, though he outranked me.

"Goodbye, Rob." The words sounded so final.

"Goodbye, Phin," I choked around the growing lump in my throat.

"I'm glad you didn't wait. I'm not ever going back. I reckon neither of us will." He saluted me again and turned, tossing me one final look over his shoulder before he blended into the milling crowd.

The general was in high spirits when I found him in his office after midnight. It had all gone off without a hitch, from the demonstrations on the field to the final boom and crack of the fireworks over the river.

The Red House was finally quiet, our guests settled in their quarters, and the general was sprawled in his chair, humming a tune the band had played, his face relaxed in the candlelight. He'd removed his boots, and his uniform coat and waistcoat were tossed over another chair, his neckcloth and banner as well. The bottle of brandy I had placed on his desk was open, a half-filled glass in his hand.

I was wilted and weary, having traipsed from one end of the garrison to the other all day, attending to endless needs and countless tasks, and my bad leg throbbed in time with my sore heart. I had not recovered from my encounter with Phin. I didn't worry he would expose me, but I was badly shaken all the same.

Seeing the general's contentment soothed me greatly.

"Ah, there you are," he greeted.

"Here I am," I sighed. "Do you have everything you need, sir?"

"I realized about an hour ago that I did not make sleeping arrangements for myself . . . or for you," he said. "I was so busy making accommodations for everyone else that I forgot that the commander would be in my quarters."

"'Tis not your duty to make arrangements for me, sir."

"Samson." He rolled his eyes skyward. "Of course it is."

"I saw to it, sir."

I had placed two pallets on the thick rug and moved some of our clothing from his quarters before General Washington arrived. The pitcher was filled with water for him to wash, and I'd made sure there was a tray of ham, cheese, bread, and fruit, in case he'd worked up an appetite. I'd pilfered it from the feast, worried that he would not sit down long enough to eat. I had not sat down all day.

"Yes. I can see that you have. And I am grateful, for the brandy too." He raised his glass. "You are remarkable. An excellent aide, although this arrangement"—he tipped the glass toward our bedding—"is not . . . ideal. You should have some privacy."

"I am accustomed to the lack of privacy, sir."

"I am aware," he grumbled, but he said nothing more, and I took that as acceptance of the accommodations, intimate as they were. I sank onto the little settee by the door and removed my boots, biting back a grateful groan as I tugged them off. My hair had begun to escape its tie, and I pulled it free, shrugged off my coat, and unwrapped my neckcloth.

"You are weary," he said.

"I am." I had visited the toilet and washed at the pump, and I wanted only to lie down on my blankets and rest my aching leg.

The general rose and picked up the tray, but instead of sampling the selection, he sat down beside me and placed it between us.

"Eat," he ordered, and I complied without a word.

"No argument? You must be exhausted," he muttered, laying a piece of ham on a slice of bread and taking a huge bite. I gave him a rueful shrug, and we ate in silence, making short work of the excellent repast.

"It went well, sir. You should be very proud," I commented, revived by the meal and his company. "Everything was perfect. The colors, the sounds, the weather. All of it was wonderful."

"Yes. It was."

"And you even danced," I said, giving him a small grin.

"Mrs. Knox would not take no for an answer, and she couldn't find you," he answered, wry. "It is easy to see why she and Henry suit. They both have dogged wills."

"You did very well. And yes. Mrs. Knox is frightening. I would dearly love to be her friend someday."

The general laughed out loud.

"I've never cared much for dancing. Elizabeth adored it so I did it for her, and she was never wanting for partners. Do you know how to dance, Samson?"

"Of course I do, though I have never been to a ball like that one."

He brushed off his hands and rose to his feet. "Come then. Up you go. I've made you eat. Now I will make you dance."

"Sir? We have no music," I said, but I scrambled up, thrilled by the prospect.

My hair was loose, but I did not bother tying it back. Decorum at such a late hour, when we were alone behind a closed door, seemed unnecessary. And the general was as rumpled as I. The balmy air and the hours of dancing in the hall had turned his normal waves into curls that fell across his forehead and escaped his messy tail. Our feet were bare, and looking down at them, I saw our difference was marked. My feet were narrow and my ankles slim. His feet were large and sprinkled with hair. I curled my toes and averted my eyes, but not before he took in the contrast as well.

"You should always wear your shoes, Samson. Even your feet give you away."

"But you already know who I am."

He cleared his throat. "Yes. Well . . . give me your hand."

"I cannot think of a single melody," I said, placing my palm against his. My hands were big, but his were huge. "The Thomases only sang the hymns."

"Ah. But I know a hymn that will work." He began to hum "Praise to the Lord, the Almighty, the King of Creation" in a waltzing, three-count tempo and extended his hand with a small bow.

I hummed along with him as we found our rhythm and matched our steps.

"You are trying to lead, Samson. Stop that. You must be the woman or we will collide."

"I *am* being the woman. You went the wrong way. Is it because you are left-handed?" I argued.

"You are not doing the woman's part. You are doing the same thing as I am. I'm going to tread on you."

Footsteps moved down the hallway, and we froze, fearing we'd been too loud. A door opened and closed, and the footsteps receded.

"Let's try that again," he demanded.

We clasped hands and stepped left-two-three and right-two-three, left-two-three and right-two-three, all while whisper singing "Praise to the Lord" and chortling, trying to keep from honking too loudly.

"You are still doing the man's part," he hissed, laughing.

"I was afraid I might have to give one of the officer's wives a turn around the room, and practiced a little. Now I'm confused and can't remember which is which."

"We should really choose a different number. How about 'Yankee Doodle'? It's catchy," he suggested.

We immediately launched into a much more vigorous version of the same steps, up-tempo and energetic, singing softly, and I managed to perform the correct steps, right up to the end, where I forgot to curtsy and we bowed at the same time and knocked heads.

"Ouch! Dammit." The general laughed, clutching his brow. He rubbed my head with one palm as he massaged his own.

"Sorry, Samson. That must have hurt."

I had only meant to tease him, to pull a prank as friends do, but when I moaned and staggered, planning to fall on my bedroll like the collision had truly done me damage, his arms shot out, and he eased me down to the floor, searching my head with his fingers and patting my cheeks while supporting me against his chest.

"Deborah. Curse it all. My mother said I had the biggest, hardest head of any child she'd ever seen. She said it was a wonder that she survived my birth. If I'd have been the eldest, my sisters would never have been born. It's a great stone club, is what it is," he worried, holding me in his arms and staring down at me as though he expected my eyes to flutter into a dead faint at any moment.

I crossed my eyes and stuck out my tongue. "I'm fine, John. I was just teasing you."

He sat back on his heels, but he didn't release me. "You were just . . . teasing me," he restated flatly.

"Yes. But now I'm quite cozy. Do you think you could rock me to sleep . . . perhaps a lullaby too? You have a beautiful voice." I grinned up at him, needing desperately to laugh a little longer, but his eyes had narrowed. And for a moment I thought something had shifted, or perhaps I only mirrored what I felt.

"You called me John," he muttered.

I had. *Was he angry?* "Yes. I'm sorry, sir. I forgot myself for a moment."

Neither of us were smiling anymore. But he didn't let me go.

"It is late," he said.

"It is."

He released me abruptly and stood. He retreated to the pitcher and poured himself a glass of water before refilling the cup and bringing it to me.

I took a few sips and handed it back. I knew better than to fill my bladder when it meant traipsing outside in the dark when the entire garrison—the entire hillside—bristled with visitors.

He set the cup down, blew out the candles, and dropped onto his pallet. I did the same, too warm to burrow into the blankets and too aware of the man beside me to contemplate sleep.

I considered telling him that I'd seen Phineas and immediately dismissed the thought. The general would stew and fret and talk of sending me home again. And I did not want to talk about Phineas. Not yet. I didn't want to even think about him. But Phineas had asked a question I didn't have an answer for.

"Sir?" I whispered.

"Yes?"

"Why did you ask me to be your aide? Aren't aides usually chosen from the officers?"

He was quiet for a moment, and I wondered if I would get the truth or any answer at all.

"You impressed me. And intrigued me."

It was my turn to lie in silence, hoping he would continue.

"I realize now . . . you have always intrigued me. Even as a voice on a page, you were like no one else I had ever encountered. Elizabeth thought you were a marvel. She would read bits of your letters out loud and shake her head. 'How am I to respond to that, John?' she would say."

"I never wrote of girlish things," I said.

"No. You didn't." There was laughter in his voice.

"I was supposed to be practicing the art of letter writing and proper conversation. But I wanted knowledge more, and when I discovered Elizabeth was willing to speak of serious things and deep thoughts, I was overjoyed."

"She said she felt like she was being interrogated by a seasoned solicitor and turned them over to me. That's how . . . that's how I got involved. I didn't mind. Writing to you about the lead-up to war actually helped me solidify and clarify my own beliefs."

"Your letters were my favorite. I think . . . if I had not been born a girl, a servant girl, I would have liked to study law. Were there women in your classes at Yale?"

"No. But I've no doubt you would hold your own."

"Are women allowed at any of the colleges?"

"No. They aren't."

"Perhaps after the war . . . if I remain Robert Shurtliff, I could go to school." My heart started to pound. I had not even dared dream beyond the days I was now living. But maybe I could simply live as a man indefinitely. Or at least until I'd accomplished all I wanted to do that required a pair of pants and bound-up breasts.

"You would continue this charade?" he asked softly. "Is there nothing about being a woman that appeals to you?"

"Many things," I murmured, but I did not list them. I yearned to feel the swish of a skirt around my legs and the weight of my hair as I brushed it. And there were many things that interested me now that had not compelled me before I met him.

The mere thought made my breasts ache and my belly thrum, but I ignored that impossible longing, distracting myself with conversation.

"Nathaniel told me once that I should stop trying to be something that I am not. But that's not what I'm doing."

"No?" he snorted.

"No. I'm trying to be something . . . that I am." He let the statement settle, uncontested, so I continued. "Elizabeth told me I would someday be a woman who inspired much admiration. She was very kind to me."

"She was kind to everyone," he said.

"Hmm."

"What? What is *hmm*?"

"That does not comfort me. If she was kind to everyone, it is not nearly so special that she was kind to me."

"Ahh," he murmured. "Well, I know of no one else she wrote to the way she wrote to you," he said. "You were dear to her."

Emotion stung my nose. *What a day it has been.*

"She answered my letters for almost a decade. And you did too," I added. "Though . . . you were very different in your correspondence."

He was and he wasn't, but I had discovered that I liked to tease him. It was a suitable outlet for my affection and a good distraction from the ache in my chest.

"I hope so. I was not writing to a soldier. I was writing to a precocious young girl."

"You were kind to me too."

"Of course I was."

"But I expected you to look like Reverend Conant. Or Deacon Thomas. Or even . . . George Washington."

He snorted.

"Maybe Benjamin Franklin?"

He began to laugh.

"Have you met Mr. Franklin?" I asked.

"I have indeed. He is quite popular with the ladies."

"It is his intellect."

"Oh yes?"

"A smart man is always attractive. What a life he has lived!"

"Indeed." The general yawned, and I yawned in response.

"Good night, Samson. You made me proud today."

My emotion welled again, and this time it ran over, trickling down my cheeks. I turned onto my side, away from him, so he wouldn't see.

"Good night, John," I whispered. It was only as I drifted into sleep that I realized I'd done it again. I'd called him John.

~ 22 ~

A Long Train of Abuses

For a lazy two weeks, the garrison at West Point was self-satisfied and sleepy, caught in the afterglow of a successful operation. Flags were taken down, artillery was stored, and normal schedules were slowly resumed. It wasn't too hot. It wasn't cold. It was peaceful and quiet and almost easy, and it didn't last. Heat and boredom are almost as miserable as marching in the snow, and idle hands and minds are more prone to discontent.

Temperatures soared the first week in July, and a hundred men from General Paterson's brigade decided it was time to have a party of their own. Fed up with the inactivity and the months without pay, they'd abandoned their posts in the dead of the night and congregated in White Plains, sending word to the general that they would return to work when they'd been given what they were promised.

The Point was in chaos, and General Paterson sent Agrippa racing north to New Windsor to deliver a message to the commander in chief, while he assembled a force from various encampments up and down the North River to go after them and defuse the situation.

General Washington wanted to avoid an attack or provocation, but the sooner it was tamped out, the better, and he gave General Paterson full authority to handle the situation as he saw fit. By nightfall of the same day, all light infantrymen in the garrison had been assembled, a plan was in place, and we headed out.

We had just crossed the river and debarked at the Peekskill encampment when the sky rumbled and the winds kicked up. The general had intended to gather another 250 men from lower encampments, doubling our numbers, with the intention of intimidating the insurgents into immediate surrender. Instead, he instructed the men he'd already assembled to lighten their packs and button their capes, and be ready to move out immediately.

"We're going now. No wagons. No horses. No drums. No warning. They won't think we're coming. Not on a night like this. And maybe we can end it without anyone getting hurt."

He wanted me to follow behind with Agrippa and another slower detachment. They would bring wagons, horses, and supplies, and I could ride Common Sense.

"Your leg still troubles you. You cover it well, but it is not healed."

I frowned at him, affronted. "Do you not know me at all?"

"I know you too well," he muttered.

"I will keep up, sir. I am your aide. I must go."

He shook his head and relented, though I knew he wanted to argue. Colonel Sproat had arrived at the encampment an hour before us, and within minutes, he'd culled from his regiment twenty-five men who were accustomed to such rigors and who wouldn't balk at the unpleasant mission ahead. No one liked mutinies.

We moved fast and hard for twenty miles, rain in our faces and the earth sucking at our feet. My boots were so heavy at one point, I considered abandoning them, but feared falling behind when I stopped to pull them off. Plus, the general had warned me to keep my feet covered, and none of the other men were removing theirs.

I kept up, but not without considerable suffering. The general stayed at my side, but we did not converse—the storm made that impossible—and he did not offer me aid, though I wouldn't have accepted it if he had.

Perhaps it was the cover of the torrential rains and the howling winds, or perhaps the mutineers didn't expect for the general to move on them so quickly, but while they huddled in tents that didn't keep them dry, nursing the flames of their discontent, we started to form a perimeter around the insurgent camp.

We were covered in mud and wet to our skins when we made our presence known, but by the time the sun rose and the storm had broken, the mutineers were completely surrounded.

Colonel Sproat and his twenty-five rousted the inhabitants of each tent with bayonets drawn while the rest of us maintained a tight circle around the encampment. No one tried to run or fight, but no one begged for mercy either.

General Paterson ordered them to line up in rows of ten and asked those responsible to step forward.

"Who leads this rebellion?" General Paterson asked, projecting his voice so all could hear.

No one moved or spoke, knowing that the ringleaders would most likely be executed before the day was done.

The general was grim, his face mud-spattered, and his hair in rivulets beneath his sodden hat. When I'd shaved his face the day before, he'd sent for Reverend Hitchcock, the chaplain attached to his brigade, and asked the reverend to pray with him.

"Will you include the mutineers?" Paterson had said. "Ask that their hearts will be softened and no blood spilled. And ask God to help me know what is just."

Justice and mercy were a delicate balance, one he rode well, but he was troubled.

Reverend Hitchcock was not here now, and the mutineers were hard-eyed and unrepentant, and nearly as wet and miserable looking as the rest of us. No hearts had been softened. None of them wore shoes or hats. Most wore breeches and nothing else. It had stormed, but it was still July, and they'd likely shrugged them off before retiring.

It was then that I saw Phineas. He wore a shirt, unlike many of the others, and his dark hair lay about his shoulders and obscured his scarred face. If he'd noticed me, drenched and dirty as I was, I did not know. His eyes were on the general, his chin high, his eyes sullen.

"All of you have suffered for a cause that has lost its shine," General Paterson said, raising his voice to be heard. He pointed at the armed soldiers encircling the mutineers' camp. "All of them have suffered too. And they suffer now, as they are forced to contend with you, fellow soldiers, brothers, patriots. And that is what is hardest for me to forgive. They shouldn't have to fight you too. This is not the way. We've come too far. And if I do not punish those responsible, this will happen again. And men like them—" He pointed at the soldiers, their muskets drawn and their eyes shadowed, who'd marched through the wet darkness to mete out a punishment they wanted no part of. "Men like them will suffer."

"Then they should join us!" someone yelled from the middle of the formation.

"Come forward, soldier," the general demanded. The men shifted, looking at each other, but the dissenter did not reveal himself.

"I would ask you, as soldiers and men who have been charged to uphold and defend, to do what you agreed to do," the general entreated.

"You have not done what you agreed to do," another man spoke up. "None of you."

The general nodded, his mouth set, and he asked once more, "Who is responsible for this uprising?"

Every head bowed and every man was still. Then, from the back of the line, Phineas stepped forward and said, "I am responsible."

My bad leg buckled and the bile in my stomach became ice. Phineas looked at me then and shook his head, the movement almost imperceptible, but the general saw it.

"What is your name, soldier?"

"Lieutenant Phineas Thomas. Colonel Putnam's regiment. General Paterson's brigade." His mouth twisted in mockery, and a few men snickered as he added, "We are all in your brigade, General."

General Paterson's brow lowered and then cleared as the name registered. "Phineas Thomas," he murmured, but Phineas heard him.

"Yes, sir."

"And you are responsible?"

"I am."

"And who else?" the general asked again. "Does Lieutenant Thomas speak for all ninety-eight of you?"

More shuffling.

"And will you let Lieutenant Thomas take your punishment as well?"

No one else stepped forward.

"General Paterson," I blurted. "May I speak on behalf of Lieutenant Thomas?"

My heart was pounding so loud, I could only hear my voice inside my head, but the men had all turned to look at me, so I knew they had heard. Phineas was shaking his head and General Paterson was perfectly still.

"Lieutenant Thomas has served since 1775. He is one of ten brothers, all of whom enlisted. Four of them are dead. No family has given more than his. I would ask that you show him mercy," I pleaded.

Phineas shook his head, vehement. "No. I don't want mercy. I want justice."

"I can't give you justice," the general said. "I can't give any of you justice."

"Then why are you here? Why are any of us here?" Phineas shouted.

The mutineers at his back rumbled in agreement.

"Why indeed?" the general shot back. "It is something I have asked myself every single day since this conflict began. Why am I here? What is it all for? That is something each man must answer for himself."

The men looked at each other and back at Phineas, and the general spoke directly to him.

"There is nothing I can do to repay you, Lieutenant. Nothing anyone can do to compensate you for what you've given and what you've lost. There is no justice for that. It doesn't exist. But I will give you my back and let you take your vengeance." He took off his coat and threw it down and proceeded to unbutton his waistcoat and shrug off his shirt, until he stood, naked but for his boots and his breeches.

"Hand Lieutenant Thomas the whip," the general instructed Colonel Sproat.

The silence was absolute, but my horror was reflected on the face of every soldier.

"Sir?" I protested, but the general didn't acknowledge me at all, and I bore down on the howl that crouched behind my teeth.

"Give Lieutenant Thomas the whip!" the general repeated.

Colonel Sproat nodded to one of his men. A moment later, a lash was brought forward.

"It is not you who has wronged me, General Paterson," Phineas protested, stunned, but he accepted the whip.

"If not me, who? I lead your brigade. I make sure you are paid. And fed. And heard. And you have not been paid. Or fed. Or heard. None of you have. You have not been adequately thanked. And you are weary."

Phineas nodded, his chin wobbling and his eyes bright. "Yes, sir. I'm tired."

"So take your vengeance, Lieutenant. You took responsibility, and I will take responsibility too."

General Paterson turned and offered the broad expanse of his naked flesh to the ninety-eight men who still stood in their lines and to Phineas, who was frozen in place.

Terror sat sour and unsettled in my belly, and I moved closer to the general, my musket loaded and raised, afraid that his vulnerable position would be seen as an opportunity to scatter or attack. Colonel Sproat seemed to have the same idea, and we stood in the ready position on his left and right.

"Stand back, Shurtliff," the general demanded, raising his gaze to mine. "Sproat, you too."

Phineas tested the weight of the lash and gave it a practice snap. Any boy raised on a farm had learned to use a whip.

"How guilty are you, General?" he asked softly. "How many men have you let down?"

"At least ninety-eight," the general said.

"You have no post to cling to," Phineas hedged. "How do I know you will not run?"

"Proceed, Lieutenant," the general ordered.

Phineas drew back, his teeth bared, and let the whip crack against the general's back.

"One!" he yelled.

I closed my eyes. He drew back again. "Two!"

By the time he reached ten, I had begun to shake and my face was wet with sweat and tears, but the general had not stopped him, and Phineas seemed completely unaware of anything but the power in his hand and the pleasure of the motion.

"That's enough, Lieutenant Thomas," Colonel Sproat roared, raising his musket. Phineas ignored him and struck again. From where I stood, I could not see the damage being done on the general's back, but the mutineers, to a man, stood with bowed heads, taking no delight in the display. The soldiers who guarded them were as distressed as I.

"Enough, Thomas," Sproat repeated. "Put the whip down."

"He still has eighty-seven lashes to go," Phineas said. "I want justice for these men too."

"I'll not have an innocent man taking my stripes," a man burst out. He marched forward and placed himself in front of the general. "I'll take my own."

Phineas's chin sank to his chest and his shoulders fell, as though he'd suddenly become aware of himself again.

"Has justice been served, Lieutenant Thomas?" the general asked.

"Yessir," Phin answered, weary.

The general straightened and turned toward the men again. His back was sliced and bloodied, but he didn't appear weakened or faint.

To the man who had stepped forward, he asked, "Are you responsible for this uprising, soldier?"

"I am responsible for my own part in it, General Paterson, and I will take responsibility for the five men in my company who are here because of my example. I have not been paid for months. The paper money I have received is an insult . . . it's an insult to all of us. It's only good to wipe my arse, and I have a wife and five daughters at home who have been too long without me. My three years are up, but my colonel says I signed till the end of the war."

"What's your name, soldier?"

"Captain Christian Marsh, General, sir."

"What justice can I give you today, Captain Marsh?"

"I'll take ten lashes for my men. No, eleven. Same as you. And I'll go back to my post and I'll stay to the end of this godforsaken conflict. I'll stay to the end if you do, sir."

"Agreed."

Captain Marsh stripped to the waist, and with a set jaw and clasped hands, took eleven lashes from Phineas Thomas with the same stoicism the general had exhibited. Other officers among the mutineers stepped forward and negotiated their own terms, much the same as his: eleven lashes, immediate return to duty, and a promise to stay as long as the general remained as well.

Phineas was soaked in sweat and weaving on his feet, but he did not want to relinquish the whip. It wasn't until several more men stepped forward, pledging their recommitment and extracting a pledge from the general in return, that Phineas finally surrendered the lash to Colonel Sproat. He was then given water and returned to the line.

Each man signed his name or his mark to paper, and General Paterson put his name beside each one. By midafternoon, every mutineer had been seen, heard, and punished according to his own judgment. All had agreed to return to duty, reassured by the promise that General Paterson would continue to fight for them.

Every man who had taken part in the uprising would need to be escorted back to his post and remanded to the custody of his commanding officer, and until they were, they would be guarded like mutineers. No weapons were returned, the men were divided up according to their companies and encampments, and assignments were given to their guards.

The heat and the humidity, especially for those with open wounds on their backs, was unbearable, and the weariness of the soldiers who had slogged through twenty miles of rain and mud the night before was severe. The detachment with wagons, horses, and supplies had not yet arrived, but the consensus was to head back toward Peekskill Hollow, with the hope that we would intercept them before too long and rest once we had reinforcements.

I'd been watching Phineas throughout the afternoon, and had often caught him watching me too. The mutineers had been allowed to gather their possessions and take down their tents, and most were sitting quietly, waiting to move out. He'd pulled down his tent, but the effort seemed to drain him, and I'd refilled his canteen and brought it to where he sat, his elbows to his knees. He asked for my rum ration, but I'd used it to wash the general's wounds, and told him as much.

"I could tell everyone who you are, Rob," he murmured, his dark gaze speculative. "I could tell the general. But I think he knows. He doesn't look at you the way a man looks at another man. And when you spoke up for me . . . he didn't like that."

"Why would you do that, Phin?" I asked, my voice soft, my eyes hard.

"To save you."

"For what?"

He frowned. "Don't you mean *from* what?"

"I'm here, Phin. If I wanted to be saved from it, I never would have come. And if you tell on me . . . where would I go?"

"Maybe I don't want to be saved either," he said, and stared at me, baleful.

His possessions were strewn beside him, his blanket in a heap, his feet bare. He drew a long hunting knife from his rucksack and approached the general, leaving everything else behind.

"Phin? Leave the knife in your pack," I commanded, but he ignored me.

"I didn't sign your paper or accept your pledge, General Paterson," Phin shouted.

General Paterson had put his shirt back on, but the straps from his gear would rub against his wounds, and I'd given his rucksack and cartridge box to another soldier to carry, as well as his musket and the belt he strapped around his waist. He was unarmed and distracted, and he wasn't paying attention to Phineas.

"I said I didn't want mercy!" Phineas shouted, and the general finally gave him his attention. Phineas had begun to breathe hard, and he wasn't blinking. Colonel Sproat cocked his musket and took a small step back. I did the same.

Phineas looked from me to Colonel Sproat as if testing our readiness, and then he slowly withdrew his knife from its sheath with a steady hand and a set expression.

"You have served long enough, Lieutenant Thomas," General Paterson said, voice measured. "Go home. Or continue. I will give you a full and honorable discharge. It is your decision."

"I was not lashed like the others."

"No. I took your lashes for you."

"Lieutenant Thomas," Colonel Sproat warned. "Put the knife down."

"I don't think I will, Ebenezer," Phin said. "You won't tell my mother about this . . . will you? You'll tell her I was a hero. You'll tell her I died bravely. Like my brothers."

"Phineas Thomas, you put that down," I demanded, sounding like the sister I'd always been.

"I didn't want to tell you, Rob, but Jerry's gone too. He's gone too. You might be the only one of us left."

He darted forward, teeth bared, knife high, eyes on the general, and I screamed in denial and rage. But I pulled the trigger too. The force sent him hurtling, his knife still clutched in his hand, his dirty feet briefly leaving the ground, and I was chasing him again, like I'd done all those years before, trying to catch up, trying to catch him before he fell. But he won.

I collapsed at his side, hoping I'd simply grazed him, hoping somehow I'd missed him altogether. But I hadn't. And neither had Ebenezer Sproat.

"I will never forgive you for this, Phineas Thomas," I cried, pressing my hands to the holes in his chest.

"I don't want to be saved, Rob," he wheezed. The blood bubbled up on his lips, and he smiled at me like old Phineas. "It doesn't even hurt. Just feels like flying. Didn't you use to . . . dream about . . . flying?"

I grabbed his hand, but he was fading, and it was already growing cold.

"I'm not running anymore, Rob. You win."

The general was barking orders for Dr. Thatcher, who had just arrived with the second detachment. A moment later Colonel Sproat knelt beside me with bandages and rum, but it was too late. Phineas died with his eyes open and a smirk on his lips, like he knew exactly what he'd done and what he wanted.

Sproat closed his eyes with a gentle touch. "You didn't kill him. Neither did I. He killed himself. You know that, don't you, Deborah Samson?"

I did not even react. I was too broken. Too stunned. But Sproat continued softly, even kindly.

"It took me a while to place you. I probably never would have figured it out if you hadn't spoken up for Phineas today. He called you Rob, and I remembered the skinny servant girl who lived with the Thomases. I remembered the story my father wrote me about Deborah Samson trying to enlist and getting hauled out of his tavern by the church deacons to sleep off a drunk."

He chuckled like we hadn't just killed a boy we'd both known since childhood. Ebenezer Sproat had been out here too long. Or maybe he'd just seen it all. He wasn't even surprised by me.

"Did that happen?" he pressed softly.

I didn't admit it or deny it. I just stared at Phin's dead face and his dirty bare feet and waited for Sproat's verdict, completely numb to it all.

"Way I see it, you're a fine soldier. A damn good soldier. And any soldier who wants to be here is one I want to keep. God knows, we got enough of 'em who don't. I won't say anything to anyone. Even my pa, though he'd dearly love to hear all about it." He patted my shoulder. "Maybe someday, huh?"

"Are you awake, Deborah?" the general asked when he finally came to bed. Dr. Thatcher had seen to his back, but he'd spent the evening among the mutineers, and from the quiet in the encampment, it seemed he was the last to retire.

His use of my name was my undoing, a reminder of my life before, of the people I had loved and who had loved me, though it had never been enough. I had promised myself I would not cry, but I was unraveling.

I swallowed and steadied myself to answer. "Yes, sir."

I'd washed Phin's blood from my hands and changed my shirt. Then I'd pitched the general's tent and prepared us a small meal, and when there was nothing more to do, I crawled under my blanket and wished for oblivion. But it had not come.

The general didn't lie down on the bedroll I'd put out for him, and his broad back was rounded in defeat. He sat, his elbows to his knees, his head bowed, a dark shadow limned by the pale wall of the tent.

He needed reassurance. He needed comfort. He needed me to talk to him, the way I'd done riding behind him on Lenox, trying to keep him from falling off. But I was too heartsore, and I could do nothing but grit my teeth in the stifling silence and crumble as quietly as I was able.

"He wanted to die," he whispered, and though I wasn't certain he was even talking to me, I choked out an answer.

"Yes, sir. I know."

"I gave him mercy, but he wanted relief."

"Yes, sir." It was all I could say, but he sounded so pained, like a man being stretched on the rack, that I sat up and moved to the bags I'd placed along the wall. I took out a tin cup, filled it halfway with grog, and crouched in front of him.

"Drink it, sir. It will make you feel better."

"I am not the one crying," he said, raising hollow eyes to mine.

"Perhaps you should be."

"Will it help?"

"It will ease your sorrow."

He handed the cup back to me, untouched. "If I start . . . I will not stop."

"Drinking, sir? Or crying?"

He stared up at me, battle worn, but I urged the cup on him again. "I will not let you have too much."

He raised one brow, as if to say, *You couldn't stop me*. But he took the cup and drank down the contents, shuddering at the taste and the burn, but he insisted I have the last swallow. I took it, simply to avoid the argument.

"I have put your canteen there beside your roll, should you need it. It is full, and the water is sweet and cold." I rose and slipped the tin cup back into the pack.

"Thank you."

I returned to my bedroll and lay down upon it, but I faced him.

"He recognized you. He called you Rob."

"Yes. He knew I was . . . here. He saw me the night of the dauphin's celebration."

"And you saw him too."

"Yes. I spoke to him."

"And you did not tell me."

My tears became a torrent, and I could not answer. He waited, head bowed as if I'd betrayed him, and that made my anguish all the worse.

"It hurt too much," I said, gritting my teeth against the waves that just kept rising.

"Why?"

"He w-was so changed."

"We are all changed. And none for the better." His voice was plaintive. "Is it so hard to trust me, Samson?"

"It is not trust, sir. It is fear."

"Fear of what? I know who you are."

"Fear of this," I choked, and touched my cheeks. "Fear of breaking. Of weeping. Of grieving. There is a lifetime of grief inside me. It is in my chest and in my belly. It is in my head and in my arms. My legs ache with it. My feet too. It is beneath my skin and in my blood, and I can't . . . hold . . . anymore."

"Oh, Samson," he whispered.

He moved to my side and stroked my hair and dried my cheeks, though he was the one who was wounded. I tried once to rise, and he pressed me back down and brought me the canteen I'd filled for him.

I drank and cried, and drank again, but he did not leave me, and when the shuddering stopped and my chest was emptied, he moved his pallet close to mine and stretched out on his side, his chest to my back, and pulled me close, cocooning me with his body.

"Are you in much pain, sir?" I whispered, so weary I could not lift my head.

"Shh. I'm fine. Sleep," he murmured. I thought he pressed a kiss to my crown, but maybe it was just his breath, stirring my hair.

"I am afraid to sleep. Afraid to dream. When I close my eyes, I keep seeing him fall."

"Tell me about young Phineas," he said.

I did, tiptoeing through the early years, my voice slurred and my stories brief, but the fear retreated in the face of sweet reminiscence.

"Phineas Thomas, the boy who was bested by the magic breeches," John said. "That is the boy you must remember."

"He said death felt like flying," I murmured, and let myself drift toward sleep. "He said Jerry was gone too. I believe him. I've felt it for a while, since Tarrytown, but didn't want to admit it."

"Oh, Samson," John whispered again, knowing how I felt about the youngest of the Thomas brood, my other half, my best mate, but I was beyond words. I wanted only to rest in the comfort of his arms.

I dreamed of roads and wildflowers and racing through the trees, and Phineas soared above them, but I did not see Jeremiah. He'd already said his goodbye.

~

When I rose the next morning, I was emptied out, but instead of feeling gutted, I felt cleansed, even whole. Perhaps my grief had begun to distort me into someone else, and I'd returned to original form. I felt numb.

Poor General Paterson did not.

He was not beside me when I woke, and I doubt he'd slept much at all. Every movement reopened the welts, and the salve Dr. Thatcher applied wasn't as good as the one Morris had given me. Still, I carefully daubed it on the crisscrossed wounds and bandaged them tightly, and we began the long walk back to the Peekskill encampment, even though our horses had arrived with the wagons and the second detachment.

"It feels better to walk than to ride," he said, and I insisted on walking beside him. We trudged along, letting the others pull ahead.

"You should ride, Samson. Your walking doesn't make me feel any better."

"I am walking with you, sir. All the way."

"You are so headstrong," he complained. "It's tiresome."

"Deacon Thomas said the same thing. But I am not headstrong. I am strong-minded."

He chuckled, which I had intended. "What is the difference, pray tell?" he asked.

"One is a virtue. One is not."

"Ahh. So that's how it works. We take our faults and reframe them. How clever."

"It is a very important distinction. You, sir, are not harsh, but you are austere. You are adamant about rules. You have to be. Your men suffer when you aren't."

"How so?"

"Rationing saves lives in winter. So does cleanliness and thrift and guards that aren't drunk." I swallowed. "And delivering painful justice because mercy would encourage wolves."

"I don't know that my experiment in mercy went so well yesterday."

We were quiet then, caught in the tangle of mercy and justice and which was which.

"They always send you, don't they?" I asked. "When there's a rebellion or a traitor or a conflict that must be resolved. They send you."

"It is, oddly, the story of my life. Faithful and dutiful above all else. Old Reliable. Do you know that is what my mates called me at Yale? I was always the one who got everyone else out of scrapes. I was the staid one. The stern one. When they were planning something, they wouldn't tell me about it, because they knew I'd try to talk sense into them. But I was always the one they came to when it all fell apart."

"Elizabeth said you were likely to get pulled into the fray wherever you went, even though you wanted to avoid it. She said, 'He has wide shoulders, a level head, and a patriotic heart.' Like Solomon, but with no desire for a crown. I think she is right."

"She gave me too much credit. You do as well."

"No." I shook my head. "No. You are the best man I've ever known, John Paterson."

"And you are the most remarkable woman."

~ 23 ~

Provide New Guards

Back in March, an officer named Captain Huddy of New Jersey had been assigned to guard a blockhouse in Monmouth that came under attack by a regiment of loyalists. Captain Huddy, after expending all his ammunition, was taken hostage and brought into New York. A few weeks later, and without any trial or warning, he was brought to the New Jersey shore, late at night, and hanged from a tree.

A letter pinned to Captain Huddy's chest read, "*We, the loyalists, having with grief long beheld the cruel murders of our brethren, therefore determine not to suffer without taking vengeance for these numerous cruelties. We have made use of Captain Huddy as the first object to present to your view; and further determine to hang man for man while there is a loyalist existing. Up goes Huddy for Phillip White.*"

Further investigation had revealed that Phillip White, a loyalist soldier, had been taken prisoner in a skirmish after Captain Huddy was already in confinement. Phillip White had also, after surrendering, taken a musket and shot the son of a colonel before escaping. He was recovered and once again brought into custody only to escape once more. One of his pursuers, after repeated warnings to him to stop, struck him across the head with a broadsword, which killed him instantly.

The outcry from the inhabitants of New Jersey to Congress as well as General Washington himself over Huddy's death was so strident, General Washington called on all the general officers and those commanding brigades or regiments to assemble and deliberate on what should be done.

The previous vote had taken place in June. Now it was September, and the commander in chief had assembled his officers back at Robinson's house, this time to discuss the sorry circumstances they now found themselves in.

I took the opportunity to look in on Morris and Maggie, who in spite of our shared reticence and reserve, had become friends of mine. I had little experience with friendship, and the two of them seemed to have even less, but an unspoken understanding had emerged, one I did not overanalyze or rely on. I simply enjoyed it and asked after their well-being whenever I was able.

General Paterson had been in meetings all morning, but he'd stomped from the house during a recess, desperate for some air and exercise. I'd seen him exit and had rushed to his side.

"Should I get the horses, sir?"

"No. General Washington has asked me to remain. There is another matter I am to attend to, but he is conferring with General von Steuben at the moment. I am going for a walk."

"Should I come with you?"

"If you wish." The general's voice was terse and his stride long, but I loped after him.

"Your limp has worsened since the march to White Plains," he muttered. "You should have listened to me. Both times."

The day Phineas died our relationship changed, though I hadn't allowed myself to draw conclusions from the intimacy we'd shared. We didn't speak of it, and I was surprised he brought it up now.

"I will get some more salve from Maggie. It should help with the ache."

He stopped abruptly. "You did not tell me you were hurting."

"It isn't constant. I can keep up, General."

"Yes. But you would not win any races. Even in your magic breeches."

I pushed my hat back so I could better see his eyes. "You know the fable of the tortoise and the hare, don't you, sir?"

"Yes, Samson. I do."

"Who wins the race?"

"The tortoise."

"That's right. I have lost some speed, but I have not lost my stamina."

His gaze on my face softened, and he let me set the pace as we began to climb the hill behind the house. As we ascended, he relayed what had transpired in the strained meeting.

"Last June, without any discussion, we all put our opinions on the Huddy matter in writing and gave them to General Washington. He did not want us swayed from our own feelings by the sentiments of others. Unfortunately, the consensus was to retaliate in kind and hang a British prisoner of the same rank."

I gasped. I knew the fate of poor Huddy, but I'd known nothing of the vote.

"Is that what you wanted?" I asked, trying to keep any judgment from my question.

"No. I was, as usual, the voice of dissent. Captain Huddy was an innocent man. To hang another innocent man in retaliation for his death seemed absurd, not to mention immoral. I said as much."

I should have known. "What did you suggest?"

"I said we should punish the perpetrators if we discovered who actually carried out the hanging of Captain Huddy. Until then"—he shrugged—"I recommended we do nothing. No one liked that idea. I suggested we put all our efforts and attention into ending this damnable conflict instead of creating new atrocities."

"That was June. What's happening now?"

"Now, General Washington is embroiled in a mess."

"How so?"

"All of the imprisoned British officers in Lancaster of the same rank as Captain Huddy were brought into a room and the circumstances explained. They drew lots." The general paused, pained. "A twenty-year-old captain by the name of Asgill is to be the unfortunate victim. He's a member of the British guard from a noble family." He exhaled and shook his head. "General Washington is beside himself. It is the execution of John André all over again."

Major John André had been the British liaison between Benedict Arnold and Sir Henry Clinton, the British commander in New York, when Arnold plotted the treasonous surrender of West Point in October of 1780. Arnold had failed but escaped, and John André had been captured and subsequently hanged. One man was a traitor, one man a patriot, though he fought for an opposing side. That the patriot was hanged and the traitor remained free in the bosom of the British Army continued to be a painful thorn in the American conscience.

"But I said my piece." The general sighed. "Then and now. General Washington does not need an 'I told you so' from me."

The general sat down on a boulder that appeared to barely cling to the side of the hill, though it had likely been thus for eons. It was big enough that I could sit beside him, my hands in my lap, my eyes on the view laid out below us.

"It is too hot for such exertions," he said, but he didn't appear winded at all, and the tension around his pale eyes and mouth had lessened, making the effort well worth it, in my opinion. His back had healed quickly, but the pressures on him had not ceased.

"What do you suppose Beverley Robinson was thinking when he built his house here?" I marveled. "It is not the most hospitable spot, though there's something to be said for the view."

We could easily see the back of Robinson's house and the outbuildings and orchards now heavy with fruit. I'd spent an hour there, filling a bushel. I took a pear from my pocket and handed it to the general, who took an enormous bite. We traded it back and forth, chatting as we shared.

"Robinson's wife, Susanna, brought the land into the marriage. Her name was Philipse before she married Beverley. She and her sister, Mary, were the heiresses to thousands of acres up here."

"An heiress. How lovely for her," I murmured, licking my lips.

"It's rumored that Washington was in love with Mary, the sister, at one point. She married someone else instead."

"And now Washington is here, and the land is his."

"Knowing him, I've no doubt he would have preferred to have the woman. And it is hardly his." The general tossed the core of the pear as far as he could, watching it soar and then bounce, as if returning back to the orchard from whence it came.

"Well it's certainly no longer hers," I said dryly, uncapping my canteen so we could wash the juice from our fingers and faces.

The general wetted his thumb and swiped at the corner of my mouth, not waiting for the canteen. I licked at it, and he instantly withdrew his hand and averted his eyes.

"No. But it ceased to be hers the moment she married," he said, rising.

I took a deep breath, ready to rail against that infuriating injustice, sticky chin and all, when John asked, "What do you think that's about?"

He pointed toward Billy Lee, Washington's African valet, who was rarely far from the commander's side, even in battle. Lee was on horseback, emerging from the trees at the edge of the huge expanse of green that had once been a deer park, though large game had been greatly reduced by the hungry army quartered nearby. But he had trapped something.

He held a pistol and his reins in one hand and a rope in the other. The rope was looped around the midsection of a man who was trailing unhappily behind him, his face slick with sweat, his blue uniform coat unbuttoned over a bare chest, his breeches bloodied.

"That's Davis Dornan," I breathed.

The general began descending the rise we had just climbed, half running, half sliding on his haunches to get to the bottom, and I mostly kept up, my musket slapping against my back as I bounced my way down.

An alert had gone up, and a moment later, two dozen regimented officers and their aides exited the house, General Washington among them.

"This man tried to kill me, General," Lee said simply, his eyes on Washington. He leaned down and released Dornan from his bind. The man's eyes darted left and right, as if considering a run for it. "He put a musket ball through my hat," Lee added, brandishing the injured article.

"It was an accident," Dornan wailed. "You startled me."

Lee continued without inflection. "Looks like he's been living in an abandoned caretaker's cottage at the edge of the property around the back of Sugarloaf. I was just out for a little ride. It's taken me an hour to walk him back here."

"He shot me!" Dornan moaned, clutching at his buttocks. He was walking just fine, so it must have only grazed him, but the left side of his breeches was soaked through in a merry red bloom.

"Had to," Lee said, unapologetic.

"Are you Davis Dornan?" General Paterson asked.

The man frowned and looked from the general to me and then down at his worn shoes. Three of his stockingless toes peeked out above the soles.

"Private Dornan deserted last May," General Paterson explained to the others. "He's in Captain Webb's company, Colonel Jackson's regiment. He was thought to be one of the ringleaders of the planned mutiny following the dauphin's celebration."

"I wasn't planning anything, General Paterson, sir." Dornan shook his head, adamant. "I ran because I was afraid of getting blamed for it. I knew Shurtliff was talking."

He swung his attention to me, and his fear immediately turned to derision.

"You're a liar, Shurtliff. I know it was you who told. Can't trust the pretty ones. You think we don't all know how you got promoted?"

"Are you a deserter, Private Dornan?" General Washington asked, interrupting Dornan's accusations. Washington's voice never rose above the quiet rumble that caused the men around him to lean in.

"I didn't go far," Dornan whined. His eyes were doing the shifty thing again.

"Did you shoot at Mr. Lee?"

"I did. But I didn't know he was your man."

General Washington motioned for the soldiers in his guard to take Mr. Dornan into custody.

Dornan panicked and swung at me, clearly thinking I would be the easiest to get past. His fist glanced off the side of my face as I shifted and lunged—the way I'd done in a thousand maneuvers—and brought the butt of my musket against his head with a firm crack.

He crumpled like I'd paid him to perform, his knees buckling inward, his head at my feet, and I was back in Tarrytown, sick and dizzy, looking down at the first man I'd killed.

The men around me were only silent for a moment.

"I say, Shurtliff. Well done," von Steuben chortled, but General Washington had already moved on.

"Paterson," he said. "We have just been made aware of a problem in Philadelphia. If we are done here, we have a few more deserters to attend to."

"I'll see that Mr. Dornan is escorted back to the Point," Colonel Jackson offered. Dornan was hoisted up by his armpits and hauled toward the hospital on the other side of the house, his head lolling, his feet dragging all the way.

General Paterson wore two spots of vivid red high on his cheekbones, and his pale eyes glittered as he looked at me. "Your nose is bleeding, Samson," he said, impassive. "Get that salve from Maggie, and ask Dr. Thatcher if he can spare some ice for your cheek. You're going to need it."

He and the other officers immediately dispersed, following General Washington back in the house, and I was left, still gripping my musket in a two-handed carry, my knuckles white on the barrel and the stock.

"You're going to have a black eye," the general commented as we left Robinson's house an hour later.

"Yes, sir." My cheekbone throbbed slightly, and the skin was starting to bruise, but it was not something that would bother me much or for very long.

He started to respond and seemed to think better of it. A small detachment traveled with us, including Colonel Jackson, who'd informed us that Davis Dornan needed a night in the hospital, but would be brought back to the Point, under guard, as soon as he was fit to be tried. The circumstances were not ideal for conversation, especially of a private nature, and the general did not address me again.

General Washington was sending us to Philadelphia, and General Paterson was agitated and impatient as we waited for the ferry to take us to the other side of the river. A detachment of the Pennsylvania line, all newly levied soldiers, had barricaded themselves inside the state house in Philadelphia and threatened to destroy it and harm the members of Congress if their demands were not met. To make matters worse, the city had been gripped by an outbreak of yellow fever over the summer, and the city could ill afford the chaos. General Paterson, General Howe, and fifteen hundred men were being sent to quell the uprising and restore order.

"My entire brigade will leave for Philadelphia first thing in the morning," General Paterson informed Joe, the stablemaster, when we swung from our saddles back at the Red House. "Agrippa and Colonel Kosciuszko will travel with us as well, and Kosciuszko—and his mount—will not be returning at all. Our horses will need to be ready before dawn."

Joe nodded, never a man who needed much instruction, and led Lenox and Common Sense toward the stables, mumbling to them as they clopped along beside him.

"What do you need me to do first, General?" I asked.

"Come with me, Samson," he clipped. His stride was long, and he tugged at his neckcloth as he walked, as though the heat of the day had finally gotten to him. It was loose before we reached his office, and he tugged it off as he tossed his coat aside and began to roll his sleeves.

I walked to the pitcher and poured him a glass of water, catching a glimpse of my face in the mirror above the cabinet. It didn't look too bad. No swelling. No deep discoloration. I doubted it would last longer than a day or two. I'd looked worse.

The general took the glass without a word and drank it down before he stepped to the basin and washed, giving a terse assent when I excused myself to briefly wash as well. He sat down in his chair and opened his ledger as I left, but when I returned only minutes later and sat down across from him, he continued to stare out his window, his elbows on his armrests, his hands steepled beneath his chin.

"General?"

"Yes?"

"What's bothering you, sir?"

He inhaled deeply. "I do not like what was insinuated by Private Dornan," he said, his voice low and hard.

I didn't need to ask which insinuation. I knew. It had bothered me too. Embarrassed me. It had also given me the burst of anger I'd needed to knock him flat. But I was surprised the general had confessed his feelings so easily. I typically had to wheedle and wait him out, but he continued, still staring into the gathering dusk. The sun was setting and the clouds were violet against the green crags, but I didn't think the general was arrested by the purple sky.

"General Washington doesn't spend five seconds worrying about who his officers select as their aides," he muttered.

"Sir?"

"Von Steuben's predilections with his aides are well known, but he is a brilliant military man, and I have no doubt God sent him to us, all the way from Prussia. That is what matters to General Washington."

"So why are you so upset?" Turmoil billowed around him, heated and confused.

He turned his head then, pinning me in his gaze. "Do you expect to survive this adventure, Deborah?"

I was so taken aback by the question, I simply stared at him, but he supplied his own answer.

"I don't think you do. I think that is part of the reason you are so bloody brave and so damned competent that it stuns me. I've watched you now for more than a year, continually doing things that would terrify anyone, not to mention a woman who had never before seen or engaged in battle. But you don't seem afraid of anything. I think it's because you expect to die, and you are at peace with that ending."

"I have survived this far because I've had your protection for much of it."

He shook his head, rejecting my answer. "No. That's not true. You don't give yourself nearly enough credit, and that's not an answer."

I tried again, being as honest as I was able. "I resolved, in the very beginning—when I saw men stripped down at the whipping post and tied together to be shuffled onto prison ships—that I would end my life before I allowed myself to be captured or publicly exposed. I would rather die. As for an ending . . . I do not think about it. I do not want to think about it. I am only here. In this moment. And I do my best to think of nothing else."

He began to shake his head, slowly at first, and then more adamantly, his eyes never leaving me. "I cannot do this anymore," he said.

"General?"

"You are so dismissive of your own life, so unbothered by your own safety." He slapped his hands on his desk. "Well, I can't be. I have lost Elizabeth. I won't lose you. And I cannot do this anymore," he repeated, punctuating each word.

"You are angry with me," I summarized, bereft.

He covered his mouth with his palm, gripping his cheeks like he was holding himself back. When he spoke again, I could barely hear him behind his hand.

"I am *angry* because I should not feel this way. I am angry because I should not need you. I am angry because you are here, and I know you should not be. I should have sent you to Lenox long ago. But instead, I have kept you here with me."

"I *want* to be here with you," I confessed in a rush.

"That doesn't make it better," he roared. "Goddammit!" He shoved everything from his desk, swiping at it like a great bear. His inkpot shattered against the wall and his ledger slid drunkenly to the floor, pages splayed.

I stood and walked briskly toward the door, thinking it might be better for me to retreat. I was clearly not helping matters.

"Stop this instant! I did not dismiss you," he commanded, rounding his desk like he'd been shot from a cannon. I had never seen him so overwrought. John Paterson always had a firm hold on his temper and his words, and both were applied with precision instead of passion.

I froze, my back to him, my hand on the handle. He crossed the room in three strides, and slammed his hands against the door, his chest to my back.

"I do not want you to go," he said, and his anger had suddenly become anguish.

"Then I won't," I whispered, and for a moment we simply breathed together, harsh inhales and rasping exhales, standing pressed together against the door. Then he tugged on the tie that bound my hair and let it fall to the floor. Cradling my head between his hands, he tangled his fingers in the shoulder-length strands, gathering it into his fists.

I did not protest. Or breathe. Or even dare hope.

"How does no one see it?" he asked, bleak, and he dropped his brow to rest it on my head.

"See what, General?" I asked, composed. Calm. Pretending nothing was amiss.

"How does no one see you?" he whispered. "You, Deborah. Your skin. Your eyes. Your mouth. The length of your neck, the wisdom in your words. You are a *grown woman*. How does no one see it?"

He was so close. His lips and hands were in my hair, his length pressed to my back, and I closed my eyes, trying to find my shield and my strength. But I found nothing but naked longing.

"I don't want them to see me . . . to see the woman," I whispered. "I am a soldier in Washington's Continental army, and an aide-de-camp to a great general."

"And what else?"

"What do you mean, sir?"

He inhaled deeply, as if summoning his own strength, and on the exhale, he asked, "Do you have feelings for me, Samson?"

It did no good for me to deny it. It was there between us, the tension that I'd called kinship. The knowledge that I'd insisted was trust. The intimacy that I'd convinced myself came from shared suffering and near escape. It coiled in my breasts and burned in my belly, and he knew it.

"Yes, sir. I am in love with you."

The shudder that ran through him coursed through me. It was like cold water down my parched throat, and I reveled in the relief of my confession.

"So bloody brave," he whispered.

He released my hair, and I turned toward him, raising my face to his. Triumph and torture warred in his eyes. He pressed his forehead to mine, ground it there, like he wanted to push me from his thoughts, but then his mouth descended, and his lips caught mine.

It was not a sweet press of mouths or a stamp of approval like I'd received from Nat. It was not a pursed peck or a careful aligning of our noses. It was immediate warfare, and it didn't matter that I had not battled thus before. The kiss—if it could be called that—was as instinctual and guttural as an infant's first cry. We wrestled with our mouths, a desperate duel of lips and longing, panting and pursuing, clutching at each other, bowing and bending, until my head collided with the door, disconnecting us.

I gasped and he cursed, and we immediately broke apart. The general took a step back like I'd slapped him or he'd inadvertently caused me pain. It was not pain; I had no name for what I felt.

"We will leave in the morning for Philadelphia." He wiped the kiss from his mouth, and I wanted nothing more than to make it wet again. I was reeling. Reeling and aching.

"And I will go with you," I insisted.

"Yes." He nodded once. "Yes. You will come to Philadelphia with me . . . as my aide. But I am dismissing you as soon as the situation there is resolved so that you don't have to return to the highlands. It will be an honorable discharge. The war is all but over. It is time, Samson."

"But . . . I want to be with you."

"No." He shook his head, vehement. "No. I can't be around you. I should never have allowed you to stay."

He'd tricked me. He'd asked me if I had feelings for him, and I had readily confessed. Now he was punishing me for it.

"I can't be near you . . . like this . . . anymore," he whispered. "Clearly, I cannot be near you."

"You asked me how I felt," I cried, dismayed. "And I have embarrassed you."

"No. That's not it. I embarrass myself." His cheeks were stained with red, and his jaw was tight.

"I feel like a lecher," he explained, urgent but quiet. "And I don't like it. I don't trust myself. On the one hand, I look at you, and I see courage and competence and strength. I see a valued companion. A brave soldier." He choked on the last word, and the stain deepened. He ran his hands over his face.

"On the other hand, I see only Deborah. I see the line of your cheek and the bloom on your skin. I see the changing colors of your eyes, and I want to . . . to . . ." He paused and took a deep breath. "I loved my wife," he said, sounding almost desperate. "I loved everything about her. She was elect in every way. And you are *nothing* like her."

I gasped, and he flinched. It was the worst kind of rejection because I knew it was true.

I immediately wrapped myself in my accomplishments, in my triumphs, the way I'd always done. The way I'd always had to do. I'd had to value myself and better myself because I knew no one else would.

"I am smart like she was," I argued. "And I am capable . . . and strong." I grasped at the items from my never-ending lists. "I am . . ." My voice hitched, and I made myself stop, mortified.

"Yes. You are all those things," he answered immediately, even contritely. "But I would never have looked at you the way . . . the way I look at you now. You would not have been the type of woman to garner my attention. Your eyes are too piercing. You are too thin. Too tall. Too . . . bold. And yet . . . I am . . ." His voice trailed off like he was searching for the right words, but I didn't want to hear anymore.

"Why do you tell me this? It's not as if I don't know." I was near tears, and I despised myself for it. I turned, grappling for the door handle. Just like before, he was there, pushing the door closed again, but he gathered me against his chest and rested his cheek on my bowed head. I did not turn in his arms. I couldn't. My love yowled and my back bristled, and the need to claw my way free was overpowering.

"Forgive me, Samson. Forgive me. I am a man still grieving for a wife who deserved more than I gave her. I loved her. I will always love her. So to look at you and feel the way I do is . . . troubling to me."

"I would like to leave now, sir." I gulped, my eyes clamped closed, my hands fisted, clinging to my control with everything I had left.

"Deborah. Look at me. Please. I am trying . . . to explain." He made me turn toward him.

"Explain what?" I did not raise my eyes.

"That I find you impossibly, undeniably, irresistibly beautiful. In fact, you are the most beautiful woman I have ever laid eyes upon. And I cannot do this any longer."

Maybe he intended for us to laugh together. He would smirk and I would shrug, but I was in no mood to be the butt of his joke. Especially not when it was the same ribbing I'd taken from the Thomas brothers for so many years. But when he let the words settle around me, final and firm, I lifted my gaze to his. He did not smile or take them back. We just stared at one another.

"The hated highlands have stolen your sanity, General," I said, but my heart had begun to race, and the need to weep had intensified for entirely different reasons.

"Perhaps," he whispered. "Because I am mad about you. Crazed, in fact."

"Crazed?"

"Beyond all reason. But what I am trying—very poorly—to say is that I love you too."

"You are in love with me?" I asked, tremulous.

"I am in love with you. Desperately. And I am afraid everyone will see it."

Had he not confessed his feelings—even as tortured and tangled as they were—I would never have dared do what I did. I stepped in close to him, raised up on my toes, and pressed my cheek to his. I didn't try to speak, and I didn't seek his lips; I wouldn't survive another kiss like that. Not right now.

With my face pressed to his, I was shielded from his eyes but not from his pounding heart, and I wrapped my arms around him, holding on to him with all the devotion I'd never allowed myself to express. To anyone. And his arms encircled me in return.

We did not converse. Our hands didn't rove. We simply stood, cheek to cheek, his breath tickling my neck, our arms locked in a fierce embrace. And it wasn't until we heard boots in the corridor beyond that he cradled my face in his hands, pressed his mouth to mine once more, and let me go.

He retreated to his desk, and I answered the knock that came seconds later, admitting Colonel Jackson, who stepped past me without a second glance, even though my hair was tangled about my face.

"We will leave for Philadelphia in the morning, Shurtliff," General Paterson instructed from his desk. "Make sure we are prepared. I don't know how long we will stay."

"Yes, sir." When I looked back, the general was seated, Colonel Jackson obscuring him from my sight, and I stepped from the room.

~ 24 ~

The Patient Sufferance

The four-day, 150-mile journey to Philadelphia on horseback was markedly different from the march I'd participated in the year before. The heat was the same, as were the colors that lit the valleys, changed the leaves, and warmed the hills, but this time I rode at General Paterson's side, and the tension I felt was entirely new. The general was careful to never look directly at me when others were around, but Agrippa sensed the disturbance immediately. He rode with Colonel Kosciuszko but sometimes fell back or spurred his horse forward, depending on his desire for certain company or a particular conversation. When General Paterson moved up beside General Howe for a brief conference, Agrippa drew his horse alongside mine.

"Did you upset the general again?" Agrippa asked me, frowning. "He's not himself."

"It is the constant mutinies."

He scrunched up his face. "No. That's something else. He's on edge. And it's always when you're around, I noticed. I asked him if he wanted to make a switch."

"Agrippa?"

"A switch. I take care of him. You take care of the colonel. He said that wasn't necessary. But I'm wondering if it is."

I was stunned into silence, unable to protest, and Grippy saw my distress.

"You've taken good care of him," he rushed to add. "If you didn't, I would insist. The general is my best friend. He looks out for me. I look out for him. You do a good job, Bonny. But sometimes people just don't mix. Oil and water."

"It is my leg," I blurted out. "He has tried to give me less to do so I will heal. I've argued with him on the matter. I am fine. But he won't hear it."

"Huh." He chewed on his lip. "That sounds like him. Maybe that's it." He frowned at me. "You'd best not argue with him. He's a gentleman, through and through, but a stickler for the rules. Once he's decided, it's done."

I knew that to be true. John Paterson *was* a gentleman, and I had put him in a situation that was untenable. I was breaking all the rules, and he was abetting me. What was worse—and simultaneously wonderful—was that he claimed to *love* me, and I spent the hours traveling beside him in a state of thrilled horror at the thought.

The first night, I placed my bedroll as far from his as I was able and put his saddlebags near the opening of the small tent. I was half-terrified that he would walk all night to avoid me and alert Agrippa and anyone else paying attention that something was amiss, but he slipped inside when the camp was quiet and removed his boots before stretching out on the bed I'd made for him.

The next morning, I scolded him while I shaved his face, relaying what Agrippa had said to me. "He thinks I have upset you. He says you are on edge whenever I am near."

"I am." He raised his pale blue eyes to mine, and I removed the blade from his skin in case the tremor in my belly became a trembling in my hand.

The second night he dined with General Howe and returned when the moon was high. I'd been waiting for the camp to go to sleep and the night to deepen so I could retreat to the trees and visit the river. I rose and made to slip out as he watched.

"Samson?"

"I need to wash," I said simply. "And there are other needs best attended to in the dark."

"I will come with you and stand watch."

"General . . ."

He raised one finger and hissed between his teeth, silencing me. "I will come with you."

I waited obediently, clutching my washcloth and soap to my chest as he pulled his boots back on his feet. I'd removed the binding over my breasts so I could better clean myself, and wore only my breeches and my shirt. I would not submerge myself; my clothes would not have time to dry if I washed them.

I did not need to tell him how odd it would look for him to be standing watch over me, but he folded his arms and waited as I moved deeper into the trees to relieve myself, and he was still there, in exactly the same position, when I returned.

"I am continually amazed that you have managed so long," he said quietly. "I shudder when I think what these last eighteen months have been like for you."

"I chose to be here. Everything is easier when one chooses it."

We walked to the shore and removed our shoes and I rolled my sleeves. The general shucked off his shirt, tossing it over his boots. Clearly he had decided to wash as well. I crouched beside the water and wetted my cloth, suddenly warm and a little breathless. I proceeded carefully, washing beneath the billows of my shirt while the general splashed away, unimpeded. He was muscled and long and lightly furred on his chest, with not an ounce of extra around his middle. I peeked at him as he finished and turned back toward his discarded clothing, shaking himself as he went.

"I will be just a minute more," I murmured.

"And I will wait."

"Will you step away?" I asked. I needed to wash my nether regions, and doing something so undignified, even beneath my clothes, was more than I could endure with him watching.

I heard him move up the bank, swatting at a mosquito and shaking out his shirt. It had been a wet spring and a hot summer, and the water drew the bugs. I loosened the ties on my breeches and managed to wash below my waist without dropping them. It was not a bath, but it would suffice. When I was finished and my cloth was rung out, I turned to see if he still waited. He was there, silhouetted and still, but he turned as he heard me pick my way up the bank.

My clothes were damp and sticking to my flesh, and my hair had come loose around my face. My shirt was so wet it was sheer in spots, and I covered my chest with one hand while my shoes swung from the other. I dropped them in the grass and shoved my feet into them, not bothering with the buckles, but when I straightened, his back was rigid and he was turned away. I plucked at my shirt, pulling it from my skin. I'd lost the tie for my hair.

"You must not let anyone see you," he murmured, his voice strained.

I did not need to ask why.

He followed me into the tent and tied the flap closed with shaking hands.

And then he reached for me.

The ferocity of his embrace lifted me off the ground, thigh to thigh, belly to belly, chest to chest, and my shoes fell from my feet, landing with muted thumps.

His mouth against mine was immediately familiar and strange. I knew the shape of his lips and the sound of his voice, the rasp of his breath and the smell of his skin. I'd studied his features in detail many times, but kissing was another matter entirely, and we came together the way we'd come together before, frenzied and frantic.

"Dear God, Samson. What am I going to do with you? What the hell am I going to do?" It was a whispered wail against my lips, and he dropped his mouth to my throat, as if he needed breath or fought for control, but I could not bear to share his attention with that part of me, and I grasped his face and brought his lips back to mine.

"I do not know how to do this," I said, and I tightened my grip so that he would teach me. "But I want to learn."

I felt his jaw clench beneath my palms, a battle to slow down, to savor.

"You want to learn?"

"Yes. I want you to show me."

He groaned softly, and I reveled at the sound.

"Do what pleases you," he whispered.

"I do not know what pleases me," I said, but he shook his head, rejecting my words, and the caress of his mouth, so soft and light, pleased me greatly.

"Yes, you do," he countered.

His heat pleased me. His texture. His very presence pleased me, and I touched my tongue to his cupid's bow to see if that pleased me too. And then he was tasting me the way I tasted him, his lips seeking and supping, and I forgot to tally the wonders and matched him parry for parry.

I am convinced nothing is so intimate as a kiss, not even the joining of flesh or the taking of vows. When mouths commune, there is little that can be hidden, and I had no desire to hide anything any longer. Not from him.

His hands flexed and fisted in my shirt, and his fingers danced beneath it, stroking the smooth skin of my back. He palmed the curve of my hips and the swell of my buttocks and ran his thumbs across the peaks of my unbound breasts, but when I thought perhaps we would sink to our knees and surrender to the ever-intensifying drumming of our flesh, the general dragged his lips from my mouth, wrapped his hands around my wrists, and ground his rough cheek against mine.

"Deborah, please. Please, help me. I cannot do this. I will not do this."

I nodded immediately and stepped back, aching but obedient, and not at all certain what he could not do. We stood in the sticky darkness, breathing and battling, and when he let go of my wrists, we parted, retiring to our pallets. But when we had settled, our eyes fixed on nothing and our ears keenly attuned to each other, I spoke, my voice pitched lower than the murmur of the camp.

"What can't you do, sir?"

"Woman," he pleaded. "Do not call me *sir*. Not now."

I swallowed the "yessir" that bubbled on my tongue.

"I will not put you on your back and plow you like a camp trollop," he vowed, his voice almost inaudible. "That is what I will not do." He was trying to shock me and to chastise us both, and for a moment it worked.

"There are camp trollops?" I asked.

"There are. You have not been involved in the type of engagements that would allow for it. The march to Yorktown was too fast. And you are light infantry, who lead the army. The trollops trail behind. I am actually worried about what will happen to them when all of this ends. It's gone on so long that it's become a way of life. Some of them have children that are now six and seven years old. They trail the army too. They have nothing to go back to."

"Just like me," I whispered. "I suppose I am already a camp trollop."

"Don't say that."

We were quiet for a time, but neither of us slept.

"Did you . . . ever have need of their services?" I asked.

"Need? Yes. Partake? No. I would not do that to Elizabeth."

Guilt swelled and my conscience was pricked. "John?"

"Yes?" He sounded pleased that I had used his name.

"What would Elizabeth think . . . of us?"

"Ah, Samson. Are you fretting over that?"

"Yes, sir," I confessed.

It was a moment before he said anything more, and when he did his voice was thoughtful and the tension in him had eased.

"Of all the things I torture myself over, that is not one of them. I have not betrayed Elizabeth and neither have you. Elizabeth would approve. She adored you."

"She adored *you*. I think I loved you long ago, simply because she did. Her love was in every line and mention, in every letter."

He did not agree nor argue, but simply waited for me to continue.

"But what if she had not died? What if she were here?" I asked.

"She isn't." His voice was gentle. "And she never will be again. Nothing we do—or don't do—will bring her back."

I pondered that truth so long, I thought he might have drifted off.

"I should not love you like this, should I?" I asked.

"Like what?"

"I loved Sylvanus. I loved him dearly. And I loved Deacon Thomas, though I didn't always *like* him. I loved Nat and Phineas and Jeremiah. I loved—love—them all. I loved them in different amounts. Small piles and great piles. I do not love you the same way. This feeling is new. It is a mountain, and it has fallen on me. I didn't know it would feel this way to love."

"It doesn't," he whispered. "God forgive me, but it usually doesn't."

~

I was not repulsed by the general's talk of camp trollops.

I was bewitched.

That he'd used such vulgarity to describe the act probably should have dampened my romantic feelings. I knew it was what he'd intended. Instead, I was strangely affected by it. To be desired in such a way was something I'd never envisioned for myself. And for the general to want me—a man that I loved so desperately—felt miraculous. I could think of nothing else.

The next night, the general walked and I quaked, waiting for him to return. When the flaps parted long after the camp grew quiet, I rose and met him at the door, desperate to touch him and afraid he would leave again as soon as I did.

"You're still awake," he accused.

"Yes, sir—yes, John."

His chin hit his chest, but he reached for my hand as though he couldn't help himself.

"I want to kiss you again," I whispered, shameless in the darkness.

"I want to kiss you again too. I want to do a great deal more than that. Which is why I can't start."

"You can," I said. "I mean . . . I want you to."

"Deborah."

"I am not . . . physically . . . very w-womanly," I stammered. "Does that bother you?"

His grunt was almost a laugh. "I think my body knew you were female, even before I did."

I gasped. "Truly?"

"I have been surrounded by men of all shapes, sizes, and comeliness . . . or lack of. Not once has my flesh taken notice of the lot of them. But I noticed you. I thought it odd, and it made me look again to determine why." He shook his head, sheepish. "I have been cold. Hungry. So sleep-deprived I could have closed my eyes and dozed on my feet. But not once has a man made my body twitch. You didn't fool me for very long, I just didn't care to admit it. My body knew even when my mind refused to accept it."

"Does the twitching happen in the vicinity of all women?" I squeaked, amazed.

"No. It doesn't. But again . . . not once has it happened in the vicinity of a fellow. I have had great admiration for many men. Great fondness. Even hero-worship for a few. Henry Knox, General Washington, Nathanael Greene. I look on them with considerable awe, and awe feels a little like falling in love. But not once have I wanted to tup one of them or see what their mouths felt like beneath mine."

I almost moaned out loud, and he turned to go. "I thought I would hate kissing," I admitted in a rush.

He stilled. "Why?"

I shook my head. It was impossible to explain. "Because . . . because . . . I thought it signified bondage. Ownership. I didn't know it would feel like this."

"Like what?"

"Like flying . . . and transforming and . . . and freedom. And I never thought I would want . . ." I cleared my throat, searching for the proper words.

"Want what?" he pressed softly.

"Want . . . you. All of you. My body wants yours. My skin wants your skin. My mouth wants your mouth. I am not repelled. I am not disgusted. In truth, I have never wanted anything so much in my life."

He smiled, the bloom of it so wild and wide, I thought he was laughing at me. I covered my face with my hands, and he peeled them away, the glorious beam still splitting his cheeks. And he kissed me again, mouth fervent, hands splayed over my back, my hips tucked against his, and the embarrassment I felt evaporated. We sank down to the pallets, arranged side by side, and he kissed me until my eyes would not open and my lips would not close, until my body thrummed like a one-stringed lute, and I implored him for relief.

"What is this wanting?" I panted, quaking. "You must help me, John."

I could not move, and I could not stop moving. I could not draw breath, and I could not release it. He found the pulse beneath my clothes, the place where all my longing originated, and when I writhed with wonder, he held me fast, his mouth on my mouth, his hands on my body, until the climb that had begun with his kiss became a free fall, a weightless hurtling, and a miraculous landing.

Then he released me, boneless and senseless, and threw himself from the tent and out into the darkness.

~

The night before we reached Philadelphia the general was so weary that we vowed we would stay apart, and I kept my word, but he did not.

"I can feel your eyes," he muttered.

"You cannot."

"I can. And it is unsettling."

"I will close them."

"It won't help. *You* are unsettling." He rolled onto his side and traced my profile in the darkness, dragging the tip of his finger from my hairline to my heart. When his fingers drifted to the peaks of my breasts, he withdrew his hand with a hiss and rolled onto his back, vibrating like a coiled snake.

"I have a plan," he announced.

"That is why you are a general. You are very good at making plans." I was trying to soothe him, but he ground his teeth like I was provoking him instead.

"There is no privacy anywhere. At any moment, an aide or an officer could come barreling in. And I am in a state of constant . . . discomfort . . . when you are near me. My sister Anne and her husband have a home on Society Hill, not far from the center of town. You and I will stay with her while we are in Philadelphia."

My eyes widened in the dark.

"Her husband is Reverend Stephen Holmes of the Pine Street Church." He took a deep breath. "They have no children and plenty of room. Anne is lonely much of the time. I will ask Stephen to marry us while we are there. And you will stay with them until the war is over, and I can come back for you."

Of all the things I thought he would insist upon, marriage was not one of them. I sat up slowly and he did the same, turning to face me, his eyes glowing and his mouth set.

"But I have not been discharged," I whispered, as if that was the most important thing.

"I will discharge you. Honorably. It is within my authority to do so."

"B-but my term of enlistment is three years or the end of the war. It hasn't even been eighteen months. And I w-want to be where you are."

"No." His voice was firm. "You can't be where I am. Not like this. Not anymore."

I had thought he would relent as he'd done before. Especially now, when parting would be excruciating. I had been so sure he would let me remain beside him until the end.

"You are a soldier under my command. You are my aide. And it does not matter if I know who you are. It matters who *they* think you are." He indicated the camp, the men who slept beyond our canvas walls.

"They think I am Robert Shurtliff."

"Yes. And I am in a position of authority over you. That is a responsibility, not an opportunity. I have never sought positions of power or glory, and I can happily live out the remainder of my life, however long that is, without either. But that doesn't mean I'm not proud. Or that I don't care what men think about me . . . or say about you."

He paused, and when he began again, his voice was riddled with remorse. "But mostly . . . if someone were to see me with you, like this, with a young *man* who is my aide, what would that say about my relationship with my wife?"

It was not where I had expected him to go, and my breath caught and my guilt welled.

"It would suggest—" His voice broke. "It would suggest," he began again, more strident, "that I stayed away from Elizabeth for all those years and that she died without me because I preferred a different kind of company. It would diminish her sacrifice. And mine. I did not join this fight to escape Elizabeth. And I will not dishonor her, or this cause, by doing anything to make people think that I did."

His words, even as softly delivered as they were, resonated like cannon fire, and for a moment I could only sit in silence, recovering, wondering if I would ever hear again. I was afraid if I spoke, I would shout or cry, unable to gauge my volume, and the whole camp would hear my voice.

"So you would marry me," I whispered. "That is your solution."

"Yes."

"But . . . we will be apart."

"Yes. For a while."

I sank back down on my pallet and stared up at the shadowy folds that blocked out the stars. For a moment, I wished that I could simply float up, the way I did in my dreams, and leave it all behind. See what I wanted to see. Go where I wanted to go. And feel nothing but the vast quiet, no beginning and no end.

"I do not want it to be over," I mourned aloud, for that was the truth at the heart of it all.

"If you marry me, it won't have to be over. Ever."

"I do not want the *war* to end," I whispered, and made myself meet his eyes.

He stared at me, dumbfounded. Wounded. But he did not understand. The woman he thought he loved did not exist anywhere else but here.

"Forgive me," I begged. "I know it is selfish. There has been far too much suffering. Your children need you. And you need them. But . . .

but I won't ever get this time back. This freedom. This life. And I will be Deborah Samson again."

"I am in love with a woman who has no desire to be a woman," he marveled, almost to himself. "Dear God, what a disaster."

"That is not true. I desire to be a woman." My voice was small, and he scoffed, unconvinced.

"I do," I said, this time stronger. "I want to be a woman. I want to unbind my breasts and put on a fine dress. I adore pretty things and beautiful fabrics. I want to walk on your arm and dance with you and . . . and . . . kiss your mouth and lie beside you. I would like to have your children."

My cheeks were flaming, but my voice grew stronger with each word. "I want those things. I do not hate being a woman. I simply hate that a woman can't go to Yale or be a statesman or help draft a constitution. I hate that I can't travel to Paris without a husband or even walk down the street alone. I hate the limitations that nature has placed on me, the limitations that *life* has placed on me. But I do not hate being a woman, and I would not hate being your woman."

He was suddenly there, looming over me, his hands cupping my face, his vow abandoned again.

"Then you will marry me. And we will end this charade."

"But . . . it is *not* a charade," I lamented. "Not to me."

He wilted, his back bowing as though I'd lashed him, and he laid his brow against my breast, defeated. I wrapped my arms around his head and for several long minutes we lay in silence, my heart pounding against his lips. My yearning for what he offered was as fierce as my impending loss.

"And Robert Shurtliff will just . . . disappear?" I whispered, weakening. He lifted his head and stared down at me.

"Yes. My sister will help us. Robert Shurtliff will go into her home. And he won't come out again."

"Hidden away."

His hands tightened on my jaw and his thumbs moved across my lips, as if he wanted to erase my reservations.

"I am not hiding you because I am ashamed of you. I am hiding you because I want a life with you. I cannot have a life with Robert Shurtliff."

"And then what? After you have made me disappear . . . then what?"

He ground his teeth in protest of my description, but he did not argue my point. "When I have been released of my command, we will go to Lenox."

"Oh, John," I mourned.

"What, Deborah? What?" He was growing increasingly vexed.

"I don't think you understand," I whispered.

"What don't I understand?" he hissed back. "Do you think I don't know exactly who you are?"

I closed my eyes and breathed him in for a moment, allowing myself to bask in his affection before I warned him away. "In Middleborough, and probably Taunton and Plympton too, Deborah Samson is a laughingstock. No one knows what I've done, but they know what I tried to do. They know I put on men's clothes and tried to enlist. They know I drank too much in Sproat's Tavern, and my name was taken off the rolls of both churches."

He grinned and threw back his handsome head, laughing silently, but his smile faded when he saw my anguish.

"Perhaps it is you who doesn't understand," he murmured. "You won't have to go back. Ever. You will come home with me. You will be Deborah Paterson. You will be my wife."

"But I won't ever cease to be Deborah Samson. Eventually someone will make the connection. It is the same colony, after all. People will talk about Deborah Samson, the woman who dressed up like a man and tried to join the regimentals. The men you have served with will find out. People in Lenox will find out, and they will shun me. They might shun you. They might shun your children."

That gave him pause. He stared down at me, suddenly bereft.

"Have I not given enough for my country?" he asked. "Must I have nothing for myself?"

"Have they—have your children—not given enough? Do you want your children to have me as a mother? Do you want your family to have *me* as a sister?"

"Yes," he retorted. "I do."

"Oh, John. You don't have to do this. I am not your responsibility."

"Is that what you think this is? You think I am being selfless? You think I feel responsible for you?" He stretched out atop me, his big body covering mine, his arms braced on either side of my head. I could not breathe, I could not escape, and I did not want to. He kissed me then, suckling my lips as if he would draw submission from my throat.

"You do," I panted against his mouth. "You feel responsible."

"Deborah," he warned, withdrawing enough to shake his head. "Cease this."

"It is an admirable quality. And one I understand." I wrapped my arms around him and buried my face in his throat, nuzzling the hollow I'd longed to kiss a hundred times. It tasted of leather and salt. It tasted of him, and I loved him so much it was all I could do not to sink my teeth into him and swallow him whole.

He groaned into my hair. "So it is all well and good if *you* take on every responsibility. It is nothing that you constantly shoulder more than you should be able to carry, that you've done so all your life, and done it well. I love you, desperately, but somehow it is wrong if I also feel responsible for you?"

"It is enough for me that you love me."

He reared back onto his knees, breaking my embrace, depriving me of the weight and the press of him, the flavor and the heat. And he glowered down at me.

"It should not be. It should not be enough for you, Samson. It is certainly not enough for me."

I reached for him, but he shook his head in warning. "Stay there, dammit."

He fisted his hands in his hair and closed his eyes. I was convinced he prayed, though his mouth didn't move and his head didn't bow.

"We will marry," he said when he finished, resolute.

"General . . ."

"You will marry me, Deborah Samson. So help me God."

"That is really what you want?" Joy and trepidation filled my chest. "Truly?"

"I have never wanted something so much in all my life."

~ 25 ~

The Necessity Which Constrains Them

We arrived on the morning of October 3, fifteen hundred men from four regiments, along with General Howe and his aides, only to learn that the mutineers had been dispersed and the conflict was over. We rode into the city to survey the damage, but left the troops camped at the edge of town. I would have liked to explore, but the general was immediately swept into meetings, and I attended at his side, marveling at his patience and the respect he commanded.

"The commander has asked that you stay in Philadelphia, Paterson, and conduct the hearing and sentencing of those most responsible," General Howe informed him at lunchtime. "You are a barrister, after all, and we all respect your prudence. This will not be as hard a task as the last. These soldiers have not earned the compassion others have. They are all new recruits, not one of whom had suffered the years of toil and lack. They should be heard, swiftly punished, and dispensed with.

"I will return to West Point with our men day after tomorrow. The sooner we leave, the better. The hospitals are full of yellow fever, the barracks in the city center have been converted to a temporary ward, and we don't need to add fifteen hundred troops to an already overwhelmed system."

Colonel Kosciuszko's home was in Philadelphia, and he invited us to stay with him until the proceedings were concluded. He would not be going back to West Point. The great hall had been his final project, his enlistment had expired, and he was excited to return to the city he'd called home for twenty years. He had asked for Agrippa to stay in Philadelphia with him and continue on as his personal valet, but Grippy was undecided.

"Kosciuszko lives in Society Hill," Agrippa told me. "Fancy place. Fancy people. The colonel comes from money back in Poland, though you'd never know it. When the British took the city in '77, he thought they'd burn the whole neighborhood down, but the house is his again, minus a few treasures, and he has big plans. I guess those plans include me."

He sighed and rubbed at his brown cheeks, ruminating on the decision. "General Paterson says it's my choice. I've been there once, but I don't really want to make it my home, no matter how well the colonel treats me or how much he wants me to be his valet. But it sure beats the barracks, and it sure beats a tent while we're here. He's invited the general to stay at his home too."

But just as he planned, General Paterson politely refused the invitation.

"My eldest sister lives on Society Hill as well. She is expecting me and Private Shurtliff. We will remain there until matters in Philadelphia are resolved. But Dr. Thatcher will be assisting at the temporary hospital in the barracks until we return to the Point. I am sure he would appreciate an invitation, Colonel," General Paterson added. He simply patted Grippy's shoulder and reminded him that the decision was his.

"You will always have a place with me, Agrippa Hull. Your room in the Red House is yours for as long as you want it."

"You have Bonny," Agrippa grumbled, shooting a look at me. "I need to be useful."

The general said nothing more, though he hesitated like he wanted to speak. Instead, we mounted our horses, and with a promise to return in the morning, he and I made our way through the streets toward the colorful rows of merchant houses and businesses lining the busy docks. We passed a wagon filled with sick people in differing states of distress. A woman, flushed and moaning, held a child who was already dead, and a man vomited over the side, the contents of his stomach splashing on the cobbles.

A shop owner grumbled as they passed, and he tossed a pail of water over the vomit, diluting it, and went on with his day. The city was unfazed, and business continued. Perhaps it helped that yellow fever was not contagious, but Philadelphia had experienced one upheaval after another, and no place in the country was more ready for it all to be over.

The general dismounted in front of a dressmaker's shop on Elfreth's Alley and tied his reins and mine to a hitching post as I slid off Common Sense.

"General?" I asked, my eyes wide. We had not discussed any of this.

"You cannot be married in your uniform," he said beneath his breath. "I will say the purchases are for my wife."

My breath caught. "I keep expecting you to pinch me like the brothers used to do and tell me it is all a grand prank," I murmured, but his gaze was filled with challenge.

"You must get everything you need. Shoes, stockings, a dress—several dresses, I would think. A wardrobe." He wrinkled his brow. "I don't know exactly what that entails."

I didn't know either. I knew cloth, and I knew quality, but I had never purchased anything from a dressmaker's shop. Mrs. Thomas and I had sewn our own frocks, but I followed the general inside.

"I will not take Continental dollars, sir," the gentleman warned as we entered his establishment.

John nodded, as though he expected as much, but the statement tightened his mouth. It was not the shopkeeper's fault that the paper had no value, but it reinforced the injustice of paying the troops in that currency.

"I need a wardrobe, ready-made, for a woman, tall and slim," the general said.

"How tall and how slim? We would need to do a fitting, sir."

The general frowned at me, and I frowned back. "That is not possible. We are in town only briefly. Her maid can make minor alterations, but she is in need of a formal gown as soon as possible. And perhaps two more dresses that can be worn about the house."

The shopkeeper stroked his chin, as if in deep deliberation, but his eyes gleamed.

"A sea captain ordered a wardrobe for his new bride. Gave me a deposit. Brought the woman in for a fitting. She was tall. And slim. But with a bit of a bosom." He cupped his hands beneath his chest and bounced them, as if gauging weight. It amazed me how differently men talked to one another when they believed no women were present. The general flushed, and the man dropped his hands.

"But the captain and his bride died from yellow fever. His ship is still docked in the harbor." He shook his head sadly, but the gleam was still present. "I will sell it all to you, sir. For your missus. And I will do all the alterations for free."

"There is no time for your alterations. I will need to pay someone else to do them," the general countered. "And my wife is a lady with discriminating tastes."

I almost snorted but managed to control myself.

"We will have to see the gowns," the general finished.

The shop owner shrugged, and the haggling began. The chest was opened, the contents revealed—velvet and lace and stripes and bows—and a price settled upon. I followed General Paterson from the shop a short time later, the new owner of a wardrobe fit for a sea captain's wife. It would be delivered to the address on Society Hill within the hour.

~

John had sent a message to his sister the moment we arrived in Philadelphia, with the instructions for the courier to await her response. Anne Holmes had replied with effusive warmth and welcome, according to the general.

"What did you tell her?" I asked as we climbed the hill lined with stately homes and pretty carriages that was only minutes, and a great deal of money, from the shops near the wharf.

"I told her I was in Philadelphia and that I was getting married to a young woman I have known for many years. A friend of the family. I asked her if Stephen would perform the marriage. He is accustomed to such things. He was an army chaplain in the early days of the war."

"And you asked her if we could stay?"

"I didn't have to ask. She insisted."

"Oh, John," I breathed. "I do not feel very good."

"Courage, Samson," he said softly. "And I like very much when you call me John."

Anne Holmes did not wait for us to knock on her big black door, but flew down the drive and threw herself into her brother's arms before I'd even slid to the ground. I gathered the reins of both horses, standing quietly by until a servant strode from the house, clucking at Mrs. Holmes, and took the horses around the house to the stables, promising to remove our packs from the saddles and have them delivered to the general's quarters. He did not ask my name or question my status, and I turned back to the general and his sister, who was ushering him toward the house, chattering all the way.

"I have been beside myself with excitement since I received your post, brother. All is in order. Stephen has use of the church, as you know.

You will stay here tonight, of course. And for as long as you need. The servants have been advised, though I see you have your aide. The reverend and I leave first thing in the morning for Trenton. I'm so glad you came today! I would have missed you. The house will be yours . . . but when will we meet Miss Samson? How lovely that she knew Elizabeth. That will make it better for the girls. Do they know?"

"No. No one knows, Anne. Just you. I will tell you everything. But let's go inside."

He waited until we were settled in the sitting room where tea had just been laid out. I was hungry and terrified, and I sat perched on the end of the settee. The cup Mrs. Holmes gave me rattled in my hands, and I set it down immediately. She didn't seem to notice. I took a bite of a biscuit and it was powder in my mouth. I made another attempt at the tea and managed to splash my coat and miss my lips.

"Deborah?" John said quietly.

I raised my eyes to his and realized he'd said my name more than once.

"Yes, sir?"

"Deborah Samson, this is my sister Anne Holmes. Anne, this is Deborah."

His sister looked at me, baffled, and her cup began rattling on its saucer as well.

"Have you lost your mind, little brother?" she whispered. "You said you were bringing a woman. To *marry*. Who is this boy?"

"This is Deborah Samson, my aide-de-camp, and my wife-to-be."

I took off my tricorn hat and tugged the tie from my hair, but it wasn't enough. Like everyone else, Anne Paterson Holmes simply saw a lean-cheeked, square-jawed boy in army dress. That I was anything else was too impossible to believe.

She actually moaned, poor woman. "John. I don't understand. Am I to dress your aide as a woman . . . or is your aide dressed as a man?"

I did not flinch. I'd learned not to, but for the first time since I'd begun my quest, I mourned that she could not tell.

"I am Deborah Samson, Mrs. Holmes," I said quietly. "It is a pleasure to meet you. I may be out of practice, but I am indeed a woman. I would appreciate all the assistance you can give me. It has been a while since I wore a dress, and I've never been especially skilled with my hair."

Her mouth formed an incredulous O, and she looked from me to her brother and back. "What are you up to, John Paterson? This is not at all like you."

"No. It isn't like me. So I would ask, darling Anne, that you trust me. I don't have much time, and very little of it is my own. I would like to wed Deborah before the day is done. And the Reverend Stephen Holmes, bless his righteous heart, will not perform the marriage if my wife-to-be is wearing breeches."

She moaned again. "Stephen! What will Stephen say?"

"Anne." The general's voice was sharp, and he leaned forward on the settee, demanding her attention. "Help us. I came to you for a reason. There is little you haven't seen and no one I trust more. You have been a patriot, through and through. From the beginning."

She exhaled slowly, her eyes clinging to her brother's face and then to mine.

"Do you trust her?" she asked.

"I have known her since she was a child."

"That is not an answer, John," she contended. "You know what many of us went through in this city with Benedict Arnold and that terrible Miss Shippen. I had known *her* since she was a child. That means nothing."

When the British had withdrawn from Philadelphia in '78, Benedict Arnold had been assigned military command of the city. Not long after, he'd married Peggy Shippen, a young socialite from a wealthy, loyalist family who was thought to have encouraged and even arranged his defection.

"Arnold was ambitious, arrogant, and selfish, but she was a spoiled snake," Anne Holmes continued, vehement. "They bankrupted the city and sold us out. So I will ask again. Do you trust this woman?"

"Yes. I trust her," John said. "And I need you to trust me."

~

"What is *this*?" Anne Holmes asked me, frowning with distaste. She picked up the band I'd fashioned to wear around my breasts. It was fraying and soiled on the edges and almost unrecognizable in its current condition.

"It is a corset," I said. I was in a tub filled with all manner of salts and scents, every inch of me scrubbed and pink and naked. Once Mrs. Holmes had decided she was on board, she'd set her jaw and thrown herself into my transformation with a vigor that rivaled my own.

"Half of one?"

"Yes, ma'am."

She had demanded that I talk, and talk I had, sputtering as water was poured over my head and blushing from head to toe as she examined the scars on my leg and the long, puckered line on my arm. She'd allowed nothing to go unexamined, and I endured it all. John had been sent to ready himself, and he could not save me.

The trunk had arrived from the dressmaker as well, and Anne had investigated every last piece, muttering to herself.

"These will have to be redesigned. They do not suit at all. Perhaps if we remove the ruffles and bows and remake the sleeves," she mused. "You are angular and your features are bold. You need solid color and simple lines. Nothing that will compete. You do not need to be dressed up or disguised. You need to be . . ." She wrinkled her brow, looking for the word. "You need to be . . . displayed. But this will do nicely."

The dress she held up was a brilliant colonial blue, not unlike the blue of my uniform. It even had gold buttons marching in parallel rows down the front, all the way to the ground.

"You will have to wear an underskirt. It is not long enough, but with white fichus at the neck and in the opening of the sleeves, it will work."

I had nothing to add and simply rose from the water, toweled myself dry, and let the preparations begin. Anne summoned two maids, and I was bundled and pinched and tortured and teased from head to toe for what felt like hours.

"You are thin but so beautifully shaped, and so magnificently tall. We will make you even taller still. They are powdering their faces in France, but I find the look revolting. You have beautiful skin and astonishing eyes. We will rouge your cheeks and your lips, just a touch, and dress your hair high."

I didn't argue and she did not ask permission, but when she declared me ready, dismissed her servants, and led me in front of the looking glass, I was stunned at the result.

"I cannot breathe," I said.

"Nor can I. You are breathtaking."

"No. I cannot breathe. This corset is too tight."

"You're not supposed to breathe. You're supposed to sip."

"Sip?"

"Yes, dear. Sip at the air. Don't you remember? You have worn a tourniquet around your lungs for a year and a half. This should be easy in comparison."

"I might be a better soldier than I am a woman," I said, striving to do as she advised.

"A woman is not a corset or a gown or a pile of curls. You've always been a woman. And a remarkable one, it seems."

Her pronouncement stunned me, given our rocky introduction. She met my gaze in the mirror and gave me a small smile.

"My brother does not do anything without considerable fore-thought. He thinks things through and around and over and back. And then he decides, and that is that. But he does not resolve to do anything that he has not settled in his mind. If he does not doubt you, I cannot doubt you either."

"He is extraordinary," I whispered. "And I don't know why he wants me. But he does." I shook my head. "So here I am."

She laughed and turned me around.

"So here you are. And here we go."

"I cannot make her blend in, brother. She is too tall," Anne declared as we descended the stairs. John awaited us at the bottom, his dress uniform brushed, his epaulets gleaming.

He gaped at me, his lips parted and his head cocked, and I would have wilted if I'd had a choice in the matter. My posture was dictated by the cinch at my waist and the twin rods up my back.

"She is a beauty," Anne said. "She just needed a wee bit of grooming."

"'Beauty' is too tame a word," John breathed. "I don't know where to put my gaze."

"What if we are seen?" I worried. "What if someone recognizes me?"

Anne laughed and John shook his head.

"Tonight you will be by my side as Deborah Samson. That is how I will introduce you. That is who you are."

"And why would you be with the likes of Deborah Samson? What business have I here?"

"You are an old family friend. Close to my late wife. A descendant of one of our founding fathers. And in an hour's time, you will be my wife. That is your business here."

"But . . . what if someone recognizes me?" I insisted again.

"Recognizes you?"

"As your aide. As Robert Shurtliff!"

Anne spoke up, reassuring me. "They won't. To be a beautiful woman and disguise oneself as a sixteen-year-old boy, that is the difficult part. This will be easy."

"This is not a disguise." John touched my cheek and pulled away again, very aware that his sister was observing us. "This is real. No one will look at you and see anything but Deborah Samson."

"You keep saying that. It isn't true," I whispered.

"What part?" Anne interjected.

"I am not beautiful. That is why Robert Shurtliff was so believable."

"He was believable because it was madness to believe anything else!" Anne exclaimed, but the general was shaking his head.

"Your beauty, even as a boy, was noted. Why do you think they all call you Bonny?" John asked.

"Because I didn't grow a beard. It was said with mockery."

"It is because you were—you are—comely. And not even a Continental uniform and a bold gaze could hide it. But no one will look at you tonight and see Robert Shurtliff. No one but me. And I quite adore the fellow."

I needn't have worried. We saw no one at all in our brief walk to the church on Pine Street, mere minutes from the Holmeses' residence, and no one was inside save the reverend. The church was a pillared, brick edifice that had been built before the war and gutted during the British occupation. First a hospital and then a stable, the structure had been reborn and rebaptized, according to Anne, though it was empty now but for the candles that flickered and danced. Reverend Holmes, a middle-aged man with deep brown eyes and a sonorous voice, met us with a smile for his wife and a clasp for John's hands. I don't know what he'd been told, but I was keenly aware of what he hadn't been told.

"Stephen, this is Deborah Samson," the general introduced, and the reverend bobbed his head in greeting and brought out a Bible, which we were instructed to sign. Anne and the reverend signed their names as well.

Then the pews without parishioners and the long windows with their new colored glass bore witness to a marriage so impossible and improbable, it felt like one of my dreams.

But it happened. And we were. Man and wife. John and Deborah, though until that moment, I felt Deborah had hardly existed at all.

"And in the Book of Revelation we are given this admonition," Reverend Holmes intoned, and John smiled down into my eyes. It had all begun with Revelation.

"'Write the things which you have seen, and the things which are, and the things which shall be hereafter.'"

And I promised that I would.

~

We ate supper alone in an upstairs room at Anne's house, and though the dress made me feel beautiful and left John agape, I was not at all sad when he helped me remove it.

And then he loved me perfectly and patiently, and I loved him back with all the fire and fortitude I'd applied to every other aspect of my life.

"You are not just Samson. You are Delilah," he mumbled, his mouth and his hands on my skin. "How can that possibly be?"

"You are a good teacher, sir."

"You cannot call me *sir* when we are lying here without our clothes."

"Then I will call you my dear Mr. Paterson," I declared.

"No."

"My beloved general."

He rose up on his arm and pressed his thumb to the tip of my chin and a kiss to my brow. "Better. But no."

"I always thought of you as Elizabeth's John," I confessed, and immediately hated myself for it. I had gone straight from soldier to spouse, and I'd never been a coquette.

He was sadly silent though he did not withdraw. "You are not very good at this part," he said.

"I will be," I vowed, fierce, and the sadness lifted with the corner of his mouth.

"There's the Samson I know. Bound and determined to excel in everything."

I pulled his body back to mine, desperate to practice.

"How about dearest John?" I suggested against his lips.

"Dearest John implies that there is a dear John. I want to be your only John," he whispered, coaxing my flesh to yield for him once more.

"My only general."

"Samson . . . please," he begged.

"John," I said, full of contented surrender, and he shuddered at the sound.

~ 26 ~

Let Facts Be Submitted

I had not slept nearly enough. My skin was sore and my chest was tight. I felt in equal measure wonderful and ghastly, and I missed the general with an intensity that made my eyes tear. He had left me only hours ago.

"I have become ridiculous," I whispered, but my censure did not change my feelings in the slightest. I had become a new creature. Not Deborah. Not Shurtliff. And not any version in between. I was a woman. A wife. A wanton? I nodded. Yes, that too. And like a snake shedding its skin, or a bird hatching from an egg, it was not an entirely painless experience.

John kissed me goodbye at dawn and rose, washing his teeth and tying back his hair, demanding I remain in bed.

"You are not my aide, Deborah. Not here. Not now."

I ignored him and gathered the implements to shave his face. He pulled me into his lap and wrapped his hands around my hips, and when I finally finished the task, we were both dappled in lather, and the front of my new nightgown was soaked through from his nuzzling.

"It is a wonder you are not cut to shreds," I murmured against his lips. I set the blade aside and my nightgown followed, and when the general finally left the pretty house on Society Hill, I had been thoroughly and completely ravished once more.

"I will return this evening," he said, pressing his cheek to mine. We still had not settled the details of my discharge, but I was too spent to do anything but murmur, "Yes, sir."

"John," he reminded.

"Yes, my darling general."

I fell back to sleep to the clip-clop of hooves on cobbles, my last thought of him. When I awoke again hours later, a maid had set out a dress and underthings, as well as a pair of slippers that were a tad too wide and a pinch too short. That she had entered the room without waking me set my cheeks aflame and caused me to marvel all the more. I was not myself at all.

I donned the clothes, even the corset, though I didn't lace it up as tightly as Anne had. I was flushed and sore and famished, but when I sat down to tea in Anne's drawing room, I found I couldn't eat.

I forced down a few bites, knowing I needed the strength. I was alone in the house, but for the servants, and I wandered back up to the room John and I had shared. My uniform had been laundered and was hanging in the wardrobe, my boots shined, my hat brushed, as though I had an aide of my own.

What in the world would I do with myself? I was weary, but to lie back down in the bed and sleep the day away was an idea so foreign and distasteful, I dismissed it immediately.

When we'd moved through Philadelphia on our way to Yorktown, the dust from the army had obscured my view, settled between my teeth, and coated my eyes, and I had been unable to take in the wonders of the famed city. I wanted to walk, to explore, and I could not walk about the city by myself. Not dressed this way. I would require a companion at the minimum, and I didn't want a stranger toddling along after me.

But if I wore my uniform, I could go wherever I wanted. All by myself.

I did not think about it more than a few seconds. I stripped off the dress and the cloying underthings. My halved corset was nowhere to be found. I frowned and searched the space. I didn't want to destroy the one that had been provided me. Plus, I didn't have scissors or a needle and thread to make the adjustments.

I donned my uniform without my binding, and with my waistcoat my bosom was barely visible. But I dared not risk it. The blue sash I'd worn the night before might work. I wrapped it tightly around my chest, crossing it in front and in back until I'd bandaged myself up from my armpits to my ribs. When I pushed my shirt and waistcoat over it, the effect was much more convincing.

I slipped out the front door without seeing anyone, and strode along, as giddy with my freedom and solitude as I'd been in the days after leaving the Thomases, walking through the countryside with no plan beyond enlistment.

But the joy did not last. I did not feel at all well. I looked for a place to rest for a moment, and my vision swam. Uncapping my canteen, I drank deeply, filling my belly with water. Almost as soon as I stopped, the water came right back up in a bilious flood, and a woman screamed and pointed.

"The soldier's sick with the fever. Run fetch the sick wagon," a shopkeeper cried and someone else cursed.

I felt my face. I wasn't sick. I did not get sick. I had never been sick except when I'd been tossed about on a boat on the way to Chesapeake Bay, and that was not illness. But the heat radiating off my skin was undeniable. I turned back in the direction I'd come, my only aim to reach Anne's house without vomiting again, but I'd barely gone ten steps when the world tilted, tipping me over, and everything went black.

~

I was dying—or perhaps I was dead. It was not what I expected death to be. I was in the dank, filthy room with the rows of other men who were dead or dying too, and then I was not. I flickered in and out, like a candle fighting a draft. Beyond pain but not beyond feeling, my mind hovered between my lives, the one I clung to, and the one I lived before. Two men were fighting over my boots.

"Those won't fit you. He's just a boy."

"Well his clothes won't fit neither of us. Too skinny. It's too bad. They look new."

Agrippa had insisted on the new uniform. *If you are going to be the general's aide, you can't be dressed in rags.*

Would I ever see the general again? That thought brought horror, but I was too weak to react.

How would he find me? Would he even want to?

The arguing above me faded, and I was ten years old again, riding on the back of a plodding horse, Reverend Conant shielding me from the cold.

I couldn't go back to Middleborough. I'd shamed the Thomases. But there I was, and Reverend Conant was there too, though both were an impossibility. He was dead. Perhaps I was too. And then he was speaking, his voice just as I remembered.

"There will always be a place for you here, Deborah," he said.

"Where is here?" I asked him.

"Here is where I am."

"And Elizabeth?"

"Yes."

"And what of Nat and Phineas and Jeremiah? Are they here too?" My longing to see them engulfed me, and I saw the fields where we'd run and the house where we'd grown, and the places I'd named and loved.

"They are here, yes."

I could see the Thomas house, smiling window eyes and an open door, and boys spilling from the farm and the fields, waving and calling to me, and love overwhelmed me.

I slid down from the horse, eager to greet them, to reunite, to embrace my brothers.

They were all there, the loves I had lost—Nat, and Phineas, and Jeremiah. Even Beebe and Jimmy and Noble were there, as if they too had returned to the Thomas farm after falling at Tarrytown.

But John was not there. John was not racing to greet me, calling my name, arms outspread.

I turned back to Sylvanus, who still remained on his old horse, reins in hand, looking down at me in sympathy.

"Don't be afraid, Deborah," the reverend said gently. "You will not be mistreated here." It was what he'd promised before, all those years ago. And he'd been right.

"Where is the general?" I asked.

"He is not here. He promised to stay to the end."

"But I am his aide. I am his . . . wife. I cannot leave him."

"Then you must go back. You must continue to battle."

"I will only bring him shame," I mourned, doubtful. Weak. "Maybe it is better this way."

He shook his head. "It is not better. Only easier. But you are a warrior."

"I am a woman," I argued.

"You are both," he said, but I had already turned back, tumbling from the warm sunlight into the dark tunnel of the space between. My skirts tangled around my legs, and pages, like those torn from a book, floated up in the murky green that was suddenly all around me. I was not in the fields of Middleborough. I was in the harbor. I was drowning in the harbor with Dorothy May Bradford, and she was crying for her son. For her John. Cold which has no description slowed my thoughts and stole my breath, yet I did not fight. I simply waited, letting myself be drawn downward, lungs screaming, light winnowing, unable to free myself.

I'm so sorry, John. Those were the words in my head, though the voice was not my own. I added mine to it, succumbing to my fate. Dorothy May and I were connected after all.

"I'm so sorry, John. Forgive me. Forgive me."

I woke, heart thundering, my body stiff and sore, unable to move, but I was no longer in heaven or the harbor, though the room I was in could have been hell. A woman moved from berth to berth, and I tried to cry out to her but couldn't summon any sound or even lift my head. The paralysis was the worst part, the sense that I was detached from myself, that my body wasn't my body, that I was living another life or even dying someone else's death.

A moment later she stood over me, tsking.

"So young. So pretty. Poor boy," she murmured, and the *r* on her "poor" rolled endearingly. She ran a hand over my eyes, as if to close them, and I willed them open again. My lids fluttered and she screamed.

"Good heavens! You're still alive."

When I woke again, my uniform was gone and I was clean. The bedding beneath me was white and the sheet atop me was crisp. I still had no strength in my limbs and barely a thought in my head, but someone was beside me, and when I willed my head to turn, I saw two doctors in deep conversation. One of them was Dr. Thatcher.

"The soldier was brought in a few days ago," the unknown man said. "He collapsed on the street. No one knew who he was beyond the uniform."

"His name is Shurtliff. He's one of ours," Dr. Thatcher said. His voice moved over me, but I couldn't keep my eyes open. "Is he going to die, Dr. Binney?"

"I've thought he was dead a number of times. But . . . he . . ." The doctor seemed to struggle over the word and gave into it reluctantly. "He is holding on. I don't know how. He's a strong one, to be sure."

"What else can be done?"

"At this point . . . the soldier either lives or he dies. Only time and rest will tell. But sir . . . I must tell you what I've discovered. For . . . her sake."

I moaned, wanting to protest, but no sound escaped my lips. Tears leaked from my eyes and dripped down my cheeks, but I couldn't raise a hand to wipe them. I prayed for death or, even better, annihilation.

"Private Shurtliff is a woman, Thatcher. She wore a garment to bind her breasts, and it looks to me like she sustained a fairly serious wound in her thigh at some point. She has a terrible scar. Someone removed a bullet, but not with any skill. It wouldn't surprise me if she dug it out herself. I don't know how she's gotten this far without discovery, but she's clearly gone to great lengths to keep the secret."

Silence filled the room, and I thought perhaps they had gone, or I had gone, that Robert Shurtliff had truly died, and I was dreaming. But then Thatcher spoke somewhere else, as if he paced.

"I d-don't believe it," he sputtered.

"I examined her myself, Thatcher. It is as I say. The nurse who found her in the morgue brought it to my attention. I had her moved here, to this room, to give her some privacy."

Thatcher seemed dumbfounded, but Dr. Binney pressed forward.

"Was she a good soldier, Dr. Thatcher?" he asked.

"By all accounts, yes. Exemplary. She is the general's aide-de-camp, for God's sake."

"An aide-de-camp?" Dr. Binney cried. "To a general?"

"Yes. General Paterson. He commands all of West Point. He . . . he must be informed. That is . . . if he hasn't left the city. General Howe left days ago with a full battalion."

"And what will happen to her now?" Dr. Binney worried.

"If she doesn't die . . . I don't rightly know," Thatcher responded. "But this . . . this is . . . I can't believe it. General Paterson must be informed. He will have to make that decision."

"Please," I whispered. "Please."

Both men scrambled to my side, and Dr. Binney tried to help me sit up, but I was unable to do anything but list to the side, and he propped my head instead and dribbled a bit of water into the pool of my cheek.

"I have never seen someone so ill with the fever who has come back from it," Dr. Thatcher said.

"Dr. Thatcher," Dr. Binney said, censure in his low voice. "She has defied the odds thus far. In every way."

"What is your name, madam?" Dr. Thatcher insisted, peering down at me. "You must tell me this instant. General Paterson will be made aware of your duplicity. I will let him decide what will become of you."

"Please don't tell him," I said, and somehow managed to form the words. "The general . . . didn't . . . know."

If Dr. Binney gave a response, it was not audible, and I was past caring anymore. It was finished. Over. And I let myself slip away, hoping this time I would not wake. Surely it would be better for John if I did not wake.

~ 27 ~

All Allegiance

I was moving but not flying, not soaring untethered above the earth as I'd longed to do. I heard wheels over cobbles, the screech and jostle immediately identifiable as well as the man who carried me.

"Almost there, General. Almost there," Grippy called. It was night, or maybe the darkness was just the weight of my lids over eyes that couldn't open.

"John?" The tremor in his arms and his chest ran through me. I was terror and hope mixed with humiliation. He tightened his embrace and pressed his lips to my brow.

"Hold on, Samson."

"Does . . . Agrippa . . . know?"

"Yes. He knows you are my wife."

"Oh, John. I'm so sorry."

"Do not say that." His voice shook with temper, or maybe it was grief. The darkness of the carriage left me guessing.

"Did . . . Thatcher?"

"Yes. Thatcher told me where you were."

"I cannot go back to West Point," I mourned.

"No," he whispered. "I doubt either of us can."

"Forgive me, General," I begged. "I wanted . . . only . . . to stay with you."

"Do not leave me, Samson," he choked out. "Promise me you will not leave me."

I was able to form simple sentences. That was a great improvement, and I would have told him—promised him—had I not drifted off again, cradled in his trembling arms.

~

"John?"

The weight of his hand was in my hair and on my cheek, stroking and steady, and I turned my face into it, seeking the scrape of his palm and the scent of his skin, and he said my name. I was stronger every time I woke, and every time I did, the general was there, seeing to my needs.

He brought me a glass of water and insisted on feeding me a bit of broth and bread, though I insisted I was capable of feeding myself. The candlelight flickered, and I'd lost all sense of time, and I desperately needed a toilet, a bath, and a bit of fresh air.

When I asked, all were provided, John refusing to leave any of the tasks to his sister or her servants. It was odd, lying naked in his arms without passion, odder still to be washed and dressed and fed, but he ignored my protestations, feeble as they were.

When he tucked me back into our marriage bed, opened a window, and sat down beside me in the chair he'd hardly left, I fought off the pull of exhausted slumber and reached for his hand. I needed an accounting of events. He was deeply subdued, and I feared the worst.

"Tell me what has happened," I insisted.

He breathed in deeply, as if he too had needed the airing out, and began to speak.

"Dr. Thatcher came and found me Wednesday evening and told me you were lying in a hospital bed near death. He could hardly look at me when he reported that you were not what you seemed." He cleared his throat. "I was shocked, and he misinterpreted my . . . response . . . as surprise. I did not correct his assumptions. He still thinks I didn't know."

"Praise God," I whispered. "I feared you would confess all."

He battled for control and lost it several times, his hand gripping mine, before he spoke again. "He said you begged him not to tell me. Why, Samson? Why would you do that?"

"I only wanted . . . to protect you," I breathed, and he laid his head down on the bed beside me, his big shoulders shaking, and groaned into the mattress to drown out the sound of his own torment. I laid my hand on his head, needing to touch him, unable to do more.

"I thought you had run," he cried. "I came back here, to Anne's house, and you were gone. Anne and Stephen had left for Trenton, and the servants did not know where you were. And I . . . I was convinced I'd scared you away. Your uniform was gone. I thought you were gone too."

"I do not scare so easily, General." I tried to smile, to coax him to smile, but he did not lift his head.

"Why did you leave?"

"I wanted to walk about on my own. I have no freedom in a dress. I did not know I was ill . . . really ill . . . until it was too late."

"My father died of yellow fever," he whispered. "It hits fast. He fell unconscious, just like you. And he never woke."

"I am so sorry, John." It was the only thing I could say. And I was. Desperately, truly sorry. I was so weak I could hardly move, but my mind was clear, and I knew I would recover. I wasn't sure the general would. He had not raised his head from the mattress, I could not see his eyes, and despair radiated from him.

"My uniform is gone," I murmured. "They took it from me." It was not the most important thing, but it signified something deeper, something we had to face. John was not wearing his uniform either.

"No." He shook his head. "I have it. I knew you would want it. Grippy carried your things. I carried you. No one even saw us leave the hospital except for Dr. Binney. He was worried about what would become of you. He is a very . . . decent . . . man."

The general had thought to retrieve my uniform. In that moment, I loved him more than I'd ever loved him before, and tears began to leak from the corners of my eyes and wet the pillow beneath my head. For several silent moments, I wrestled my emotions back the way I'd bound my breasts, wrapping them so tightly they would never expose me. But those days were done, and I had a new mission.

"What *will* become of me?" I asked after several minutes of weighty silence. "And what will become of you?"

Finally he raised his head. "I told Dr. Binney and Dr. Thatcher that I would see to your welfare and no charges would be brought. It felt like a betrayal not to claim you . . . or explain you . . . but I saw no benefit to either of us to make our relationship known or to expose you further."

I studied him, eyes wet, hardly breathing. He stared back, his gaze bleak, his jaw tight.

"I have seen to matters here in Philadelphia. My work here is finished, and I requested a thirty-day furlough. But I will resign when it is up. And we will go to Lenox when you are well. If that is what you want. Is that what you want, Deborah? Am I what you want? Or have I simply trampled over your wishes to reach my own desires?"

"Oh, John," I breathed. "You are the only man in heaven or earth that I want. But you cannot resign. You would never forgive yourself. And I would never forgive myself."

"Why?" he gasped.

"I will not be the reason you break your word. You made a pledge to your men. You promised you would stay, all the way to the end. You promised Phineas."

He rose from the chair, agitated, torment in his every step, and made a slow circle around the room, stopping to pull the night air into his lungs before he returned to my bedside.

"I have clearly made more promises than I can keep. I made one to you nine days ago, a promise before God. And you were taken from me the very next day. I cannot leave you, I can't do it. Not now. I don't have the strength. And you can't come with me to West Point. Dr. Thatcher's discretion will only go so far. He will not be silent if we try to continue as we have. A newspaper printed something very similar to our circumstances today, though names weren't used."

"Dr. Thatcher knew me when I was a child. He knew Deborah Samson. Yet he did not guess?"

John shook his head. "He did not."

"So Grippy . . . is the only one who knows . . . everything?"

"Yes. He and Anne. She and Stephen returned today. I will let Anne handle the reverend, though at this juncture, he only knows that you've been ill."

"Will Agrippa talk?"

"No. There is none more loyal than Agrippa Hull, though he is still in a state of shock. I think he feels a little . . . foolish. And awed. He says he should have known. He said he knew you were running from something, he just didn't know what. And he can't believe I married you."

"Yes . . . well. He can't be more shocked than I was."

The general was silent then, studying me, morose.

"Will he stay with you? And watch over you?" I asked. "He can serve as your aide."

"I cannot go back to the highlands," the general argued, but that was his love talking, not his duty, and John Paterson was nothing if not valiant. He knew what he had to do. He simply did not want to do it.

"You can. And you must, General."

His groan was more like a bellow, a warding off of reality.

"There was a time I wanted to be someone," he said. "When I dreamed—albeit quietly—of my name being bandied about and my actions recounted among the men. Benedict Arnold wanted to be someone too. And he was." He ran his hands through his loose hair and shook his head. "He'll always be someone . . . that's the odd thing. He has exactly what he wanted. He has fame. No one will ever forget the name Benedict Arnold."

"God has a sense of humor, doesn't He?"

"He gives us what we ask for," he replied, nodding. "Every unrighteous, foolish desire. So I have learned to ask for nothing. I didn't even ask for you. I just took what I wanted. And look what has happened."

"What has happened, John? Tell me."

"No one will remember the name John Paterson, and I don't care a whit. You know that. But the way I have served—the effort, the sacrifice, the time—I have to believe it matters, that it all matters. The glory is not mine. Or even ours. The glory is what God makes of our sacrifice. But you are one sacrifice I am not willing to make. And He knows it. I cannot lose you . . . and I am convinced that is exactly what will happen."

"You won't lose me. I would follow you anywhere."

His eyes filled and his hands clenched. "But you cannot follow me, Samson. You cannot follow me anymore. You can't even stay here, in Philadelphia. Do you understand?"

"Yes," I whispered.

"I want to be with you. I want to be with you so much that I bound you to me so you wouldn't—so you couldn't—get away. And still . . . you almost died." He shook his head. "I am not in control here. Not at all. I never have been."

"I am right here, my beloved general," I said, and his mouth trembled at the endearment. John Paterson had not been loved nearly well enough, and I reached for him, desirous to rectify the deficiency, but he took my hands and pressed a kiss to each palm before he let me settle them on his whiskery cheeks.

"I am afraid the moment you are out of my sight, I will never see you again. But if I am to endure to the end and do as I promised . . ." He shuddered again like he could hardly bear it. "If I am to keep my word, then I can't stay with you, and you cannot be a soldier anymore," he said.

"I know. So I will wait for you. As long as it takes."

His shoulders sagged as if I'd just granted him pardon. He laid his head against me and wrapped his arms around my waist. I stroked his hair, reveling in the weight of him and the gift of another day.

"I believe some men and women are blessed to see a bigger purpose, to understand the ripples that extend far beyond their own lives," I said. "That is what gives me hope, that all of this suffering will be worth something far bigger than any of us. You are one of those men, General. And I want to be one of those women."

"Do you promise?" he whispered. "Do you promise that nothing will happen to you? That you will focus all that considerable Samson might and keep yourself alive and well until we can be together again?"

"I promise. And when this is all over, I will be waiting for you in Lenox."

~

Grippy paid me a visit before he and the general returned to the Point. I wore a dress and Anne's maid arranged my hair, but when he looked at me, brown eyes wide, hat in his hand, I was transported back to that first day at the Thomases' and the brothers openly sharing their unflattering opinions about my appearance.

"I'm still not much to look at, am I?" I asked. "Even in a dress. I've never been a bonny girl." I meant to make him smile, but his eyes got bright instead.

"I'm a fool," he muttered.

"Why?"

"I treated you badly. Poked fun at the way you looked."

"You treated me exactly the way I wanted to be treated, like every other soldier on the Point. You were my friend."

"We are friends, aren't we, Bonny?" He released a pent-up breath. "Is it all right if I still call you that?"

"Yes, Agrippa. We are. And Bonny's just fine with me."

"That's good then. I gotta get used to Deborah. To Mrs. Paterson." He shook his head like the shock still hadn't worn off.

"I lied to you about who I was, Grippy. I'm sorry. But I never lied about anything else."

"The general told me most of it." He shook his head again. "You are some kind of woman, Bonny. Didn't I always say there was more to you than meets the eye?"

I nodded, and for a moment we fell silent.

"You'll be going to Lenox now. That's good." He didn't sound convinced. I wasn't convinced either, but encouragement was not what I sought from Agrippa Hull. I needed promises.

"You'll take care of General Paterson, won't you? You'll keep his spirits up and make sure he eats and sleeps and comes back from those long walks he takes?" I asked.

"Yes, ma'am. I will."

"And you'll protect him, and his reputation, from those who might have heard about me?" I added in a rush. "I'm no Benedict Arnold, but I won't have the general tarnished by my name. Any of them. I clean up my own messes."

His eyes softened, and he began to smile. "Your secret is safe with me, Bonny. Remember what I told you? You don't have to be afraid anymore. You're one of us now, and I protect my own."

~ 28 ~

Conclude Peace

June 12, 1783

Dear Elizabeth,

The house in Lenox is just as you described it, even down to the flowers on the rugs and the colors on the walls. When I touched the railing, I remembered how you liked the way it felt beneath your hand as you ascended the stairs.

The outside is John, stately and solid with classic appeal, but the inside is a place created by and for women. John's presence is nowhere to be found in the furnishings and the decor, but his absence—eight years of absence, marked only by brief furloughs—is deeply felt.

You are here in this house. You are present in your daughters' faces. They are not little girls anymore.

Ruthie is nine years old. Polly eleven, and Hannah is almost thirteen. Hannah is tall. When John said she favored you, I thought she would be small. But she is dark and long and lovely and almost as tall as me.

Ruthie does look like John, just as he said, though she is loud where he is reserved and demanding where he is dutiful. She is the life of the household and wants all of my attention. Perhaps she, like Jeremiah, needs it the most. I think Polly must be the most like you in looks and demeanor. She is determined to do everything well, but struggles with poor health. She is all the more resolved because of it, and I have begun to teach her to weave.

Poor John will come home to daughters who have grown up without him.

I miss him desperately, but I am beginning to think this best, this time I have to adjust to your home and your walls and your footsteps still lingering on the floors and in your daughters' hearts. It makes me cross to think the general was right that I come here, to Lenox. He is infuriating that way, isn't he? Always making good choices, always knowing what is best. One might say his decision to fall in love with me was the one exception.

We have returned to our preexistence, John and I, to the days of our letter writing and letter reading. He is new and old and mine and yours when he is on the page, but I have loved every iteration of John Paterson.

I can see John in his mother and his sisters, Mary, Anne, and Sarah. They have the same pale eyes and generous brows, the bow-shaped lips and red-brown locks, though Mrs. Paterson's hair is snowy white. They are handsome people, well-made and well-mannered, and they welcomed me with open arms. In that way too, they are just like him.

Anne and Reverend Holmes brought me all the way from Society Hill in Philadelphia to Paterson House in Lenox, Massachusetts. It took us two weeks of travel in a ridiculous carriage, and had I not still been weak and trussed up in uncomfortable gowns, I would have begged to walk or ride Common Sense, who made the journey with me.

The general was responsible for many arrangements, privately and publicly. Morris, Maggie, and Amos Clay reached Lenox even before I did, a letter in hand from John Paterson declaring them freemen, along with a small contingent of returning local soldiers entrusted with escorting them safely there.

Imagine my surprise when Morris walked out to greet the Holmeses' carriage the day I arrived. I confess that I cried when I realized what the general had done, and I subjected Morris to an embrace, which he endured stoically, much the way I did when John first embraced me.

The general had not prepared either of us for the surprise, but when Morris saw me, he just shook his head, saying, "Well, I'll be. Maggie told me you were a woman, and the general's woman at that, but I didn't believe it." I should have known Maggie would see the truth. The women always did.

The day I arrived in Lenox was eerily similar to the day I arrived at the Thomases'. Both houses were brimming with strangers who needed me, and I had to find my purpose and my place. I realize now that my whole life has prepared me for this. In many ways, you prepared me too.

Unlike when I arrived at the Thomases', I had no experience in the part I was expected to play at Paterson House. I'd never been a wife or a mother, and instead of being put to work and assigned a servant's quarters, I was shown to a room that had once belonged to you, a room where all your possessions—even your clothes in the bureau and the wardrobe—still remained.

I found my letters—ten years' worth—in a wooden chest at the bottom of your bed. It is still your bed. Your home. Your daughters. Your world. Even . . . your John, though he was somehow mine too, even then. The letters are soft and faded, like you enjoyed them often. It was odd, seeing them all together, how my writing changed and grew, lengthening with me.

Hannah discovered me reading the letters beside your open chest one night and summoned her sisters to demand that I "stop snooping in her mother's things." I showed them my name at the bottom of each letter.

"Your mother was my very first friend," I said. "These are my things too."

Hannah stared at me, suspicious.

"I used to write her letters. So many letters. And she wrote me back. She was a woman of consequence, and everything I was not."

"You are strange looking," Ruthie said. "That's what Grandmother says."

"Ruthie, that is not kind. You should not repeat private conversation," Polly scolded.

"It wasn't private if we all heard it." Ruthie shrugged, unrepentant.

Polly tried to mediate. "But strange is not bad."

"Grandmother says you are arresting," Hannah admitted. "Aunt Anne says your looks are unsettling."

John had said the same thing, but I did not tell them that.

"Would you like me to read them to you?" I asked. It was late, and they should have been in their beds, but I sensed a miracle at my fingertips. A bridge between us all. They sat around me and I read, starting with that very first letter dated March 27, 1771, which began:

Dear Miss Elizabeth,

My name is Deborah Samson. I'm certain you've been warned that I would be writing. I am not an accomplished writer, but I hope to be. I promise I will work very hard to make my letters interesting so you will enjoy reading them and allow me to continue. Reverend Conant tells me you are kind and beautiful and smart. I am not beautiful, but I try to be kind, and I am very smart.

With each letter, I introduced myself to them, as I once introduced myself to you. There are so many, and we read only a smattering that night, but the girls have warmed to me in a way that would not have been possible without our correspondence, and I have wept in quiet gratitude that you kept each missive and prepared a way for me here in your life. Here in their lives. You have prepared us all.

We continued our reading the next day, and the next. They like me to read the letters out loud under the tree where you are buried. They call it Mother's tree, and I wonder if you are not there listening with them. They laugh at the ninny I was and the ninny I am and marvel that you were once my dearest friend. I marvel at that too, and Proverbs 16:9 has been ever on my mind.

"A man's heart devises his way: but the Lord directs his steps."

All my ways, all my steps, have brought me here.

—Deborah

General John Paterson returned home for good in December of 1783. When he left Lenox early on a Saturday morning in 1775, the thirteen colonies were bordered in the west by the Alleghenies. When he resigned his commission at the end of '83, Lenox was no longer at the edge of the frontier. America stretched west to the Mississippi.

He'd been back only twice in the nearly nine years he'd been gone. Once to bury his sister Ruth in '77, and once to bury his wife. He did not warn us he was coming, though we had been watching for him since soldiers had begun straggling back after the Treaty of Paris was announced.

Of course he was the last to come home. He had promised to stay to the end.

I saw him from an upstairs window, a lone figure on a white horse. Agrippa had gone left at the fork to Stockbridge and John had kept right. I saw him when he was still a ways out, just a speck on the long, straight road through Lenox.

The girl I'd once been would have tucked her skirts into her bodice and flown out to meet him, stretching the length of her leg and the size of her heart. But though my heart raced, my legs could not, and I went to the willow tree instead, needing a moment with Elizabeth before I greeted our beloved John.

It gave the others time to welcome him, all the many women in his life. I heard Ruthie shrieking and Polly sobbing and Hannah telling both to pipe down. Then there was laughter, babbling, and boisterous kissing and finally the rumble of my name on his lips.

"Where is my wife?" he asked, and I heard a frisson of doubt. Had he really feared I wouldn't wait?

"She is beneath the willow tree with Mother," Ruthie informed him and everyone else within a mile.

"She said it was only fair that Mother be part of your triumphant return," Polly said, parroting me word for word.

"Ahh." Relief resonated in the sigh. "That sounds like Samson."

"We like her, Papa," Polly said.

"I love her," Ruthie declared, always in competition with her sisters.

"I will never like her as much as I loved Mother," Hannah warned. "But she will do."

"Thank you, Hannah. And when did you get so tall?" John asked, and I could hear his dismay amid his delight.

"I have always been tall, Father. You are just enormous, so you never noticed."

Mrs. Paterson, bless her gracious heart, intervened. "Come, girls. Let's go inside and give your father and Deborah a moment."

"And Mother," Hannah reminded.

"And your mother," Mrs. Paterson amended. "Good gracious. What a strange assortment we are."

I heard them depart as his tread grew closer, and even though my back was turned, I closed my eyes just to hear him come, the way I'd done in the Red House, tracking him through the halls, waiting in anticipation for every moment I got to spend with him.

"I would like to feel that fearsome gaze on my face again," he said, pausing just beyond the tree, Elizabeth's stone between us. I reached out and touched the cold surface, an acknowledgment, and then ran my hands down the blue dress I'd worn to marry him. I'd had to wear it many times since—a good dress is not something to waste—but the moment I'd seen him from the upstairs window, I'd run and pulled it on, wanting to start our marriage where we'd left off. I'd had no time to properly dress my hair, and I'd drawn it back into a smooth tail. It was much longer than Shurtliff's had been, but I liked the combination of the dress and the soldier's queue.

"Welcome home, sir," I said.

I turned slightly, unable to hide my smile. It was better to laugh than to weep, but then I saw his face, every dear and perfect line, and I could not jest or call him sir. I could only stare and drink him in. It was impossible that a man, bedraggled and windblown, saddle-weary and uncertain, could still look like John Paterson.

Impossible.

"I can't breathe," he said. "Looking at you . . . I can't breathe."

"Nor can I," I choked. "I haven't breathed since Philadelphia when Anne turned me back into a girl."

Surprised mirth split his cheeks and parted his lips, and we laughed together amid our tears.

"Thank God for Anne," he said, wiping his cheeks. And still we stood, gazing at one another without closing the space, elongating the incomprehensible joy of reunion.

He stooped and picked up a rock near the base of Elizabeth's grave, and brushed the snow and debris from it. I thought he would set it atop the marker, an acknowledgment of his own, but he showed it to me instead, a smooth stone, ordinary and unremarkable, sitting in the palm of his hand.

“Once you told me that you loved in different amounts. Big piles and little piles,” he said.

“You remember that?”

“I do. You said your love for me was a mountain on your chest.” His voice quaked, and he wrapped his fingers around the little rock.

I nodded, and pressed a hand to my heart, afraid it would burst forth without me.

“How big is the pile today, Samson?”

I could not endure the distance any longer and flew into his arms, knocking his hat from his head and the breath back into my lungs. He braced his feet, swept me up, and kissed me without waiting for me to answer, ravenous and unrestrained, his ardor and relief matched only by my own.

“Samson himself could not knock it down,” I confessed. “Samson herself.”

~ 29 ~

This Declaration

My mother died without ever knowing my story. She lived out her days in her sister's home in Plympton. She did not seek to visit me, nor did she request that I visit her. She never inquired where I'd been or what I'd done after I left the Thomases, and I assumed she didn't want to know. I assumed no one really wanted to know. Better it be left unsaid. I wrote her letters without shape or color, consisting of short, bloodless details that encompassed my whole life, and she never asked for more.

> *I have married General John Paterson of Lenox, Massachusetts, a widower whom I became acquainted with many years ago. He has a fine home and three daughters. I am well. —Deborah*

> *I have given birth to a son. We have named him John Paterson after his father and his grandfather. I am well. —Deborah*

I have delivered a daughter. We have named her Elizabeth. We are all well. —Deborah

She wrote back in much the same way, giving me a brief accounting of the siblings I didn't know and townspeople I could not remember. And she always ended the letters the way I did—*"I am well"*—and we never discussed whether or not that was true.

Back and forth, across the miles. Across the years. Until I received a letter from her sister that was not much different from all of the other communications I'd ever sent or received. It was short and emotionless, but it ended with a slight variation.

"Your mother died Tuesday last. I doubt it will come as a shock. She has not been well."

I sent money for her burial and a bit of extra for my aunt and uncle, and received a thank-you, a bundle of letters, and a history my mother had compiled from William Bradford's journals. An inscription inside said, *For Deborah from Mother* in a wobbling hand. The letters were the ones I had written her, all bound in a ribbon, a chronicle of fifteen years. Beyond my name and careful penmanship—perfect swells and slants—there was little of me on each page. I couldn't imagine why she'd kept them.

I tried to read the history, but each word was a wound, a chastisement, and I put it in Elizabeth's chest at the foot of my bed, the place where she'd kept my letters. Over the years, I'd added my treasures to Elizabeth's chest as well. My uniform was there.

The coat would not button across my breasts when I tried it on, and it smelled like horse and campfires. Beneath the stench was a hint of lather and hair grease and *him*, and though I slept at his side each night and carried his name, my belly clenched and my blood warmed. And I missed him.

I missed me.

The uniform breeches were like old stockings, snug in places and worn through in others, but I left them on as I donned my cap. The green plume was nothing more than a wilted weed, but if I closed my eyes and nodded my head so that it brushed my cheek, it wasn't hard to remember.

The general's uniform still hung in a cloth bag at the back of the wardrobe. He'd worn it a few times. When Washington was elected president in '89 and when he went home to Mount Vernon in '97, John went to Philadelphia for the swearing in and the send-off, but I'd refused to go with him both times. I wanted to protect him, even from myself.

I made a new pair of breeches that looked just like the ones I'd worn. It took me a few attempts to get the fit right, but once I did, I fashioned more. Then I made myself a shirt and a waistcoat too, white with plain white buttons. I bought a green plume—a dozen of them—in Lenox and a black tricorn hat and tall black boots. I dyed nine yards of woolen cloth colonial blue, and lied and said it was for a new dress. I had no reason to lie, but I wasn't ready to talk, and for weeks I mulled and mourned and pondered and planned until one day Agrippa Hull stopped by to see the general and caught me chopping wood in my brand-new breeches.

"Bonny, good grief. What are you doing?" he asked, collapsing into the rocking chair on my back porch.

"I'm chopping wood, Agrippa."

"Someone might see you. Think of the general!"

"Do you suppose some people might be willing to pay to see me in breeches, Grippy?" I mused.

His jaw dropped.

I realized belatedly how that might have sounded. "I would like to put on a small production. And sell tickets. I would wear my uniform and talk about the war from the female perspective. I would call it

'Deborah Samson, the Girl Who Went to War.' Or 'Secret Soldier.' Or something similar."

He cocked his head, incredulous. "Now why would you go and do that?"

"You sit on the green and tell stories about the war all the time. Soldiers come to your house and drink that grog you make. And you talk about the Revolution. I want to talk about it too. On a stage."

"I'm not going to help you run away, Bonny."

It was my turn to gape at him. "I am not running away."

"You've got that wanderlust. Some folks do. You've always been a little wild. But you can't be running around in those breeches. Not anymore. You're not Bonny boy now. You're Mrs. Paterson."

"So why do you still call me Bonny?" I shot back. "And I should be able to go wherever I want, Agrippa Hull. I should be able to walk from Lenox with my musket and my sound mind without someone giving me permission or escort."

"*Should* is a funny thing. People talk an awful lot about the way things *should be* and not the way things are. You're a woman, and that's a reality you can't argue out of."

"I'm man enough."

He laughed at that. "Yeah. I guess you are. I guess you were. But I don't think you'll fool people like you did before. Your female is spilling out all over now. You're ripe."

My shoulders sank. It was what I feared.

"The general is one of the best men I know. Why are you running away? And from *him* of all people?"

"I'm not running away!" I insisted. "I am not running away from him."

"Then who are you running away from? And why do I feel like we had this conversation a long time ago?" He scratched his head.

"Because we did. We talked about being born free and dying free. Do you realize that you are one of the only people who truly know who I am?"

"You mean soldier Bonny?"

"Yes. I mean soldier Bonny."

"Oh, lots of people know. They just don't know what to make of it."

"They don't know Deborah Samson. They just think they do."

"So you want the whole world to know her. Is that it?"

"I want the world to *accept* her."

"Accept?" His sputtering became a great rolling laugh. And he kept laughing, throwing his head back and stamping his feet like he couldn't get enough.

His response only made me angrier.

"You may leave now, Grippy," I insisted, splitting another log and throwing it aside. "I am so very glad I have entertained you."

He didn't leave. He just kept chortling, rocking back and forth in my chair, watching me hack away at my anger.

"Oh, Bonny. That's funny. That's a funny one. 'I want the world to accept her,'" he said, pitching his voice a little higher, mimicking me. "Well go on then, woman. Go chase acceptance. When you find it, let me know. 'Cause there's a few African folk who'd really like to know where it is." He laughed again and slowly rose from the chair as if he'd worn himself out with his merriment.

"Not me, though. I already found it. It's right here." He patted his chest. "Right here."

John found me where Agrippa left me, still chopping wood, still wearing my breeches, still stewing in the emotional soup of my mother's death and finding acceptance.

"At ease, soldier," the general demanded.

I scoffed, but I stopped hacking and watched him walk toward me. Over the years, the ruddiness had continued to fade from his hair, starting at his temples and working its way back, but John Paterson was not greatly changed from the general who'd ridden onto the field at West Point to greet a batch of new recruits. My heart had stopped then, and it stopped again. Always. Every time.

He didn't slow until he'd reached me, and when he did, he lifted my chin and pressed a kiss on my mouth that was neither polite nor perfunctory.

"Why are you chopping wood, Private Shurtliff? Mountains and mountains of wood?" He looked around at my piles. "Our children will think you are building an ark."

"I am chopping wood because I can. I am good at it. And our children are not even here. John Jr. has gone into town and Betsy is at your mother's."

John's daughters were grown and married, and at fourteen and twelve, John Jr. and Betsy had busy lives and interests of their own. John Jr. had grown so tall and handsome. He looked more like a Samson than a Paterson, though he was his father through and through, dependable, devoted, and good. He would care what others thought of me. It would bother him to hear them talk, but he would be leaving for Yale in the fall.

Betsy had John's red hair and my fierce gaze, but she had no interest in books or school. She was a talented weaver and Mrs. Paterson had dedicated an entire room in her house to a loom, though we had one at Paterson House as well.

"That loom is yours, Mother," Betsy always argued. "The one at Grandmother's never gets used by anyone but me. And I am making you something. A surprise."

"You have blistered your hands." John took the axe from me and embedded it in the stump.

"They are too soft." I turned and stomped into the barn. He followed me. I grabbed the pitchfork and began turning the straw. It didn't need to be turned; I'd just freshened it that morning.

"Where did you find those breeches? Those are not mine. They fit you too well."

"I made them. Are you scandalized?"

"No. But you don't look like a boy in breeches any longer, Samson."

"That is because you know better."

His eyes narrowed and my pulse quickened. It was always thus between us. Even after two children and almost two decades. The hunger and the wanting had never faded, much to my surprise.

"You are not shaped like a man."

"Then I shall have to fashion a paunch to wear under my shirt to give my waist a little girth," I said, though the general's waist was as flat and hard as the barn walls.

"Your waist will thicken soon enough if we continue like we have. My mother had me when she was your age."

He was teasing me, but I stilled. I could not continue like we had. I could not. I had been pregnant five times and miscarried thrice, very early on. I had been determined to be as good at having children as I was at everything else, but it had turned out that I had no control or say in the matter, and I had not gotten pregnant in many years. But if John Paterson put another baby in my belly now, I would never be able to go. The thought brought me up short. I raised the pitchfork at my husband.

"Stay away from me, John Paterson. I am in no mood for coupling."

"Then you should not have donned those breeches."

He shoved the door closed, lowered the latch, and tossed the pitchfork aside. The tumble that ensued, hands grappling to find flesh, mouths seeking, proved me a liar. I was in the mood for coupling. I was always in the mood for coupling, and unlike our earliest encounter, my breasts were unbound beneath my shirt and waistcoat. John stared at them as if he hadn't seen them a thousand times—ten thousand times—before.

"You are so beautiful. They are so beautiful. They should never be bound."

"Never again. I will ride naked through the town," I challenged, sardonic even as I surrendered.

He groaned, grappling with my breeches and his own, and our heated conversation became a frantic conjoining that left us panting and loose-limbed in the straw.

"What has gotten into you, my wife?" he murmured, pulling me across his chest and tangling his hands in my long braid. I knew he did not speak of the tussle that had just occurred. That was not new. But my breeches were.

I pulled away and wiggled back into my clothes. "I want to make myself another uniform."

"Why? None of us have need of our uniforms any longer."

"I have need of mine," I said, and sudden, fierce emotion welled in my chest. "But my old breeches are too tight in the hips and no matter how firmly I bind my breasts, I can still tell I am a woman beneath my shirt. I can't even button the coat. You have made me fat, General Paterson."

"Fat?" He laughed. "Not hardly. You simply aren't bones and bandages anymore."

"I cannot run, or even walk for long distances. And I'm not as strong. I could barely pull myself up to the beam when I tried. I have always been able to pull myself up to the beam."

"What are you talking about?"

I climbed the ladder to the loft, but instead of climbing up, I swung out, clinging to the lower beam, just like I'd done in the Thomas barn with the brothers. John watched me from the straw where he still lounged, his head propped on his hand, his clothes rumpled and his expression sated.

I bellowed and strained, and managed to perform the maneuver once before I had to link my left leg around the ladder and swing back to safety.

"You're a monkey."

"I used to do ten of those without a thought."

"Come down from there."

"I am disappointed in myself," I said, still clinging to the ladder. I could not look at him. I was too close to tears.

"Deborah. Come here," he insisted.

I descended with swimming eyes and moved to sit beside him in the straw.

"Tell me what is wrong, soldier."

"Don't call me that!" I snapped.

"You were one," he said, unbothered. He picked a piece of straw from my hair and ran his hand down the length of my braid. "You always will be."

I shook my head, adamant. "I never will be."

"Deborah," he murmured, still stroking my hair. I wanted to push him away, and I wanted to draw him closer.

"The Thomases sent ten sons," I blurted. "Middleborough sent many of her sons, but no one gave more than the deacon and Mrs. Thomas."

"No one did," he agreed softly.

"It was my one regret, when I enlisted, that I might cause them more sorrow or shame. I thought I did not care what my mother believed of me. I told myself I did not care aught what *anyone* in Middleborough thought, though I scurried away like I did."

His hand tightened in my hair, like he knew to hold on.

"Reverend Conant was gone, and I was glad I couldn't disappoint him, though I'm not certain he would have been ashamed. He was not that kind of man. He was always so proud of me, in all of my peculiar stages."

"He saw the wonder of you, just as Elizabeth did. Just as I do."

I bore down, trying to hold back the water that kept rising, rising.

"I never went back. You know this. I never went back to Middleborough. I allowed the Thomases and my mother to endure the stories and speculation that must have ensued. I never explained. Never thanked them. I just left with my tail tucked between my legs. And after Phineas . . . I never felt like I could."

"I will take you to Middleborough," the general offered without hesitation. "If that is what you wish, that is what we will do. We will go to Sproat's Tavern and the First Congregational Church. And we will tell them who you are and what you've done. I will be your witness. I will attest to every word."

"You will make me respectable."

"You *are* respectable."

I challenged him with a stony glare and trembling lips. "If people knew the whole truth, I would not be. If you were not by my side, I would not be. Not to them. Not to most people."

"You did something no other woman—to my knowledge—has ever done. You should be proud."

"I *am* proud. But I am also deeply . . . ashamed."

He recoiled like I'd slapped him, but I continued on. There were things that needed to be said. So many things, and if I didn't say them now, I might as well throw myself into the harbor and let my skirts drag me under.

"You know my ancestry."

"William Bradford, Myles Standish, John Alden," he parroted dutifully. Our children had heard the stories too. I'd felt I owed it to my mother.

"Yes. I wonder sometimes if William Bradford knows me the way I've always known him. I think he might. Every soul that has ever been born is a pinprick of light in an enormous net, and his light and mine are connected."

"An enormous net," he murmured. "Yes. I think so too."

"But it is not William Bradford I think about most. It is her."

"Who?" The word was soft, and he had grown still.

"His first wife. Dorothy."

"Your grandmother."

"No. I have no relation to her at all. Not by blood. But she is the one I think about."

"She is the one who threw herself overboard, into the sea," he said, remembering. "The one who lost her hope."

"Yes. We are the descendants of his second wife, of Alice, who came to Plymouth Bay in 1623, a widow with two children. She gave William Bradford three more, and one was Joseph, my ancestor. But it is Dorothy I dream of. She haunts me. She cries and asks her son, John, to forgive her. I cry and ask my husband, John, to forgive me. And now . . . my mother haunts me too."

"Why?" he asked, wiping the tears that had begun to spill over onto my cheeks. I bowed my head and began to weep, and it was not the quiet weeping of frustration or the pained weeping of a bullet in my flesh. It was not even the sorrow of death or the reassertion of life. I wasn't sure what it was, but it was roiling up from someplace deep, from my well of miseries, a place I thought long dry.

"Deborah. Deborah," John moaned, pulling me into his arms. "Shhh. Don't do that. I can't bear it." But there were tears in his choked rebuke. I was not prone to tears, and he didn't know what to do with this version of me. For several minutes, I was too overcome to tell him.

"I have hated my mother. Loathed her. But I see now that there was much to admire. She did not abandon us or throw herself into the sea, though she could have. She was too proud for that. And she was so proud of her heritage. It has only recently occurred to me that my mother took pride in what was because she knew no pride in what is."

"I don't understand."

"The one thing my mother gave me was my name. She made me proud of my name. She made me proud of what I came from and who I was. Yet I have spent so many years hiding from my name." I rubbed my chest, battling the sentiment that surged there. "It was Deborah Samson who marched and bled and starved and served. *Me.*

But Deborah Samson is still an object of scorn and speculation when anyone thinks of me at all. And I have allowed myself to be by staying silent. I never even told my mother what I did."

I was overcome again, drowning, and John did not try to answer or even urge me to stop. He held me for a long time, the way he'd done after Phineas died, and when he finally spoke, I heard the same helplessness in his voice, the same guilt.

"You've remained quiet all these years . . . for me."

"You are my heart, John Paterson."

"And you are mine. But you are unhappy."

"No. Not unhappy. It is not so simple as that."

"You have lost your hope," he whispered.

"Yes. I have lost my hope because I have lost my purpose."

"What can I do?" he asked, his compassion evident. "Tell me, soldier."

"I know what I am asking. I know it might cost you your dignity, and it might even cost you *your* good name, the name your father had and now . . . the name of our son."

"I have never cared all that much about my name, Samson. I told you a long time ago. No one will remember John Paterson. That has never been what motivated me."

"I need to tell my story, General. I want to tell it. Even if no one wants to hear a woman speak. Even if I am run off the stage and chased out of town. I need to tell my story because it is not just my story. It is Dorothy's. And Elizabeth's. And Mrs. Thomas's. It is my mother's story and your daughters' story. We were all there too. We suffered and sacrificed. We fought, even if it was not always on the battlefield. It was our Revolution as well, and yet . . . no one ever asks us."

~ 30 ~

Divine Providence

People wanted to hear it.

I arranged the entire tour myself. I booked venues and put advertisements in the papers. I went to Boston and Providence and Albany and New York. I filled halls. The *Colombian Sentinel* said it was the first tour of its kind, a woman giving a public lecture.

I started every show with a demonstration. I wore a uniform—a blue jacket with white facing and crisp white pants. It wasn't the uniform I'd been given years before. It wasn't the uniform I'd patched and repaired. I'd fashioned myself a new one, identical to the old. The hat on my head with its jaunty feather was new too. But the musket was the same. The maneuvers too. I performed a full five minutes of drills with John calling out the commands, the snap of my gun and the whisper of my movement the only sound in the hall.

I loaded my weapon, ripping the paper cartridges open with my teeth and flying through the motions of pouring the powder, dropping the bullet, and tamping it all down with my rod, drawing a smattering of applause as I completed each demonstration of my manly skill. Then I marched back off the platform and out of the hall, only to quickly change and return to the assembly, wearing the attire of Deborah Samson, the wife of a general, my hair swept up, my dress accentuating my female silhouette. But I still carried my musket, and the crowd loved that.

I always began my speech the same way, and I always stood on the stage alone.

"It is not for the man who has everything and wants more that we fight, but for the man who has nothing." They were the words that had inspired the revolution in me, and I believed them still.

"In no place on earth can a man or woman who is born into certain circumstances ever hope to truly escape them. Our lots are cast from the moment we inhabit our mothers' wombs, from the moment we draw breath. But perhaps that can change here, in this land."

We went to Middleborough too.

Reverend Conant's old church agreed to let me speak from their pulpit, a truly revolutionary concession. The Third Baptist Church invited me too, not wanting to be outdone by their only competition, and I made my presentation on two nights, giving two consecutive performances from each church, and all four shows were full to brimming with people from Plympton and Taunton too, though I was a curiosity more than a favorite son.

Mrs. Thomas and Benjamin came. The deacon had passed, and Mrs. Thomas had grown even smaller. Her dark hair was silver, but her brown eyes were still the same. When I approached her at the end, she drew me into her arms and laid her head against my chest, as if I were the mother and she the child. Age has a way of reversing those roles.

"Oh, Deborah. Oh, my dear girl. I have missed you. I have missed you so. Will you come back to the house with us and have a late supper or at least a pot of tea and some bread and jam?"

I agreed, though I arranged to come the following day for the midday meal before we left for Boston. I spent the afternoon introducing John to the farm and the fields that had once been my comfort and my cage.

"This room is even smaller than your quarters at the Red House," he said softly, surveying the tiny space that I'd been so fortunate to have. I knew that now. I had been one of the lucky ones.

The space had been used and occupied in the years that I'd been gone, and nothing of mine remained, but I had only to close my eyes and breathe deeply, and I was twelve years old again, scratching away at my letters by candlelight.

Over a simple meal at the old table now crowded with empty chairs, we reminisced about the early years, speaking cherished names and remembering beloved faces, honoring them with our memories. Jacob had come home after the war and married Margaret, who had waited patiently for his return, but they'd moved west into Ohio, taking advantage of the land Jacob had been promised when he was made a lieutenant.

Benjamin had never married and now ran the Thomas farm, along with Francis and Daniel, who lived nearby with their own families. I would have liked to see them, but got the feeling that they'd chosen not to see me. Association was a complicated matter, and I forgave them even as I grieved.

Before we departed, Benjamin brought out a wooden box that he seemed loath to part with. He held it for a moment, his bottom lip between his teeth, and then handed it to me.

"These are yours. Everything that you left. I read all those letters to Elizabeth in your journals. Many times." His face became an uncomfortable pink, but he held my gaze as he confessed. "They were wonderful. You should compile a book."

John, always observant and always gracious, excused himself to stow the box and see to the horses while we said our final goodbyes. Mrs. Thomas embraced me again and made me promise to write.

I said I would and apologized for all my years of silence. "You were my mother. You loved me. And I left without telling you that I loved you too. Can you forgive me, Mrs. Thomas?"

She took my face in her hands and, with trembling lips and streaming eyes, gave me absolution. "I am so proud of you. I have always been so proud of you. Don't ever stop being Deborah Samson. Don't ever hide her again. The world needs to know your story."

As we rode away, the carriage bouncing over the lane I'd raced down a thousand times, John looked at me with a sad smile.

"Were they all in love with you, Samson?" he asked.

"Who?" I answered, still caught in reminiscence and distracted by old haunts. Mayflower Hill beckoned and the willow trees wept.

"Those ten Thomas boys. Were they all in love with you?"

I tsked and shook my head, accustomed to his teasing. "Jacob married Margaret."

"Yes. Pragmatic of him. But poor Benjamin Thomas is still standing in the road."

I looked back and saw that it was true. I waved again and he held up his hand, an acknowledgment that he still saw me, though he was almost out of view.

"The day you arrived . . . it must have been something," John mused. "I almost feel sorry for them."

"They said I looked like a fence post, a scarecrow, and would murder them in their beds." I laughed, but remembrance burned in my throat and tickled my nose. "They were merciless."

"No. They were totally at your mercy, poor fellows. No girl would have ever measured up after you."

I wiped my eyes and looked back, one more time. Benjamin was beyond my sight. "You don't know everything, John Paterson."

"No. But I know you, Samson."

April 29, 1827

Dear Elizabeth,

The willow tree over your grave has grown tall. There's a place for me beside you there, and I think this letter will be my last. I've written all there is to say and told you all there is to tell.

I have grown old in your house. I used to think how odd it was to walk where you had walked, to sit at your writing desk where you had once written to me, to look from your windows and see from your perspective.

I asked John once what you would think of me, stepping into your life the way I did. Stepping into your shoes.

He simply said, "She would welcome you here. But you brought your own shoes and made your own life. You didn't take hers."

And we left it at that.

John became a judge—he's been a judge for many years. He's never lost an election. I think I told you about that. He went to Congress for two years too, but it required too much time away from home, and he did not run again.

The people trust him, and he is fair. They love that he was a general and are willing to look past the uncomfortable fact that I am his wife. Once, a newspaper man asked him about me on the stump. John called me up, introduced me, and I gave the speech I'd memorized, complete with paragraphs from the declaration, my thoughts on the rights of all men and women, and my Pilgrim ancestry. I even finished with my musket and the manual of arms.

No one asked about me again.

Your daughters are grown. My children too. They call each other siblings, and it makes my heart glad. Our grandchildren run about and race and holler when they are here. We have a granddaughter named Elizabeth and one named Deborah, and they are the best of friends. They have challenged the eldest boys to a footrace, and I have fashioned them each a pair of magic breeches to make it a little more fair.

It's been twenty-five years since my first speaking tour, and I only do small engagements here and there, now and then. It's always an honor that people still want to meet me, and they are always surprised by the way I look and the way I speak. They say things like, "You must have appeared much different then," or "I thought you would be taller." I find that one remarkable, for I am still very tall. The general says they are surprised that I look like a woman. "They don't expect you to be lovely or wise or well-spoken," he says. "They expect a Samson and you are a Deborah."

I like to think I am both.

Some don't believe I ever really served. They think me a liar, and I've been the source of talk—most of it unbecoming—since I started telling my story. But John knows the truth, and I know the truth, and together we have kept hope burning.

Agrippa Hull knows the truth too, and he likes to say that change is slow, but once it comes, it stays. He is still in Stockbridge. He's as much a celebrity in these parts as I am, probably more so, though no one ever has a bad thing to say about him. People still gather around him on sunny days on the town green to hear him tell stories from the war.

He found a woman he likes to look at and one who likes to look at him. Their children are grown too, freemen born of freemen, but slavery hasn't ended, not even all these years after the war. Slavery hasn't ended, and women still have our place, and we'd best not venture out of it. Maybe it is because we are treasured, as John once said, but it is one thing to be treasured and it is another to be a treasure. One is valued, one is possessed, and people aren't possessions.

I applied for a soldier's pension and sent dozens of letters to Congress, asking to have my service acknowledged. John says I earned it, same as all the others, and I should have it, but it wasn't until 1818, even though I had letters of support from Paul Revere, who has become a dear friend, and President John Quincy Adams himself, that Congress finally relented, and I received my pay. Paul Revere delivered it personally, and the papers wrote that I was once again drinking in taverns with men, and the long-ago story from Sproat's Tavern in Middleborough resurfaced.

I've made John promise that he will apply as a soldier's spouse if I pass before he does. I put his promise in writing and made him sign it Major General John Paterson. He doesn't argue with me anymore—not on such things—but when I get too bossy, he refers to me as Private Shurtliff, reminding me he outranks me. Then he smiles that secret smile, the one that makes me catch my breath, and we remember how it was when I ceased to be Shurtliff and he became my beloved John.

I was a soldier, and I am proud of that. I am a mother too, and a wife, and I have not wished away the blessings or power of womanhood, as you once counseled. I have embraced every role, played every part, and made my mark on the world.

But the world has made its mark on me too.

In Genesis, when Jacob wrestled with God, he limped forever after. I limp too. The years have taught me that we never leave our battles, as worthy as they are, unscathed. Every cause has a cost, and so many have paid it. So many. And much of the world will never know the part they played, the part I played, a girl called Samson.

Sometimes when I close my eyes, I am marching again. Moments from those days stand out in glaring color, a red kerchief on a clothesline surrounded by wool. The memories wave at me gaily and haunt my dreams like I am there, the bare feet of the men around me leaving blood in the snow. Red and white and coats of blue. Marching endlessly back from war toward a future we will never see.

But I do not dream of Dorothy May Bradford anymore. My skirts don't wrap around my legs and pull me under. I have learned to kick them free. To wear breeches when I must. And soon I will race again.

I can almost hear my brothers calling.

—Deborah

AUTHOR'S NOTE

I did not know the story of Deborah Sampson (also Samson) until 2021 when I came across an article about women of the American Revolution. It was a Fourth of July story, one from a women's publication that I follow online. I was stunned. I once taught history! I was a schoolteacher at a school where America's history and heritage was the foundation of the curriculum, and I didn't know anything about her. I immediately went on a deep dive, as deep as I could go, considering the limited resources about her and her life. Then I wrote a proposal for my publisher, hoping they would be as interested as I was in her story. They were, and *A Girl Called Samson* was scheduled for publication.

That's when the hard work began. Deborah's tale was put to the pages back in the early 1800s by a man named Herman Mann, who is said to have interviewed Deborah at length. He didn't do a very good job. It was an almost impossible read, and Deborah herself barely peeked out from the pages, but I caught a glimpse.

I dug into other original sources from the time period, one written by Dr. James Thatcher, a doctor assigned in the final years of his service to General Paterson's brigade. In the book by Mann, Deborah is said to have known James Thatcher as a child, but no mention of her is found anywhere in the hundreds of pages of journal entries and detailed accounts Thatcher kept during the war. The Widow Thatcher, whom Deborah lived with from age eight to ten, seems to have been a relation of his, as I indicate in the book, though I do not know for certain what the relationship was.

Thatcher's journal provided not just a wealth of information on Paterson's brigade and the war in the highlands but specific accounts of Deborah's regiment. Her commanding officers, men she served with, and assignments she would have been on were all there in his entries. Thatcher was well acquainted with General Paterson and references him many times. I don't know if James Thatcher ever found out Robert Shurtliff's true identity, though he certainly knew both the girl and the soldier. Dr. Thatcher addended his record and made additions to the text long after the war was over, but never mentioned her, though Deborah's identity was exposed after her bout with yellow fever in Philadelphia. Dr. Thatcher references Dr. Binney as well.

Dr. Binney was an attending physician at the hospital where Deborah was taken, in her soldier's uniform, unconscious and unknown. It was Dr. Binney who championed her and actually brought her into his home until she recovered. In Mann's account, Deborah walked all the way back to West Point after she recovered and presented a letter to General Paterson from Dr. Binney, revealing the fact that she was a woman. At that juncture, Herman Mann claims, General Paterson gave her an honorable discharge and kept her secret, remaining a trusted confidant long after the war.

In Deborah's words, John Paterson was her dear, old friend.

He was not old at all, but I don't doubt that he was dear. When I read Herman Mann's account, I could not help but think there was something there, something very special, even if it wasn't romance. For Deborah Sampson to have become General Paterson's aide-de-camp was miraculous, and he was very much her protector. More importantly, especially for the times in which he lived, he believed in and admired her for who she was and what she'd accomplished.

I had never heard of John Paterson either. His great-grandson, Thomas Egleston, compiled and published a record of his life in 1894 using the letters and accounts available in Revolutionary War archives—mainly letters to Congress and communications with other officers—along with stories that had been passed down in the family. No mention was made of Deborah Sampson in the great-grandson's book.

Maybe John Paterson didn't talk about her, though that's almost impossible for me to believe. A female soldier who was his aide-de-camp? But no mention of her exists in 279 pages of Egleston's small print, detailing Paterson's eight years of dogged service in the Revolutionary War. Her absence felt conspicuous.

General Paterson was described as a strapping, handsome man of Scottish descent, six foot two and athletic, a man who never shirked his duty or sought attention. This is especially remarkable considering his youth; according to his great-grandson, he was one of the youngest, if not the youngest, generals in the war, and he remained in his position until everyone else was sent home. He was made a major general at the close of his duty.

An only son, the youngest in a family of five sisters, with a military father who passed away from yellow fever in service to the Crown, John Paterson was not hard at all for me to bring to life. After reading his great-grandson's stories and the military communications begging for relief for the men in his charge, I was greatly impressed. Like Deborah, I adored him. Many of the scenes and events in the book are entirely fictional, but his dedication was not. It was also evident, from the archives that remain, that he was often sent in to handle disputes and calm storms, and his reputation was stellar.

His relationship and fondness for Agrippa Hull, a celebrated African American soldier of the Revolution, was noted in the records I found as well. He was well-known and well-loved in Stockbridge, Massachusetts. The story about him donning Colonel Kosciuszko's dress uniform and painting his lower legs and feet is factual. He was a vibrant and compelling character both in this story and in real life.

According to his great-grandson, John Paterson kept detailed records, and as a general, a lawyer, a judge, and a reluctant one-term congressman, that is not surprising. However, not long after Paterson died, all his personal records and correspondence were lost in a fire.

I took liberties with the ages and relationships of my characters: John Paterson's wife, Elizabeth Lee Paterson, did not die during the war, and though it seems she met Deborah at some point, she and Deborah did not have the relationship I gave them in the book. Elizabeth Paterson outlived John Paterson and Deborah Sampson by decades and was a fascinating and stalwart woman. John and Elizabeth had five children, including one who died in childbirth and another, Polly, whom I name in this book, who suffered with ill health and died at seventeen. John Paterson has a small monument in Lenox, Massachusetts, and the home he built there was still standing when his great-grandson compiled his record.

Deborah Sampson was born December 17, 1760, not 1759, and she was indeed a descendant of William Bradford, whose accounts of the Pilgrim story have been passed down through the ages. Her heritage, on both sides of her family, began there, and it was deeply personal and important to her. She was indentured at a young age because her father, Jonathan Sampson, abandoned his family, a wife and five children. Deborah's relationship with her mother was almost nonexistent, though the Thomas family lived in Middleborough, not far from Plympton. Reverend Sylvanus Conant helped arrange the bond of servitude, which was very common in those days. Her intelligence and abilities were a joy to him, and he did his best to shepherd her and give her what he could. His sudden death in 1777 was devastating to her.

The Thomases had many sons (some records say six not ten), though I could not find a good account of their names or military records. I know several of them were lost in the war, but could not find specific, reliable details of that service. I do believe the Thomases were like many of the families in that day. All gave some, some gave all, and

I have to believe those Thomas boys made a huge impact on Deborah Sampson, both in life and in death.

Deborah's regiment, her commanding officers, and some of the names of men who served with her are all part of the historical record. James (Jimmy) Battles, Noble Sperin, and John Beebe all died at Tarrytown and were in Deborah's company. There is some doubt whether Deborah enlisted in April of 1781 or April of 1782. If she enlisted in 1782, she did not serve in Yorktown, though the book by Mann has her there. It hardly matters. Her service in the war was truly remarkable, and her stamina and grit even more so.

It is also true that she organized a speaking tour in 1802, the first of its kind, and traveled around sharing her adventures. She was the first woman to receive a soldier's pension, though she had to petition Congress for decades. Paul Revere, a friend, was instrumental in her receiving it.

Deborah married a man named Benjamin Gannet a few years after the war and had three children (Earl, Mary, and Patience) and adopted another, an indentured servant girl named Susanna. I found that especially touching. It seems our heroine never forgot who she was.

Deborah's leg troubled her for the rest of her life, though she was tireless until the end, always doing and striving. When people met her, they were often surprised by her appearance, expecting, as John states in the book, "a Samson instead of a Deborah." I think she was both. A true pioneer and a patriot, she is buried in Sharon, Massachusetts, and a small museum in Middleborough marks her life to this day.

Deborah Sampson might be my favorite rebel of all. I hope, wherever she is, she knows how greatly her story moved me. History has not done her justice, but I sincerely hope I did.

~Amy Harmon

ACKNOWLEDGMENTS

A special thanks to my agent, Jane Dystel, who is a warrior in her own right, and to Karey White, Sunshine Kamaloni, Amanda Woodruff, Ashley Weston, and Barbara Kloss, who read Deborah's story when I was scared and encouraged me when I was doubtful. I was hungry and you fed me, I was thirsty and you gave me drink. Bless you all.

ABOUT THE AUTHOR

Amy Harmon is a *Wall Street Journal*, *USA Today*, and *New York Times* bestselling author. Her books have been published in more than two dozen languages around the globe. Amy has written nineteen novels, including the *USA Today* bestseller *Making Faces*. Her historical novel *From Sand and Ash* was the Whitney Award–winning Novel of the Year in 2016. Her novel *What the Wind Knows* topped the Amazon charts for thirteen weeks and was on the top 100 bestsellers chart for six months. Her novel *A Different Blue* is a *New York Times* bestseller, and her *USA Today* bestselling fantasy *The Bird and the Sword* was a Goodreads Best Book of 2016 finalist. For updates on upcoming book releases, author posts, and more, join Amy at www.authoramyharmon.com.